THE ACADEMY GUARDIANS

Callen's Legacy

BY ARA J. EDEN

25 24 23 22 21 20   1 2 3 4 5 6 7 8

THE ACADEMY GUARDIANS
Copyright ©2020 Ara J. Eden

Unless otherwise noted, all Scripture taken from the *King James Version* of the Bible.

Published by:
Emerge Publishing, LLC
9521B Riverside Parkway, Suite 243 Tulsa, Oklahoma 74137
Phone: 888.407.4447   www.EmergePublishing.com

Library of Congress Cataloging-in-Publication Data:
ISBN: 978-1-949758-94-8 Perfect Bound

For my siblings.

You always know when to
tear the walls down.

0.

When Elohim created the world, he gifted a select number of humans with the ability to fly and appointed them Caledons—guardians of his world. All of the guardians were given various talents in addition to their wings, and although the talents were equally important in function, they were not equal in size and power. Over time, some of them grew jealous and greedy, sowing discord among their peers. Eventually there was an uprising. Elohim's loyal guardians fought with diplomacy, but the rebels desired bloodshed. Brother murdered brother, and friends betrayed friends, until Elohim put a stop to the fighting. The rebels were exiled and became known as Lacquers. With his heart and mind heavy with sorrow, Elohim withdrew from the world, leaving behind the promise to one day reunite them through his son.

As the years passed, the Caledons grew in strength and number, dispersing throughout the earth. Talents were passed down through the generations, but they remained dormant in the vast majority. The handful of Caledon offspring who did discover their wings and talents were trained as future guardians. The Lacquers also grew in number; however, their talents became warped and defiled with each generation. They drew their strength from sheer numbers, reproducing many and often. Lacquers and Caledons were the only two groups of humans with wings, and like their talents, the conflict between them continued through the ages.

One day, a female Lacquer and a male Caledon became friends. They grew to love one another and eventually married, despite immense disapproval from all sides. Shortly after, they were forced to flee the persecution, finally settling down in a quiet land far from both their home territories. They lived a peaceful life, cherishing each other and working out their differences.

Two years after their union, a daughter was born. They couldn't have picked a worse time to have a child. Word had just begun to spread about the birth of Elohim's promised son, which meant the emergence of a new era in which the Caledons would once again become guardians of the earth. A desperate search for Elohim's son commenced from both Caledon and Lacquer communities. While the Caledons were overjoyed, the Lacquers were deathly afraid. Out of the conflict that ensued, two leaders emerged: Loren and Jaden.

Loren was hand chosen by Elohim to gather the Caledons together on a mountain he consecrated for his followers. The Lacquers were charmed by Jaden's charismatic leadership and elected him to be their leader. Under Elohim's guidance, Loren called off the search for Elohim's child and set to work building Elo's Academy, a place to prepare the next generation for the inevitable war. Jaden continued the search for Elohim's son, travelling far and wide, and he came across rumors of the existence of a half-Caledon-half-Lacquer child. Obsession with the concept of a half-breed child consumed him, and he immediately set to work acquiring it.

After several attempts at deception, he convinced the mother to sell her young daughter to him for the price of safety and shelter in the Lacquer community. The child's disposition was a mixture of her mother's mischief and her father's gaiety. Her intelligence and quick thinking were impressive, and she was adept at escaping. She became Jaden's favorite little pet and was raised at his side. He called her Moriana. For the next six years of her life, she lived entirely as a Lacquer and without knowledge of family, friends, love, hope, or trust. She only knew self-preservation, fear, rage, and hate.

As Moriana matured, Jaden aggressively developed her Lacquer talents, hoping to suppress any Caledon tendencies. But compassion stole through at the most unexpected moments. The more hate Jaden poured into her, the more powerful those stolen moments grew. For six years, she was Jaden's favorite. Then a new Lacquer child showed up. He was male, he was angry, and he was thoroughly spiteful—exactly what Jaden wanted.

∞

Jaden perched on his self-erected throne atop a steep rock terrace dotted with soft moss. His chin rested against his palm as he studied the winged-child practicing aerial maneuvers before him. "Moriana," he called in a bored tone. She stopped in mid-air and focused her dark, intelligent eyes on him. "Starting tomorrow, you'll be training alongside Aeron."

Moriana's voice was an equally flat timbre. "Who is Aeron?"

The corners of Jaden's mouth curled upwards in the slightest way. "My new pupil." He rose gracefully and beckoned her toward him. They walked together to a balcony overlooking the vast Lacquer community he lorded over. He pointed out a solitary child with dark emerald green wings—a color so deep, it was almost black. "You and I will train him together. He's much more talented than you are." He paused as a hummingbird flitted across their vision.

Moriana followed the tiny bird's progress as it hovered over the flowered vines winding down the ledge. Its erratic flight took it closer and closer toward the ground where another set of eyes also watched. The hummingbird touched the last flower and sped into the open sky.

A burst of activity suddenly erupted. Aeron, who had been intensely tracking the bird's movements, pounced on it when it drew near and clasped it between his palms. Moriana, who had read his movements a split second too late, catapulted herself off the ledge and tried to prevent the bird's capture.

Aeron transferred his hostage into one hand and held it up triumphantly.

Moriana clenched her fists. "Let it go."

In response, the boy tightened his fingers, and the hummingbird let loose an array of terrified chirps.

"Let it go!" she screamed, launching a full-bodied assault on him.

They tussled on the ground for several intense seconds before Jaden calmly intervened. He grabbed Moriana by the back of her tunic and tossed her aside. Then he knelt and gently picked up the limp form of the hummingbird lying in the dirt. He stroked its vibrantly colored feathers and said in a thoughtful voice, "Aeron also has a better attitude."

Moriana's eyes cut murderously to the boy now standing at Jaden's side. "He's hateful. Is that what you mean?"

Aeron lifted his eyes from the bird's still form and set his jaw. "You're the one who killed it."

"Liar!"

"Enough!" Jaden thundered. He straightened and crooked his finger at the girl. She got to her feet and approached cautiously. "You're too soft, Moriana," he said with regret. "You hurt easily." He slid the bird into her open palms with a look of dissatisfaction on his face. "I hate the Caledon in you. I've trained you to suppress it, but it's growing. I see it come out every time you act without thinking. I *despise* it."

Moriana stared at the lifeless body in her hands. She was furious, sad, and afraid. "Are you going to send me away?"

"No," he answered with resignation. "I'll tolerate you because I love you, despite your poor qualities."

"Jaden, what is love?" Moriana asked, careful not to show the relief she felt.

"It's power," he answered with fervor. "As master over the community, only I possess it."

She looked him dead in the eye. "I met a mentor who claims to also have love. He says I do as well, but I need to awaken it."

Jaden crossed his arms. Only Caledons were mentors. "This mentor, where did you meet him?"

"Outside the eastern border."

His eyes narrowed dangerously. "How many times?"

"Every other day," she answered indifferently.

"So that's where you've been running off to," he said in a cold, hard voice.

Moriana blinked. "I didn't think you'd notice."

"Is that so?" Jaden's fist lashed out and sent the girl flying across the air. "Insolent half-breed!" he roared in fury. "You dare disobey me! I told you not to step outside our borders!"

"Why not?" she asked sullenly from where she had landed.

"These rules are meant to protect the ones I love most!"

Moriana smirked haughtily. "You're lying."

Jaden stalked forward, yanked the girl roughly to her feet and slapped her without restraint. "Do not disobey me again."

Moriana's cheek smarted, but the betrayal inside burned like wildfire. She was hit and thrown often by those around her, but Jaden himself had never laid a hand on her before. "You slapped me ..."

"I did, and I will do so again," he stated with contempt.

"You only hit those you say you hate," she ground out.

Jaden backhanded her. "I **hate** the Caledon in you."

Defiance flashed in the young girl's eyes.

"I will **never** love the Caledon in you," Jaden growled again. He whirled back for the thoroughly forgotten Aeron, who flashed Moriana a look of alarm before being hauled away.

Moriana wiped the blood off her cheek and sat up slowly. She almost felt sorry for Aeron. Little did he know what Jaden had in store for him. Kneeling, she dug a grave with her fingers and buried the body of the little bird deep into the earth. A spark of hatred ignited within her, and she allowed it to consume her from the inside out. She grew insolent and derisive, lashing out with her words and fists without warning. To especially goad her master, she kept meeting with the Caledon boy outside the eastern border.

One day, the boy came to see Jaden. Moriana was turning twelve in six months—a good age to enroll in Elo's Academy. Eaerien wanted to take her home with him, but Jaden wouldn't negotiate. He had the fifteen-year-old boy brutally beaten and dumped outside the borders of the Lacquer community. Then he locked Moriana in her room without food or water in an attempt to break her into submission.

When Moriana escaped after three days, she immediately went in search of Eaerien. If he was beaten badly, he couldn't have gotten much of a head start. Maybe he would still take her with him. She had recently discovered that sometimes the cuts she touched healed themselves. If she could figure out how that worked and was able to fix him up a little, maybe she could use that to convince him. She flew as fast as she could in her weakened state to their usual spot. To her amazement, Eaerien was waiting for her. "You look awful," she greeted him.

Eaerien was sitting and leaning against a tree trunk, covered in bandages, and didn't attempt to stand. "Jaden had me beaten pretty bad, but I'm on the mend. What about you?" His eyebrows furrowed as he took note of her thin frame and sunken eyes. "What did he do to you?"

She shrugged carelessly. "Nothing he hasn't tried before. I escaped."

"Are you all right?" he queried with concern.

"Never better." In truth, the isolation hurt worse than any beating she had ever endured. The Caledon boy gave her a small, knowing smile, and Moriana realized he saw through her bluff.

"I tried to come back sooner," Eaerien explained. "But…" He glanced meaningfully at his injuries.

She folded herself down next to him. "Jaden said you left for good."

Eaerien tilted his head and studied her expression. "I told you I wasn't leaving without you."

She scoffed and averted her face. "Jaden isn't going to let me go. I came here to tell you that."

He raised his brows. "Are you sure you weren't planning on running away?"

Moriana bristled.

"I was hoping you would come looking for me," Eaerien continued without missing a beat. "I brought Loren back with me this time. He's with Jaden right now, and he won't take no for an answer." He waved his bandaged hands in the air for emphasis.

Moriana caught one of Eaerien's hands and sandwiched them between hers while asking, "Who's Loren?" She slowly squeezed his hand as hard as she could.

"You'll meet him soon enough—ow!" Eaerien yanked his hand out of the girl's grasp.

Moriana jumped to her feet and pounded on the tree. "It didn't work!"

Eaerien winced at the throbbing in his hand. "What didn't work?"

"Nothing!"

"Well I'm sure it wasn't the tree's fault," he reasoned. He covered his throbbing hand with his other hand and closed his eyes as the pain slowly subsided.

Moriana picked at a loose piece of bark. "I wasn't trying to hurt you," she stated testily.

"I know." A little grin sprang to his lips, and he patted the ground beside him.

Moriana was too on edge to sit. "What do you mean Loren won't take no for an answer?" she pressed, tearing off chunks of bark from the tree. "Jaden could kill him."

With some effort, Eaerien pulled himself to his feet and placed a hand over her restless fingers. His expression was kind and a little bit teasing, and he spoke with confidence—as if he harbored a great secret. "Jaden won't kill Loren." Then he leaned his head back against the tree and relaxed.

Moriana watched him with mounting irritation. How could he be so calm?

"Here he comes now," Eaerien said, lifting his head.

She spun around and watched a tall, broad shouldered man move briskly and assuredly in their direction. "He's big for a Caledon," she remarked critically.

Eaerien patted Moriana's hand gently. "He isn't entirely Caledon."

She gave him a sharp look.

"His father was human."

Moriana eyed the man almost upon them. He was older than his movements suggested.

Loren stopped before them and smiled warmly. "Our business here is finished." He turned a piercing gaze on the small girl, who stared boldly back at him. "My name is Loren," he said in a deep, rumbling voice. "I am pleased to finally meet you, Genesis."

Surprise and confusion spread across her features. "How do you know that name?" she demanded.

Loren spread his hands. "It's the name your father gave you."

"My father." She spoke the words slowly, as if testing a foreign language. "Did you know him?"

"I met him once, a long time ago. You had just been born."

The girl tried to swallow, but her throat was too parched. "Jaden gave me a new name."

Loren's eyes hardened imperceptibly. "Jaden is no longer your master. Elohim has freed you. If you do not mind, I suggest you reclaim the name you were originally given."

It was quiet for a few moments as Genesis tried to make sense of Loren's words. Finally she lifted her eyes to his and replied, "I don't mind."

Loren's expression softened. "Well then, Genesis, shall we go home?"

1.

Genesis was finishing her lessons at the table in the aerie she now called home. Eaerien sat nearby, waiting for her to finish. The girl had ditched her classes—not for the first time—but this time she had at least brought her work back with her. An impish light danced in his eyes each time she scratched her head in confusion or sighed with frustration at the assignments in front of her. Still, she refused to ask for help.

"Genesis, do you like school?" he finally asked.

"I hate it." She pressed the tip of her quill into the parchment with such force that the end of it snapped off.

Eaerien cocked an eyebrow. "Don't you think it's necessary to attend?"

Genesis stared woodenly at the broken quill. "I don't see why I need to go there to study."

He lifted an edge of the table and pulled out another quill from the compartment within. "Where will you study then?" he wondered, twirling the instrument in her face.

Genesis snatched it out of his grasp. "Here."

Both of Eaerien's eyebrows shot to the sky. "Who will teach you?"

She fixed her gaze pointedly at him.

Eaerien shook his head slowly in disbelief. "You don't even listen to me, Genesis."

"If I listen, will you let me stay?" she bargained.

Eaerien's smile was gentle. "You can stay on *no* conditions."

"But you want me to go to school," she remarked grudgingly.

He leaned against the back of his chair and crossed his arms behind his head. "That's correct."

Genesis stood abruptly and paced away. "Why?"

"It will help you grow."

She paused to narrow her eyes at him. "Grow the Caledon in me?"

"No." Eaerien dropped his arms and straightened in surprise. "It will help you grow as *you*."

"I don't understand."

He scratched his chin thoughtfully. "Your mother is Lacquer and your father is Caledon, which makes you both. There is no need for you to exchange one side for another. Elohim has embraced you just as you are, and I follow his lead."

She rolled her eyes. "I don't know this Elohim you speak of."

Eaerien rose from his seat and moved toward her. "Elohim is our king. He created this world and designated this place especially for us. He gave us our home. More importantly, it's a place for us to find him when we need him." He saw the hope and doubt warring her eyes. "This is why you need to go to school," he reiterated. You need to learn our history. It will better prepare you for our future."

"You keep saying *our* history and *our* future," she burst out, jabbing herself with her finger. "I am no Caledon! I am a child of Jaden—*your* king's enemy! I don't belong here!"

"You belong!" Eaerien gripped her shoulders earnestly. "Elohim came to me and told me about you. He is the reason I went to find you on the forest border. " He searched her eyes. "When Jaden wouldn't listen to me, Elohim showed Loren the way to free you. You belong to Elohim now."

Genesis pushed his hands away. "I don't want to belong to anyone!"

Eaerien let his hands fall to his sides. "We all belong to someone, Genesis," he said quietly. "I know that Jaden treats his followers poorly. He is not a good master to serve, and I wish—" Eaerien's voice cracked, and he took a deep breath. "Elohim is a good king. Remember how we talked about love? You will see what that word really means after meeting *our* king." Impulsively, he pulled her into a hug.

Genesis stiffened. Any invasion of personal space usually resulted in pain, and she had to fight the reflex to lash out. Eaerien wasn't hurting her.

"What are you doing?" she demanded. She could feel his laughter resounding through his chest.

"I'm hugging you." He leaned back and grinned.

"What does it mean?" she asked uncertainly.

His eyes crinkled at the corners. "It can mean many things: a greeting, goodbye, affection, joy, comfort."

"And in this case?"

Eaerien pulled her into another hug. "In this case, a hug is needed because words are not enough."

Genesis held very still for a brief moment. "You can't hug me if I'm at school?"

"I can, but it would be more difficult."

She wiggled away from him. "Then I will go to school."

Eaerien's laughter rang out, and he released her.

Genesis quickly gathered her books and hurried out of their aerie located high on a cliff behind the Academy. The sound of her mentor's laughter floated down the cliff with her, and she almost smiled. As much as she fought against it, Eaerien was growing on her, but the thought of another betrayal kept her on guard.

For the next couple of weeks, Genesis tried valiantly to honor Eaerien's pleas to attend school. She never felt more alone than when she was among her schoolmates. No one dared to approach her except to taunt her or provoke her into a fight. She gave up eventually and decided that if she were meant to be alone, she would rather be alone *away* from people.

∞

Eaerien walked away from Loren's office feeling defeated. Why would Elohim put him in charge of someone as tempestuous and unpredictable as Genesis? Shouldn't a mentor with more wisdom and experience be her guardian? Was he being punished for all the pranks he pulled as a student? The young man inhaled deeply of the clean mountain air and pondered his next move. Genesis had stopped showing up to school entirely, but Eaerien hadn't realized it because she still left the aerie every morning with her homework completed. She had also given him no indication that anything was wrong at school.

He ambled over to a massive tree that indicated the start of the Academy's training grounds and peered into its thick foliage. "Hey, Genesis, come down here!"

Genesis dropped lightly to the ground. "What is it?" she asked impassively.

He put his hands on his hips and surveyed his young student with a critical eye. "Loren tells me you've been cutting class again."

She looked away and kept silent.

"I thought we had an understanding," Eaerien reminded her.

Her lips pressed into a thin line, but still she didn't answer.

"If you don't pass your first year, I won't be able to take you on any assignments outside of the Academy or the community," he pointed out. "Weren't you the one who said you were excited about helping me?"

Genesis gritted her teeth. "It doesn't matter because I won't go back," she muttered.

"What happened?" Eaerien prodded.

"As if it really matters!" she suddenly erupted. She spun away and scrambled back into the tree.

Eaerien followed her with his eyes, surprised by her outburst. "What in the world?"

"If you don't like me, then send me back to Jaden!" she yelled over her shoulder.

The young mentor frowned. "I didn't say I don't like you." He took a steadying breath. It wouldn't do any good to lose his temper. If he yelled at her, she would fight back; if he remained silent, she would walk away. "Please come back down."

She turned resolutely away.

He felt the frustration mounting and tamped it down. "If you won't talk to me, how am I supposed to help you?"

A few moments of silence passed.

"I'm coming up," he said decidedly.

Genesis climbed higher.

"You're not running away that easily," he muttered, climbing slowly and struggling with the branches. He knew very well that she had intentionally picked a tree with branches too close together to spread one's wings in—Caledons were lousy tree climbers. It was a classic Lacquer evasive maneuver.

"Give it up, Eaerien," she called down.

Was she talking about climbing the tree or herself? "I'm not giving up on you or this tree."

"You're a fool."

Eaerien paused to wipe the sweat off his brow. "Some may think so, but Elohim agrees with me. You wouldn't call *him* a fool, would you?"

Genesis hesitated. "Why would Elohim go so far to save someone like me?"

"Because life is precious to him."

"You're young, Eaerien," she commented. "But you talk like an old man."

Eaerien chuckled and resumed his awkward climbing. "I'm sixteen. Compared to you, I am old."

She scoffed, "Compared to me, you're still a baby."

A sad smile formed on his face. "You've been through a lot, haven't you?"

"Feeling sorry for me won't do any good," she advised emotionlessly. "It just makes it harder to forget."

"Instead of forgetting it, why don't you let it shape who you are today?" He groped for another branch and hauled himself onto it. "Easier said than done, but you have to try to learn from it."

Genesis leapt lightly down to him. "What is there to learn, Eaerien?" she asked in a quiet voice.

Eaerien smiled in relief and touched the tip of her chin. "Let your past motivate you to become who you are meant to be and not who others say you are."

Her expression hardened. "You think the real me is being suppressed by my Lacquer blood?"

"No," the young man answered. "I told you this before. Your mixed bloodline may have influence on your personality, but it is not your defining feature."

"Explain."

Eaerien leaned against the wide tree trunk. "Caledon blood and Lacquer blood are like water and oil—they simply do not mix. Don't spend your entire life trying to find a happy medium between the two. Instead, develop their different strengths and use them for good."

"What kind of advice is that?" Genesis demanded, unsheathing long, deadly talons from between her fingers and brandishing them. "Just look at these! You might as well ask me to put out a fire and stop a flood at the same time. How am I supposed to do both?"

"You can stop a fire with the right amount of water, but can you revive the flame once it has been extinguished?" Eaerien asked instead. "Can fire stop the flow of water? How much of one element do you need in order to keep the other element in check?"

"And how am I supposed to find that out?" the young girl asked exasperatedly.

"Learn to control them," Eaerien replied, tapping her on the forehead. "It may be difficult, but you have the ability."

Her talons retracted. "Do you really believe that?"

"I do," he stated with conviction. "I also believe the first step is completing your education. Remember that it's *mind over matter*. The stronger your mind is, the easier it will be to control your body."

Her face contorted in despair. "I can't stand the way they look at me!" she blurted. "They think I'm a monster, Eaerien! Everywhere I go, everyone looks at me the same, everyone treats me the same. I didn't ask to be born!"

Eaerien pulled her into a tight embrace. "We don't hate you, Genesis," he whispered softly, his heart breaking for her. "But we are afraid of you."

"Even you are afraid of me," she said hopelessly.

"Of course," he replied matter-of-factly. "You're the first Caledon-Lacquer offspring the world has ever known, and we're not sure of what you're capable of."

"I'm only twelve, Eaerien."

He patted her encouragingly on the back. "You're wrong, Genesis. Even a child can change the course of history."

"A child?" she scoffed.

"Shall I tell you a story?" he offered, loosening the circle of his arms.

She rolled her eyes and found a comfortable spot on the wide branch. "Why not."

Eaerien sat beside her and tucked her against his side. His heart warmed when she relaxed against him. Little by little, she was learning to trust him. "Thirteen years ago," he began. "Two babies were found dangling from a tree in twin baskets. A lonely, newlywed young woman discovered them and brought them home to her husband. They named the boy Callen and the girl Marian. The boy was evidently older. The husband and wife raised them as their own in the traditions of their community. Four years later, the woman gave birth to a son, whom they called Caeden ..."

2.

Thousands of miles away, in the early hours of the morning, a boy stood inside an oversized, barn-shaped birdhouse. Housed within the bird-barn were four spacious enclosures that contained up to five birds each. The boy walked up and down the length of the barn, counting the birds and checking for any signs of injury. There were two breeding falcon pairs, five falcon juveniles, and one newly fledged eagle.

Enclosures 2 and 3 were located at the front of the barn and housed the juvenile birds—three females and two males. These birds were used for hunting and sporting purposes, and they weren't fed until after they had worked. Enclosure 1 was deeper in the barn and separated from 2 and 3 by heavy double doors. It was further sectioned into two cages that contained one breeding pair each and their respective hatchlings. These birds received regular meals to ensure the survival of all the chicks. After tossing a dead rabbit carcass into each of the enclosures, the boy moved on.

The fourth and last enclosure was positioned at the back of the barn. It was considerably smaller than the others and contained a lone occupant. The boy watched the cage for a moment. From inside his prison, the juvenile male eagle glared back with fierce brown-grey eyes.

The boy entered the enclosure and extended his arm toward the bird. Gracefully, the eagle stepped off his perch and curled his massive talons around the boy's arm, which was bare beneath his long-sleeved tunic. Sitting down where he was, the boy ran the back of his fingers down the eagle's solid white breast. "Today's your day," he whispered eagerly. "Make it count."

The majestic bird let out an answering trill, eliciting a carefree laugh from the boy.

"Callen," a deep, commanding voice resonated through the oversized birdhouse.

From within their enclosures, the raptors screeched and flapped their wings in response. The bird on the boy's arm merely cocked his head and snapped his beak in clear disapproval.

"You know that voice as well as I do," Callen remarked with a grin. "But why don't you show the same respect?"

"Because you've spoiled him, Callen."

Callen got to his feet respectfully as a man in his prime moved into view. "Father."

Kael gave a brief nod to his son. "You're up bright and early, as usual. I trust everything has been prepared for the eagle's first hunt?"

"Yes, Father. You only need to choose the location."

"Why don't you choose today?" Kael suggested. "After all, he's your raptor. You know his strengths and weaknesses better than anyone."

Callen's eyes brightened. "Yes, Father."

The man's eyes rested on the boy's unprotected arm. The eagle seemed to be aware of the danger his talons presented, gripping loosely and shifting his weight gingerly with the boy's movements. "I will wait for you on the training field. Caeden will help you bring the other bird out."

"Yes, but where exactly *is* Caeden?"

Kael's eyes snapped up and his voice hardened. "Hasn't he been in here yet?"

With regret over his words clear in his eyes, Callen admitted, "I haven't seen him all morning."

Kael sighed in exasperation. "Callen, I put him under your guidance for a reason. He should've been up hours ago, helping you with the morning chores. Why did you not wake him?"

"He was exhausted from yesterday," he hastily explained. "So I let him sleep a while longer, but when I went to wake him, he was gone."

"You'd better find him then," Kael stated, turning on his heel. "Remember, Callen," he advised as he walked away. "The student can only learn if his teacher is willing to teach."

The boy's shoulders sagged. "Yes, Father ..."

It was always like that. Whenever Caeden did something wrong, Callen took the blame for it. He usually didn't mind, but lately his father's favoritism had taken a whole new turn and watching over his younger brother had become more of a babysitting job than an instructional one. To make the situation worse, Caeden was feeding off of their father's favor, and his attitude was starting to reflect it.

Resigned, Callen returned the eagle to his perch. "I'll be right back."

∞

"Caeden! Are you in here?" Callen stuck his head into the main living area and frowned at the empty room.

"Brother, is that you?" a sweet, girly voice called from the kitchen.

Callen moved into the kitchen. "Marian? What are you doing in the kitchen?"

"Making breakfast," she announced happily, her arms deep in a mound of lumpy dough.

"Is that why you didn't come to the birdhouse this morning?"

"No. It's because I overslept. How are the birds?"

"Healthy," Callen replied absently, his eyes fixed on the hideous mass his sister was kneading.

Marian paused and studied her brother for a moment. "Shouldn't you be training with Father right now?"

"Yes," he said, lifting his gaze from the strange mound. "But I can't find Caed. Have you seen him?"

Marian started to shake her head when the outside kitchen door slammed, and a little boy came running in.

"Marian," he panted. "Has Callen—Uh, oh ..."

ARA J. EDEN

Callen glared at the younger boy. "Where have you been? Did you forget you had chores to do?"

Caeden's eyes widened. "It was an accident!"

"There are no such things as accidents at this point," Callen chastised. "I won't be around much longer, and if you don't learn your responsibilities by the time I leave, you're going to be useless to Father. Do you understand that?"

Caeden drew back and clenched his fists, shouting, "Father will never think I'm useless! I'm his favorite son, and you can't yell at me like that!"

"I don't care if Father thinks of you as a prince!" Callen hollered back.

Tears sprang into the younger boy's eyes. "You're a tyrant! I'm glad you're leaving."

Callen brushed the remark aside. "Take your corrections like a man and stop crying. I'll see you in front of the birdhouse in five minutes."

Caeden sniffed loudly and glared at the older boy's departing back.

Marian wiped the flour from her hands and patted the little boy's head gently. "Don't cry, little brother. Callen's hard on you because he cares about you. He wants you to live up to Father's expectations."

"Expectations?"

"Yes," the young girl smiled brightly. "Father expects more from you than he does from either Callen or me."

"Why?" Caeden asked, screwing up his face.

"You know how important Father is to our community, right?"

He nodded solemnly.

"Well," she explained patiently. "Since Callen's leaving, you're going to take over his responsibilities. And one day, you're going to take Father's place as head of the community. All good leaders are responsible leaders."

Caeden shook his finger in the air. "Brother's coming back to marry Faye—that's what Mother always says. Why can't he be head, then?"

"Because you're special, Caed. You're the only child here who is already home."

"Father is the head of this community," he argued. "If he wants brother to be his apprentice, he can!"

With a slight shake of her head, Marian went back to her dough. "It's not that simple, little brother."

"Why not?" he pressed, moving closer conspiratorially. "Did Callen do something to fall out of his favor?"

"Of course not," Marian said firmly, nudging him back with her elbow. "You mustn't think that. This is just the way it is."

Caeden crossed his arms. "I don't know that I can agree with that."

"When you take over for Father, you can change things," she said pragmatically.

"I'm only nine years old, Marian. I'm too young to take Father's place."

"Even so, you're never too young to learn responsibility." She prodded him toward the door. "Go on. Callen's waiting."

The little boy nodded and obediently ran out the door.

Marian abandoned her dough and leaned against the doorframe, watching until her brothers reappeared from the barn with the young eagle. She continued to watch until they disappeared into the forest and a wistful sigh escaped. If it were up to her, she would be right beside them. She was, after all, quite the falconer despite being female and having only received second-hand training from her older brother.

"Hey, Marian!" a girl called from the other side of the house. "Come on! We're going to be late for school!"

"School, already? But I haven't even finished making breakfast!" she exclaimed. "Mother, I'm leaving for school now! Can you finish the morning meal for me?" Marian waited for a response, but there was none. "Mother!" she called, running through the house. "Mother, where are …?" She halted abruptly at a door.

There was a woman inside, sitting on the bed, tears trickling down her face.

"Mother, what are you doing in Callen's bedroom?" she asked in surprise.

Startled, the woman stood up.

Marian hurried to her side. "What's troubling you?"

"Oh, darling, everything is fine," the woman quickly assured her.

"Then why are you crying?" Marian prompted worriedly.

The woman forced a cheerful smile on her face. "I was tidying Callen's room—you know how he gets—and it suddenly hit me that he's almost of age. I'm going to miss him terribly when he departs."

Marian's eyes were moist. "I'm going to miss him too, Mother."

"Yes, you're also going to miss school if you don't leave soon."

"The morning meal—"

"I'll finish the meal," the woman reassured her. "And remember, Marian, young ladies don't run around the house yelling for their mothers. They handle things calmly and purposefully."

"Yes, Mother, I'll remember." Marian walked serenely until she was out of her mother's sight, then sprinted to her room and quickly gathered her books. Her two closest friends were waiting in the courtyard.

"There she is," Faye exclaimed.

"It's about time," Sara commented. "What took you so long?"

"I'm sorry," she said, falling into step beside them. "I woke up late and started the morning meal late and ran out of time."

"Late night?" Faye wondered.

"Yes, I had a hard time falling asleep."

"What were you doing?" Sara inquired.

"Nothing," she replied. "I just couldn't stop thinking about … something."

Faye gave her a knowing look. "Something that has to do with your brother?"

Marian nodded.

"What is it this time?" Sara prodded. "The same thing?"

"Don't you think it's unusual that my father hasn't mentioned anything? Callen's turning fourteen-and-a-half in a few weeks."

"Stop worrying. Callen's the most talented boy in our community," Sara reassured her. "Your father probably has so many offers from all over the country that he can't decide who to choose from. Everyone knows your brother's special, so I wouldn't be surprised if your father was being extra careful about his future."

"I guess you're right," Marian reluctantly agreed, exchanging a sidelong glance with Faye. Sara didn't know yet that Marian and Faye's fathers were arranging a marriage between Callen and Faye. What Marian couldn't understand was, why would her father delay giving Callen his coming-of-age speech if he was already making plans to marry him off to someone in their village?

"Of course I'm right. Besides," Sara added teasingly, "Callen's too cute for anyone to resist."

"What do you mean?"

"The men want him in their shops because he'll attract more customers, and the women want him in their villages because he might end up marrying one of their daughters someday. What's wrong with your face, Faye?"

Faye's face had turned pink with embarrassment.

"We're not supposed to talk like this in public," Marian explained hastily.

"I was only teasing," Sara returned. "Since when were the two of you so concerned about being lady-like, anyway?"

"Young ladies aren't supposed to be temperamental. We're supposed to give the atmosphere a pleasant feeling," Faye quoted with sarcasm.

Marian blew out an exasperated breath.

Sara laughed. "That's more like it."

"Our mothers would be mortified," Faye commented with a mischievous smirk.

"I must admit that I will be sorry to see both your brothers go."

Faye jostled the girl good-naturedly. "You don't have to include my brother out of pity, Sara. We all know Callen's the one you're going to miss."

"Not just Callen," Sara protested. "Liam too! By the way, Faye, stop telling people I have a crush on Callen because I don't!"

Marian's eyes grew wide. "Faye never said that. But you do, don't you?"

"Of course she does," Faye remarked dryly. "Just like every other girl in our village."

"How do you feel about my brother, Faye?"

The girl blushed again. "I like him as a friend. He's nice, and he doesn't make me feel like I have to put on an act. I can just be a thirteen-year-old girl who likes to run and yell and climb trees."

Marian mused over her words. "You're right, Faye. He doesn't make me feel like I have to act older than I am either." She frowned and added, "I wish he'd act that way with Caed. He's so hard on him sometimes."

"Caed has some pretty big shoes to fill," Faye commented. "If he doesn't grow up quickly, your father might be pressured into taking on an apprentice from another community."

"There's talk of merging several villages into one great community under one leader with a team of supporting advisors," Sara added. "I heard my father discussing it with my brother before he left. It gives me hope that I'll see him again one day."

"I have a feeling we'll be seeing all our brothers again one day," Faye declared.

∞

Later, during the hottest part of the day when the entire village was quiet and out of the sun, Faye's brother Liam—also Callen's closest friend—stopped by for a visit. He went by the main house to greet Callen's parents then trekked into the forest. He found his friend sitting in the middle of a meadow. "I knew I'd find you here," he called in greeting.

Callen raised his arm in response.

Liam threw himself down next to Callen and let out a deep sigh. He was visibly worried about something. "Has your father given you the 'coming-of-age' speech?" he inquired.

"No, I don't think I'll hear it for a few days yet."

"Well, that makes you the last one for this year. I heard mine yesterday."

"Yesterday?" Callen repeated. "Why did you wait so long to come over?"

Liam plucked a flower from the ground and twirled it between two of his fingers. "I had a lot of sorting out to do. I guess no matter how prepared you think you are, some things still shock you." The boy spoke with a reflective expression on his face. "Some things he said really bother me."

"I could've helped you," Callen offered. "We've always talked about everything."

"Not this time, Callen. I couldn't burden you with this. Not when you—" Liam paused momentarily. "I came here for a reason."

"What is it?"

He held up a finger. "Let me warn you first that I can't help you. Maybe Marian can, but there's not much anyone else can do for you."

Callen didn't like the sound of that. "What are you talking about?"

"I know who you are, or rather who you are not."

Callen's head started to spin. "How? My father hasn't even spoken to me yet."

"We"—Liam gestured in a large circle in reference to all the boys their age—"all know. Why do you think all the others left without a word of goodbye to you, and the rest have been avoiding you?"

"I thought they were waiting for me to come of age."

"Trust me, they're not." Liam faced his friend squarely. "They'll never think of you as a friend again, Callen; nor will the rest of the village view you as one of us."

Callen's face paled and his stomach tightened.

"You're not one of us." His voice dropped to a whisper. "You're not even one of the distant relations. *No one* knows who you are."

The weight of Liam's words hung heavily between them for several tense moments.

Callen's mind was reeling with the information. "Are you here to say goodbye, Liam?" he finally asked. "Are you abandoning me as well?"

A small, regretful smile crept onto the other boy's face. "I spent all night thinking, and I've decided I don't care if you popped out of a cow. I rather enjoy your company, and to dump fourteen and a half years of friendship over something like this would be a waste." He shrugged dismissively. "Anyway, I always knew you were different."

"How?"

"Your shoulder blades."

Callen burst into laughter.

Liam chortled with him. "Maybe it's not *just* because of your shoulder blades, but I'm serious, Callen. No one in our village has shoulder blades like yours. They stick out like wings."

"Marian has them," Callen stated, sobering. "You said she might be able to help me. She's different too, isn't she?"

Liam nodded reluctantly.

"What are they saying about her?"

"Your father has agreed to consider giving her to one of our allies as a wife to one of their sons."

A small flame burned in Callen's eyes. "He's going to separate us."

"As your friend, Callen, I think you should take her with you when you leave."

When. Callen understood. It was inevitable that he would leave—if not by his choice, then by force.

Desert communities ensured peace and unity between villages by exchanging children at birth. Families were made up of a father, mother, and two foster children—one boy and one girl. Tradition declared Callen a man once he came of age at fourteen-and-a-half years old. Typically, he would be informed who his birth parents were and sent to them to learn the family trade. If his parents were no longer alive, he would go to the next immediate family member. On rare occasions, if only distant relations remained, then any of them could take Callen on as an apprentice. If his foster family wished for him to return, they would petition the tribe leaders and betroth him to a young lady of their choice. After learning his family trade, he would return and marry his betrothed, solidifying his adoption into their village. With absolutely no family to speak for him, tradition declared Callen a stranger, and the tribe did not allow strange men to dwell among them. They would not honor the marriage between a stranger and a tribe member either.

"Where will you go, Liam?" he asked his friend.

"To the village in the northeast. My family's trade is farming."

Callen grinned. "It suits you."

"I leave tonight when the moon comes up. I thought since you and I would be the last to come of age, we would travel together during the next full moon." He gave Callen an apologetic look. "Now I understand why the others were delayed last month."

At the full moon of each month, the boys in the village who had come of age would travel together by night to their new homes. They avoided the heat of the day and used the stars to navigate.

"You will be there to see me off?" Liam asked eagerly.

"Of course."

"And Marian?"

"We'll all go."

Liam sighed with resignation. "Your brother's lucky he won't go through the same process. He won't have to leave everything familiar behind and go to a strange place with strange people and try to make them family. I envy him."

"I don't." Callen's eyes sparked. His little brother *was* special. Caeden was child number three for their family and for a reason unknown to all of them, he had been allowed to stay with his birth parents. Maybe that was another reason Caeden had developed a superiority complex. "I like adventure. The world we live in is small. There are greater things out there."

Liam chuckled. "You and I are opposite in that sense. I'm more sentimental than you." He swung his gaze over the familiar landscape. "I'll miss this place."

"You'll miss Marian," Callen corrected.

A faint blush colored Liam's ears. "Oh, I'll miss her all right. I never imagined I'd have to say goodbye to her like this. I always thought ..." He shrugged.

"We all thought the same."

"You and Faye won't be betrothed either." Liam clenched his fists at the sudden realization. "How can I leave now? My little sister's future is no longer set, and I may never see you or Marian again." He shook his head slowly. "I suppose I'm too emotional?"

Callen put a comforting hand on his shoulder.

In response, Liam gripped his hand. "Come find me one day, Callen. Promise me you'll let me know you and Marian are all right."

"I promise."

"I wish I could help you," he said, relaxing once more. "But I don't know how."

"Don't trouble yourself over it," Callen said kindly. "You've already helped by being here."

Liam nodded and got to his feet. "I'd better go. They asked me not to speak to you, but ..." He shrugged again and grinned.

Callen grinned back. "You've been a good friend, Liam. Thank you."

"Try not to worry, Callen. You will turn out all right. I know it."

Callen watched his friend walk away from him and resisted the urge to run after him and beg him to say it was a hoax. He dropped his head into his hands and attempted to sort the thoughts swirling around like a whirlpool. He would find a way to live, but what was he to do about Marian?

3.

Marian met her brother at the gate leading into the courtyard of their home. "Brother, where have you been? Mother's been worrying."

Callen glanced toward the house. "I told her I was going out."

"You've been gone a long time," she commented, studying his expression. "You're nearly late for supper."

He grinned cheekily. "That means I'm right on time."

Marian didn't buy it but decided not to press him. "Barely. I've just come to call Father. I made our meal tonight."

"Did you now?" His thoughts went immediately to the mass he had seen her working on that morning. "What did you make?"

"All your favorites," she announced with a laugh. "Well, the side dishes anyway. Caed wanted corn chowder."

"You can't go wrong with corn." He waved her ahead. "Go on inside. I'll get Father."

"No," she protested. "You're almost a man. I'll get Father, and you can sit down."

Callen felt a flash of annoyance. "I don't care if I'm a man or not. You're still my younger sister, and you'll do as I tell you."

"Fine then!" Marian shot back. She walked away with her nose in the air.

The boy blew out an exasperated breath and went in search of his father. He met him coming from the direction of the village center. "Father," he greeted him cordially, "supper's ready."

Kael rested his palm briefly on his stomach. "Wonderful. A nice warm meal will be perfect."

Callen fell into step beside the man. "It's corn chowder, Father."

"Mmm, my favorite."

"It's Caed's favorite, as well."

The man smiled slightly. "Like father, like son."

"Marian prepared the meal tonight," Callen added.

"Is it her first?"

"Yes, Father."

Kael nodded approvingly. "Then I am anxious to taste it. Callen, tell Mother to set an extra plate. I've invited a guest to dine with us. Also, tell her to dress formally and keep the food warm until the guest arrives. Caeden may eat if he chooses."

"He will wait if I tell him to, Father," Callen offered.

"No, Callen. As his father, I will be the one giving Caeden instructions from now on."

The comment stung, but Callen bowed his head respectfully and hurried off to do as he was told.

∞

Marian glumly listened to her mother's last-minute instructions. Callen was never cross with her. Where had he gone and what could have happened?

"Remember to serve Father first, then guests if we have any, and your brothers after," the woman reminded her.

"And you, Mother?"

"It depends whether your brother has come of age or not. Do you know?"

"I know Callen was irritable when I met him coming home," Marian replied, her upper lip curling.

"Where has he been all day?"

"Mother, I don't know." She flipped her palms up and spread her hands wide. "Callen and I have not exchanged more than a few sentences all day."

"Well, what did he say when you met him earlier?"

"He said it does not matter if he's a man or not," the girl recited drily. "I shall do as he says for I am younger."

"That doesn't sound like Callen," the woman commented thoughtfully. "See if you can catch him before he sits down."

"He'll come to the kitchen. He always does."

"Marian, do as I say."

"Yes, Mother." Stepping outside the confines of the kitchen, Marian took a deep breath and checked her temper. Something was either wrong with everyone today, or she needed to reevaluate her attitude.

Callen stepped around the corner and raised his hand in greeting.

She stopped abruptly and eyed him warily.

He raised his eyebrows in response.

"What can I do for you, dear brother?" she asked with exaggerated politeness.

"Father says to set another plate," he said, stopping before her. "He's bringing a guest. Where's Caed?"

"Setting the table, why?"

"Never mind." He propelled her into motion. "Is Mother in the kitchen?"

"Where else would she be?"

Callen cocked his head to one side. "Marian, I'm sorry for snapping at you earlier."

You should be. She wanted to hold onto her anger a little bit longer, but her brother was smiling at her as if he could read her mind. "I forgive you," she relented.

"I'm forever grateful," he said with a wink. His sister bit back a smile. "Wait a moment. I have something to tell Mother from Father."

Marian tried to eavesdrop on their conversation, but couldn't make out their words over the din of pots and pans moving.

Callen came out a moment later looking unsettled. "Where did you say Caed was?"

Marian pointed to their younger brother skipping down the hall. "Right there."

The younger boy came running. "Callen! Did Father give you the speech?"

In an unusual display of affection, Callen reached out and ruffled the boy's hair. "Not yet. Marian prepared corn chowder. Father says you may eat now if you wish."

Caeden hesitated momentarily. "Does that mean we have a guest?"

"Yes."

Caeden thought for a moment. "What would you do?"

"Does it matter?"

He nodded.

"I would wait for Father."

"Because you love him and want to be with him as much as you can before you go to your biological father?" Caed inquired enthusiastically.

Callen chuckled with amusement. "Not exactly, little brother."

The boy furrowed his brow. "Why? Don't you love Father?"

"Caeden," Marian warned.

"I'm sorry, Callen," he apologized automatically. "You don't need to answer that question."

"It was a good question, Caed. Unfortunately, the answer is complicated, so I'll save my answer for another time."

Caeden nodded acceptingly. "Okay, I'll wait and eat with everyone," he decided.

"Good, now go wash up." Callen hesitated a moment, the look of unease returning to his face. "You too, Marian."

"Did Mother mention what I should wear?" she asked innocently.

"She said to look nice, but not too nice."

Marian frowned. "I'll just double check with her."

"No!" Callen grabbed her arm and swung her around. "I'll help you. Mother's busy making sure everything is perfect for Father's guest. He sounds important."

"You're acting very strange, Callen."

"No stranger than usual," Caed chimed in.

Callen turned on him. "Didn't I tell you to wash up?"

The younger boy made a face at his siblings before scurrying off.

"Why did you say that to Caed?" Marian wondered as they walked together back to their rooms. "It sounded like you were saying you don't love Father."

"I was questioning where he got the idea that I would wait for Father because I wanted to spend time with him," he explained. "I wasn't questioning his assumption that I love Father."

"Yet you know that's how he interpreted it."

"I meant something different."

"What did you mean?" Marian pressed.

"I would wait for Father out of respect, not love," Callen answered with resignation.

"How can you say that?" Marian exclaimed with surprise. "Don't you respect Father because you love him?"

"I wouldn't call it love."

Marian gaped openly.

"Don't stare at me like that, Marian."

"I don't understand—"

"Let's talk about it later." He nudged her into her room. "Remember, you want to look nice but not *too* nice."

"I don't even know what that means!"

"Pick something out and show me," he advised. "I'll let you know if it's the right kind of nice."

"Mother is never that vague," she said doubtfully. "What aren't you telling me?"

Callen gently maneuvered her away from the door and pulled it shut without answering her question. When he had stopped by the kitchen a moment ago to deliver his father's message, his mother had made her first mistake by wondering out loud if Father's guest was there to negotiate a marriage agreement for Marian. She had then made another mistake by asking him to make sure his sister dressed appropriately just in case. Callen alternately gritted his teeth and clenched his fists. He would make certain she looked like the cheerful *thirteen-year-old* girl that she was.

After making his sister change several times, Callen finally approved an outfit.

"Are you sure what I'm wearing is appropriate?" Marian asked for the umpteenth time.

"Don't you trust me?" he asked with feigned indignation.

Marian swirled her brightly patterned, floor-length tunic around her ankles. "It's not very becoming."

Callen grabbed her hand and propelled her back toward the kitchen. "How becoming do you think a thirteen-year-old can be?" He tossed a warm grin over his shoulder and added, "You look beautiful."

"Do you think Faye is beautiful too?" she asked smartly.

He stopped abruptly. "What?"

"Faye and I are the same age," she pointed out. "You didn't complain about her being only thirteen when Father arranged your marriage to her."

"What does marriage have to do with your dress?"

Marian counted off on her fingers. "I'm old enough to be betrothed, Father's bringing a mysterious guest, and Mother wants me to dress up. I'm not clueless, Callen!"

"First of all, your friend has nothing to fear from me," Callen retorted. "I didn't complain because it's not going to happen. Father's guest, on the other hand, has everything to fear from me if he so much as—"

"There you are!" Their mother appeared out of the doorway and glanced them over with a critical eye. "You two have taken far too long to get dressed. Marian, you look lovely, but you should've picked a more mature color scheme."

Marian gave her brother an I-told-you-so look.

Callen answered with a smug grin. It was too late for any of them to change. His mother's small sigh told him she had reached the same conclusion.

"You'd better bring out the bread, Marian. Callen, hurry ahead of your sister."

Callen walked a few steps away, then turned around and went back to his sister when she emerged from the kitchen. He took the large bowl from her and glanced at the small loaves. He smiled in relief. "You made this bread?"

Marian squinted at him. "*No*, Mother did. She said I'm good with flavor, but I have to work on making it *look* appetizing."

Callen snickered, and she shook her head. Several feet from the dining room, he handed the bowl back. "Is it too heavy?" He glanced once more at the bread and grinned.

She grinned back. "No. It's only bread."

"All right." He took a step forward only to turn around again. "Wait a few moments after I go in."

"I will," Marian assured him. "Go on already. I don't want them to wait long."

Callen nodded and hurried into the dining room.

Kael hailed his son at the doorway. "Callen, you are late."

"I'm sorry, Father," he apologized with a slight bow.

"Come and apologize to our guest. His name is Jaden."

Callen turned to the handsome stranger sitting at the opposite end of the table with another slight bow. "I apologize, Jaden."

Jaden nodded graciously and continued to eye the boy.

Kael gestured for Callen to sit. "Where have you been today, Callen? Your energy seems to be lacking."

Callen slid into the empty seat next to the stranger and across from his mother's usual seat. The seat intended for Marian. "Nowhere of any consequence, Father," he replied, avoiding Jaden's intense gaze.

"Well, tell us on any account," Kael urged. "Jaden was just expressing a curiosity of what boys your age do all day."

Callen glanced uncomfortably around the table, briefly making eye contact with his younger brother, who scratched his head in confusion. Callen subtly lifted an eyebrow in response, knowing that Caed would be the only one to catch it. "I took care of the raptors, went hunting with Caeden, and exercised the dromedaries."

Marian entered the room with a bright smile. "Good evening."

"Ah, here she is," Kael smiled gently. "Jaden, this is our daughter, Marian. She prepared her first meal tonight. The bread smells wonderful, Daughter."

"Thank you, Father." Marian set the bowl in the center of the rectangular table.

Callen nodded appreciatively. "Looks just like Mother's!"

Marian's eyes rounded with innocence. "Thank you, Callen! What a wonderful compliment!"

Callen furrowed his brow and pressed his lips together, fighting back laughter.

"And where is Mother?" Kael inquired.

"On her way," Marian answered politely. "She wanted to check on the meal one last time."

"Very good. Have a seat, Daughter."

Marian sat across from Caed, next to their father. Callen silently congratulated himself. Once their mother took her seat, Marian would be entirely out of Jaden's view.

Kael directed the conversation back to his eldest. "Now, Callen, continue."

The boy looked up in surprise. "That's all I did, Father."

"How did Caeden do with the birds?"

Callen swallowed, and Caeden stifled a giggle, both recalling the failed hunt. Fortunately, Kael had been summoned by the elders of the village during their training session and missed the disastrous event. "He's not exactly—"

Then Mother made her entrance, diverting the attention from the children. Much to the boys' relief, the conversation was never resumed.

∞

That night when the full moon was up, Callen snuck into his sister's room.

"Marian, wake up," he said, shaking her.

She swatted him away and said reproachfully, "You're not allowed in my room." Now that she was old enough to be betrothed, no males—not even her brothers—were allowed to step into her private chambers.

"Since when have you cared about that?" Callen wondered.

"Right now because I am trying to sleep."

Callen shrugged and walked toward the door. "Fine, but you're going to miss Liam's departure."

Marian sat up immediately. "He's leaving?"

"He came of age yesterday."

Marian looked disappointed. "He didn't tell me."

"I only found out before supper. Besides," he pointed out with sarcasm, crossing his arms. "You're not allowed to meet him unsupervised anymore."

"All these rules," she grumbled, throwing off her covers. "Is that where you ran off to earlier?"

"Yes." He held out a hand.

Marian took it. "Why didn't you tell me?"

Callen helped her to her feet. "I'm telling you now."

"Are Father, Mother, and Caeden joining us?"

"They'll follow. I've asked permission to leave earlier."

Marian still hesitated. "What of Jaden?"

"What of him?" Callen inquired indifferently.

Marian handed him her boots and coat. "I'll meet you outside in ten minutes."

"Five, Marian. The moon is already up, and the ceremony will be starting soon."

She rifled through a chest of drawers. "Why didn't you wake me up sooner?"

"Because I was stuck trying to have a conversation with our guest," he muttered as he left the room.

"Can we take Flander?" she called, referring to her favorite dromedary. The departure ceremony was always held at the outskirts of their community at the edge side of the forest. It was too far of a walk from their home, which was located at the center of the village.

"Creed's faster," Callen reasoned.

"Flander is smoother," she argued. "I don't want to show up looking tossed around."

Callen shook his head. "Marian, you are impossible."

"And I suppose you're not?" she retorted.

"Three minutes, Marian," he called, shutting her door. "Otherwise, I'm leaving you."

The girl ignored her brother's threat. The last thing he would do is leave her.

4.

"Callen, Marian!" Liam dropped his bags and hurried to them with a broad smile on his face. "I'm so glad you made it!"

Callen frowned. "I said we'd come, didn't I?" Even if the villagers shunned Marian and him for being orphans, he wouldn't have missed saying goodbye to his best friend. Even now, he saw the clear disapproval in the elders' faces.

Liam's grin faltered.

"Callen," Marian tugged on his arm. "What's gotten into you?"

"Not to worry," Liam's grin turned wry. There was no need for false niceties between them. "Have you told her?"

"Not yet."

"What are you waiting for?"

"There hasn't been time," Callen answered hesitantly. "I'd like to have a few words with you privately before you depart."

Liam nodded understandingly. "After the ceremony. Let's exchange words at the gate. I saved you and Marian a seat near mine. Shall we?"

Marian discreetly elbowed her brother. "What's troubling you?"

"Ah, I'm all right, Marian," he smiled softly. "This might be the last time you see Liam. Don't waste it worrying about me."

"I'm going to miss him."

Callen touched his sister's hair lightly. *He's going to miss you too.*

∞

After the coming-of-age departure ceremony, Callen disappeared to talk to his friend one last time. When he returned, he climbed wordlessly onto Flander's back and settled a sleepy Caeden in front of him. Marian took hold of his hand, and he pulled her up behind him. She slipped her arms around Callen's waist as Flander kept pace with the small carriage bearing their parents and Jaden.

"I don't like the way he looks at us," Marian whispered near Callen's ear.

Caeden's head drooped, and he tilted dangerously to the side. For a moment, Callen's attention was diverted as he tucked the sleeping boy securely to his chest. Then he tilted his head toward his sister. "I don't like it either."

Marian rested the side of her head against his back and stared into the night. "Who is he?"

Callen shrugged. "No one you need to worry about, Marian."

"Maybe he's here for you and not me," she suggested.

"He's not," Callen stated.

Marian lifted her head. "You don't know that."

"I do know," he answered firmly.

"How?" she pestered. "Father wouldn't discuss those kind of things with either of us."

"Leave it alone, Marian," Callen answered crossly.

Marian stiffened and loosened her grip on him. "You've been so ill-tempered all day, Callen. I think I'll ride with Mother."

Callen grabbed her arms at his waist. "No, I'm sorry." He let out a long exhale and softened his voice. "Please, Marian. Just trust me, okay?"

"Okay, Callen," she acquiesced, relaxing against him.

Callen gently squeezed her arm. "Thank you." He turned his eyes to the stars above, wondering what in the world he was supposed to do next.

Unbeknownst to them, Jaden's cold eyes carefully watched their every movement.

When they reached their home, Callen helped his siblings dismount then assisted his father in detaching Creed from his harness.

"Callen," Kael spoke as they worked. "I advise you to display your skills to our guest tomorrow morning. You would like that, wouldn't you, Jaden?"

The stranger nodded from where he stood idly by.

Callen was beginning to wonder if Jaden could speak. The man had done nothing more than nod occasionally when he had tried to engage him in conversation after supper. "If it pleases Jaden, I shall show him my falconry skills as the sun rises."

Jaden nodded his assent once more.

"Father?" Callen ventured hopefully. "I'd like to enlist Marian's help."

"Granted," Kael replied without hesitation. "Marian may accompany you; however, why do you not ask for Caeden?"

"Marian's skill surpasses Caeden's by three years," he explained. "She has accompanied me often enough to spot an error on my part. Caeden's inexperienced eye may not be so quick."

"Wise decision, Callen."

∞

The next morning, Marian was in her brother's room well before the sun. "Callen, are you not awake yet? Come, we must hurry."

"Marian, hours have yet to pass before the sun rises," a groggy Callen protested.

She ripped his blankets off. "Aren't you excited?"

"Apparently not as much as you are," he replied, burying his face into the pillow.

"It's only because I hardly get a chance to go anymore," she explained. "My household education is taking up all my time."

Callen opened sleepy eyes. "Have you been keeping up with your studies? I know you miss school often."

Marian pulled her ponytail out and started to braid her hair. "Honestly, Callen, I would rather be in a classroom practicing algebra than cooking inside a kitchen."

"Then why don't you go to school more?" he wondered, sitting up.

"I can hardly keep up with all the housework, Callen, much less my schoolwork." She could tell her brother was awake now.

"Get your school books and meet me in the barn in ten minutes," he said, climbing out of bed and pushing her out of his room. He dressed quickly and gathered a stack of papers. On his way to the barn, he stopped in the kitchen for a bowl of warm broth.

"Do you mean to teach me?" Marian wondered, glancing at the papers in his arms. "This early in the morning?"

He put the broth into her hands. "The best time to study is in the morning, and you have two hours to learn five lessons in algebra. Drink this and get to work."

∞

Two hours later, Marian was scribbling down the answers to the last few questions.

Callen was preparing his eagle. "Are you finished, Marian?" he called.

"Yes," she replied, flinging her pencil down. "I didn't understand several questions though."

"I'll look over them later. Come and help me with these jesses. I've tangled them again."

The girl snorted. "For a skilled handler, you are rather incompetent with the jesses."

"How can I be skilled then?" he returned with a smile.

"You have a rare connection with the birds, Callen. I can't tell who's enjoying themselves more—you or them." The jesses came loose under her capable hands, and the juvenile eagle suddenly lifted his wings and flew straight out of the open door.

"Watch out!" they yelled simultaneously, running after the raptor.

Outside the barn, Jaden stared openly at the large bird circling above him.

Callen held out a gloved arm, and the eagle descended gracefully out of the air.

Kael came running out of the main dwelling. "Callen, do you have control over that bird?"

"I do, Father," the boy quickly apologized. "I'm sorry to have disturbed you."

Kael threw a brief glance toward their guest then shook his head. "Mind yourself, Callen," he cautioned before returning inside.

What does that mean? Callen wondered before answering. "Yes, Father."

∞

At the northern edge of the forest, Callen and Marian stood with Jaden, watching the juvenile eagle circle high above.

"What has he been trained to do?" Jaden spoke for the first time. He had a melodious voice—smooth and enchanting.

Callen watched the bird with pride in his eyes. "He can accomplish many tasks, Jaden."

"Can he bring me a live hare?" the man challenged.

"He can," Callen answered confidently.

Jaden smirked. "I doubt it."

"Do not doubt his abilities," Marian quickly defended. "Only doubt the eagle's response to your commands. He only responds to Callen's signals."

"I shall not doubt once I've witnessed Callen's mastery, Marian," Jaden replied generously.

Callen calmly leveled his gaze at the man. "We're up to the challenge."

Jaden glanced at the boy. "Do it then."

Callen walked a few paces away and signaled the bird. He disappeared into the clouds and a few moments later, shot through the air with deadly precision. Moments later, Callen rejoined the group with a quivering rabbit in one hand, and the raptor rested comfortably on the other arm.

"Who trained the bird?" Jaden asked suspiciously.

"I did," Callen replied.

Jaden scoffed. "Not a likely answer, Callen."

The boy was silent.

"Who helped you, Callen?" Jaden asked again.

"My sister."

"Impossible!" Jaden shook his head. "Females are not given the privilege of learning falconry."

"My sister is a natural," Callen explained patiently. "She points out many faults no one else seems to notice."

"What sort of falconer makes many mistakes?" the man challenged.

Marian was quickly losing patience with the stranger's superior attitude. "Callen's falconry skills far surpass any other in the village. He is known for it."

"And you, Marian?" Jaden turned on her with glittering eyes. "Does your father know of your part in training the birds?"

""Yes," she replied, taking a half step away from him. "He's aware of the time I spend with them."

"How interesting." Jaden walked a slow circle around them and smiled sardonically. "A thirteen-year-old girl handles her older brother's falcons."

Callen stepped into Jaden's path. "Do you have a problem with that, Jaden?"

"No, but your father will," he answered coolly, stepping closer.

"Father does not object," Callen repeated with a hard edge to his voice.

"We'll see about that," the man taunted, stepping to the side.

"Don't you dare," Callen warned, turning his head to follow the man's new path. Something in Callen's voice triggered the eagle on his arm, and he leaped into the air, circled once, and free fell faster than a bullet, slamming into Jaden's back. The force of the impact knocked the man to the ground where he lay still. Marian started to scream, but Callen hastily clamped his hand over her mouth. "He isn't dead, Marian," he said in a rush. "He's only unconscious."

"What have you done?" she cried.

Callen called the bird back to him. "I don't know. Fortunately, his talons did not cause any harm."

Marian looked worriedly at her brother. "Did you give him a signal?"

He lifted his shoulders. "I must have. Why else would he attack?"

"You don't know?" she asked incredulously.

Callen scratched the back of his head with his free hand. "I don't recall anything."

Marian glanced at the man, perplexed. "What shall we do with him?"

"Wait until he wakes up." Callen sighed. "Hopefully, he won't remember what happened."

Marian stared at him. "Callen, you do understand the consequences." Guests were considered royalty in desert communities.

"Tell me."

"Father can send you away—in the night."

In the night was a phrase used by the village children to mean disowned or disinherited without being informed of who their biological parents were.

Callen regarded her with a strange light in his eyes. "There's something I haven't told you. Something Liam told me that will affect both of us."

"Something to do with Jaden?" she guessed.

"I don't know," he answered honestly.

"Well," she demanded, propping her hands on her hips. "What is it?"

The boy looked at the stranger's still form. "Let's move him into the woods. Then we'll talk."

5.

"Do you have any idea who our biological parents are?"

Callen and Marian were nestled in a large oak tree. Jaden's sleeping form lay in a covert clearing some feet off. From their perch, they monitored the man's progress. The eagle sat regally on a high tree, keeping one eye on his master.

Callen waited for his sister's response to his question. She appeared to be thinking it over, but he knew better. The fidgeting, averted eyes, and slightly rounded shoulders all indicated his sister's hesitance to delve into the topic.

"Callen, must we discuss this subject?" she finally asked. "It has never been a favorite of mine."

"Nor mine," he admitted. "But we have to talk about it."

"What for?"

He blew out his breath in uncharacteristic frustration. "You are really starting to show your youth."

Marian brought her eyes up sharply, but her quick retort halted on her tongue.

Callen watched her with a bemused expression. Her eyes went first wide with near panic, then narrow with disbelief, and finally round with wonderment.

"What are you?" she finally asked in a breathless voice.

"I'm not sure. I was hoping you might know."

"I can't imagine," she breathed. "Is Liam one too?"

"No, but his words started this."

Marian couldn't tear her eyes away. Coming out of her brother's back was a large set of wings with pure white feathers. "I don't understand."

Callen took a deep breath. "Yesterday afternoon, Liam came by and asked to talk. He tipped me off about this—" He pointed to his wings and then the sleeping figure below them. "—and that."

"How did Liam know?"

"All of them know, except those of us who haven't come of age in my group."

Marian made a face. "You're the only one who hasn't."

"Right."

She scooted around him and reached out a tentative hand. "It draws your blood."

"It does sting a little," he admitted, trying not to flinch.

"And Father?" she questioned. "Does he know? He must."

The boy took a deep breath and gave her a somber look. "He will never find our parents, Marian. But he still has to send us off."

They involuntarily turned their gaze to the sleeping form below them.

"That's where Jaden comes in?" she asked hesitantly.

Callen sighed. "Father is re-arranging your marriage to Jaden's son."

"*Re*-arranging?" she repeated incredulously. "I've already been spoken for?"

"Liam wanted to come back to the village and marry you. It was all arranged until the Council realized that we're …" He shrugged.

Marian hugged her knees to her chest. "I would've liked being Liam's wife, I think. Faye and I would be sisters. Is there nothing I can do?"

"No, but I have a plan," Callen said decidedly. "I'm leaving. Come with me, Marian. Father won't approve because it goes against tradition, but we are no longer bound by their standards."

Marian smiled sardonically. "That's a frightening thought."

"It isn't frightening," Callen argued. "It's unbinding. We're as free as the birds in the air."

"Some birds are bound even when they are not physically tied down," she pointed out practically.

Callen glanced at the eagle nearby. "He isn't bound by anything, Marian. He chooses to stay of his own accord. This is what he knows, and—and he trusts me." Realization dawned, and he turned to his sister with excitement. "I see it now, Marian. The raptors respond to me whether I give a signal or not because they and I are connected. We understand each other."

Marian shook her head. "I don't know, Brother. This is a lot to take in. Where would we go? How would we travel? What do we do about Jaden?"

Callen stretched his newfound wings. "We fly."

She gave him a skeptical look. "Even baby birds can't fly when they're first born. And you just discovered yours ...?"

"Yesterday afternoon."

"What did Liam say to you last night before he left? You had an odd look on your face."

"He said, 'I will survey the heavens for your sign.' I think he knows even more than what he shared with me. More than even the Council."

"His father *is* in charge of history," Marian pointed out.

A low moan followed by a curse reached their ears.

Callen jumped out of the tree—his wings disappearing in the same motion—and knelt beside their guest. "Jaden?"

Something dark flashed in the man's eyes before it was replaced with what he intended as a charming, wounded look.

Callen swallowed his disgust. How could Father entertain the idea of sending sweet, kind, loving Marian to **him**? "Are you all right?"

Jaden nodded, glancing up at the raptor still perched in the tree.

Marian stepped into his view. "I must beg your forgiveness, Jaden. It was my error—"

"Marian!" Callen said sharply, yanking her away from him. "It was not her fault, Jaden. If you remember, I was the one handling the eagle."

"I remember." His gaze slid from brother to sister and back again.

A shiver ran down Marian's spine.

"Shall we head home for the midday meal?" Callen suggested. "I understand you have important things to discuss with our father."

"I do." Jaden stood and brushed himself off carefully. "Marian, my dear, would you see that my hair is in order?"

Callen narrowed his eyes. *She's not your dear.*

Jaden locked eyes with Callen before bending his head down to Marian's level.

Callen's hands balled into fists as he watched his sister pat down a few straying hairs.

"There," she announced, stepping back toward her brother, who caught her hand in his and maintained his grip the entire way home.

Jaden noted with grim amusement that the boy hadn't even bothered to give the raptor further instructions, but he followed them home anyway. He would have to keep a close eye on the boy. Maybe plan another visit in the near future. As for the girl … A calculating gleam shone in Jaden's eyes. She would make a fine, submissive wife for his heir.

6.

A week after Jaden's visit, life in the village had settled back to its usual quiet pace.

Callen and Marian were still unsure of what to do about their newfound predicament; however, neither had had much time to dwell on it. Callen was busy training his younger brother, and Marian was still trying to balance school and house duties.

Wandering into the kitchen early one morning, Callen found Marian preparing the meal alone. "Marian, let's talk," he said, seizing his chance to try and convince her of his plan.

She gave him a shrewd look. "We're not running away from home."

Callen held out his hand, and she put the ladle in it. With a chuckle, he put it into the pot and stirred whatever soup she had concocted that morning.

Marian tapped her foot impatiently. "Why can't we work it out with Father?"

"It's not Father I'm worried about convincing," he admitted reluctantly. "It's the village elders who came up with the rules in the first place."

"Father's the head of the community, Callen," she reasoned. "He doesn't have to do what the elders tell him to."

Callen abruptly doused the fire and set the lid on the pot. "Father's just a mediator between the villagers and the elders," he stated bluntly. He walked to her with his hands outstretched and palms up. "Come with me, Marian," he pleaded.

Unable to resist, Marian took his hands, but planted her feet. "Where will we go?"

He tugged her after him with a happy smile. "To the forest."

"I'm not running away," she reiterated, dragging her feet.

His smile turned cajoling. "Just for a few hours. Please?"

She looked back into the kitchen. "What about the morning meal?"

"It's not even dawn yet," Callen replied. "And your soup is already finished."

Marian finally conceded. "We can watch the sunrise like we always used to."

Callen grinned, and they ran hand in hand toward the trees in the distance.

∞

"Do you smell that?" A female voice muffled by a protective face cover spoke.

Her companion took a whiff. "No, is it blood?"

The girl nodded and took to the air.

Quickly following suit, her companion joined her in scanning the desert for signs of life. "I can smell it now."

Glancing down, she replied, "It's coming from the trees." As soon as she said it, she made a face.

The young man beside her grinned. "Who ever heard of trees in the middle of the desert? They must be cultivated."

"Of course they are," she retorted. "But who has a water supply large enough to water these trees?"

Her companion shook his head in exasperation. "If you had read the research I gave you before our journey, you would not be asking such a question. Those trees are the southern border of the largest of the desert communities. The desert people use a hidden water supply that is believed to be unlimited."

"Where could they possibly conceal that much water? It makes absolutely no sense," she protested.

"That's why it is a big mystery," her companion replied. "Now keep a lookout for any movement from below." He pointed. "There! Did you see it?"

"That was just the leaves rustling," she scoffed.

"Have I taught you nothing the last two years?"

She waved his comment off dismissively. "Are you going to lecture me, or are we going to check it out?"

"You are going to check it out," he replied, hovering in the air. "I will wait here for your report."

Without a word, the girl obeyed.

From below, Callen watched their movements closely. He had inadvertently rustled the leaves when he leaped from the tree to the ground, which had caught their attention. He wondered who they were. When the smaller of the two dove toward the trees, Callen instinctively ran for the nearest clearing.

Catching sight of his movements, the winged creature followed in close pursuit. The smell of Caledon blood was all over the boy.

In the middle of the clearing, Callen whirled around to defend himself. Then, remembering he was weaponless, he exclaimed, "What am I doing?"

"What are you doing?" a voice reiterated near his head.

Callen spun around in surprise. "Who are you?" he demanded, backing away.

"Relax," a low-pitched, but distinctly feminine voice spoke.

His steps faltered. Stepping forward, he pulled down the protective face cover revealing—"A girl!"

A very angry girl. Her dark eyes glittered with rage. "How I wish I could rip you apart," she growled. "But I'm going to prove Eaerien wrong by letting you live."

"Who's Eaerien?" Callen asked, glancing cautiously around and backing slowly away.

Genesis remained where she was and slowly dropped into a crouch. "My mentor."

"And you are?" he prompted.

She still looked like she wanted to damage him. "Genesis."

"Your name is too gentle for your face," he blurted.

Genesis spread her wings and her eyes blazed. "I ought to—"

"You ought to do nothing," Eaerien cut in from behind the boy.

The hair on the back of Callen's neck tingled. Who were these people? Where had they come from?

"What did I tell you about your temper?" the young man continued, his eyes on the girl.

"I didn't kill him, did I?" the girl retorted, straightening back up and replacing her face cover.

Eaerien gave her a look that silenced her. Turning to the boy, he asked softly, "What is your name?"

Callen was silent.

Eaerien ran his eyes over the boy, noting his strengths and weaknesses. His expression was wary, but there was no evidence of fear in him. Looking into his eyes, the young man read the sadness lurking beneath the guarded gaze. "My name is Eaerien," he offered. "You have already met my hot-headed fledgling. We have come for you. It's time for you to come home, Callen."

Callen exhaled sharply and stared with wide eyes.

Then another voice reached their ears.

"Callen?" Marian stepped out from the shelter of the trees. "Who are you talking to?"

Without a word, the boy backed up, keeping his eyes on the pair until he reached his sister. Then he turned and ran, dragging her along mercilessly behind him despite her protests.

Eaerien and Genesis watched them go.

"Looks like he's got a girlfriend," she remarked drily.

"No," Eaerien corrected her. "He has a sister."

Genesis shrugged. It made no difference to her. "Aren't we going to stop them?"

A soft smile crossed the young man's lips. He too had a sister back home.

"Eaerien?" the girl prompted impatiently.

"Let them go," he decided. "He's probably from the community nearby. We'll spend the night there and look for them in the morning."

∞

"Callen, will you stop?" Marian's pleas fell on deaf ears.

They had been running for their lives for a mile now, and she had no idea why. Besides, she was exhausted. Yanking her arm out of her brother's grip forced him to stop.

"Finally," she sighed with relief.

"What are you doing? Why are you stopping?" he demanded, grabbing for her hand again.

Marian collapsed tiredly against a tree and tucked her arms close to her body. "Because I can't run anymore! What happened back there?" She was gasping for air, while her brother did not even appear winded.

"We have to get out of here." Callen held out his hand.

She straightened but shook her head with determination. "Not until you tell me what's going on. Who were those people?"

Callen caved. "They weren't people. They were—"

Someone was crashing through the bushes in their direction.

"Marian, don't!" Callen reached out to stop her, but she quickly eluded him and went straight for the noise.

"Only one person can make noise like that, Callen," she claimed. "It's—"

"Caeden!" he exclaimed as a their younger brother burst into view. "What are you doing here?"

The younger, fair-haired boy approached, breathing hard. "I've been looking for you," he gasped. "Caledons were spotted in the air not too long ago. Father's gone to greet them."

∞

Callen, Marian, and Caed stumbled into the kitchen, breathing hard.

Marian glanced cautiously out the door. "We almost ran into them."

Callen reached over her and shut the door. "You'd better warm up breakfast."

"What about us, Callen?" the younger boy asked. "We have our morning chores."

"Let's go."

Suddenly, an attendant came running. "Young masters, your father wants to see both of you in the courtyard immediately. You have guests he would like you to greet."

Callen straightened his shoulders and walked stiffly after the attendant.

Caeden exchanged a desperate glance with his sister and followed.

"There they are," Kael exclaimed, holding out an arm in his sons' direction. "These are my boys, Callen and Caeden. My daughter, and their sister, is inside preparing the morning meal."

Callen glared at the two strangers for the second time that morning.

The young man stepped forward. "My name is Eaerien, and this is Genesis."

Callen eyed them with open hostility. "Why have Caledons suddenly appeared in our land?" he asked with stiff politeness. "And why do you come so discreetly?"

Kael frowned at Callen's tone.

Eaerien bowed his head. "Please forgive us for not informing you of our arrival ahead of time. We came upon some unexpected difficulties on the way and had to make an abrupt stop."

"What sort of difficulties?" Kael questioned. "Nothing serious, I hope."

"No," Eaerien reassured him. "We were merely unprepared for the weather, or rather, we underestimated its effect on us."

Callen narrowed his eyes.

"Callen," Kael prompted patiently. "Please show our guests to the house."

The boy's expression morphed instantly into one of detached politeness. "Yes, Father." He nodded to the Caledons. "Please, follow me."

Eaerien turned to Kael. "Thank you for accommodating us under such short notice. We are indebted to you. If there is anything we can do for you during our stay, please do not hesitate to tell us."

Kael held a hand to his chest. "It is our honor to have you as our guests. If you will excuse me." He nodded to the same attendant still hovering nearby. "I'm sure our guests would like to rest. Please prepare their rooms. Callen, I leave them in your care. Caeden, come with me."

"Excuse me, sir," Caeden asked even as his body turned to follow his father. "Is that a girl?"

Callen stiffened visibly. *Caed, you idiot.*

Eaerien chuckled. "Yes, Genesis is a girl."

Caeden paused his footsteps. "She doesn't resemble any girl I've ever seen before."

Callen put a hand on his brother's shoulder and squeezed hard. "Father said to go with him," he reminded his brother through gritted teeth.

Caed scowled. Turning to the girl, he bowed apologetically.

She glanced disinterestedly at him.

"Genesis," Eaerien prompted.

She glanced up at the man for a moment before giving Caeden the same bored look.

Eaerien chuckled with exasperation. "Don't mind her. She's not exactly the sociable type."

"If you say so," Caeden replied agreeably and took off after his father.

Callen led them through the main house and to the guest home at the back of the property.

Eaerien gestured toward Marian as they walked past the kitchen. "Is she the girl from earlier?" he asked.

Callen tensed. "Our sister."

The young man smiled warmly.

Genesis shrugged indifferently. Sister, brother, family, and friend: none of those words held any special meaning for her; they were just words—concepts—that she could not comprehend. There was Jaden, and now there was Elohim. Of course there was Eaerien, whom the girl liked but did not understand. Genesis rolled her head from side to side and stretched her shoulders. She was growing impatient with all the formalities.

Callen led them to a smaller home adjacent to the main one and up a flight of stairs. "This staircase is the only way in and out of the guest rooms, so you can't get lost."

"How old are you?" Genesis asked suddenly.

"Fourteen."

"Almost time for your coming-of-age ceremony according to desert customs," Eaerien stated.

Callen nodded.

"Where are they sending you?" he inquired lightly.

Callen took a deep breath. "It seems you already know the answer to that question."

7.

"So, what do you think of him?" Eaerien inquired casually while making himself comfortable on a sofa inside the guesthouse.

Genesis didn't reply at first. She was busy looking out of the single large window in the room.

Curious, Eaerien joined her and saw a group of children running around.

"What are they doing?" the girl asked.

"They're playing."

She looked perplexed. "Playing?"

Eaerien nodded. "See the ball they're tossing around? They're trying to keep it away from the little girl. It's a common game among children."

"I've never played it before," she stated matter-of-factly.

Eaerien looked surprised for a moment, then grinned invitingly. "Want to play?"

She gave him a look of disdain and moved away from the window. "Don't be a fool."

"Why not?" he asked, following her. "You don't need more than two players. Let's try it."

"No," she replied flatly. She sprawled onto a sofa and turned her back to him.

Eaerien's shoulders sagged in disappointment. "But it's fun."

"What could possibly be fun about it?" Genesis retorted. "All they're doing is teasing that girl with something she wants but can't have. That's not fun for her; it's frustrating."

The young mentor studied the tense set of her shoulders. "You're angry."

"I'm not," she answered without inflection.

Eaerien sat beside her. "I can see why you're angry."

Genesis's voice dropped into a growl. "Shut up."

Eaerien plowed on, seemingly oblivious to the warning in her voice. "You're angry because you can relate to that little girl; always striving for something just beyond your grasp. It's frustrating, isn't it? Frustrating and lone—"

In an instant, Genesis flipped into a sitting position and released her talons right underneath his chin with the tips just barely touching the delicate skin. "I said, 'shut up'," she reiterated in a dangerously calm voice. "If I'm angry, it's because of you."

"All I meant to say was," Eaerien began.

The door suddenly swung open and a small head appeared.

Genesis glanced at the intruder with annoyance. "Try knocking next time," she suggested sarcastically.

Caeden's eyes grew wide at the sight of Genesis's talons pointed at Eaerien's chin. "Ahh!" he screamed. "Callen! Father! Marian!"

Genesis nonchalantly retracted her talons and lay back down while muttering, "How annoying."

An equally calm and vaguely amused Eaerien settled back to watch the scene unfold as if he had absolutely no part to play in it.

Callen reached them first, skidding to a stop just before the doorway. Right behind him, Marian sidestepped to avoid colliding into him. "What happened?" she demanded.

Caeden kicked the door open all the way and pointed accusingly at the girl. "She was going to kill him!"

Callen gazed at the girl, who was regarding them with a bored expression. "Are you sure?"

"Of course I'm sure!" Caeden shouted. "How dare you question me? I clearly saw her holding daggers to the man's throat! Do something!"

Callen glanced first at Genesis, then at Eaerien and shrugged.

"Well?" the younger boy demanded impatiently. "Aren't you going to stop her?"

"What is there to do, Caed?" He gestured at Genesis's relaxed air. "She's not doing anything."

Caeden's eyes were as wide as saucers. "You're not—!" Turning to Marian, he asked in a meeker voice, "Marian?"

Genesis tilted her head curiously at the younger boy's change in tone.

Marian answered gently. "It's all right, Caed. I'm sure everything's fine now."

"But I saw! Don't you believe me?"

"I believe you saw what you did," Marian replied diplomatically. "But I don't think she was trying to harm him."

Kael mounted the stairs at a more subdued pace. "Is everything all right?" he asked when he'd reached the top. "One of the attendants said you screamed, Caeden. What happened?"

"I—I—" the boy stumbled.

Callen spoke up. "Father."

Her interest piqued, Genesis sat up. She was expecting the older boy to get the younger one into trouble especially with the way the younger boy had been treating him.

"It was a misunderstanding," Callen explained simply.

Kael's expression darkened. "Is this true, Caeden?"

Caeden hung his head. "Yes, Father. I apologize for causing a scene and jumping to conclusions."

"Don't apologize to me," the father corrected. "Apologize to our guests."

"I beg your pardon," Caeden recited in a strangely formal tone.

Genesis directed her gaze to Eaerien, who replied, "No harm done."

Kael gave them a parting nod and directed his younger son back to the main house with him.

Callen offered them a civil smile. "Father's guests are free to roam the premises. If you'd like, I'll arrange for someone to show you around."

"Oh, no, that won't be necessary," Eaerien returned warmly.

"No, really, I insist." Callen pushed his sister gently out the door ahead of him. "After all, the sooner you find what you're looking for, the sooner you can leave."

Genesis's temper flared, and she was tempted to slam the door shut before the boy was even clear of it.

"Genesis," her mentor sighed, collapsing dramatically against the back of the sofa. "Try not to frighten anyone while we're here."

"It was an accident," she replied unapologetically. "He's right though, Eaerien. We shouldn't overstay our welcome. This place ..."

Eaerien understood the girl's uneasiness. Her sense of danger was keen, and Eaerien had long since learned to trust it. "Well then, what are your thoughts on the boy? Shall we take him home with us?"

"And what makes you think he'll come willingly?" she challenged. "He's not an object you can just take. Besides, even I can tell that he's not the type who'll be easily convinced."

"You may be right." Eaerien smiled grimly. "But he doesn't have much of a choice."

∞

At dinner, Genesis couldn't keep herself from staring at the boy called Callen. He was supposed to bring the Caledons back together again? He didn't look like much.

Callen didn't mind the staring at first, but as the evening progressed, the girl's stare turned into more of a glare but somehow her expression remained bland. He shifted uncomfortably in his seat.

Noticing the boy's discomfort, Eaerien leaned discreetly over and spoke quietly, "Don't mind her. She's just trying to get a handle on you."

Callen openly eyed the young man. "Why would she want to do that?" he asked slowly.

"Well," Eaerien explained, "she's curious, as am I. Does it offend you?"

"Yes," he answered curtly.

"Callen," Kael reprimanded sternly. "I'm surprised at your manners. What has gotten into you?"

"He's tired," the woman—evidently their mother—sitting beside Kael explained gently. "He worked hard all day teaching Caeden his studies, as well as his chores."

Her husband relaxed slightly and softened his voice but remained firm. "I understand you're tired, Callen, but you mustn't be rude to your guests. They've traveled a long way to see you."

Callen stared woodenly at the half-eaten meal before him. "Why?" he asked quietly. "I don't know you. What business do you have with me?"

"True," Eaerien agreed. "You don't know us, but we know who you are. As far as our business with you, I'd like to finish discussing that with your father first. I hope you don't mind."

Callen glanced across the table at his father and mother. "I don't mind," he replied. "But before all that, how about telling us something about yourselves?"

Eaerien nodded willingly. "I will gladly share my story, but I'm afraid I can't promise the same from my fledgling. She's not very responsive to personal questions."

Marian piped up. "Excuse me, sir."

"Call me Eaerien."

"Eaerien," Marian colored a little. "What *does* Genesis respond to?"

The young man threw a quick glance at the girl. She was detached as usual, so he replied, "She likes to train. Running drills is her favorite."

Genesis's eyes cut murderously to the young mentor, who chuckled.

"Actually, she hates running drills."

"Oh."

Eaerien appeared to be having a hard time coming up with an answer. "Well, she likes ... That is, what she's interested in is ..." He cleared his throat. "She likes to be entertained, I suppose." He threw Genesis another questioning look, but she was absorbed with watching the wall. "I'm not quite sure how to explain this, so perhaps another question?"

Marian nodded. "Of course. I didn't mean to ask such an awkward question."

"Oh, no," the young man protested. "It wasn't awkward, but it's a little difficult for a teacher to explain the likes and dislikes of a student he doesn't fully understand sometimes."

"Genesis is your student?" Kael asked.

"Yes," he answered. "For almost three years now."

Kael leaned forward. "If you don't mind me asking, how old are you?"

"Nineteen. Genesis was put under my care when I was sixteen."

Kael's wife blinked in surprise. "How old is Genesis?"

"Fourteen."

Kael exchanged a look of surprise with his wife. "You're so close in age. You couldn't possibly be her guardian."

Eaerien gave them a lopsided smile. "That's correct. I am her guardian, as well as her mentor."

"What sort of relationship does that encourage?" Marian couldn't help but ask. "Father-daughter, student-teacher, or brother-sister?"

"A bit of all three." His smile spread into his eyes. "I am very fond of her."

It was Genesis's turn to be surprised. Eaerien had never said that in front of her before.

Caeden flinched at Marian's next question.

"Genesis, do you feel the same way about Eaerien?"

Genesis turned cold eyes on the bubbly girl and frowned. She didn't like being asked questions about herself, especially in front of Eaerien. Despite her mentor's easygoing manner, she knew he was actually sensitive about it. "I am grateful to him," she replied stiffly.

Marian nodded.

"How awkward," Caeden muttered under his breath.

Callen abruptly stood. "Marian, let me help you serve the dessert."

Their mother also got up and began lighting the evening candles positioned around the room.

Only Caeden and Kael remained seated.

When he reached his brother's place at the table, Callen nudged him impatiently. "Everyone's helping out. Get up and clear your plate, then refill the water glasses."

Caeden started to protest, but their father cut him off. "Do as your brother says, Caeden, and do not complain."

Without another word, the young boy did as he was told. Caeden's hand shook a little under the weight of the jug, causing him to spill some water on Eaerien's lap as he brought it back up. "My apologies!" he blurted with a horrified expression, nearly dropping the jug.

Callen took it from Caeden so the boy could hand Eaerien a small cloth.

The young man chuckled quietly. "No harm done."

"Are you sure? Will it stain?" Caeden questioned anxiously.

"It's just water, Caed," Callen reminded him. "Here, try again."

Caeden accepted the jug with reluctance. "I'll spill again, and she'll be angry," he fretted.

"No, you won't."

Caeden finished filling the rest of the glasses without spilling. After the last one, which was his own, he sighed with relief. "I finished!"

Callen held the jug in one hand and patted the boy on the head with the other. "Good job, Caed."

The young boy beamed happily at his brother's praise. "I did well?" he called after him.

Callen paused briefly at the door. "You did well."

"Did you hear that, Father?" the boy announced gleefully. "Callen praised me!"

Kael offered him a small smile. Soon enough, you'll be taking on all of Callen's responsibilities, and you may even do them better."

Caeden's expression fell. "Yes, Father." Then a determined look emerged. "Father, about Callen's situation. He should stay. You know as well as I that we need him."

"Caeden," Kael interrupted quietly, but coldly. "Do not speak of matters that do not concern you."

"Father—!"

Callen stepped back into the dining room. "You are so loud, Caed!" he exclaimed. "I can hear you clearly from inside the kitchen. I wonder what our guests think of the next head of the community."

Caeden's face burned. "Why do you have to say it like that?" he demanded. "Can't you pull me aside and tell me the way Father does? Besides, you are the louder one!"

"I'm not your father," Callen nonchalantly replied. "I'm your brother. I enjoy embarrassing you." He laughed at Caeden's crimson face. "Are you mad or are you embarrassed?"

Genesis braced herself, waiting for the younger boy to lash out in anger, but to her surprise, Caeden forced out a stiff smile instead.

"I can't decide if I'm mad at you or not," he answered with passive resignation. "I should be mad."

Callen studied the younger boy curiously. "You're not mad? How unlike you."

Caeden glanced away and lowered his eyes. A gentle hand descended on his head and lightly ruffled his hair. Caeden glanced up at his older brother. Callen wasn't smiling, but his eyes were kind and reassuring. Somehow, it was enough to soothe the younger boy's spirit.

8.

The night air was cool and refreshing—a sharp contrast to the scorching heat of the day. The tensions that had built up during the day seemed to vanish in the dark sky lit up by millions of twinkling stars.

As usual, Genesis was unable to sleep. She glanced toward the door, hesitant. Normally, she would wake her mentor, but tonight she wanted to go off on her own. It was the first time since leaving her former master that Genesis wanted to be alone. Imbedded deep in her heart was a mixture of fear and hate for the master who had first driven her into a corner and then carelessly tossed her aside. Traces of his presence lingered in this village and particularly in this home. Anger welled up inside as she remembered the memories she had purposefully buried away. No longer hesitant, Genesis slipped out the open window and ran across the shadows of the courtyard.

Unbeknownst to Genesis, a pair of watchful blue eyes followed her progress. Eaerien knew very well that Genesis had been unable to sleep; he too was restless. Traces of Jaden's presence lingered in the community. Eaerien also understood the turmoil that was beginning to resurface in the girl's mind. The Caledon that Elohim had commissioned them to find and bring home had turned out to be a boy, and Genesis had been discarded by her last mentor-figure in favor of a boy. Even so, Eaerien wasn't Jaden, and Callen wasn't Aeron. Eaerien lifted his gaze to the star-studded night sky. He had an undeniable feeling that this boy would change their lives forever.

∞

Genesis didn't stop running until she reached an open field. It was grassy and quiet. She sat down at the edge of the meadow within close range of the shadows. It was safer there than in the open, and she sensed someone else's presence in the meadow.

Callen lay flat on his back at the heart of the meadow, gazing thoughtfully at the night sky. He sat up after a while and glanced around. His eyes came to rest on the figure by the trees.

Half-hidden in the shadows, Genesis watched as the boy exposed the vulnerability of his location by standing up and stretching. *Fool*, she thought.

Without hesitation, Callen approached the girl and seated himself a few feet away from her.

They sat in silence for some time.

Finally, the boy spoke. His voice was gentle and light, matching the night breeze. Unwillingly, Genesis listened carefully to catch his words. She felt an unbearable loneliness coming from him.

"Why did you come here?" Callen questioned softly. "Your timing was too precise to be coincidental."

"It wasn't a coincidence," Eaerien answered from behind them, surprising neither the boy nor the girl. "But it wasn't exactly planned either."

Callen stretched out on the grass once more and breathed deeply. "I'll go with you," he whispered decisively into the night air.

Does he have a choice? Genesis mused.

∞

"Callen's going away?" the young boy repeated slowly. He gazed searchingly into his father's eyes. "Why?"

His father sighed quietly. Explaining this was going to be harder than he thought. "Caeden, your brother can't stay here anymore. He's going to come of age soon, and some people have come to take him home with them."

"But, Father," Caeden protested in disbelief. "You said brother didn't have anyone to go home to. You said you'd let him stay and work here with us. You said he'd be part of our family for good."

"I know what I said," the man replied in low voice. "But it can't be helped. We don't have a choice in the matter."

The young boy turned and walked jerkily away. Then as if struck by something, he whirled back around. "Father," he asked angrily, "does that mean Callen agreed to go with them?"

Startled, Kael glanced up. "Caeden," he began.

But the boy cut him off. "Did he?"

"Try to understand. Callen has very few options—"

"Please answer the question!"

Kael sighed. "Yes, he has agreed to go."

The boy's eyes grew wide with disbelief and anger. Ignoring his father's attempt to explain, Caeden stormed off in search of his brother.

Inside the bird-barn, Callen sat with his head on his sister's shoulder and his arms limp at his sides. The expression on his face was a mixture of weariness and sorrow.

Caeden threw open the door and stormed in, stirring up a brief furor among the birds. His sister glanced up slowly, but the older boy didn't budge. "Hello," he greeted them icily.

Marian gazed at him with sad eyes. "Caed," she whispered.

Taking a defiant stance before his brother, the young boy smiled sarcastically. "I heard you were leaving. Good riddance."

Callen wearily lifted his head and lay down with his face toward the wall. He didn't want to deal with his younger brother's attitude at the moment.

Marian's eyes filled with tears. "Caeden," she whispered reproachfully. "How can you say that?"

"Don't cry for him!" the boy shouted angrily. "It's not like he fought to stay! He wants to go! He doesn't care about you!"

The girl shook her head. "Stop it, Caed. You don't understand."

"I understand all right!" He glared daggers at Callen's back. "He's going to leave you behind, Marian. He'll forget you, and then that guy who came to visit a week ago will come back and—Agh!"

Shocked, Marian watched her younger brother fall back suddenly, holding his cheek. She looked to Callen with wide eyes.

Callen withdrew his hand slowly and sat up. "You are such a child," he said quietly, his voice edged with anger. "I don't care how angry you are at me, but don't take it out on Marian."

Caeden gritted his teeth as tears unexpectedly crept into his eyes. "You're always like that!" he yelled furiously. "Always defending Marian and taking care of her, but when I—!" He broke off, burying his face in his arms as tears spilled over and sobs shook his body.

Callen watched his brother for a moment, a small war raging inside. Kneeling beside him, he took the boy into his arms and rocked him gently. Caeden stopped crying after a short time, but Callen didn't let him go.

"You can let go now," the younger boy said quietly. "I won't cry anymore."

"Stay like this with me, Caed?" Callen beseeched him. "Just for a little while longer."

"I'm too old to be treated like a baby," he muttered even as he put his head on his brother's chest and relaxed. "You haven't hugged me in a long time."

"I know," Callen whispered into his brother's hair. "I thought I was protecting you by not letting you get close, but I was wrong. I'm sorry, Caed."

Caeden's arms snaked around Callen's body. "I never wanted you to leave," he admitted. "I hate that rule."

Callen rested his cheek against Caed's hair. "You can change those rules. It's your birthright."

"What's yours?"

Callen held him tighter. "That's why I have to go, Caed. I have to find out who I am."

Marian slipped out quietly. Her brothers needed some time alone. They hadn't been getting along lately due in large part to Caeden's rejection of his brother, but Callen had been frustrated too and had given up trying to understand the younger boy. It was time they talked things out.

Callen and Caeden were absent for a while. It was long past suppertime when they finally emerged from the birdhouse.

"It's dark," Callen commented.

"I'm hungry," younger boy replied.

As they made their way to the house, Caeden walked close to his brother, glancing up at him occasionally. They were at the door when he finally mustered up the courage to voice the question that had been nagging at the back of his mind for hours. "Um, Callen?"

Callen paused and looked down questioningly.

"Are you ever going to come back?"

"I'll come back," he smiled reassuringly.

"When?"

"I don't know," he answered honestly. "Probably not for a while."

"How long?" Caeden pressed.

"Years, maybe."

Caeden blanched and felt sick. "Everything's going to change."

Callen nudged his brother. "Change isn't necessarily a bad thing. It would be kind of boring if everything stayed the same all the time, don't you think?"

"Probably," he agreed. "But I don't want you to change, Callen. Even though Father says we can't be brothers anymore, you won't treat me differently, will you?"

"I don't really care what anyone says," Callen replied slowly. "You're my brother, Caed. That won't change."

The little boy's frown broke and was replaced by a delighted grin.

9.

Callen stood facing the vast desert. There wasn't much to see except gallons and gallons of sand. Behind him stood Eaerien and Genesis, his new travelling companions. He was beginning to like Eaerien's matured yet somewhat boyish personality, but Genesis didn't seem to care anything for him.

"Are you ready, Callen?" Eaerien asked.

The boy turned to face the young man and silently shouldered the offered pack. He fingered the strange cloth around his neck before pulling it over the lower half of his face. To his surprise, he breathed easily through it. It covered his ears and extended from the bridge of his nose to the base of his neck, and was designed to protect his face during long stretches of flight. They would walk until they were out of sight of the community, then they would fly. Callen didn't know how he was going to pull that one off, but he didn't want to tell them that, especially if it would elicit more caustic remarks from Genesis. What was her problem anyway?

Callen couldn't have known it then because he had never seen another Caledon until Eaerien, but Genesis was only half Caledon, and she was used to being sneered at for it.

As for learning how to fly, Callen was praying that it would come naturally.

"All right!" called Eaerien. "Saddle up!"

Genesis shook her head slightly and retorted, "We're not pack animals." She looked at Callen, who was staring up at the sky. "You might want to take your pack off before opening up," she suggested with mild sarcasm.

The boy gave her a blank look. "Then how do I get it back on?" he wondered.

Without a word, Genesis reached over and unfastened the straps on his pack.

"Oh," he responded in a small voice. The scathing look the girl gave him left no doubt in Callen's mind what her opinion of him was.

Eaerien joined them. "Have you ever used your wings, Callen?"

"No, sir," the boy replied.

"Don't call me 'sir.' Call me Eaerien," the young man replied. "Don't worry. It'll be easy for you to learn. Pretend you're a bird—what's your favorite species?"

"The eagle."

"Good. Mine happens to be the swallow, and Genesis likes—Genesis, tell Callen what your favorite bird is."

"Hummingbird," she reluctantly replied.

Callen glanced at her with curiosity. He never would have guessed she liked such a tiny bird.

"Callen, I need you to open your wings," Eaerien instructed.

With little difficulty, the boy did as he was told.

"Now, strap your pack back on."

Callen had trouble strapping it back on because his wings wouldn't cooperate. Every time the pack touched them, they contracted involuntarily.

Eaerien cocked his head and raised an eyebrow. "Well, I guess we'll be walking today," he decided. "Genesis, help him strap his pack back on."

"Can't you do anything by yourself?" Genesis grumbled from behind the boy.

"Does it help to complain?" Callen challenged.

In response, Genesis pulled the straps as tight as they would go, causing the boy's wings to contract, smacking her from both sides. Genesis shoved them away.

"It's your fault," Callen muttered as he readjusted the straps himself.

Watching them, Eaerien sighed. "You two aren't starting off on the right foot."

They glared at each other.

Eaerien watched them stare each other down. Suddenly, an idea hit him. "Genesis," he said. "You teach Callen how to fly in three days, and I'll let you lead the way home."

Genesis grinned mischievously. "All right, I'll do it." She turned to Callen. "We start now." Grabbing hold of the boy's arm, she dragged him away from their camp.

Eaerien watched them go. Although he had only known Callen for several days, he had seen him interact with Genesis long enough to realize that the boy would not be able to stand taking orders from her for very long. He would learn to fly within three days, Eaerien was certain of that.

Callen pulled away from the girl's grasp. "Let go!"

Genesis whirled around, a fierce expression on her face. "You're going to learn to fly in three days, or I'll rip your feathers out."

"If you rip my feathers out, you'll have to carry me the rest of the way!"

"Maybe I'll drop you off a cliff then."

Callen gestured to the endless stretch of sand around them. "Look around, Genesis. There aren't any cliffs!"

"Then I'll bury you in the sand!" she yelled.

"Hey, you two!" Eaerien shouted at them. "Keep it down. I'm going to find some water. Stay out of trouble!" Quietly he added, "And try not to kill each other."

Genesis waved at the young man in acknowledgement. "Let's try this again," she suggested with a slightly less murderous tone of voice.

"Try what?" Callen asked in a flat voice. "You haven't taught me anything."

The girl's eyes spit fire again, but the flames quickly died down. Apparently, she was determined to keep her cool. "First, take off your pack. Can you move your wings on your own?"

Callen tried and found that he could not.

"It's like a muscle. Concentrate," she instructed.

Callen's wings twitched.

"Keep doing it until you can flap them."

While the boy was at it, Genesis sat down and watched. "You have to flap them," she pointed out. "Faster. You're going so slowly, and you're barely moving them," she criticized.

Callen concentrated even harder. Why were they so heavy?

"I said—"

"I'm trying," he grunted. "They won't go."

"You're not doing it right."

"I'm doing it right. They feel stuck."

He turned around, and Genesis immediately noticed the problem. "Your wing slits are still partially sealed," she stated.

That meant nothing to him.

"I'm going to have to cut them open," she restated.

Callen's eyes grew wide. "No! You don't have to!"

"I have to. It's the only way."

"I don't believe you."

"Then ask Eaerien!" she responded angrily and turned to sit back down.

Callen relaxed. "Fine, I'll ask him."

"You're wasting my time," Genesis muttered. In one swift motion, she was back and running a talon down the insides of his wing slits.

Callen didn't even have time to call out before he felt something warm trickle down his back. "Genesis!?"

"It didn't hurt, did it?"

He hesitated. "No, but what's that—"

"Blood. Don't overreact. It's only a little that was trapped; it'll stop soon. Try moving them again."

Callen flapped them easily, but slowly. "Aren't feathers supposed to be light?"

"Yeah."

"Then why are mine so heavy?" he exclaimed.

"I don't know. Caledon feathers are heavy for some reason. You'll get used to it." She pointed to the gaps forming between the feathers. "Don't spread your feathers when you upstroke. If you accidentally lift off before your wings are strong enough, you'll drop to the ground like a rock."

"Don't spread my feathers?" he reiterated questioningly.

"Just try to keep as little air as possible from going through your wings."

∞

On the morning of the third day, Eaerien approached Genesis who was crouched in the sand several yards away from camp. "When are you going to let him stop?"

"Soon."

They stood side-by-side in companionable silence, watching the boy struggle on.

"I can't believe he kept on this long," the girl remarked.

"You underestimated him. Has he even slept?"

Genesis nodded. "Right before he's about to collapse, I let him sleep for several hours, and you keep shoving food and water down his throat. He's fine."

"Don't tire him out completely," Eaerien advised. "Or you'll be the one to carry him all the way back to the Academy. I'll get breakfast ready," he said, walking back to camp.

Genesis waited until Eaerien's back was facing them before running to the boy. "Hey," she called. "Hey!" Callen couldn't seem to hear above the noise of his wings beating, so Genesis grabbed them and held them down. "You can stop now."

"Finally," he breathed, collapsing into a heap.

"You should probably get up," Genesis suggested.

Callen eyed the girl and sat up. He'd learned to take her warnings seriously. "I'm hungry," he stated.

"Eaerien's preparing a meal." She tilted her head toward camp and walked off. Callen dragged himself after her.

Eaerien welcomed the boy with a friendly grin. "How do you feel, Callen?"

"Hungry."

"Of course you are." He handed the boy a large white bread roll. "There's meat inside."

As they ate, Eaerien rifled aimlessly through their packs.

"Something wrong?" Callen finally asked.

Eaerien cleared his throat. "We don't have any more food left."

Callen glanced at the remaining bread in his hands. "Okay."

"Okay?"

The boy shrugged unconcernedly.

Genesis cautiously studied the boy. He had grown progressively quieter as the days passed, and all the elaborate politeness in his words had disappeared as well.

"Do you like him better this way?" Eaerien whispered softly, interrupting her thoughts.

She bit angrily into her bread bun. "I don't care either way."

A ghost of a smile passed through Eaerien's lips. "Well," he spoke up. "You and Callen take the day off and rest. We leave bright and early tomorrow morning." He reached out to pat the boy on the shoulder. "Smile a little. You're making me lonely."

10.

Their arrival at the Academy was a quiet one. It was the dead of night, and they were famished and exhausted. Loren and Kaven were waiting for them just outside the gate.

Eaerien and Genesis landed first—silent and soft as feathers.

"Only two?" Kaven wondered in surprise.

Suddenly, a third figure crashed to the ground behind them.

"You spoke too soon, Kaven," Loren remarked wryly. The pair turned around in unison and caught sight of the boy inside the gate.

Kaven ran forward immediately. "Are you all right?" He dug in his pocket for his key to the gate. "Why didn't you land on this side of the gate?"

Eaerien was at Kaven's side in an instant. "He hasn't gotten the hang of a smooth landing yet," he whispered. "He only learned how to fly a few days ago."

Kaven gave him a startled look. "He what?!"

Eaerien abruptly flung his arms around his friend. "Long time no see, Kaven!"

"Eaerien," Loren's deep voice rumbled behind them. "Where have I encountered this situation before?"

The young mentor faced the old Caledon with a bright smile. "It won't happen again."

The old Caledon merely shook his head.

"I'm sorry to interrupt," Kaven said. "Loren, what should we do about the boy?"

"Nothing," Genesis answered promptly, stepping forward. She picked the gate's lock without hesitation and let herself in. "He didn't know," she repeated, stopping beside the boy to face them.

Callen reluctantly picked himself up. His entire body was screaming at him.

Eaerien came forward, pulling Kaven along. "Don't fret over the lock. She didn't break it."

"Eaerien, what have you been teaching Genesis all this time?" Kaven chided.

"I didn't teach her that," Eaerien replied. "She taught me. Come now, Kaven. Don't be so distracted." He nodded at the boy. "Callen, I'd like you to meet the chancellor of Elo's Academy, Loren, and his apprentice, Kaven."

"He's just a boy," Kaven commented.

Loren approached the boy, who was watching them tiredly. "Welcome home, Callen."

Callen glanced at the girl beside him and spoke in a barely audible voice. "I'm tired."

Genesis, in turn, looked expectantly at Eaerien, who turned imploring eyes on Loren.

The old Caledon nodded graciously. "His room has been prepared. Kaven, see to it—"

"It's not necessary," Eaerien interrupted mildly. "Genesis can take him." He tossed a smile at Genesis, who was already ushering the boy away. "Loren, I would like to discuss something with you."

"Right now?" Kaven asked in surprise. "Eaerien, you look exhausted. Why not wait until tomorrow?"

Eaerien shook his head. "Before you put those two back into regular classes, there's something you should know."

∞

The next day, Eaerien woke Genesis from her sleep.

She blinked and stretched. It was already the middle of the afternoon.

"It's rare that I'm awake before you, isn't it?" he laughed. "I've brought you food. I noticed you didn't eat anything when we arrived last night." Genesis seated herself at the small table in her room and, without a word, accepted the proffered meal. She and Callen had fallen asleep before Eaerien had even made it up to the aerie. *Strange*, she mused, biting into a slice of bread and jam—her favorite. She never fell asleep that easily.

Eaerien smiled broadly and mussed her hair. "You did well, Genii."

She ducked away from his hand. "What happens now?"

"I'm going to meet with Loren and revisit our discussion from last night. When you're finished, please make sure Callen eats something."

Genesis narrowed her eyes.

"He's still asleep," he explained. "I'll return later this evening."

"What am I supposed to do until then?"

Eaerien shrugged. "Whatever you do, keep him inside the aerie. I don't want him running into the others quite yet. Where are you going?"

"I'll wake him now."

"Let him rest, Genii."

"You have something to say to him, don't you?" She waited for the response she knew wouldn't come. "I'll wake him."

∞

Callen opened his eyes and found himself in an unfamiliar environment. He wasn't surprised.

The past few days burned brightly in his memories. It had taken Genesis and Eaerien two years to find him, but only seven days to return. There was a step at the door, followed by a soft knock. The boy sat up slowly, minding his tortured muscles. He didn't bother to respond to the knock and merely glanced toward the door.

Genesis opened the door and regarded him with an unreadable expression. "Eaerien," she called, then disappeared without waiting for an answer, leaving the door open.

Callen let his gaze roam, noting the contents of the room with an equally unreadable expression. The ceiling was high, and the walls were bare. Across from his bed was a honey-colored desk with attached bookshelf and a matching dresser not too far from it. Callen glanced at the bed underneath him. It was large, white, and comfortable. The frame was also made of the same honey-colored wood. The pillows were plump and firm, but easily moldable with the right amount of pressure. Lying back into them, Callen realized the stiffness of his limbs was due in part to sleeping in the same position all night. He sighed inwardly, enjoying how the entire bed seemed to conform to the exact shape of his body.

A low chuckle sounded from the doorway, and Eaerien came to lean against the desk. "Sleep well?"

In response, Callen exhaled with satisfaction.

"Callen," the young man began. "I'm going to speak to Loren about your circumstances."

"What do you need from me?" the boy inquired with detached civility.

"Your preference. Do you want to live with me and Genesis?"

"I don't care," he replied without any apparent consideration.

Amused, Eaerien shook his head and left, closing the door behind him. After he had gone, Genesis quickly finished her meal and changed clothes. Then she picked up the remaining tray.

Callen opened his door before the girl had a chance to knock. He stared at her in surprise.

"What?" Genesis demanded.

He abruptly shook his head and stepped aside to let her pass. *She looked like a boy this entire time,* he thought to himself.

"Are you going to eat or not?"

"Eat?"

Genesis nodded toward the food she'd laid out.

Callen dove in eagerly. "And you?"

"I ate." She moved back to the doorway.

"You look different without the … face protector," he said. "You surprised me."

Genesis turned away distastefully, and he saw that her dark hair was tied in a simple braid hanging all the way down her back.

"I meant it as a compliment."

"I don't care," she retorted.

Callen finished his food, reflecting on the disparity between Genesis's attitude and her actions. He was growing increasingly curious about her.

Genesis glanced at his empty plate over her shoulder. "There's clothes inside the dresser," she suggested.

Confused, the boy glanced down at his clothes. *Pajamas?* His eyes darted quickly to the large dresser. Intrigued, the boy opened the drawers one at a time, studying their contents. "I've never worn clothes like these before."

Genesis shrugged. "I'll be in my room. Do what you want, but stay inside the aerie."

"Okay," he replied absently. As he began pulling clothes out, another idea hit him, and he padded quickly to the adjacent bedroom.

Genesis was lounging at her desk when Callen burst in. She glared irritably at him.

"Before you found me, did you already know of my circumstances?"

She stared at him, debating. Her mentor had known, but he hadn't shared the information he carried with her. Instead, she had read it behind his back, which he must have known she would do. "I did."

"You knew I wouldn't have another option?"

"We didn't know the details. The only records we have of you are that you were born some time ago and found in the desert. No one knew how old you were; that's why it took us so long to find you. We never suspected that you'd be this young."

"How old …?"

"Personally? Old," she admitted. Callen stood there, looking uncertain. In a way, he reminded her of Aeron. He too had looked at her with the same vulnerability once. She summoned up whatever kindness she had left inside. "You can have that room. No one was using it before."

"How do you know I'm staying?"

Genesis responded with an ice-cold expression.

∞

When Eaerien returned, he found both young Caledons holed up in their rooms. "Genesis, Callen, come out here," he called.

Two bedroom doors creaked open, and two expressionless faces appeared.

Eaerien glanced from one to the other. *Both of them?* "Come here and sit down." He patted the sofa and waited until they had complied before beginning. "Callen, you're probably wondering about a lot of things that I, fortunately, cannot give you answers to."

Callen watched the young man through guarded eyes.

"First things first," he grinned. "Welcome to the Academy, and welcome to our aerie. In time, you will find the reason why you are here, so please don't let that trouble you anymore."

The boy remained silent.

"As for you, Genesis," Eaerien continued. "Lessons start again tomorrow. Please, try to get along with everyone."

A dark look crept into the girl's eyes.

"School?" Callen questioned.

"Yes. You won't be attending just yet. I need to catch you up on the fundamentals first." He crossed his arms and studied the boy carefully. "How does your body feel?"

Callen hesitated. "Fine."

"Eaerien," Genesis started.

"It's alright. You come too, Genesis," the young mentor invited with an eager smile. "Let's go, Callen."

Callen threw a questioning glance in the girl's direction, but Genesis ignored it.

∞

Eaerien gave Callen a quick tour of the school, ending at the training grounds. There, he taught him a simple drill and made him repeat it one hundred times. By the end of the drill, Callen was dragging his wings on the ground. "You'll develop other skills once you've mastered flying."

"What sort of skills?" Callen questioned.

"Every Caledon is born with a unique set of skills. For example, I can focus my vision to see miles away, and I can heal simple wounds. Genesis, so far, has skills characteristic of both Caledon and Lacquer. Loren thinks she may have a few more skills that have not been awakened yet. It will be interesting to find out yours."

"I've been meaning to ask. Why did you travel the desert for two years searching for me?"

"Because Elohim asked me to go."

Elohim?

11.

Life at the Academy was vastly different from life in the desert. For one thing, Callen didn't have any chores to do. He spent most of his time attending classes or group training sessions. Randomly, Eaerien would invite him to train with him and Genesis. Those were Callen's favorite moments. Afterwards, he went home to Eaerien's aerie, where he had been temporarily assigned.

The Caledon aeries were cavities built into the cliffs that bordered the Academy. The entrance was just large enough to admit one person at a time and was followed by a narrow, curved tunnel that led to the door. The door opened to a circular living area with high ceilings. Three adjacent doors lined the wall opposite the entrance, leading into bedrooms with individual washrooms. Immediately to the left and right of the entrance were cozy nooks with wide, narrow ledges that opened to the cliff and allowed for airflow into and out of the aerie. Having lived in a house built from the ground all his life, Callen expected the aerie to feel claustrophobic, but it was rather cozy. And it felt like home.

Eaerien was easy to be around. He didn't ask too many questions, but he seemed to understand those around him well. He was a late riser and not easily woken. Genesis, on the other hand, slept fitfully and infrequently throughout the night. Her perpetually shadowed eyes testified to that. She barely spoke to him at the aerie and avoided him at school. At times, she disappeared for hours, but Eaerien never seemed to worry about it.

Callen enjoyed his classes. Back home in the desert communities, boys stopped attending school at twelve years of age and any further education depended on their parents. His Caledon schoolmates fascinated him. They were full of life and evidently close knit. In between classes, the sky-lit hallways were filled with wings, laughter and games. They welcomed him but shied away from Genesis. Callen couldn't figure out why since she moved unobtrusively among the other students, keeping her words and thoughts to herself. Unable to tolerate anyone being left out, Callen started following Genesis around, much to her chagrin.

"Stop following me," she confronted him one day between classes.

"Why?" he wondered, keeping pace with her quickening strides. "Am I bothering you?"

"You are," Genesis bluntly replied. To drive her words home, she spread her wings and significantly widened the distance between them with one easy stroke.

Callen broke into a dead run after her.

Genesis's temper flared. "Go away!" she yelled at him.

He stopped short right in front of her, bringing with him a gust of wind that rocked her back and ruffled her feathers. Callen tilted his head, regarding her calmly and with mischief alight in his eyes.

Infuriated, Genesis snapped her wings back into place. "Don't make me ask you again," she ground out.

"Then don't ask because I'm not leaving," he returned evenly.

Genesis could detect no challenge in the undercurrent of his words, and the heat of her temper ebbed away. A dead-eyed look replaced the fire in her eyes.

Callen held his breath, wishing she had more words for him. She so rarely spoke to him, but he often heard her conversing with Eaerien. He wanted nothing more than to crack that expressionless mask she constantly presented to everyone around her.

"Don't do this to yourself," she advised quietly.

"Do what?" he pressed.

"They," she gestured vaguely around at the empty corridor, "seem to like you. Make some friends while you can."

Callen arched an eyebrow and made a show of looking around. "While I can?"

Genesis rolled her eyes. "If you keep following me around, no one will dare befriend you."

He shrugged indifferently. "I'll have you."

"I'm not your friend," she growled, the spark returning to her eyes. "Not now; not ever."

He didn't rebut her words, but a tiny smile peeked out of the corner of his mouth.

Genesis's sharp eyes caught it, and interpreting it as a challenge, she snarled and backed warily down the hall.

This time, Callen made no move to follow her. He stayed rooted to the ground for a long time, contemplating her behavior. Something must have happened during Genesis's first days at the Academy or not long afterwards. Why else would she be so determined to remain alone and everyone else comfortable ignoring her existence?

∞

Eaerien found him there on his way back to the aerie. "Something wrong, Callen?"

Callen turned to see his mentor looking at him with worried eyes. "Eaerien," he greeted with a smile.

Eaerien clasped him on the shoulder. "How long have you been standing here?"

Callen glanced at the deepening sky above. "A while."

Keeping his arm around Callen's shoulder, Eaerien gently guided him in the direction of the aeries. "What's on your mind?"

"Why is Genesis so cold to me?"

"She isn't exactly cold," Eaerien mused. "She just doesn't express herself well."

Callen shook his head. "She avoids me and when she can't avoid me, she ignores me. She doesn't speak to me unless she's forced to either. She does that with all our classmates, but we *live* together. And still, I know nothing about her."

"I wouldn't say that," Eaerien amended. "Let's say I asked Genesis to prepare dinner tonight. What do you think she would make?"

"A salad," he immediately responded.

Eaerien dropped his arm from Callen's shoulder and clasped his hands behind his back. "Why do you think so?"

Callen backtracked over the last few months. "That's all I ever see her eat."

"And how often do you take your meals with her?"

"Every morning and evening."

"Mhm," Eaerien nodded. "What about the noon meal?"

A troubled look crossed the boy's face. "I don't know. I've never seen her in the dining hall."

Eaerien glanced at the sky now darkening to blues and purples, and picked up his pace. "What about during class? What does Genesis usually do?"

Callen lengthened his strides to match his mentor's. "Stares out the window. Sometimes she reads when the lecture hall doesn't have any windows."

"Is that all?" Eaerien prompted, leading them out to a small courtyard and spreading his wings.

Callen hesitated, winced, and followed suit. "She seems uncomfortable in the classroom," he remarked as he flew with Eaerien to their aerie. "Actually, any situation that involves sitting in one place for an extended period of time makes her either fidget or be still as a rock."

Eaerien chuckled at the boy's keen observation. "Every lecture is another trial for her," he explained. "Sometimes it becomes unbearable and … well …" He glanced at the boy. "Have you heard what the other students say about her?"

Callen looked uncomfortable.

"You don't have to repeat them, but I'll admit that most of the rumors have a basis of truth in them." Eaerien sighed. "The details are obviously exaggerated."

Callen was incredulous. "In what way could they be true?" Rumors of violence, destruction in the classrooms, and deafening cries in the middle of the night circulated around Genesis. He remembered Caed accusing her of trying to kill Eaerien.

Eaerien found the boy's disbelief amusing. "Most people are blinded by their preconceived notions and biases, and they fail to see Genesis's true character." He folded his wings and alighted into the tunnel leading to their aerie. Turning, he gave Callen a warm smile as he steadied his still-awkward landing. "You are not one of them."

"Thanks." Callen's wings quickly disappeared underneath his shoulder blades, and he leaned against the tunnel wall next to his mentor. "How do you see Genesis?" he asked.

"I see her as a fragile little girl, barely holding herself together by the seams. She's been through an unbelievable amount of emotional and physical trauma. She does have a frightening temper," he admitted. "But her silence is what kills me, and what I have to offer her is not enough." A half-grin formed on his face. "Elohim said to be patient because there is someone who can help her, but I've never been a very patient person."

"Can't Elohim help her?"

"Yes, but Elohim works in mysterious ways. No one can fully comprehend his plans."

Callen scuffed the rock wall beneath his moccasins. "Is it true that Genesis is half Lacquer and that she was abandoned by her father?"

"He didn't abandon her," Eaerien explained, "he was called away, and when he returned, Genesis and her mother had left."

"Where are her parents now?"

"Serving their masters." Eaerien held up a hand when Callen started to ask more questions. "Better to hear the story from Genesis herself." He started walking to the door and beckoned him to follow. "Tell me about school. How are you enjoying it?"

"I like it," Callen replied monotonously.

Eaerien was unconvinced but didn't press him. "Train with us tomorrow," he invited, stepping into their aerie. "Midnight. Across the e44444

lake." He grinned at the girl sprawled across the sofa. "Genesis will guide you there."

"Across the lake?" Callen repeated. "That's beyond the Academy grounds."

Eaerien leaned forward conspiratorially. "That's the exciting part."

∞

After classes the following day, Callen was summoned to the chancellor's office.

"Have a seat, Callen," Loren invited, pulling out a chair. "How are you?"

Callen sat. "Fine."

Loren spread some papers across his desk and pointed as he spoke. "These are evaluations submitted from your academic instructors. You're doing well in school and—" He pointed to a sheet with a single check mark across the entire page. "—according to Eaerien, you are progressing quickly through your training. How are you getting along with the other Caledons?"

Callen didn't answer immediately.

Loren folded his hands together and eyed the boy knowingly. "Who do you spend most of your time with?"

The boy's voice hardened. "I think you already know the answer to that question, Chancellor."

"You are correct, but why the defensive tone?"

Callen dropped his gaze apologetically. The professors had been aggressively encouraging him to spend less time with Genesis. They continually quoted a prophecy to him about Elohim's son returning to reunite the Caledons and lead the war against Jaden. Callen didn't know who Elohim's son was, but apparently, this 'chosen one' was supposed to be careful with the company they kept, but all Callen could think about was that his sister might end up married to the wrong side.

Loren spoke again. "I know these past few months have not been easy, Callen. You must have many questions."

Callen studied the old Caledon in front of him. How much did Loren know? Would he be able to tell him if Marian was safe? Would he dissuade him from building a friendship with Genesis? Callen thought carefully how to phrase his question.

"The professors teach us that Caledons and Lacquers are enemies, but why haven't we tried being friends?" he finally asked.

Loren leaned back with a satisfied look. "There was one attempt at peace—a union between a Caledon and a Lacquer. However, neither Caledons nor Lacquers were ready to accept it. Their offspring now bears the weight of the divide."

"And the parents?" Callen questioned eagerly. "Where are they now?"

"They have returned to their kind."

Callen was outraged at the injustice. "And the offspring? What did they expect for her?"

Loren looked sadly at the boy. "They were young and foolish, Callen. There was no forethought to the consequences of their actions."

"Genesis is not a consequence!" he shouted.

"Callen, you misunderstand," Loren corrected gently. "I mean to say there was no wisdom in their decision to marry. The consequence is the torment they left their child in, not the child herself."

Callen raised his brow slightly. "Chancellor, you don't shun Genesis the way others do?"

"Oh no, Callen," he reassured him. "Elohim has very special plans for Genesis. She does not realize how beloved she is."

Callen's brow came down into a crease. *Elohim again.*

Loren changed the subject. "I understand you are training with Eaerien tonight."

Callen nodded.

"Then I won't keep you much longer." He gathered the papers into a pile. "Your three-month evaluation date has been set for the beginning of fall. Be prepared."

Callen nodded again. "Yes, sir."

"Good. You may go."

He was halfway out the door when he heard Loren speak again.

"Oh, and Callen," the old Caledon said, "call me Loren."

∞

Genesis was waiting for Callen outside the Academy gates. "You're late," she scowled, crumpling up her homework and stuffing it in a crevice in the wall just inside the gate.

Callen folded his homework and carefully set it inside with hers, then placed a narrow stone over the crevice. "Loren sent for me."

She kicked off the wall and set a brisk pace in the direction of the lake. "Your evaluation?"

"Yeah," he said, hurrying to keep up. "In the fall."

"So is mine."

Callen gave her a confused look. "You've only been at the Academy for three months?"

She tossed him an impatient look. "They evaluate us four times during our first year, then three, then two, then one. It's their way of making sure we're not slacking on our training."

Callen smiled to himself. It was surprisingly easy to converse with the girl when she was in the mood.

"What?" Genesis demanded.

"Nothing." He stuck his hands into his pockets. "Why do they do they check up on us so often?"

"They're preparing us for something, but Eaerien won't say what it is."

"Does Eaerien tell you anything?" he asked lightly.

Without missing a beat, Genesis swept the boy's feet out from under him.

Callen flew forward, his hands still buried in his pockets. He twisted at the last minute and landed on his hip. "Ouch!"

Genesis smirked and shot off into the forest like lightning.

Callen picked himself up and shook his head with exasperation. He followed her deep into the forest and to the edge of a lake.

Eaerien was waiting for them, and he was uncharacteristically serious. "Two conditions," he said without preamble. "Do not lose sight of each other and do not wander. Outside the Academy grounds, there are creatures that do not uphold Elohim's ways. Are you ready?"

They nodded. Callen could feel his pulse accelerating.

"What's our assignment?" Genesis asked.

"We are going to explore."

Callen started. *We are risking our lives to explore?* He caught Genesis's eye, but she simply shrugged.

They flew unhurriedly across the center of the lake. Callen was pleasantly surprised at how easy it was to cruise through the still night air beside Eaerien and Genesis. His broad wings stretched long and white across both sides of his body. He felt the now-familiar trickle of blood down his back, but little pain. He made a mental note to ask Loren about it the next time he saw him.

Something glinted in the moonlight, catching his attention. Mesmerized, Callen stared at his mentor's silvery wings shimmering gracefully in the moonlight. He had learned that Caledon wings highlighted the strength or character of their bearer. All were unique, but none glimmered the way Eaerien's did. It seemed a fitting design for his mentor, but Callen could not explain why. He cast a glance at Genesis. Lacquer wings were mostly identical: small, narrow, sharp and with dark feathers. Genesis's wings were an enigma: long and tapered to a point like a Lacquer's but broader; although not as broad as a Caledon's, and obsidian black with a velvety softness.

On the opposite shore, they landed in the open.

Genesis peered anxiously into the trees. "Did we have to fly directly across the lake? Anything could have seen us."

"We are guardians, Genii. We are supposed to be seen," Eaerien replied with amusement.

Genesis glanced at Callen. "Stick close."

"Are you worried about me?" he teased.

She gave him a dark look.

Eaerien walked toward the trees, gesturing them to follow.

Callen blinked in the darkness of the forest. It was his first time in a forest at night without a light, but he could see surprisingly well. Could he always see this well at night? None of the Caledons carried lights around at night, and he finally knew why. As they strolled deeper into the trees, he marveled at the life around him.

They walked quietly for the better part of an hour. All the while, Genesis kept a close eye on Callen. The boy wandered all over the place, curious about everything and sometimes moving out of sight. Eaerien moved as silently as always, and Genesis could sense rather than see or hear him. She took a deep breath and tried to calm her pulse. She was nervous. Lacquers dwelt here, and being on the ground left them horribly exposed.

Eaerien scanned the trees. He could see Lacquers moving restlessly among them. It would not be long before they tired of remaining hidden and instigated a confrontation. He stepped to Genesis's side and saw that her eyes were shut. It was time to go. He took her hand and looked around for Callen.

Genesis's eyes popped open and her blood ran cold.

The boy was gone.

12.

Callen was scared and on the verge of panic. Neither Genesis nor Eaerien were anywhere in sight, and he was surrounded by a crowd of jeering, vicious Lacquers. He backed as far as he could into the hollow of a giant, ancient tree and wished for invisibility. Lacquers did not see well in the dark, but they had a keen sense of smell for blood, and he was bleeding everywhere.

Callen threw up—he couldn't help himself. *The only thing Eaerien asked was for us to stay within sight,* he berated himself. He had not realized how far he had wandered until he had been attacked from behind. He must have also drifted out of earshot or the Lacquers would not be making so much noise. Callen had no idea how to escape from this predicament. None of his training sessions thus far involved combat. To make matters worse, his wings were in shreds.

He flattened himself against the wall of the cavity. *Please, help me,* he begged silently. *Eaerien, Genesis!*

"I smell you!" a malicious voice exclaimed.

"He's in the hole!" another one called out.

A chorus was raised.

"Go get him!"

"Don't let him get away!"

Desperate, Callen rushed at them. He wasn't about to let them drag him out of his hiding place.

They had him pinned to the ground in no time and were fighting over each other for a chance to run their claws down his back when Genesis miraculously dropped out of the sky like an atomic bomb. She wielded her talons like a thousand swords as she descended on the gang of Lacquers. Chaos ensued. The ones holding Callen down scrambled frantically out of reach. Furiously, she chased them down, dragging them from the trees and exacting her vengeance. The Lacquers hastily retreated. They knew about Genesis. They feared her and hated her, but they were forbidden from touching her. She belonged to Jaden.

Genesis followed them a short distance, snarling fiercely, "Cowards!"

Eaerien ran after her with Callen in his arms. The boy was a bloody mess, and his wings were in tatters.

A fresh wave of rage engulfed her. "I'll kill them!"

"Genii," Eaerien called urgently. "Give me your tunic." He knelt, cradling the boy's head. "I'll heal what I can."

Genesis pulled off her outer tunic and tore it into pieces. She wrapped up the deepest wounds while Eaerien worked quickly to seal the many smaller, bleeding cuts.

A tear slipped silently down Eaerien's cheek. *Oh, Elohim, what have I done?*

∞

Callen blinked and squinted his eyes.

"Morning."

He turned his head slightly and saw Genesis perched nearby. *Where am I?*

"You're in the hospital," she answered.

His eyes opened fully. *Did I say that out loud?*

"No," she answered, her expression mirroring his. "I can hear you."

Callen tried to sit up. "Owwch."

Genesis jumped off her perch and attempted to be gentle as she pushed him back down. "You're still injured. Just lay down, okay?"

He groaned. "What happened?"

"You don't remember?" she asked incredulously.

Callen moved his head carefully from side to side. "How did you find me?"

She pulled a chair close and sat cross-legged onto it. "Eaerien didn't hear you call last night. He found you with his eyes, but I heard you yell my name when you were inside that tree."

He stared at her. *You heard me yell? Inside my head?*

She held his gaze and nodded slowly.

Can I hear you? Callen waited for a response. Then he said aloud, "I can't hear you thinking. Wait, can you think?"

Genesis made a motion to hit him.

Callen started to laugh and ended up contorting his body in pain. When it subsided, he lay still and turned weary eyes on his teammate. *Why can you hear me, but I can't hear you?*

Genesis furrowed her brows. "I don't know. I'm pretty sure you're the one who opened the connection."

Callen shut his eyes and thought carefully. *I was pretty desperate last night.* He waited, but she didn't respond, so he tried a question. *Can Eaerien hear me too?* Still, she gave no answer. *Genesis!*

"What?" she asked.

Did you hear what I asked?

"No."

He opened his eyes. "You can only hear me if I'm focused on you. Where's Eaerien?"

"With Loren," she answered curtly. "He blames himself."

"It's not his fault," Callen said as regret washed over him, "I wandered off."

Genesis gave him a cold look. There was no doubt in her mind whose fault it was.

"I'm sorry." He closed his eyes again.

Her eyes softened imperceptibly as she studied Callen's drawn face. Even if Eaerien blamed himself, the one suffering the most was the boy before her. "They've never attacked a Caledon unprovoked before," she stated quietly. "Eaerien wouldn't have brought us there if he knew."

Callen nodded, and his breathing slowly deepened.

"Are you in pain?" she asked with worry lining her voice.

"Only when I move," he admitted. "How bad is it?"

She remembered the state of his wings, and a small wave of nausea hit. "You won't be able to fly for weeks. They really tried to maim you."

Thank you for saving me, he said with his thoughts.

Genesis shook her head then remembered his eyes were closed.

Callen's eyes fluttered open briefly. "You're not like them," he said softly.

"I'm half of them."

You're not half anything. You're just you …

∞

Eaerien returned soon after Callen had fallen asleep again.

"How is he?" he asked, coming to Genesis's side.

"He woke up." She looked inquiringly at her mentor. "He didn't seem traumatized. Is that possible?"

"With him?" He adjusted the boy's blankets. "My guess is that anything is possible. Were you able to hear his thoughts again?"

"Only when he was speaking directly to me. Eaerien, do the Lacquers know something that we don't?"

Eaerien raised his eyebrows.

"What aren't you telling me?" she demanded.

"I've shared with you everything Elohim has told me."

"No." Genesis stood, tension evident in the stiffness of her movements. "You know something. Something he didn't exactly say to you, but you've figured out. What is it?"

"Genii," he tried to placate her. "My thoughts are just thoughts. They have no weight unless they've come from Elohim."

"I know how close you are to Elohim," she insisted. "Your thoughts aren't usually far off from his, so why won't you share them with me?"

Eaerien took the seat she had vacated and propped his chin on a hand before replying. "There are things that are meant to be told and things that you simply must learn on your own." He reached for the girl's hand. "Don't be afraid to get to know him, Genii. We *are* able to love more than one person at a time."

Genesis pulled her hand away and thought involuntarily about Aeron and Jaden. She had once held Jaden's favor, but he had cast her aside when Aeron showed up. She knew that Eaerien had not immediately taken on a second fledgling in consideration of her. But now Callen was here. She acknowledged that he was different from the others who scorned her, but Genesis had too much experience with the fickleness of emotions to trust anyone. She turned away from Eaerien. "I'll wait at the aerie."

13.

Eaerien couldn't find his eyases anywhere. A week had passed since Callen's run-in with the Lacquers across the lake, and with the exception of his wings, he had fully recovered. Genesis and Callen had been instructed to meet Eaerien under the massive oak tree at the center of the Academy courtyard, and he had been waiting for an hour already. The young man sighed and closed his eyes reluctantly. He had been using his eyes too often lately, resulting in a near constant throbbing at his temples. When he opened his eyes again, they had changed from deep blue to an ice blue color. He scanned the surrounding area and located them immediately.

Genesis and Callen were sitting in a tree at the edge of the forest.

"Are you sure this is all right?" Callen asked for the twentieth time that hour. "Maybe we should've stayed near the rendezvous point."

"You said you wanted to know how his eyes work," she remarked unconcernedly.

"I could have just asked him."

Genesis didn't respond.

"We should go," Callen insisted. He started to jump off the branch, but Genesis pulled him back. He sat down hard.

"He's here," she jutted her chin toward the sky. "Look."

Eaerien landed silently next to the tree and looked up at them.

Callen watched, fascinated, as his mentor's light blue eyes darkened to their usual shade.

"Is that all you wanted to see?" Eaerien teased.

Callen felt color rise in his cheeks.

"Come down here and let's start the lesson."

They slid obediently from the tree.

"You're pretty adept at moving through trees?" Eaerien asked Callen.

"Like a monkey," Genesis commented.

Callen glared at her, but she pretended not to notice.

"That makes two of you," Eaerien remarked. He chuckled when Genesis gave him the same glare Callen was giving her. "Go on, back into the tree." After they obeyed, he called to them. "Keep your wings sheathed. This is your warmup: race to the lake and back. Stay within the treetops. Ready?" Without waiting for their reply, he shouted, "Go!" He followed their progress with his eyes. Genesis was faster in the air, but Callen matched her speed in the trees. They were still rather slow compared to Lacquers though. When they turned back at the lake, Eaerien closed his eyes.

Genesis glanced sideways at Callen as they raced back to their mentor. He seemed to be enjoying himself. With a sudden movement, she launched herself at him, talons fully extended. She was extremely quick, and it would have been a miracle for any creature to escape her punishing talons at such close proximity.

Callen recoiled automatically, throwing himself away from the tree and into the next.

She missed by a fraction of a hair and immediately launched herself at him again.

Callen twisted and jumped backward from the tree. *What are you doing?!*

"Training!" she yelled back with a smirk. She fixed her eyes on him and crouched.

In the next tree, Callen mimicked her posture and swallowed hard. He wasn't fast enough to avoid her. If she missed, he could run, but how could anyone miss at this close range? Hadn't the Lacquers cornered him like this the other night? *Here she comes.* He flung his arms in front of him as she hurtled toward his chest and waited for the impact.

It didn't come.

Callen peaked over his arms and his jaw dropped in surprise. Genesis was suspended in the air in front of him, looking just as surprised. They stared at each other, speechless.

"Let her down, Callen," Eaerien spoke calmly from below them.

Genesis tried to move her head to look at their mentor, and the air around her tightened.

Callen stared at his hands. *I did this?*

Genesis struggled to inhale against the constricting atmosphere. "Eaerien," she called in a muffled voice.

Callen glanced around and at Eaerien. "How do I?" Genesis started choking.

Eaerien was at his side in an instant. "Take a deep breath," he suggested.

Callen shut his eyes and tried to focus on his breathing instead of Genesis suffocating in front of him. He started to panic. "Eaerien, I can't—!"

Eaerien shoved Callen out of the tree and watched with satisfaction as both eyases fell toward the ground. He dove after them and caught them before they hit the ground. He set them down gently.

Fuming, Genesis scrambled to her feet and slowly withdrew her talons. A small, sinister voice whispered in her ear. **He tried to kill you! He wants to take your place as Eaerien's fledgling!**

Callen also stood, looking remorseful. "Are you all right?"

Her expression darkened.

Callen recognized the conflict he had grown accustomed to seeing in her eyes over the past few months. "Genesis?"

Her eyes narrowed dangerously, and she tensed like a tightly coiled spring.

Get rid of him, the sinister voice said with authority.

"Genesis, stop!" Eaerien commanded.

She froze, breathing hard and with her talons mere inches from Callen's head.

Eaerien spoke softly, "You don't want to do that."

"Yes, I do," she snarled, shivering in anticipation of the bloodshed.

Callen's eyes were locked on hers. *I'm sorry.*

"Genii ..." Eaerien prompted. She flinched and her eyes lost focus. He put a gentle hand on her head, and her talons slowly retracted.

Callen took a step toward her, but she backed warily away. "Genesis," he said imploringly.

For a moment, her tortured gaze connected with his then she spun away and ran.

Eaerien watched her go with a sad expression on his face. He put a hand on Callen's shoulder. "Let's go home."

Callen followed, a thousand questions running through his mind.

∞

Genesis was in class the next morning, although she had not returned to the aerie.

Callen took his seat next to her as she eyed him with open hostility. "Hi," he greeted unable to hide the relief he felt.

"Stay away from me," she warned quietly.

"Why?" he queried.

She clenched her jaw. "I might kill you one day."

Callen persisted. "What happened yesterday was an accident."

Genesis ignored him and twisted in her seat to stare out the window.

Callen focused his eyes on the back of her head and concentrated. *You can't ignore me forever.*

She gave no indication that she had heard him.

Callen reluctantly let it go as the lesson began.

As usual, Genesis paid no attention to the instructor. Instead she preoccupied herself with her thoughts and kept her gaze directed out the window. *Maybe I should have skipped class,* she thought idly. For some reason, sitting through this morning's lesson was more torturous than usual. She dropped her head to the desk. *I can't believe I attacked Callen. When did it get so bad that even Eaerien couldn't reach me?*

Ha ha ha ha! The same ugly voice from yesterday intruded on her thoughts.

Genesis shook her head. *Not today,* she begged.

Hello, Moriana. Did you enjoy the blood rush yesterday?

A shiver travelled the length of the girl's spine, and she willed the voice to disappear.

It's hopeless, Moriana. You know very well that you can't resist me once I've awakened. It's too bad about your new friend. I was hoping to keep him around for a while longer, but it looks like you've already gotten too attached for your own good.

No.

Don't worry, Moriana. You gave him a warning. It's his problem if he doesn't take it seriously. Now, how shall we do this? The quicker the better, since he seems to have gained a significant amount of influence over you in such a short time.

What influence?

Oh, you didn't realize? That boy was the one who pulled you back from the depths of your despair. He was also the one who reawakened me. It's a bit of an irony, isn't it?

Genesis attempted to redirect her thoughts.

Stop resisting me, Moriana. At first the voice spoke in a whisper then grew increasingly loud with every word. **It's useless to resist. You can't fight me. I always win in the end.**

Genesis squeezed her eyes shut. *I'm not that kind of creature anymore!*

You're a monster.

No! she screamed inside her mind. *Leave me alone!*

MONSTER. Your real name is Moriana. Go back to where you belong.

Genesis gripped her head in between her hands. *Make it go away,* she pleaded desperately. *Elohim!* She felt a light touch on her elbow and in an instant, a light chased the oppressive voice away, and her mind cleared like the sun peeking through the clouds. She raised her head cautiously.

Callen was looking at her with a mixture of curiosity and mild concern.

She stared back at him with a puzzled expression. "Did you just touch me?" she demanded in a loud whisper.

"Just a nudge," he explained in a hushed voice, returning his attention to the lesson at hand.

"Hey," she whispered more quietly.

He glanced at her inquiringly.

"Genesis!" the instructor called out. "Is there a matter so urgent that you must consult your teammate in the middle of my lesson?"

"No, sir," she mumbled.

"Then keep quiet or feel free to leave the classroom. You never pay attention anyway."

Genesis shrugged indifferently and turned to face the window once more.

∞

After class, Genesis and Callen were the first ones out the door.

"Genesis, wait," Callen called, rushing after her. "What's wrong?"

"Don't follow me!"

Callen ignored her and quickened his steps, walking sideways to see her face. "What happened back there? And where were you last night?"

"None of your business," she replied shortly.

"You always say that!" he protested. He caught her arm and pulled her to a stop. They stared each other down.

"Callen," someone called, breaking the moment.

Callen released Genesis's arm.

Their instructor walked briskly toward them. "You and Genesis are needed in the chancellor's meeting room."

"Chancellor's meeting room?" Callen reiterated questioningly.

"And our mentor?" Genesis inquired.

The man's eyes flickered distastefully toward the girl but didn't quite reach her face. "Eaerien is with the chancellor."

Callen felt sadness deep in his heart. It wasn't the first time he'd seen Genesis regarded with open hostility.

Genesis pushed Callen lightly from behind. "Hurry up."

∞

The meeting room was filled with mentors and elders, only one of whom Callen had never seen before. Genesis went immediately to stand next to Eaerien's chair, while Callen remained by the door.

Loren stood. "Come inside, Callen. We are here to discuss your placement on a team."

Callen moved forward uncertainly.

"Stand by my chair, Callen," Loren directed. "This is standard, I assure you. We take creating teams very seriously, as I'm sure you've heard already."

Callen looked questioningly at Eaerien, hoping for a hint.

His mentor appeared entirely unconcerned.

"Callen?"

"I'm sorry, Loren," he said apologetically. "I must have missed that lesson."

Loren frowned and directed his gaze at the young mentor. "Eaerien?"

"I did not inform him," he answered cheerfully.

There was a murmur of disapproval around the table that Loren quickly silenced. "No matter." He turned to the boy. "Each team we create gets sent on assignments or missions, the difficulty of which depends on the cumulative skill level of each member and their overall skill as a team. Unless you become a mentor, your teammate is your partner for life. Your case is unique in that you have only awoken one skill, and you will be placed on a team prior to awakening your others."

Eaerien lifted his hand.

"Ah, yes. Eaerien informed me this morning that you have another skill that has awakened, but no one here seems to know how to describe it. Have you used that skill before yesterday?"

"No, sir. I'm not entirely sure what I even did."

"Time will tell," Loren said dismissively. He turned back to face the table. "Now, shall we begin with an introduction? I don't believe Callen has met everyone here."

Kaven, Loren's apprentice, was immediately on his left. Then Shiloh, one of the three mentors. Next, a young female Caledon named Aria, who looked remarkably like her younger brother Eaerien. Three elders followed consecutively. The elder sitting directly across from Loren was Eaerien and Aria's father, Raine. After the elders sat another instructor, then mentor Tuolene, and finally Eaerien.

Callen sat woodenly as the elders spoke about a prophecy regarding Elohim's son.

They spoke about the impending war against Jaden and his followers.

Then the changes occurring in the desert communities.

The prophecy again.

Callen's potential skills that hadn't awakened yet.

Eaerien's unconventional teaching methods.

Loren's potential junior apprentice.

The prophecy.

Callen's mind was whirling. Did they expect him to fulfill that prophecy? He barely knew about Elohim, and he had never met him. Elohim was his father? How was that even possible? Reunite the Caledons? He couldn't even stand against a group of Lacquers! And what was wrong with the way Eaerien taught them?

And what about Marian? Dear, sweet Marian. She had to still be with their adoptive parents. Kael was stern and played by every rule in the book, but he wasn't cruel. He doted on Marian. Surely by now he had seen through to Jaden's true character and called off the betrothal.

The nameless instructor voiced a concern about Genesis's influence on the boy, launching another involved discussion. Callen had had enough.

When one of the elders suggested a vote, Callen stood abruptly. "If you'll excuse me," he said politely. Not waiting for an answer, he practically fled from the room.

Without consciously realizing it, Genesis followed Callen out of the office. She found him sitting around the corner with his knees drawn up, arms crossed over his knees, and face buried in his arms. She glanced around and shifted her weight from one leg to another, at a loss for what to do. She started to walk away when Callen's voice stopped her.

"Why did you follow me?" he asked, his voice obscured by his arms.

"I don't know," she admitted.

Callen peeked up at her through the hair that fell over his face. "You," he began before turning his face away again. "You didn't seem bothered by what the instructor said about you."

"I'm used to it," she said carelessly.

He's wrong.

Genesis hung her head. "He's not wrong. Did you already forget what I almost did to you yesterday?"

"That wasn't you," Callen stated confidently.

A wall started to crumble inside Genesis. "You barely know me."

Callen uncovered his face and looked directly at her. "You're here, when you always say you don't want anything to do with me."

Genesis scowled.

He studied her face thoughtfully. "Genesis, do you also think Elohim wants the Caledons and Lacquers to go to war against each other?"

She looked uncertain for a minute then sat next to Callen. "No one cares what I think," she reminded him.

"I care," he replied, his eyes crinkling at the corners.

Genesis fought back the unfamiliar wave of emotion that surged through her. "I don't think he does."

"Why do you say that?"

She fidgeted. "Elohim saves. He doesn't destroy; he redeems."

Callen inhaled deeply. "Right before you and Eaerien arrived at the village, Jaden had been there." He noticed her flinch at the name.

"I knew it," she muttered.

"He was negotiating a marriage contract with my father for my sister and his son," Callen continued.

"He doesn't have a son," Genesis explained with unusual patience. "He has an heir, but it doesn't matter. Elohim won't allow that marriage to go through."

"You're nothing like the rumors say about you," Callen said with a kind smile.

Genesis frowned and turned her face away. "You already know that I'm half Lacquer."

"You're not half anything, remember?" He nudged her playfully with his elbow. "You're wholly you. You're Genesis."

She gave the boy a curious look.

"What is it?" he prompted.

"Why did you come to the Academy?"

Callen let his head fall back and gazed searchingly into the deep blue sky. "Back in the desert," he said slowly, "they taught us that everything has a purpose. I guess I'm here to find mine."

"You knew nothing about Eaerien or me, but you followed us." She shook her head in disbelief. "You didn't even know the difference between a Lacquer and a Caledon. We could have led you anywhere."

"Your timing was not an accident even if it wasn't planned," he reasoned. "I've seen the changes in the desert communities the elders speak of. They are slowly implementing Jaden's practices into their teachings, but what he stands for is wrong. I knew right away that you and Eaerien don't follow him."

Genesis mulled over his words. The changes in the desert communities had been so subtle that the majority of the Caledons were still unaware. If Elohim had not tasked Eaerien to search for Callen, the Academy leaders would not have known of the changes for many months to come. As it was, they heard of it because she and Eaerien had witnessed it during their two-year search.

Callen stood and brushed himself off. "We'd better get back." He held out a hand toward her. "You coming?"

The meeting room, which had been filled with voices moments before, fell silent when they walked back in. Genesis returned to Eaerien's side. Callen looked to Loren for direction.

"Do you wish to say something?" Loren invited.

Callen let his gaze roam around the room. "I can't claim to or deny being the one from the prophecy." *I don't even know who Elohim is.* He continued out loud, "I believe that will be made clear to all of us at the right time. As for which team I'll be placed in … " He looked at Eaerien. "If you aren't against it, I'd like to stay with you and Genesis."

Loren glanced around. "There doesn't appear to be any objections."

Grinning, Eaerien stood. "Well then. Since we've reached an agreement, I'll take my team and officially start training immediately." He bowed respectfully to Loren before leading Genesis and Callen from the room.

14.

As the weeks passed by, there was a gradual shift in the way Genesis regarded Callen. She remained insecure of his attachment to her, but she grudgingly accepted his presence. They bickered constantly; however, like her mentor, Callen was persistent in becoming her friend.

Eaerien experimentally began giving them assignments together instead of individually. He was hoping their teamwork would improve with time, but more often than he cared to admit, he found himself questioning Elohim's wisdom in pairing them up.

"Slow down, Genesis! We have to do this right!" Callen yelled.

"We also have to get it done!" she yelled back. "Hurry up!"

Watching from below, their mentor shook his head in exasperation. Would they ever learn to get along?

This was Callen and Genesis's first aerial assignment since the encounter with the Lacquers weeks ago. They had been tasked to gather abandoned skunk eagle eggs and build a nest for them at the tree line. It was not intended to be difficult, but Eaerien was resourceful. The only time Callen was able to activate his defensive skill was when his life was in danger, so Eaerien intentionally put him in life-threatening situations. So far, it was working.

Genesis was a good thirty meters ahead of Callen, scrambling up a sheer cliff. Moving at half her speed, Callen carefully groped for handholds, unable to trust his wings that were still weak from disuse. Eaerien soared high, making a mental note to give the boy strength-training drills.

When Genesis reached the top of the rock wall, she sprinted for the tree line. At the same moment, Eaerien launched his first attack. He had given them until sunset to complete the task, which was now two hours away. He had not forewarned them about an attack.

Genesis was near the tree line when she sensed Eaerien closing in from behind. Too late to mount a defense, she threw herself to the side, using her wings for cover. They repeated their odd dance until Genesis found herself back at the edge of the cliff where he held her at bay.

When Callen finally reached the top of the cliff, Eaerien directed his attention on the boy, trying to push him back over. With Eaerien's attention diverted, Genesis initiated her own attack. Unfortunately, he saw her coming and was ready for her. Beating his wings with powerful strokes, he blew her away.

Callen took the opportunity to slip away and ran for the trees, picking up eggs that had slipped out of Genesis's sack on the way. He made it to the forest and set the eggs behind a tree trunk while he scrambled to construct a nest.

Eaerien abandoned the onslaught on his eyases and targeted the eggs. Within seconds, he had the sack in his arms and was flying toward the cliff. Genesis scrambled to her feet and sped through the air like a bullet, ramming into her mentor, who somersaulted through the air and over the cliff. Clutching the sack of eggs, she flew desperately back toward the shelter of the trees. An arm's reach from the safety of the forest, she heard Callen's warning shout. She flung the sack at her teammate as Eaerien's body slammed her to the ground.

Callen hoisted the sack into the nest. Surprisingly, the eggs were alive and whole. As he threw the last layer of earth and leaves over the eggs, an unmistakable rustle sounded above him. He looked up to see Eaerien descending on him. "No!" he yelled, flinging his arms over the nest.

Eaerien froze.

"No!" Genesis screamed from below.

Callen dropped his arms in surprise, and his mentor fell toward the ground. Genesis caught him mid-air and supported him the rest of the way down.

Eaerien sat up, gasping for air. "Good, you're getting stronger," he rasped.

"I'm sorry," Callen blurted.

"Don't be. You did exactly what I was hoping you would do." Eaerien stood and brushed himself off. "Were you conscious of it this time?"

Callen nodded. "But I can't control the strength."

"Can you reproduce it right now?"

"But how will I stop it?" he asked with uncertainty.

"If you can start it, you can stop it," Eaerien stated confidently. "Focus on my hand."

Callen exchanged a dubious glance with Genesis. "Maybe I should try it on something else."

Eaerien raised an eyebrow, chuckled, and nodded to a layer of leaves and pine needles. "Gather them."

Concentrating hard, Callen was able to gather the leaves and needles into a loose pile.

"Now try and bring a few leaves over to us," Eaerien directed.

Callen imagined the leaves floating in the air gently to their feet. Instead, an invisible fist crushed the pile into a tight ball, which hurtled toward them at breakneck speed.

Alarmed, Eaerien grabbed his eyases to his chest and enfolded them protectively into his wings.

STOP! STOP! STOP! Callen screamed inside his head.

Eaerien braced himself for the impact, but the air fist suddenly dispersed, showering them with fragments of leaves and pine needles. He gazed at Callen in awe. "You can manipulate the atmosphere! It makes perfect sense now! That suffocating feeling I had when you trapped me was you separating the gasses to create that effect!" He flapped his wings with excitement. "I have some research to do. Go straight to the aerie. Tomorrow's lesson starts early!"

"We have an exam tomorrow," Genesis called after him.

"We will meet before!"

Genesis and Callen simultaneously groaned.

15.

As promised, Eaerien pulled them from their beds before dawn. Genesis grumbled unintelligibly. Callen dragged his feet, wondering if he could fly with his eyes closed.

Eaerien was not to be deterred. "We are watching the sunrise together," he said with an excitement that grated on Genesis's nerves. Together, they flew toward a large boulder on the edge of Eaerien's favorite cliff. Near the tree line, Eaerien veered off to check on the eggs they had gathered the day before.

Callen watched Eaerien go. He had grown extremely fond of his mentor, who was as kind as he was erratic. He would disappear for days at a time, then show up at the right moment or when he was least expected or wanted. He laughed often—a light and airy sound—yet still commanded respect. Although Callen had only caught a glimpse of Eaerien's skill set, he knew without a doubt that the mentor was not to be trifled with. *Genesis,* he called.

She turned her head slightly in Callen's direction.

Exactly how far can Eaerien see? he wondered.

"Far."

No kidding.

The tiniest smirk appeared at the corner of Genesis's mouth. "I don't know the exact distance, but the narrower he focuses his gaze, the farther it goes; if he looks broadly, details aren't as distinct."

"Talking about me?" Eaerien interrupted, landing silently between them and stretching out on his back.

"How are the eggs?" Genesis asked.

"Warm!" He gave an approving pat to Callen's back. "You made a sturdy nest, Callen."

He grinned. "What will you do when they hatch?"

"The younger Caledons will rear and release them. Until then, it's my duty to protect them." Eaerien pointed to the horizon. "Here comes the sun."

The trio watched in quiet awe as the sun rose regally over the horizon, casting softly blended hues of orange, pink, and yellow over the earth.

Is Marian watching the same sunrise? Callen pondered.

Genesis furrowed her brow slightly. What was this intense longing suddenly gripping her? She glanced around and locked eyes with her mentor, who nodded at her teammate staring off into the distance. Genesis futilely tried to withstand the onslaught of emotion and quickly gave up. "Hey, stop it!"

Callen turned to her in bewilderment.

She sucked in a deep breath, then ranted at the boy, "What do you think you're doing?"

Eaerien sat up, his expression thoroughly amused.

Confusion flooded into Callen's eyes. "What did I do?"

Eaerien smiled and put an arm around the boy's shoulders. "It appears that you are also able to project your emotions onto others. That was Genesis's first experience with that particular emotion, and you delivered a hefty dose."

"I'm sorry. I didn't realize I was doing that."

"Apology not necessary. Shall we move onto the assignment?" Eaerien bounded eagerly to his feet and waited expectantly.

His eyases nodded reluctantly.

"Today is get-to-know-your-partner day!"

There was no response.

Unperturbed, he explained the parameters. "You must remain within five feet of each other at all times. That is all."

"For how long?" Genesis demanded.

"Until the sun has completely set." He grinned at their disbelief. "I trust you can find your way back. Enjoy!"

After their mentor had gone, Callen turned to his sullen teammate. *What now?*

"Get out of my head."

He looked affronted.

Genesis felt a slice of guilt cut into her. She started to leave, but Callen caught her arm then quickly dropped it at the glare she gave him.

"We're supposed to stay within five feet of each other," he reminded her apologetically.

"We can't even fly that close together!" she shot back.

"I'll fly below you," he suggested.

Genesis gritted her teeth and took off without warning. She flew fast and recklessly. To her amazement, Callen kept up.

They arrived as the breakfast bell rang. Callen walked directly into the dining hall, but Genesis stopped abruptly at the door. She had not eaten breakfast with the rest of the students since her first week at the Academy almost three years ago.

Callen went back to her. Without hesitation, he took her wrist in his hand and led her to a table with a single occupant. "This is Mead," he introduced simply.

Mead's round eyes widened as they took seats across from him. "Hi," he said. Like the rest of the students, he kept a safe distance from both Callen and Genesis. In part because he was afraid of the girl, but also because she and Callen made an intimidating pair. Genesis had escaped Jaden, and Callen was rumored to be the son of Elohim.

Genesis sat in stony silence while Callen placed bread and jam in front of her.

When she didn't move to take any, he narrowed his eyes. *Don't make me feed you.*

She bit her tongue and started to eat.

"This is the first time I've seen you at mealtime," Mead said in a hushed voice. "Not that it's a bad thing," he added with a hesitant smile.

Genesis ignored him.

"Well, look who it is!" Bruno exulted, slamming his palms on the end of the table. "Finally decided to crawl out of hell, eh, half-breed?"

Callen stood abruptly, startling even Genesis. "Move along, Bruno."

Bruno sat slowly, challenging Callen with his eyes. "If I may," he said with mock politeness.

The entire room went cold in an instant.

Genesis rose to her feet and tilted her head ever so slightly toward the entrance. Her teammate caught her drift and turned to leave.

Bruno had other ideas. He grabbed Callen's arm roughly. "I heard you *chose* to stay with the half-breed and that crazy mentor."

Callen pulled his arm out of his grasp. "Yes, I did."

"I don't care what they say about you being the 'chosen one,'" Bruno spat. "You're a fool to stick with a monster whose own ugly mother didn't want—!"

In a flash, Callen had Bruno by the collar. "You're the fool," he said in a low, dangerous voice.

Genesis put a hand on his arm. "Let it go. He says that all the time."

"He's wrong," Callen stated. He let him go and stepped away, but Bruno remained frozen in space, eyes wide with fright.

Genesis tightened her grip on her teammate's arm. Her eyes darted between Bruno, whose eyes were beginning to pop out of his head, and the dining hall rapidly filling with other Caledon students. Instructors were moving quickly in their direction, their eyes fixed on her. *I have to get out of here.*

Callen threw her a questioning look. In his distraction, Bruno crashed to the floor gasping for air.

Genesis seized the opportunity and, still gripping her teammate's arm, fled from the scene.

"Why did you run?" he asked her when they finally halted at the edge of the training grounds.

"I don't want any trouble," she replied, striding up to the enormous tree. She grabbed a low hanging branch and pulled herself up.

Callen climbed up after her. "But I'm the one involved."

Genesis didn't answer and continued climbing.

Callen pulled even with her and studied her profile. "You're not a monster," he said quietly.

She gave him a startled look.

"What was it like growing up?" he continued in a voice laced with hurt. "For you to be calloused to words like that?"

"I'm not calloused," she answered honestly, but without inflection. "You just reacted before I had the chance to."

"They're wrong," he insisted.

Genesis shrugged indifferently. "It's true that my mother didn't want me."

"If she only knew."

Genesis rolled her eyes.

Callen planted himself in front of her. "Why is that so hard to believe?"

Her temper flared. "Because, look at me!"

I am looking at you, he said, locking eyes with her.

Genesis broke eye contact. She sheathed and unsheathed her talons with irritation. "You're annoying and stubborn."

Callen crossed his arms. "Why won't you accept how good you are?"

"Because I'm not—good. Will you drop it already?"

Callen refused. "Who in the world had such an impact on your life that you still believe their words to this day?"

"My mother!" she yelled in frustration. "She told me from the beginning that I wasn't meant to be born. That I am the worst mistake this planet will ever know."

"And your father?"

"He left one day and never came back," she answered in a hollow voice.

For a moment, Callen caught a glimpse of the pain heavily protected by her anger. *Genesis ...*

She averted her gaze and backed away when he stepped toward her. "Leave me alone!"

"No way," he stated.

She wrapped her arms around herself. "What do you want from me?"

"Nothing," he said, holding his hands up in surrender. "I want to be your friend. We're a team: we're bound in service to Elohim, together, for life. That's a long time."

"It doesn't have to be," she challenged.

"Why do you do that?" he asked impatiently.

"Do what?" she demanded.

"Push me away."

Genesis clenched her jaw.

"One chance," Callen offered. "That's all I ask."

"Fine," she ground out.

Callen's countenance lit up.

Genesis sighed heavily and found a comfortable place to sit. She waited for Callen to join her. "We might as well do what Eaerien asked."

"Will you tell me your story?" he asked carefully. "How you came to the Academy?"

"There's not much to tell. Elohim sent Eaerien to find me, and when he did, he brought me here."

Callen waited.

"That's it."

Callen suppressed his amusement and posed another question. "Where did Eaerien find you?"

It occurred to Genesis then that Callen had either ignored the rumors about her or deliberately chosen not to believe them. Well, she was about to confirm them. "He found me with Jaden."

"What happened to your mother?"

"She sold me to Jaden to regain acceptance with the Lacquers."

Callen gave her a pained look. "How old were you?"

"Six. Before that, we lived on the outskirts of their territory near the community she was raised in. My father disappeared when I was four, and my mother wouldn't talk about him." She read the question in his eyes. "They didn't care that she had married a Caledon or served Elohim for a few years. The only thing they couldn't forgive her for was bringing me back with her."

A crease formed on his brow. "What was she like?"

Genesis dropped her head and stared at the wide branch they were perched on. "She tried, but it was hard on her. Every time she fought for me, she fought for her life too." Her fist curled involuntarily. "Lacquer fledglings aren't like Caledons. They gang up on each other until the weak ones give up and die, so all that's left are the worst ones. Do you remember the ones that tore up your wings? They weren't much older than fledglings."

Callen smiled faintly. "I've never met a fledgling of any sort."

Genesis gazed thoughtfully at him. "Not all Caledons discover their wings. Some remain bound to the earth, like the community you grew up in."

He cocked his head. "What do you mean?"

"Your father. Did you know he's a Caledon that doesn't fly?"

"Father is?" he asked with surprise. "How do you know that?"

"He's the head of the village, correct?" At his affirmation, she continued. "Caledons are Elohim's appointed guardians. They have been placed in positions of influence all over the world. Those with wings are commissioned to protect peace, and those without wings maintain it." She scoffed at him. "What do they teach you in the desert?"

Callen laughed. "The only thing I learned about Caledons and Lacquers growing up is that they exist, and the Academy doesn't offer history classes at our age. But that doesn't matter now. What happened after she sold you?"

"I was Jaden's apprentice for six years, but he always hated me for being half Caledon. He said it made me kind, which made me weak." Her mind flashed back to the hummingbird she had buried as a child and her gut twisted. "The more he tried to break it, the more it grew. He abandoned me just before Eaerien came along." Her voice noticeably softened at their mentor's name.

"Eaerien seems young compared to the other mentors," Callen commented.

She nodded. "He was fifteen when Elohim appointed him."

"Appointed? He didn't just graduate?"

"His schoolmates were Kaven, Shiloh, and Tuolene, but he mastered his skills years before they did. Loren was trying to figure out what to do with him when Elohim returned, appointed him, and sent him on a mission."

"What mission did Elohim send him on?" Callen asked.

A distant look crept into her eyes. "To find me and to mentor me."

For the first time since they met, a companionable silence surrounded them.

Callen lost himself in his thoughts. *All of this makes perfect sense. If Father—Kael—serves Elohim, does that mean he wasn't fooled by Jaden when he paid us a visit? What about Marian's betrothal? Will all of this play a part in Elohim's plans?*

"What are you thinking about?" Genesis surprised him by asking.

Callen willingly shared his thoughts with her. It came naturally to impress them to her, and he was learning to read hers, as well, during the rare times she let her guard down.

Genesis withdrew from him. "Can't you leave your emotions out of it?"

Sorry.

She put her head in her hands, attempting to sort through the rush of emotions and thoughts he had projected to her. She understood excitement and wonder, but hopeful anticipation was foreign. She couldn't find fear or anxiety—emotions she was familiar with. That was interesting. She shifted through his thoughts next.

While he waited, Callen plucked a small branch and began to whittle. As he whittled, he started to whistle a simple, gentle melody.

Genesis stopped thinking to listen. *Who are you?* she wondered. A small, ugly voice started to speak. She tried to ignore it, but it grew louder and louder. Soon, it overpowered the melody Callen was whistling. "Go away," she begged, clutching her head tighter.

Callen grew quiet and watched her with concern. When she continued to struggle, he reached out his hand and placed it gently on her head. The effect was instantaneous.

Genesis raised her head as peace filled her. "How did you do that? You did that before—in the classroom."

He searched her face. "What happened?"

"Nothing," she answered, not wanting to expose her secret.

They sat quietly for a moment, listening to the bell in the distance.

Suddenly Callen sprang up. "Genesis, the exam!"

∞

By the time they made it to the classroom, the exam was well under way. The instructor frowned disapprovingly and handed them their papers, saying, "I will not allow you extra time."

Callen quickly started on his, but Genesis stared absently for a few minutes. When the time ended, he stared at the almost completely blank exam in her hand.

She shrugged unconcernedly and handed it in.

"Why didn't you answer any of the questions?" he asked curiously as they walked down the hallway together.

"I don't take the exams," she answered simply. "I only went today because we have to stay within five feet of each other, or Eaerien will probably make us run drills again."

Callen winced at the thought. Their mentor had a rather special talent for inventing grueling drills. "How are you supposed to get promoted next year?"

She gave him a sidelong glance. "You still don't you know anything about the grading system?"

"Should I?"

Genesis blew out an exasperated breath. She was not really surprised that Eaerien had not explained it to Callen. He hadn't thought it important to educate him on Caledon history either. "It's simple. We get promoted to the next year based on a cumulative point system. They score us individually based on our performance during exams and evaluations. As a team, we earn points through assignments at the Academy and missions outside the grounds. They don't require a specific number of points from either category, so technically we can fail all our exams and make it up during the evaluations."

"And that's what you do."

She nodded.

He was about to ask why when Mead caught up with them. "Aria sent for Eaerien, and I ran across him on my way out. He wants you two back in the aerie right away."

"Did Eaerien look ok?" Genesis asked.

Mead nodded. "As far as I could tell, but all three of you are enigmas to me, so don't take my word for it."

Callen chortled. "Enigmas?"

"Enigmas. And for the record, Genesis, I never disliked you. I'm just scared of angry people."

"That's true," Callen remarked. "I don't see you around Bruno very much either."

"So what changed?" Genesis asked stiffly.

Mead glanced between her and Callen. "Ever since Callen showed up, you don't seem as angry ... and ... and you haven't destroyed any classrooms since, either."

Callen raised his eyebrows at her. She was staring at Mead, who backed slowly away.

"Well, since I've delivered the message, I'll be off. See you around!"

∞

Eaerien returned to his aerie that afternoon feeling worn. His meeting with Aria had not been a good one. As his older sister, he respected and admired her for her fortitude. But as an instructor, she was unrelenting and unforgiving. They could not be more at odds.

He had listened quietly through her tirade about his erratic, unconventional, reckless teaching methods and his equally undisciplined fledglings. She blamed their behavior on his habit of pulling them out of their classes whenever he felt like it. He had no defense for their tardiness to the exam, but he did not fault them for their actions in the dining hall that morning. When he had voiced that opinion, Aria had accused him of compromise and leniency.

Eaerien shook himself in an attempt to shed his mood for a brighter one. All would be revealed in due time. He remembered the promise Elohim had given him years ago and was comforted. When he opened the door to the aerie, a broad grin split his face. His fledglings were waiting for him.

Callen returned his mentor's grin, but Genesis looked worried.

"My wayward eyases!" he greeted.

Callen laughed.

"What happened?" Genesis questioned.

Eaerien ruffled her long, dark hair, hanging loose. "You actually showed up to an exam!"

"I didn't exactly have a choice," she muttered.

"Callen, you received top marks in that exam," he said, turning to him. "But you were tardy, so you had points taken."

"That's fair," Callen replied agreeably.

"All in all, you both did well this morning." Eaerien paused to let the meaning sink in.

Callen raised his eyebrows and glanced at Genesis, who shrugged.

"Loren has given us a mission," Eaerien continued dramatically. "It will be our first as a team, and it will not be easy, but I have assured Loren that we will handle it."

Worry crept back into Genesis's eyes. Their mentor was notorious for exaggerating minor details and downplaying the major ones.

Eaerien grinned again. "We are going to the sea!"

16.

In the morning, Callen woke and found a slip of paper beneath his door. He stretched as he slid out of bed and nabbed it off the floor on his way to his dresser. He recognized Eaerien's elegant handwriting and realized that it was a list of supplies. Dressing quickly, he slipped his pack on and opened his bedroom door but a quick glance around the aerie told him he was alone. He took a few strides toward the door, noticed Genesis's crumpled homework on the table, remembered his, and doubled back for it, grabbing hers on his way out again. They were leaving for the coast in a few days' time and would remain there for the summer. Their official task was to monitor the various communities scattered there. Eaerien had confided in them that he was hoping those communities were still free from Jaden's influence, so that they would have freedom to focus on training.

Callen left their homework in Kaven's mailbox and made his way to the Academy gates. They were excused from school until they returned from their mission, but were expected to keep up with the lessons. Callen was curious how Eaerien was going to handle that part. As he strolled through the courtyard, he belatedly thought to ask someone directions. He knew there was a city tucked between the mountain peaks that provided all the Academy's supplies, but he'd never been there before. He was on the verge of turning around when he saw Genesis waiting by the gates.

He waved at her, and she held up her own note in response. When he reached her, they wordlessly exchanged notes. "Front gate 9 o'clock," he read aloud. He flipped it over. "That's it?"

"None of these will be in the storeroom," she commented, scanning his list. "Come on, I'll show you where the city is."

"We have a storeroom?" Callen questioned.

Genesis rolled her eyes dramatically and walked away.

Laughing, Callen followed her. "So what's in the storeroom, and where is it?" he asked curiously.

She waved her hand vaguely behind her head. "Over there. It has some food staples, school stuff, extra bedding, furniture, and essential travel equipment."

Callen nodded to the list in her hand. "None of those are essential?"

"Fresh bread? Fruit? *A Guide to Understanding the Atmosphere?*" Genesis asked incredulously. "Are you kidding me?"

He gave her a teasing grin. "To each his own?"

She crumpled up the list and chucked it behind her.

Callen caught it and pressed it back into her palm, closing her fingers over it. "I'm kidding," he said with another grin. "Truce?"

"Don't mess with me," she threatened, yanking her fist out of his grasp.

Callen bit his tongue. "Where's Eaerien?" he asked instead.

"He went to visit his mother."

Callen's eyes lit up.

"You won't meet her," Genesis stated bluntly. Then added in a less harsh tone, "Not today, at least."

His expression gentled at her attempt to soften her words. "Have you met her?"

"Once."

"What was she like?"

They walked a few steps before Genesis answered. "Kind."

Callen smiled and turned his gaze to watch the path before them. It narrowed and steepened, and was soon only wide enough for one person to walk at a time. "I've never gone into the valley before," he remarked, slowing his steps to walk behind her. "Who lives down there?"

She shrugged. "Lots of different creatures."

"What happens if we run into someone coming up the cliff?" he wondered.

"We won't. It's one way."

He craned his neck and leaned away from the rock wall bordering one side of the path. He couldn't see the Academy anymore. "We fly back up?"

Genesis nodded.

"Why don't we fly down?"

She paused and, using her finger to draw a path from the top of the mountain to the valley, said, "If you saw a Caledon diving at you from that height, wouldn't you think something was wrong?" Then without waiting for an answer, she resumed walking.

Callen chuckled. "So who goes into the city?"

"Mostly Academy students to visit their parents. Or the instructors." Genesis twisted her neck to look at him over her shoulder. "Do you ever run out of questions?"

He crumpled his face good-naturedly at her. *I'll let you know when I do.* She turned back around with a small shake of her braid, but not before Callen caught the small smile she tried to hide.

They walked in silence for a while, lost in their own thoughts. Finally Genesis halted and pointed ahead. "Do you see how the path widens? That's the start of the city. Stay close to the road, and you won't get lost."

He stared at her in surprise. "You're not coming with me?"

She shook her head. "I'll wait here."

Callen hesitated.

"Go," she commanded.

There was a small shuffling noise ahead of them, and Genesis sidestepped behind Callen as a young child came into view. A little girl, not more than five years old, skipped up the path. Callen called out to her and gave her a friendly wave. A bright smile lit up her face, and she ran to them.

"Hello," he greeted, crouching to her level. "I'm Callen."

"I'm Petra." She pointed up the path. "You're from the Academy?"

"That's right."

Petra peered over Callen's shoulder at Genesis, who averted her gaze.

"This is Genesis," Callen said.

Petra nodded solemnly. "She's the half-breed Eaerien brought home."

Callen's heart sank. "Petra, she's not a half-anything. She's Genesis."

"What's a Genesis?" she asked innocently.

Callen pointed to his companion.

Petra nodded her acceptance. "Okay!" She gave them both another bright smile.

Genesis held out the list. "Can you help him find these?"

The little girl took the list shyly. "I learned how to read this year." She tucked her small hand into Callen's. "Come with me!"

Callen rose and turned to Genesis once more, but she backed away and hopped out of sight behind a boulder. Petra took him along the scenic route. For the first time, Callen saw the entire valley and its view of the Academy. It was breathtaking.

Nestled against the base of the highest peak, the valley was protected by the mountain on three sides and was filled with a vast forest of lush trees standing tall and proud. The far side gave rise to a volley of low hills that dropped severely off the side of a cliff. The homes were built deliberately into and around the trees, rendering them invisible from the air. Looming watchfully above was the Academy. It was built into the rock face of the mountain, and unlike the city, it was easily seen for miles around.

Petra took him around the market for the supplies he needed, chatting merrily about life in the shadow of the Academy. Callen listened with fascination at the wealth of knowledge already accumulated in her five-year-old brain. By the time he walked her home, the sun was past its apex. He had kept Genesis waiting too long. Jogging back to the base of the mountain, he found her right where he had left her. He smiled sheepishly. "Petra showed me the whole valley."

Genesis took the bread he offered her and dismissed his apologetic expression with an unconcerned shrug. "It's beautiful, isn't it?"

"Let's go together next time," he suggested eagerly. "There's a path that skirts the city. Petra said it's seldom used because the risk of falling off the cliff is too great. Will you come?"

Genesis agreed and then made a confused face as if realizing what she had just done.

Callen happily spread his wings and strapped his pack on, something he hadn't been able to do a few months ago. "Ready to go?" he asked her with an easy smile.

Genesis nodded brusquely, and together they flew back up to the Academy.

Eaerien met them at the gate. "We are on patrol duty this afternoon!" he announced, chortling at their chagrin. "Change quickly and get something to eat. I will not have you running drills on empty fumes!"

∞

Callen, Eaerien, and Genesis stood atop an ancient redwood. Eaerien was leaning against the trunk, leisurely surveying the area. Genesis was bent over with her hands on her knees, and Callen was down on one knee. Both were breathing hard and not paying the slightest attention to their surroundings.

"Eaerien," Callen gasped. "Aren't we supposed to *patrol* during patrol duty?"

The young mentor gave him a bemused smile. "That's what I've been doing."

"Did you ever stop to think," Genesis cut in irritably, "that if we did run into trouble, we'd be too tired from running drills to do anything about it?"

"That is what adrenaline is for," he replied with an impish grin. Sobering, his eyes turned half a shade lighter. "There's something crawling through the bushes 300 meters to your right. See to it and report back here in half an hour."

Genesis straightened and tossed her head defiantly. "You're the one with the most energy left. You check it out."

Callen slowly rose to his feet, gaping at her, and his eyes cut to their mentor, who had yet to get angry in front of him.

Eaerien brushed aside her outburst and stated evenly, "I'll be waiting."

Without another word, the two eyases leaped away.

"I wonder ..." Callen began as he leaped through the forest from branch to branch. He shook his head and bit back the rest of his words.

Flying above him, Genesis's mood darkened. "You're wondering if Eaerien really did see something, or if he sent us on another practice drill," she finished for him.

Callen nodded.

Genesis dropped onto a wide branch several meters ahead. "I've had it," she fumed. "If he thinks he can get away with this—"

"You once told me that Eaerien has a method to his madness," Callen interrupted wearily, landing beside her in a crouch.

Genesis studied her teammate carefully before replying. "True, but this intensity is on another level. I don't feel like speeding anymore."

Something in her tone caught him off guard and his expression grew brighter. *Are you worried about me?* he asked with his mind.

Her defenses came up instantly. "I'm not carrying you back if you faint," she answered sharply.

Callen tried not to smile but failed. "Fair enough." He leaped from the tree branch and landed precariously onto the next.

Genesis followed him, watching his unsteady progress with a hint of amusement in her dark eyes. When Callen's next leap fell short, she caught him under the arms and steadied him. "You have a death wish, don't you?"

Callen grinned ruefully. "I'm tired."

She forced him to sit against the tree trunk. "Wait here. I'll go."

He opened his mouth to protest.

Genesis pinned him with her glare. *You're slowing us both down.* Without waiting for a reply, she sprang into the air and was gone.

Callen stared after her with wide eyes. "I heard you!" he yelled excitedly. He pumped his fist in the air triumphantly, then leaned his back against the trunk, grateful for the respite.

She was back within minutes, carrying her tunic in a bundle, which she promptly tossed at him. "It's a mutt."

"What happened?" Callen asked, eying the charred marks crisscrossing the garment.

"That little monster lit himself on fire and tried to burn me up," she explained hotly. "I almost tore him apart."

"I'm glad you didn't," Callen returned mildly. *I heard your thoughts by the way.*

Genesis blinked, caught off guard by the abrupt change in subject. "I know." She jutted her chin toward the bundle in his arms. "I'm not sure he's going to make it."

Callen cautiously lifted a corner of the tunic and found himself staring into a pair of hostile black eyes. His expression softened.

The small dog bristled and sparks flew from its fur.

Callen tucked the corner back down. "He's got plenty of fight left."

"Not for long," Genesis retorted callously. "Let's go."

He carefully secured the small bundle inside his jacket and followed her.

17.

"It's a dog," Eaerien stated, handing the bundle over to the chancellor.

"Why is it wrapped so securely?" the old man inquired with interest.

"He's alive," the young mentor assured him. "Be careful, Loren. He might blow up in your face."

Loren paused in alarm, his hand hovering over the edge of the cloth. "I beg your pardon?"

"Look what he did to Genesis's tunic," Eaerien pointed out. "Give him air, and he will light himelf on fire."

Loren raised his eyebrows. "And you want me to examine him?"

All three members of team Eaerien nodded.

The old man laughed.

Callen stepped forward. "I might be able to contain him."

Loren's eyes danced with humor. "You are certainly welcome to try, my boy."

Callen carefully unwrapped the dog, encompassing him within a pocket of limited oxygen. *Please don't let me suffocate him.*

"What unusual markings," Loren murmured, unable to mask his delight. "A sort of burnt brindle, wouldn't you say?" The little animal trembled. Rubbing his hands quickly together to warm them, Loren placed them an inch above the dog's head, moving slowly down the length of his body.

Callen glanced at Genesis. *What's he doing?*

Her eyes flickered in his direction. It still made her jump a little when his thoughts reached her mind. *He's gathering information*, she communicated back. *He did the same thing to you a few weeks past.*

Callen searched his memory. *I don't think I was conscious.*

Obviously, she retorted dryly.

Callen inadvertently snorted a laugh. Eaerien raised an eyebrow and glanced meaningfully between them. Genesis's face went blank, and Callen dropped his gaze to the floor.

Loren cleared his throat and folded his hands. "He's weak from exhaustion and dehydration, but he's got a strong will to live." He pointed to faintly glowing red streaks in the dog's fur. "Even now, he's trying to defend himself."

"May I take him?" Callen asked suddenly.

Loren shifted to have a look at the boy. "You mean to keep him?"

Eaerien was smiling. "Go ahead and make him comfortable, Callen. I'll bring up some food in a moment."

Callen gingerly cradled the little dog in his arms and left. With a nod from Eaerien, Genesis followed her teammate out of the room.

"What are you thinking, Eaerien?" Loren wondered. "He can't possibly keep that animal inside the school. You know the rules."

"They both could use a friend right now," he said persuasively.

Loren regarded the young man with a fondly exasperated expression. "Eaerien," he said. "I have always supported your decisions, but that dog is no pet, which are also not allowed inside the grounds."

"Please consider it," he insisted quietly. "This is the first time Callen's asked for anything."

"What's going on in that mind of yours, Eaerien?"

The young mentor laughed. "What are you talking about, Loren?"

Loren formed a steeple with his fingers. "Give me one good reason, Eaerien."

∞

Genesis was waiting for Eaerien when he emerged from the chancellor's office. She held up a package of finely ground meat by way of greeting.

"What's this?" Eaerien exclaimed with delight. "You went to the kitchen yourself?"

She shrugged and fell into step with him. "You were taking so long, and I needed something to do. What did Loren say?"

Eaerien draped his arm around her thin shoulders. "The dog stays."

"On what condition?" she queried.

"No condition, Genesis. He's not the type."

"Then what *reason* did you give him to convince him?" she persisted.

Eaerien chuckled. "I merely pointed out that we're leaving for the coast in a few days. The dog will stay with us while he recuperates, and if he so happens to become an essential member of our team, then Loren will see no cause for him to leave."

Genesis furrowed her brow. Turning yourself into a ball of fire was a pretty impressive skill, but how would that benefit them as a team? The idea of using a living creature as a weapon rankled her. She shook her head to clear her thoughts, a habit she had picked up from Eaerien. He would never exploit another being. He wasn't Jaden.

∞

They left for the coast a few days later. It would normally take three full days to reach the town they planned to stay in, but if they piggybacked on the winds, it would save both time and energy. Eaerien soared high and disappeared through the clouds. Genesis settled on a course just above and behind Callen, watching her teammate.

Callen barely moved his wings, and he flew with his eyes closed and one hand resting on the bulge at his chest. In the days preceding their departure, he had gained the little dog's trust, and he was content to rest in Callen's tunic. Eaerien had helped him construct an inner pocket to secure the dog in during flight. "I call him Madden," Callen had told Genesis just that morning.

Genesis shook her head at the memory of it. The boy had a knack for making friends with the most unruly creatures.

Eaerien appeared out of the clouds and joined her. He gestured to Callen. "Sleeping?"

"Seems to be."

"How about you?" he asked lightly.

Genesis gave him a shrewd look. "What did you see?"

"Nothing out of the ordinary," he replied.

"What were you looking for?" she amended.

Eaerien looked pleased. "Always the observant one, aren't you?"

"Tell me the truth."

"Always."

"What's the real reason why we're going to the coast?"

Eaerien threw a cautious glance at Callen coasting ahead of them. "Jaden got wind that a young male Caledon of unknown origins and with an impressive set of skills recently arrived at the Academy. He's coming for him."

An ominous chill settled into Genesis's bones. "He would dare come to the Academy?"

Eaerien took her cold hand into his warm one. "Elohim is there now. He sent us away because neither you nor Callen are ready to face Jaden."

"What about the school and those in the city?" she asked in horror. Jaden was ruthless. Once, Genesis had saved a hatchling, raised it, and set it free. In a fit of rage against her "Caledon-ness," he had hunted down the same bird and murdered it before her eyes. She shuddered at the painful memory.

Eaerien's heart broke for her. Her expression told him that she had unwillingly recalled something terrible she'd experienced at Jaden's hands. He took her hand again and motioned for her to fold her wings. When she complied, he pulled her into a tight hug. "Elohim is our best defense," he reminded her.

Genesis tried to find comfort in his words, but the bone-chilling terror would not easily go away. She remained in the shelter of Eaerien's wings for several miles, comforted by the warmth and safety they offered.

When Callen finally opened his eyes, the sun was directly overhead. He patted the lump at his chest affectionately.

"You're really impressive," Genesis spoke from his right. Her tone held a hint of sarcasm. "You've been asleep while flying all morning."

"Did I stay on course?" he wondered.

"For the most part," she admitted. Callen stretched lazily and did a barrel roll at her, which she dodged effortlessly.

"Let's pick up the pace," Eaerien called from above them. "There's a forest ahead."

Genesis signaled that they'd heard him and with a mischievous glint in her eye, tornado-rolled directly at Callen. He clutched the little dog close to his chest, barely evading her as she sped by him. He beat his wings with powerful strokes and raced after her. With an amused grin, Eaerien followed.

They touched down at the edge of the forest and quickly ate their midday meal. Callen let Madden out to stretch his legs, but the little dog took one look around and climbed back into his pouch. After replenishing their water supplies, they returned to the air. Eaerien set a grueling pace the rest of the day, finally landing on the side of a mountain well after the sun had set. Both Callen and Genesis collapsed wearily beneath a tree with low-hanging branches, but Eaerien appeared even more vigilant.

"I'll take the first watch," he offered and disappeared into the treetops.

Genesis woke a few hours later and stretched stiffly. She looked for her teammate and saw Madden wide-awake and standing guard on Callen's chest. When she drew near, he dove into the boy's tunic and eyed her suspiciously. "I'm not going to hurt him," she muttered. She shook the boy's shoulder. "Wake up."

Callen sat up automatically, squinting into the dark.

"It's time to switch with Eaerien," she said.

He nodded groggily and followed her into the trees where Eaerien was perched.

Eaerien greeted them with a smile and his icy eyes faded back into deep blue. Everything's quiet so far." He patted the top of Genesis's head affectionately. "Wake me at dawn."

Callen made himself comfortable next to Genesis and gazed at the stars. Madden stuck his head out and surveyed the area with bright, glowing eyes. Callen scratched his chin, and the little animal closed his eyes appreciatively. His thoughts drifted to the family he had left behind—a lifetime ago.

Lost in her own thoughts, Genesis contemplated telling Callen what Eaerien had told her that morning. He had a right to know that one of the greatest rulers on earth was hunting him down. But what good would it do? Callen had barely begun to develop his skills. All his life he had been sheltered in the desert; now suddenly the responsibility of leading an entire people to victory was thrust upon him. All this, yet Elohim had not even confirmed his identity. As she studied Callen's profile in the moonlight, a sense of peace stole into her being, overpowering her anxious thoughts and driving the fear from her mind.

Gazing into the night sky always calmed Callen's mind. Whatever turmoil was playing out on earth, the heavens remained untouched through time and space. If Elohim was the true king of the earth, then was he also ruler of the heavens? If Elohim was his father, and he was indeed the child of the prophecy, then that would make him the rightful heir. Overwhelmed, Callen released a deep sigh.

"What are you thinking about?" Genesis asked softly.

Callen dropped his gaze to his hands. "I was thinking about Elohim."

She sat up straight with interest. "What about him?"

"Do you think I'm his son?"

Genesis relaxed back into a slouch. "You're better off asking Eaerien or Loren that."

Maybe, he thought conversationally, *but I'd like to hear your answer just the same.*

"It doesn't matter what I think," she retorted. *What do I know about anything?*

He poked her side with his elbow. "It matters to me." *I think you know a lot more than you give yourself credit for.*

Genesis edged away from him. "I don't want to talk about this with you."

Callen averted his face to hide his grin.

I'm serious. She shot him a glare. *Get out of my head.*

I'm not in your head, he returned, raising his eyebrows. "I'm sitting right here."

"You know what I mean," she protested, moving further away. "Stop listening to my thoughts."

"I can't hear your thoughts unless you let me," he reminded her cheerfully.

Genesis glowered at him, but his mirth was infectious. Or was he projecting it onto her? "Callen," she said warningly.

Callen laughed. "I haven't learned how to stop it."

"You've stopped it before!"

He shook his head. *I never stopped it. You shut me out.*

Genesis pushed herself to her feet. "You need to focus on something else," she said decidedly. "How about we split up? You stay here."

"Okay," he agreed with laughter still dancing in his eyes.

Genesis moved to the next tree and settled on a branch away from Callen's prying eyes. She could still feel his laughter rippling through her and wondered how someone as innocent as Callen could stand against a cold-blooded murderer.

18.

Genesis woke with a start. Her heart was hammering out of control, and she was overwhelmed with an ominous feeling. The sky was just starting to lighten. Her eyes darted wildly and came to rest on her teammate, who was watching her actions with curiosity. "Did you hear that noise?"

"I didn't hear anything." He peeked through the treetops. "I don't see anything either."

Genesis rubbed her temples. She couldn't shake the feeling of doom.

Callen took her head in both of his hands.

"It's not helping." She shook his hands off and disappeared below, resurfacing with Eaerien.

He scanned the area, but didn't find anything. "Did you fall asleep?"

"We took turns," Callen explained. "I was watching, but didn't notice anything."

"I definitely heard something," Genesis fretted. She looked suddenly at the little dog peeking from Callen's tunic. "Do you think Madden heard anything?"

Callen shook his head.

"Even if he did, it may not have registered as something dangerous to him," Eaerien said. "Since we're all up, we may as well get a move on."

∞

Genesis felt better when they were in the air.

They traveled fast and arrived at their destination late in the afternoon.

Callen took one look at the sea and a huge grin split his face. He set

Madden down and shed his tunic. Leaping into the air, he dive-bombed into the water.

Genesis turned disinterestedly away, while Eaerien watched with fascination. He had never seen a Caledon propel himself in the water the way the boy was doing.

Callen bobbed in the water, grinning with delight. "Join me!"

Eaerien shook his head. "I don't know how to swim." He pointed to his wings. "And I don't believe these function the same underwater."

Callen pulled himself out of the water and flapped his wings, spraying water everywhere.

Eaerien shielded himself behind his own wings. "I didn't know you could swim."

"I can teach you," Callen offered, stretching out onto the warm sand.

"No, thank you. I was raised in the sky, not the sea."

"There must be a reason I was raised with earth-bound men."

Eaerien looked thoughtfully at the boy beside him. Callen was more aware of the events occurring around him than he let on. He had a gentle, quiet, focused and easy-going personality—completely opposite of the terrifying power he was capable of.

What is it? Callen asked him.

I was contemplating what you said, Eaerien answered easily with his mind.

Callen jumped to his feet in astonishment. *You can answer me!*

Of course I can. Eaerien chuckled. *I've been waiting to hear your words for some time now.* A rush of Callen's thoughts filled his mind. *You seem most curious about Genesis.*

Why won't she let me get close to her? he asked, sitting back down again.

Eaerien patted his knee. *She is. Trust me.*

Callen gave his wings one last shake and tucked them away. "Genesis told me that you were hand-picked by Elohim for a task."

Eaerien tipped his head. "Are you wondering why he chose me, or do you want to know what he asked me to do?"

Callen shook his head. *Neither.* "I want to know why you said yes."

Eaerien grinned. "Elohim demands all or nothing. We all come to a point where we must choose sides." He bumped his shoulder against Callen's. "You have already chosen yours."

"Genesis too?"

The mentor took a deep breath. *Genesis is extraordinary. She is the first and will be the last of her kind. She was born because our people lacked faith in Elohim's promise and took matters into their own hands. She has chosen Elohim despite herself, and because of that, she fights a daily battle neither you nor I can understand.*

"Despite herself?" Callen questioned, absent-mindedly digging his hands into the sand.

Eaerien stared reflectively across the ocean. "She was raised by Jaden. Her reactions and instincts were trained to his standards. Even though she is physically free, she is still in bondage mentally and emotionally." He dropped his gaze and stared unseeingly at the sand. "Every waking moment, she has to deny those instincts. You've noticed how difficult it is for her to sleep. When she sleeps, Elohim gives her peace, so Jaden does everything he can to withhold that from her."

"But how can he still reach her?" Callen demanded.

Eaerien tapped his temple. "Part of the denial process involves keeping her mind shut. That can be very difficult, and Jaden is the mastermind of infiltrating your subconscious. That's what makes him so powerful."

"I want to help her."

"You already do, Callen," he answered softly. "More than you know."

19.

The summer passed uneventfully and at the end of it, they returned to the Academy and found it just as they had left it. Eaerien ushered them to the aerie before seeking Loren out. Evaluations were around the corner—Callen's first—and Eaerien needed help. While at the coast, he had designed a variety of training exercises for Callen in an attempt to discover the limits of his skills. On one hand, Callen was now able to communicate his thoughts to an entire group at once, and his reach was potentially limitless. Potentially. On the other hand, his ability to manipulate the atmosphere had only grown more unstable and volatile. He could neither focus nor control his strength.

Inside the aerie, Genesis paced irritably inside her room. Classes were starting again, and she was not looking forward to it. Her teammate obviously was. She could hear him whistling through the walls, and it chafed her already raw nerves. Even worse, Eaerien had somehow convinced them to attend every class, at least until the evaluations were finished.

The whistling stopped all of a sudden, and Callen's head popped into her room. "What exactly happens during evaluations?"

Genesis planted her feet and crossed her arms. "We fight."

Callen moved to lean against the doorway and mimicked her posture. "Who?"

"Each other." She uncrossed her arms and resumed pacing. "You can't hurt your opponent. If you do, you're automatically disqualified."

"Why do we have to fight at all?"

"Would you prefer to test your skills in actual combat?" she asked sarcastically. As soon as the words left her mouth, she clamped her jaw shut and screwed up her face. "I mean …" She blew out her breath and plopped onto her bed. "It's their way of measuring how well we can control our skills."

Callen pulled out her desk chair and sat down with a perplexed look on his face. "Are you saying that we keep the peace by force?"

Genesis gave him a scathing look. "Elohim doesn't force anyone to follow him. We're guardians. Protectors. Defenders. We have to be ready to do that at a moment's notice. Anyway," she said, swiftly changing the subject, "the better we do, the more points we score and the more missions we get to go on."

"How many points do we need?"

"I don't know. I just aim to win."

Callen raised an eyebrow. "How often do you win?"

She gave him a smug look. "I've won all of them so far."

He burst into laughter, rocking the chair. "That's why you can turn in blank tests!"

Genesis felt his mirth seep into her mind, filling her with an unfamiliar lightheartedness. She moved uncomfortably away from him.

Callen sobered. "Will you become a mentor when you graduate?"

"No. Mentors are second in rank only to the chancellor. They get chosen. That's why Eaerien gets away with the things he does. Only Loren or another mentor can tell him to stop."

"Who comes after mentors?"

"Instructors, like Aria."

Oh, I like Aria, he thought.

"You like everyone," she retorted, still maintaining her distance. "After instructors are the other Caledons. The ones with wings go on missions. They break up conflicts and protect peaceful communities. The ones without wings, like the father who raised you, manage designated communities."

"I see." Callen stared at her for a moment, then asked. "What are you hoping to become?"

"None."

What? He asked in surprise, unconsciously speaking from his mind.

Genesis shrugged and answered, *We're being prepared for war, Callen. We're not going to have those options* … Her voice trailed as she tried to decipher the expression on his face. *Why are you looking at me like that?*

A small, affectionate smile raised the corners of his mouth. "That's the first time I've heard you say my name."

Genesis felt unexpectedly awkward. At some point, she had started viewing Callen as her teammate—someone she could rely on. "Do you have a problem with that?" she blustered.

He shook his head, an amused light in his eyes. "So how many fight simulations do we have to run?"

"It depends," she replied guardedly. "The less points you start off with, the more opponents you go against. Since you've been here the shortest, you might have to go up against everyone."

Thankfully, there were only a handful of students in their class.

∞

Shiloh carefully surveyed his fledglings. They were physically fit, mentally competent, and emotionally opposite. Mead accepted everything philosophically, believing that something was to be learned from every situation. Dar, on the other hand … "Dar," he called. "Get over here."

Dar ran quickly over but stopped out of arm's reach. "Yes, Shiloh?"

Shiloh pointed to the ground before him.

With one last suspicious glance, Dar obeyed.

Shiloh smacked him on the shoulder. "I told you to fix your attitude! I can still hear you complaining about last year."

Dar kicked at the earth.

"I'm seriously reconsidering allowing you to participate in this round of evaluations, Dar. Why are you so gloomy all the time?"

"I'm not a fighter, Shiloh," he complained. "I'm ok when I'm with you and Mead, but I'm completely useless by myself. How am I supposed to pass?"

Shiloh tapped his foot impatiently. "Historically, you've done well, and I wouldn't exactly call you useless. What's the problem?"

"We're going to war, Shiloh!" he wailed. "I can't even fight my classmates. How am I supposed to fight against the Lacquers?"

"It's all in your attitude, Dar." He poked a finger at his fledgling's forehead. "You are your own worst enemy. You can't hope to win a fight if you enter it expecting to lose."

Dar flung up his arms and pivoted away. "How am I supposed to win against Callen or Genesis?"

"So that's what this is really about."

Dar pivoted back. "Shiloh, I'm going to die! I can't do long-range combat the way those two can!"

Shiloh fought down an exasperated sigh. "This is not a fight to the death. If you were paying attention, you would have seen that Genesis does not have any long-range combat skills either. She merely uses her speed to her advantage."

"What about Callen smashing and crushing everything he looks at? When he's not even trying!"

"Callen is new to his skills." Shiloh smiled cajolingly. "I'll pray that you don't go up against him."

"Shiloh!"

Shiloh grabbed his shoulders and shook him. "Dar, you must calm yourself." He released him with a little push and glanced at his more stoic fledgling listening nearby. "If anything, Mead will go up against him."

Mead grimaced.

Shiloh nodded at them encouragingly. "Stop worrying and focus on your training. Loren knows what he's doing."

∞

That evening, Shiloh found Eaerien at the top of the arena. "Thought I would find you here," he greeted. "It's been a minute."

"Shiloh," Eaerien beamed, holding his arms out for a hug. "Did you see the lineup?"

"Is it up?"

Eaerien tipped his chin toward the judges' table.

"You know I can't see from here," Shiloh stated flatly. "Show-off."

Eaerien grinned. "Poor Dar. He has to go up against both Callen and Genesis."

Shiloh groaned. "I'll never hear the end of this. Dar is panicking that Genesis will kill him on purpose, and Callen might on accident."

"I can say confidently that neither of those will happen," Eaerien reassured him. "Callen's first opponent is Bruno."

"You think it'll be a problem?"

"I don't know," he admitted. "Callen isn't easily provoked, but Bruno seems to know how to get the job done."

"Ah." Shiloh nodded understandingly. He had watched Callen train, and his skills were impressive; however, his physical control left much to be desired. "Eaerien, you know I like Callen, and I trust you and Loren, but—" Shiloh rubbed the back of his neck. "—I've never seen a more dangerous, out of control level of energy, and Bruno …"

"You don't have to say it," Eaerien interrupted, crossing his hands behind his head. "Callen already knows Bruno likes to push his limits. He won't fall for it."

"What if he accidentally disintegrates the entire arena?" Shiloh pondered aloud half-jokingly. "He can't seem to put a stop to the energy he releases, once it's been released."

Eaerien nodded. "That's exactly the problem. Anything past a small burst of energy opens the floodgates of destruction." He rubbed his temples with uncharacteristic frustration. "I've asked Loren for help, but he is convinced that the key is not in the control, it's in the release."

"Meaning?"

"I have no idea." He looked helplessly at his friend and saw the same humor reflected in Shiloh's eyes.

Shiloh laughed. "Oh, help us all. By the way, I noticed Callen's still carrying around that little combustible dog. Have you found a good use for him yet?"

"Yes," Eaerien answered confidently. "He makes a wonderful companion."

"And what does Loren think of that?"

Eaerien lifted his shoulders slightly and grinned mischievously. "He didn't ask."

Shiloh's laughter filled the air once more. "It's good to have you home, Eaerien. This place is never the same without you."

"It's good to be home. Everything went well?"

"Of course." Shiloh answered reassuringly. "Elohim is never far from the Academy, so we were never in any real danger." He glanced curiously at his friend. "Why did Elohim send you three away anyway?"

Eaerien clapped him on the shoulder. "Because it's not yet Callen's time."

20.

Callen fell back against a tree, struggling for breath.

"Take a rest," Eaerien commanded. "You've worked hard enough today."

Callen forced himself to take slow, deep breaths. "I'm not finished yet," he muttered. Evaluations started tomorrow. Drawing himself into a kneeling position, he willed himself to stand. He was on the verge of succeeding when Eaerien pushed him back down.

"You just don't know when to stay down, do you?" the mentor stated quietly.

"I said I wasn't finished yet," he insisted stubbornly.

"And I say you are. Look at you. You can hardly sit up. How do you expect to even participate tomorrow if you're laid up in bed from overexertion?"

Callen squinted at his mentor from under tired eyelids. "I don't think I can get up."

Eaerien shook his head with exasperation. "Just a minute ago you were forcing yourself up, and now you can't move at all?" He called to another fledgling training nearby. "Mead! Please help Callen back to our aerie."

Mead approached obediently and held out his hand to Callen, who grasped it with a tired smile, and he pulled him to his feet. He draped Callen's arm across his shoulders and asked, "Ready?"

"Yeah," Callen answered, struggling to maintain his balance. "Thanks."

Moving slowly, they made their way off the training field.

"Hey, Callen!" Bruno called as they passed by. "You're looking pretty wimpy today! Did you spend the summer getting beat up by that beast you call your teammate?"

Callen tensed but did not engage him.

With a scowl, Bruno turned away.

"How does Pax get along with him?" Callen marveled. "I keep forgetting to ask."

"He doesn't," Mead chuckled humorlessly. "He just stays away."

"Hey, wait up!" Dar called, running after them. "I wanted to ask you something, Callen."

Callen looked at him with mild curiosity.

"Are you nervous about the evaluations coming up?" he asked. "Is that why you're training so hard?"

"I'm just trying to catch up to everyone."

Dar looked slightly disappointed with his answer. "Right. Where did you come from again?"

Despite his fatigue, Callen managed a small smile. "The desert."

"Got any family in the city?"

Callen shook his head.

"Listen," Dar said. "I know you must've had it rough, but we're all family here. We take care of each other, including Bruno even though he can be obnoxious."

"What about Genesis?" Callen asked softly.

Dar was nonplussed and his steps faltered. "Well, she—she," he stuttered. "She's different. She said she doesn't want to be included."

Callen gave him a penetrating look. "She said that?"

"She didn't say it, but she made it really clear. You've seen the way she acts."

Callen was silent.

"I'm not saying it's her fault," Dar blabbered on. "She can't help it. She's got Lacquer—" He stopped talking at the warning look Mead gave him.

Callen straightened and stepped unsteadily away from them. "Thanks for your help, Mead." Turning to Dar, he spoke kindly but firmly. "Don't judge what you don't understand."

Genesis waited until the others had turned away before stepping out of the shadows to help her teammate. "You overdid it."

Callen leaned gratefully against her as she hauled him, half hopping and half flying, up to the aerie. "It's getting harder and harder to control," he confided to her. "Eaerien thought that if I built up my stamina it would be easier." *But it's getting worse.*

"How can it possibly get worse?" Genesis asked, kicking the aerie door open and wrestling under his sagging weight.

Feels like a river after the glaciers have melted, he shared with her. *It just keeps growing and growing until there's no more ice left to melt.*

They barely made it to his room where he collapsed wearily into bed. Callen closed his eyes and immediately passed out. Genesis paused to catch her breath. Emerging from his hiding spot, Madden leaped onto his chest and eyed her warily. Ignoring the small animal, she moved to the end of the bed and pulled Callen's shoes off.

Eaerien appeared and leaned against the doorway. "Will you stay with him? I'll have Loren look in on him this evening."

"Where are you going?" she asked, dragging Callen's desk chair next to his bed.

"I have some business to attend to." He reached out and rested his hand briefly on the top of her head. "I'll have some food sent up. Make sure he eats."

Genesis nodded and watched her mentor depart. She listened for the sound of the aerie door shutting then turned back to her teammate's still form. Madden blinked lazily at her from where he was curled up on Callen's chest. The little dog laid his chin near the boy's heart, listening to the electrical currents running through it as Callen's heart started beating faster and faster. He placed his paws over it, absorbing the heat being generated.

A few hours later, Callen opened sleepy eyes to Genesis shaking him awake.

"You need to eat," she stated, holding out a bowl.

He groaned and sat up to take the bowl, and Madden hopped lightly out of the way. Callen stared at her. *I can't move my arms.*

Genesis put the bowl down, and both their gazes fell to his arms. "Here," she said, raising the bowl again and holding it to his lips. She tipped it forward as he drank the contents in one long gulp.

"Thanks." He flashed her a grateful smile and wiped his chin on his shoulder. "Why can't I move my arms?"

Genesis tentatively touched her fingertips to his forearm. "Are you in pain?"

"No."

"They feel like wood," she remarked, poking at them experimentally. "Loren is coming by later tonight to check on you, but I don't think this can wait."

∞

Bruno stared bitterly at the picture of Callen, Genesis, and Eaerien on the wall by Loren's office. What right did they have to make it on the wall? They were the worst team at the Academy! If they weren't fighting, they were destroying everything. He jabbed his finger accusingly at Callen's face. "I can't believe both of you took her side." Then he spit on the photograph. "Take that—! Augh!" He was suddenly off his feet and flying headlong down the hall. "Where did you come from?!" he hollered, crashing to the floor.

Genesis silently wiped his spit off the picture and stepped to Loren's door.

Bruno rubbed the part of his face he had landed on. "Filthy half-breed!" he spat.

She fought the temptation to respond, her hand poised to knock. The only indication she gave that she'd heard his words was the telltale whitening across her knuckles.

Bruno scrambled to his feet and ran at her. "You should know your place! You and that half-breed-loving-good-for-nothing teammate—"

Genesis was in his face in an instant with her talons hovering centimeters from his head. "Say it," she dared, her dark eyes flashing dangerously.

Loren's door swung open. "What is the meaning of this?" the chancellor thundered over their heads. "Guardians fighting amongst themselves! You should be ashamed!"

Bruno and Genesis automatically stepped away from each other and hung their heads submissively.

"Genesis," Eaerien said in a rebuking tone, "I asked you to stay with Callen."

She snapped her head up. "I came for Loren."

"And you, Bruno?" Loren questioned. "What brings you to my office?"

"I was running an errand for Tuolene," he replied sullenly. "When I got side-tracked."

"Go on then. Finish your task." Loren waited until Bruno was out of sight before giving Genesis a hard look. "Genesis, what were you planning to do to Bruno?"

"Threaten him," she answered honestly and with her face devoid of emotion.

"Is that an appropriate action to take against a friend?"

She bristled. "We're not—" Her eyes abruptly cut to her mentor, and she snapped her jaw shut.

"You're not—what?" Loren prompted.

Genesis shook her head and ground out, "I apologize for my behavior."

Loren patted her shoulder. "Apology accepted." He waved Eaerien forward. "Come. I am intrigued as to what is happening to Callen that has you both worried."

∞

Callen could move his fingers if he concentrated hard enough, but they were completely numb. His chest was also starting to hurt. He heard the aerie door open and shut, and he glanced up at the small dog perched nearby. Madden whined softly in response.

The bedroom door opened, and Loren walked in. He gave Callen a reassuring smile and stretched his hands toward the boy. "May I?"

Callen's eyes traveled to Genesis at the doorway, and then to Eaerien behind her, and back to Loren. He nodded.

Loren took one of his arms in both of his hands and sat quietly for a few moments. Then he took a firmer grip and squeezed. Crackling noises split the silence, and Callen cried out in pain. Loren squeezed harder.

Disturbed by Callen's cries of pain, Genesis backed away with her hands over her ears. Eaerien pulled the door shut and rested his arm companionably across her shoulders. "I think it's time you learn healing from Loren."

She looked up at him with surprise and doubt.

"It will prove quite useful, and you've got the talent," he said encouragingly. "Loren has already agreed to teach you."

"Me. A healer." She released her talons. "With these hands."

"Those hands will become my son's greatest help," said a beautiful, regal voice.

"Elohim!" Genesis exclaimed, turning to greet the Caledon king.

Elohim held out his arms and embraced her warmly. "My dear child," he said affectionately. With Genesis still in his arms, he reached for Eaerien's outstretched hand and clasped it firmly. "Eaerien, my faithful servant." Then his gaze fell on the closed door from which muffled cries of pain could be heard.

"Callen," Eaerien said softly.

At the name, a look so tender appeared on Elohim's face that even Genesis's dark heart melted. Elohim kept his eyes on the door until Loren appeared.

The old Caledon's face lit up at the sight of their king. "Elohim."

"My old friend." Elohim smiled fondly. "Thank you for diligently watching over my school."

"I'm merely doing my duty until you return."

"I am looking forward to the day I won't have to leave." His gaze turned once more to the now open doorway.

"I did what I could," Loren said, following his gaze. "But it is not enough, Elohim. The boy's power is too great to be contained."

"It was not designed for containment." Elohim turned slightly and enveloped Genesis's small hands in his large ones. "Loren, I trust you will teach these precious hands well. They will be Callen's greatest aid on this earth."

Loren bowed his head in obedience.

Elohim moved into the privacy of the room where Callen lay sleeping. He put his gentle hands on his arms and spoke softly. "My son."

Callen's eyelids fluttered open, and he looked at the stranger. *Are you Elohim?*

"I am."

His eyes widened. *You are my ...?*

"You are my son," Elohim answered with a kind smile.

All the accusations Callen had wanted to confront him with disappeared as he searched Elohim's face. There was only good in him. Callen didn't understand, but he knew with certainty that he could trust him. Still, he could not help asking the one question that would not be silenced. "Was there no other way?"

Elohim's expression fell. "If there was, do you not believe I would have taken it?"

"I have so many questions."

"All will be revealed in due time." He laid a gentle hand on Callen's head. "I ask you to trust me."

Callen nodded slowly.

"You must also trust yourself. You are my son. We are of the same heart." Sadness crept into his face. "What I ask of you will not be easy or painless. For every drop of blood you lose to save another, you will gain life. The more lives you save, the easier your pain will be to bear." Elohim touched his son's cheek. "You will also experience countless joys, and you will never be alone."

Callen felt overwhelmed. He wanted more than anything to give Elohim what he asked and fulfill everyone's expectations, but he was afraid. He thought of his limited skills and the one he had disastrous control over. *What if I fail?*

"Oh, my son," Elohim spoke tenderly. "I will only lead you to victory."

21.

Elohim's surprise visit turned evaluation day into a sort of event. The entire valley showed up for the evaluations and sat quietly on one end of the arena, while the Academy students occupied the other. The mentors sat near the judges' panel, which consisted of Loren, the city elders, and Elohim.

The format was simple. Students were ranked according to their number of individual points and matched against the student ranked immediately above them. Callen, because he was new, was ranked last. Also, because his skills were completely untested, he would be tested against all of the others.

"It's not usually this big of a deal," Mead whispered to Callen from his left. "It's because Elohim's here. He's only ever come for graduation before."

Genesis glanced pensively over at Callen from his right. He had not spoken a word since Elohim's visit yesterday evening, and his expression wasn't giving anything away either.

Concerned about me? Callen questioned light-heartedly.

Genesis's eyes slid back to the arena. *Are you all right?*

I am now.

She looked him squarely in the face, and he grinned.

Mead tapped Callen on the arm. "Watch, we're starting."

Kaven stood before the mentors—Eaerien, Shiloh, and Tuolene. "Any last minute adjustments?"

"No," they answered.

"Health checks all look fine," Kaven noted, scanning his files. "Eaerien, there's an addendum here saying Loren paid Callen a visit yesterday evening. Is everything all right?"

"Yes, Callen is perfectly healthy."

"Elohim will be overseeing the scoring. Any objections?"

Tuolene made a face. "Are you seriously asking us if we have a problem with Elohim participating in a school event? A school that *he* created?"

Shiloh waved his finger at the other mentor. "Kaven *has* to follow protocol. By the way, Kaven, why aren't you using the clipboard I got you when we graduated?"

Eaerien chuckled. "I see it decomposing at the bottom of the rubbish heap."

Kaven ignored them. He was used to their teasing. The four of them had grown up like brothers. "As you know, the first pairings in order are: Pax and Mead, Genesis and Dar, Bruno and Callen. After that will be Dar and Pax, followed by Mead and Bruno. The final set will be Callen against first Pax, then Dar, next Mead, and finally Genesis."

Shiloh whistled under his breath. "Looks like your infamous stamina drills are finally coming in handy, Eaerien."

"You sure he's ready for this?" Tuolene asked.

"It's too late for that now," Kaven cut in. "You'd better get to your seats." He stepped away and nodded to the judges before returning to his own seat behind Loren.

The fight between Pax and Mead was short. Both fledglings were long-range fighters, and neither engaged their opponents without first thoroughly assessing the situation. Pax's skills lay in information gathering. Mead had brains and brawn, but struggled with speed. Their fight simulation ended in a draw when both of them found an opening but chose not to take it, resulting in neither of them moving up a rank.

Dar and Genesis were more interesting to watch. They were both quick on their feet, but Dar formed strategies while Genesis took advantage of any opportunity. Dar excelled in defense, and Genesis was an offensive specialist.

"What are you doing?" Genesis demanded, engaging him in close combat.

"Staying alive!" he admitted shamelessly as he leaped away.

"More like running away," she remarked, pressing him. Her talons went through the top half of his tunic before he twisted away.

Dar fingered the shredded material on his chest as he dove and spun erratically in the air. She was faster than him in both the air and the ground. His only chance was to find cover and try for an ambush. He dropped to the ground and braced himself for another attack, grabbing wildly for her wrists when she jumped on him. He caught one, but he wasn't fast enough to catch the other. Taking several great leaps backward, he held one hand to the freshly shaved part of his head. Surprisingly, he felt a lot more relaxed than he had at the start of the simulation. If Genesis had really wanted to kill him, she would have already done so. It was time to even the playing field.

Genesis blinked, and Dar disappeared. One second he was beside the rock before her, and the next he was gone. She held steady for a moment, trying to pinpoint his location when the ground started trembling beneath her.

Dar's ultimate skill was tracking. He could locate anything, including things in the air, by sending low frequency shock waves into the earth. The higher up the target was, the stronger the shocks. By controlling the depth at which he dispersed the shocks, he was able to limit their damage to the surface. Right now, he was attempting to throw off Genesis's equilibrium by sending shocks that reverberated throughout the entire arena. He sent the waves in pulses to avoid damaging the foundation.

Genesis took to the air as the next series of quakes rocked the ground. She flew to the center of the arena and let out a loud, ear-splitting scream. Dar grabbed his ears in surprise, momentarily deafened with the rest of the audience. She located him moments later, still rubbing his deafened ears, and the simulation ended.

The next match was called, and Callen stepped into the arena. He faced Bruno, and the expression on his opponent's face spoke volumes. Bruno hated Callen even more than he hated Genesis. Everything about the newcomer offended him: Callen's even temperament; the way he carried himself, the way he inexplicably drew others to him, the way he had showed up out of nowhere; how quickly he was developing his skills, how everyone talked about him being Elohim's son, how he never did or said anything mean to or about anyone, and especially how Callen was looking at him right now—hopeful yet sad.

Bruno had always considered himself everyone's favorite. He had the skills, he had the power, and he had a beautiful set of wings. Then Genesis had come along and outperformed him. When he had tried to befriend her, she had set her talons on him. So he turned to goading her. And now she was chummy with Callen. It made Bruno sick.

He dug his heels into the ground. He was a combat specialist at all ranges, and he knew full well that Callen could not control his defenses. He had only to provoke him a little bit. Once the judges saw Callen's lack of control, they would stop the simulation, and Bruno would automatically win.

Callen glanced uncertainly in Elohim's direction. Seeing his opponent's momentary distraction, Bruno attacked. Anticipating this, Callen calmly shut his eyes and held up his arms with his palms forward, imagining a wall of air forming before him. He opened his eyes at the sound of a thud and saw Bruno bounce backward. He dropped his arms and felt the invisible wall disintegrate. His heart skipped a beat as a familiar tingling began in his fingertips.

Bruno was on his feet and moving toward him again albeit with caution.

Callen extended his hands again, and Bruno feinted to the side. Callen turned with him, the tingling now extending to his shoulders. His heartbeat accelerated, and Callen knew it wouldn't be long before his arms grew stiff and useless.

Bruno dodged again, and Callen took a deep breath, trying to quiet his pounding heart. As Bruno attacked for the third time, Callen attempted another defensive wall. He failed, and Bruno slammed into him, and they grappled for a few tense moments. When they finally separated, Callen had a thin stream of blood trickling down his arm.

Genesis was on her feet in an instant, but Eaerien appeared out of nowhere and fastened a restraining hand on her arm. She turned blazing eyes on her mentor, but he nodded toward Elohim, who continued watching the fight calmly.

Callen's arms were completely numb and growing stiffer by the second. Bruno was grinning at him triumphantly. Callen extended his arms out to the side at shoulder height, palms facing Bruno, and twisted around on his heel. He didn't have a clear picture in his mind of what he was trying to achieve, but he knew the simulation had to end before he accidentally hurt Bruno. He wasn't sure how many revolutions he made, but when he stopped spinning, not only was Bruno flat on his back, so were all the trees inside the arena. Callen dropped his arms and stared wide-eyed at the leveled landscape. *What have I done?*

Loren raised his arm, signaling the end of the match. Kaven, Tuolene, and Eaerien hurried onto the field. After a quick exam by Kaven, Bruno sat up, and Tuolene supported him off the field.

"Bruno's alright," Eaerien reassured Callen, while examining his arms. "His ego was the only thing harmed. This cut, on the other hand, is too deep for my skills, but I can stop the bleeding."

Kaven rushed up to them. "Callen, are you all right?" he asked, reaching for his injured arm.

Callen pulled his sleeve back over the wound. "You can heal it later." He still had trouble wrapping his mind around the Caledon ability to heal wounds. All had the ability to heal simple cuts, but some were gifted with healing hands.

Eaerien squeezed Callen's arms. "Can you feel this?"

"Just the pressure, but it's better than a few moments ago."

Kaven and Eaerien exchanged worried glances. "We can postpone the rest of the matches," Kaven offered.

Callen shook his arms out and stepped back. "I can keep going."

Eaerien gave a small sigh. "You have to know your limits, Callen."

"My skin feels a little numb, but I can still move," he insisted, demonstrating by waving his arms up and down. "Please, Eaerien."

"Fine," Eaerien acquiesced. "But be careful. You can injure yourself without realizing the extent."

"Well it won't be from leaping through the trees," Callen remarked, drawing a chuckle from both Eaerien and Kaven. Eaerien clapped him on the shoulder and returned to his seat.

Kaven gave a signal, and Pax stepped into the arena.

Pax was the smallest and the youngest in their class. He was quiet, observant, and fast. He was often sent on scouting missions to gather information about the people or land. He had paid close attention during Callen's fight simulation with Bruno, and he understood that Callen carried an incredible amount of energy but did not know how to harness it. If Callen released energy at a steady rate instead of in short powerful bursts, he would have better control over it.

Pax melted into the shade of several downed trees and stealthily made his way closer to Callen, who remained stationary. He weighed his options as he moved. He could ambush Callen, or he could try provoking him the way Bruno had. The latter left a bad taste in his mouth. When he was within several feet of Callen's back, he launched his attack.

Callen heard his opponent and, without conscious thought, threw up a shield behind him. He heard before he saw Pax ricochet off it. Wasting no time, Pax unfolded his wings while he was moving backward and flew into the sun's path. Callen took his right hand and swept the sky above him with what he hoped was an invisible hand of air. Instead, a tornado strength gust of wind captured Pax and hurtled him to the opposite end of the arena. He tumbled through the air, unable to find his wings before spiraling toward the ground.

Eyes wide with alarm, Callen sprinted for the boy, throwing up his left arm at the same time. *Stop the fall! Stop the fall!* He screamed silently. *Stop— PAX!* Pax paused in midair four feet off the ground, and sliding to a stop, Callen grabbed him.

"Thanks," Pax said breathlessly.

Unable to reply from the pounding in his chest, Callen nodded. He hugged the younger Caledon and was suddenly reminded of the little brother he had left behind.

Pax patted his arm comfortingly. "No harm done."

"Are you sure?" Callen questioned, setting him on his feet and anxiously glancing over him.

"I'm sure," Pax replied, smoothing down his tunic. "Well done, Callen," he congratulated as he walked off the arena where his mentor was waiting.

"Did you see that coming?" Tuolene asked.

"No." He glanced back at Callen and pursed his lips. "I don't think Callen did either."

Mead and Dar entered the arena together, grinning self-consciously. Callen tilted his head and raised his eyebrows slightly. Dar stepped unashamedly behind his teammate and peeked around at Callen.

Callen laughed and rubbed his arms—they were growing stiff again.

Mead picked up a small tree and tossed it casually at him. Callen blocked it with an invisible air shield. Mead tossed a second tree. Callen blocked it again. Mead picked up two more trees and tossed them both at him.

Callen meant to block them but punted them back in the direction they had come instead. He gasped as Mead and Dar dove out of the way. From where he lay, Dar sent a large tremor through the ground, and Callen jumped away from it. When Dar sent another shock toward him, Callen experimentally put his palms to the earth, pressing downward, and the quaking ceased immediately.

Callen looked up in surprise—just in time to see a tree sailing through the air at him. He tumbled out of the way and lay on his back, staring at the sky and breathing heavily. His arms felt like lead.

Mead and Dar approached warily. When Callen didn't move, they quickened their steps.

"I'm finished," Callen said when they were within earshot.

"Can you stand?" Dar asked, kneeling beside him.

"I don't think so."

Mead took a hold of his arm, and Callen groaned. "Something's wrong with your arm!"

Dar grabbed Callen's other arm. "This one too, and you're bleeding!" He beckoned wildly at the mentors.

Callen groaned again and his arms began to tremble. He shut his eyes against the pain, vaguely aware of the voices around him.

"This is worse than before," Eaerien said, scooping him up.

"Get him to the clinic," Kaven urged. He threw a quick glance at Elohim, who was calmly watching them lift Callen off the field. "I'll wrap this up quickly and send Loren."

∞

When Loren arrived at the clinic, Callen was unconscious and his arms were seizing. Loren set to work immediately. Eaerien sat quietly by his side, watching his skilled hands knead Callen's arms the way he done not too many hours ago, while pondering Elohim's statement. Callen's power was not designed for containment? He had seen Callen's arms becoming stiff during the simulation with Bruno, but when he had physically examined them afterward, they had been normal. When the boy was relaxed, he was better able to control it. But at what point did it flip out of control? He reacted instinctively during life or death situations, but it was not secondary to his emotions. What, then, was the trigger?

"Care to share your thoughts?"

Eaerien focused on the old Caledon before him and noted the beads of sweat forming on Loren's brow. "I have not seen you work so hard in years, Loren," he commented.

The old Caledon burst into quiet laughter.

Loren had been mentor to Kaven, Aria, and the three current mentors. Of all of them, Eaerien gave the most thought to all things spoken and unspoken, so it had been no surprise to any when Elohim had chosen him to mentor first Genesis and now his own son.

"Shall I ask Elohim to come?" Eaerien inquired.

Loren smiled reassuringly. "Elohim does not need promptings from us, Eaerien."

An urgent knock sounded at the door, followed immediately by the turn of the handle and a rush of air as the door swung open without invitation. Genesis hurried inside carrying a small bundle, followed closely by Pax. Eaerien watched with interest at the subdued look on her face as she approached Callen's still form.

"Pax, tell them what you told me," she ordered.

Pax pointed to the bundle in Genesis's hands. "Thermal regulation. Callen's body heat—"

"Madden!" Eaerien interrupted, jumping to his feet.

Genesis unfurled the bundle, and the little dog jumped onto Callen's chest. Loren stilled his hands and sat back. Eaerien nodded encouragingly at Pax.

Pax took a deep breath and explained. "His body temperature is directly proportional to the power he generates. When he was matched against Bruno, he was at a heightened but relatively constant temperature, which explains those shields he kept producing. When he started getting tense, he tried to relax and subconsciously dropped his body temperature, but the stress in his system resisted that change and overcompensated with more heat. He started to lose control, got desperate, and released a sudden burst of energy, ending the match. That sudden burst gave his system enough relief to reset. Similar situation when he went up against myself, Mead, and Dar."

Pax turned his eyes to the little dog stretched across Callen's chest. "This little creature survives by thermal regulation. He can light himself on fire at will using his own body heat or through heat absorbed externally. Looks like he can also regulate the body heat of others."

Eaerien laughed in delight. "Why did I not think to come to you, Pax?"

Pax flushed with embarrassment. "Who am I that you should come to me?"

Eaerien smiled with understanding. "I was the youngest in my class once too, so I should have known better than to overlook you. I apologize." *And I made Callen suffer needlessly all summer.* He smoothed the hair from Callen's forehead, grateful that the boy slept peacefully.

22.

It was unusually hot inside the Academy grounds, yet none of the students were permitted outside their aeries. Following the student evaluations, the mentors, instructors, and other winged Caledons had gathered for a week to train together. Not used to being cooped up inside, the fledglings' patience was tested. It was another first experience for Callen.

"How often does this happen?" he asked Genesis, who was lounging on a couch.

"Once every three months." She heard his unspoken question and answered. "They don't meet at the Academy often. It's too dangerous for the city."

Callen sprawled on the floor near her. "Can one of them control the weather?"

Genesis smirked. "You're the only one who can do anything close to that." Her temper flared as she watched him toying with the bandage on his arm. Bruno had broken the only rule of the simulation—do no harm—and had been expelled.

"What happens when a Caledon gets expelled from school?" he asked, reading her thoughts.

"He loses his wings."

Callen inhaled sharply. *Elohim does not take disobedience lightly.*

No, but he would have forgiven if Bruno had repented. "Speaking of wings," she said aloud. "You didn't use yours at all."

Callen didn't offer to explain. He bled and felt pain every time he unfolded them, but he didn't want to tell her or Eaerien that. He caught her staring at his arm again and held it out to her.

Genesis looked into his eyes and hesitated.

He smiled gently. "You're learning to heal, aren't you? You can practice on me."

She put her hand on the bandage. She could do so little. Callen placed his hand over her's as she was about to remove it. Her eyes widened when she realized that he was amplifying her skill with his own energy. "Since when?" she asked incredulously.

"Just now," he answered with equal surprise.

Genesis slid the bandage off. There was no trace of an injury. "You did something else in the arena. You stopped Dar's shocks. How did you do that?"

"I just did," he replied without arrogance. "I had half a thought and tried it."

She looked at him again and wondered. *Who are you?* Deep in her heart, she already knew who Callen was, and the voice in the back of her mind started to speak again. She tore her gaze from his understanding one and felt panic begin to rise. She had to go. She couldn't stay. She went for the door.

Callen caught her arm. "Wait!" *Where are you going?*

Genesis shut him out and pulled her arm from his grasp. "Leave me alone!"

"Genesis!"

She was already gone. She ran as fast as she could, and when it wasn't fast enough, she unfurled her wings and flew faster. Panic and fear drove her blindly forward.

Stop.

Someone was following her. An angry snarl bubbled suddenly in her throat, followed by a desperate sob. She was being torn apart from the inside out. She felt her talons unsheathe, but she hadn't asked for them. She heard a faint voice calling her name, and she wanted to answer but her own stuck inside her throat. She flew into the darkness. Panic mounted. She turned around sharply but could not see the way she had come. Darkness engulfed her.

Genesis put her arms around her head and screamed.

Callen winced in pain. He heard Genesis screaming, but he couldn't locate her. She had hung a dark heavy curtain between them. He felt despair for the first time in his life. *Elohim help.* He had to find her and bring her home. Why had he not realized until now just how tormented she was? *Father, please.*

∞

Moriana glared at the one before her. **Stop screaming.**

Genesis went rigid.

Long time no see.

Leave me alone.

You're in MY territory. If you want this to stop, you know what to do.

Genesis snarled.

Moriana snarled back. **If you won't take me back to him, then do us both a favor and kill yourself!**

I won't!

You won't? YOU WON'T? YOU INSOLENT—!

I won't listen to you!

I OWN YOU!

Genesis shook her head violently. *Liar!* She grabbed her knees and rocked herself. *You're lying. It's a lie. It's a lie!*

Moriana watched her with hatred and loathing. **Pathetic. Weak.**

"Enough!" a voice thundered around them.

Genesis scrambled to her feet and gaped at what she saw.

Callen stood with wings so bright they cut through the darkness. He stepped in front of Genesis and faced her enemy, his eyes glittering with the intensity of his outrage.

Moriana shrank from him. **If you hurt me, you'll hurt her too!**

"Silence!"

Moriana cowered.

"You've tormented Genesis long enough. You will not destroy her."

Moriana shrieked. **Who are you to allow or deny me? I am Jaden's disciple!**

"I am Callen, the son of Elohim." His voice was familiar, but it rang with authority that came only from Elohim. "Remember my name, and tell your master I am ready." He spread his wings, and the blinding light overwhelmed the darkness.

The last thing Genesis saw was a trickle of blood flowing down Callen's back.

∞

Genesis woke up and looked slowly around. She was in her room. She sat up and stretched. Her body felt oddly stiff for having slept in her bed. How far had she run last night? She paused and listened to the voices on the other side of her door. She recognized Eaerien, Kaven, and Loren. They must have been called away from the training session and were probably discussing what she had done the night before. With a heavy sigh, she readied herself to face them, but the door suddenly flew open.

Callen stood there looking sheepish. "I heard you get up," he explained.

She relaxed. At least he didn't sound angry.

He reached for her and pulled her into a tight hug. "We weren't sure when you would wake up."

"What are you talking about?"

He leaned away and studied her face.

Genesis turned away uncomfortably.

Callen glanced to where their mentor sat. "She doesn't remember."

She brushed him away. "I remember," she countered with a tinge of annoyance. "I ran off last night. Elohim and Callen came for me ..." Her voice trailed off at the expression on their faces.

Callen took one of her hands in both of his. "You've been asleep for a week."

Genesis's eyes widened and she threw a quick look at Eaerien, who gave her a weak smile as he came to her side.

"What's the last thing you remember?" he asked gently.

She glanced at her teammate, who had taken back his perch. "Callen chased Moriana away. He told her to tell Jaden that he's ready."

"She didn't leave that night," Callen spoke up. "I brought you home after you fell unconscious. You didn't wake up, but she did. She finally left, but you still wouldn't wake up."

Eaerien picked up the story. "Elohim came to us. He told us you had to choose, and that we were to do nothing except wait. So, here we are." His face was worn, but his eyes were bright with joy.

Genesis's mind was reeling.

Loren held his hands over her. "Lay back down, child. Let me check you over."

She laid back down on her bed and her eyes wandered back to her teammate, noting the shadows under his eyes. He must have stayed up all night and day watching over her until Eaerien returned from training. *Why would anyone do that for me?*

Callen smiled softly at the unspoken question.

"Where is Elohim now?" Genesis asked.

"He's gone, but he'll be back," Eaerien answered. "He set up a new training regimen. We've been instructed to start immediately."

"I don't understand."

"What most of us suspected, Elohim confirmed that night. Callen will reunite the Caledons and bring Jaden's influence to an end. He is Elohim's son."

23.

Callen was packing in preparation for a trip with Loren and Kaven. After the adult Caledons' training week had ended, Loren had proposed the excursion out of the blue.

Genesis leaned in the doorway of Callen's room, watching him gather his things. They would be apart for the first time since he arrived at the Academy.

"Want to help?" he asked.

"No."

"Will you take notes for me in class?"

"I'm not going if—" She bit her tongue. *Stupid.*

"You won't go without me?" Callen finished for her anyway. "What about the material I'll miss?"

"That's what the library is for." She moved to the narrow ledge on the left side of the aerie door and leaned into the crisp mountain breeze. "Besides, you started a few years late, and you're doing just fine."

A teasing smile played at his mouth. "Will you miss me?"

"Why would I?"

He chuckled and joined her at the window. "Something's bothering you."

She met the boy's gaze then looked away without responding. Something had changed between them that night he'd saved her from Moriana. They weren't merely teammates anymore. They were friends.

Callen let a small sigh escape. "You could trust me a little."

"I do" was her immediate reply.

"Genesis ..."

She turned to face him squarely.

Callen searched her eyes. "Deep down, you don't."

"It's nothing," she said, moving away.

He put a hand on her shoulder, stopping her retreat. "I want to help you."

"I know you do," she replied, carefully removing his hand without looking at him. "But I don't want you to."

"Why?" he pressed.

She swung back around to face him. "How am I supposed to get strong enough to break free from Jaden if I get more and more dependent on you every moment we spend together?"

"We're stronger together." He held out his hands. "Remember how we healed my arm?"

Genesis tucked her hands behind her back. "You can't fight my battles for me."

Callen dropped his hands, but stepped close. "Then let me fight them *with* you."

She shook her head desperately. "My life isn't worth it."

"Your life means more to me than it does to you." *You're not a burden to me, Genesis.*

Genesis averted her eyes as her chest tightened painfully. She wasn't one to pledge her loyalty to just anyone. She had been betrayed by her mother, forsaken by her father, and sold by the first master she had devoted her life to. Even now, amongst the love and care bestowed upon her by Eaerien and Loren, she didn't whole-heartedly follow after them. She couldn't fully accept Elohim either. He was so far out of her comprehension that she had doubted him in the deepest recesses of her heart. But Callen ...

Callen was honest—offensively honest—but he was gentle even in anger. He often grew frustrated by her stubborn rejection, but he stayed. He never held grudges against her, although she gave him cause to. When she had stopped fighting and started ignoring him instead, he still remained at her side. Everywhere she turned, he was breaking down her carefully constructed walls.

It was too much for her to handle.

Callen fastened his hand around her wrist. "Where are you going?"

"None of your business," she growled.

He tightened his grip, which made her fight harder. The undisguised wretchedness in her eyes stunned him, and his grip slackened enough for her to pull free.

She fled.

"Genesis, wait!"

She didn't stop.

Callen pursued her.

She could sense his presence growing and spreading around her.

He heard her thoughts and moved even faster. He was flying now, but low to the ground in the most direct line to her.

"Hurry," Genesis told herself. "Don't let him see you like this." But her feet stopped moving instead. Part of her *wanted* him to catch up.

Callen caught up to her and threw a barrier up.

Genesis clenched her fists. "Locking me in?"

"You don't have to do this," he said. "There's another way."

"If there was, I wouldn't be here."

He held out his hand. "Genesis, please."

"Don't! You don't know what you're asking me."

He took a step closer.

"The last time Eaerien tried to help me, I nearly blinded him," she snarled. "I've had enough!" She yelled into the trees, "You hear that, Jaden? Everyone will finally get what they want! I'm going to disappear for good!"

The intense self-loathing her eyes cut Callen to the core. *You need to stop punishing yourself.*

She turned her back on him. "Leave me alone!"

It's not your fault, Genesis.

"Yes, it is," she screamed, wrapping her arms around herself. "If I'd never been born, none of this would've happened!"

Callen continued his advance. *I'm glad you were born. You have no idea how glad I am.*

"Go away!" She turned pleading eyes on him and dropped her voice. "Please, you can't help me."

Yes, I can.

Genesis hated herself for hoping. "How?"

"Trust me."

A part of her screamed no, but the other part desperately wanted to take a chance. She looked at the boy just beyond her reach. She could see him clearly, but the gap between them seemed impossible to breach. To her amazement, Callen took another step closer. He was now a mere arm's length away. She looked from his outstretched hand to the kindness in his eyes.

It's your decision, his eyes seemed to say.

Genesis knew then that the barrier around them wasn't meant to keep her in, but to keep everything else out. It was simply the two of them. No Moriana, and no Jaden. She stretched her hand out tentatively and lightly touched her fingertips to his.

It was enough. Callen grasped her hand and a bright smile lit up his features. *I'm never going to let go.*

24.

They were only gone for three days. Callen didn't volunteer what had transpired, and neither Eaerien nor Genesis asked. Loren put Elohim's new training regimen into effect immediately upon their return, sending the mentor-mentee teams away for a season on various assignments.

Genesis and Callen traveled alongside Eaerien, sometimes accompanied by Loren or Kaven. They met a myriad of people groups and creatures; many took interest in Genesis's heritage, but Callen was the one they were drawn to. He sat for hours with the elders and wise men of each group, listening to their discussions about treaties and laws.

For each group that accepted Caledon rule, it seemed twice as many rejected it. Eaerien seemed more than content to relinquish his position at the table during those hours. He instead went with Genesis to survey the territory and its neighbors.

What struck Genesis the most was that many of the people they met had no idea who Callen was, and Callen did not introduce himself as Elohim's son. Both Loren and Eaerien seemed to accept his decision to do so without question. Genesis broached the subject one evening after a particularly long and heated discussion.

Callen, usually full of questions, had grown progressively quiet until Eaerien took sympathy and dismissed him. Callen immediately sought Genesis out. He found her gazing at the stars outside of the village and joined her with a sigh of relief.

Genesis studied her teammate's profile: shoulders slightly rounded forward, eyes lifted to the sky, mouth curved downward, and hands clasped protectively over the ever-present bulge at his chest. *You look weary.*

A smile curled the edges of Callen's mouth. Genesis often left her mind open to him these days. He stretched out on his back and studied the night sky, waiting for her to speak.

"I don't understand something," she began.

He turned his gaze to her.

"They should know who you are. Elohim was very clear that day. Why don't you say anything?"

Callen searched her eyes until she looked uncomfortably away. "Who am I to you, Genesis?"

"You are Elohim's son."

"What does that mean?"

"You'll fulfill the proph—" She clenched her jaw, struck by the hollowness in her words. Words she had heard over and over again. Words she believed, but did she understand what they meant? Under Callen's scrutinizing gaze, she wasn't so sure anymore. She let out a breath of frustration.

Callen laughed, but it was tinged with sorrow.

Genesis turned back to him wondering what had been said that made him sad and pensive.

"Who am I to you?" Callen asked again.

Genesis clenched her fists, wanting to answer but not knowing how. He was looking at her earnestly, and all she could think was that she was about to disappoint him.

You know me, and you believe in Elohim, Callen said to her. *These people have just met me, and even though Elohim spoke, it does not mean they heard him. If you who knows me can't answer that question, how can they?*

"Callen," she started.

His expression brightened immediately. "You said my name again."

Genesis was dumbstruck by his sudden shift in tone.

He tried to suppress a smile but failed and grinned broadly at her.

"I'm sorry," she stammered. "I—I've never—" She clenched and unclenched her fists, fighting herself. "Elohim's the king, and you're his son. Before when it was just a rumor, it was easy to hate you. But the more

190

time we spent together, the more I realized that you're not hate-able, and am I even allowed to say or think these things?" Fear crept into her eyes. Every time she opened up to someone, they abandoned her. She had withheld her doubts from Eaerien because he diligently followed Elohim. If Callen turned from her, Eaerien would follow, and that made her very afraid.

Callen gathered her hands in his. "Genesis, look at me." He waited for her to comply. "Remember how I used to follow you around even though you hated it? If I enjoyed being around you so much when you hated it, don't you think I'll enjoy being around you even more now that you like having me around?" He raised an eyebrow.

Genesis felt a twinge of annoyance.

Callen saw it and laughed.

"What if I'm using you?" she blurted.

"Why would you do that?"

"To get back at Jaden." Her insides twisted painfully as she spoke.

Anger flashed in Callen's eyes, and Madden stirred from within his tunic. "Why do you do that?"

"Do what?"

"Intentionally put yourself in a bad light."

"It's who I really am." She started to pull her hands away, but he held fast.

"Stop lying to yourself."

"You're the one lying to yourself," she declared. "I know what I am, and I've accepted it. You—you think too highly of me! I'll turn on you one day."

"Stop it." He tugged gently at her hands.

"You stop!" She tried furiously to pull her hands from his. "Don't you get it? Jaden is using me against you. I see it on everyone's faces everywhere we go. I'm the reason they won't accept you!" She saw in his eyes the pain her words caused. "I'm going back to him. Give him a taste of his own medicine!"

"No!" Callen yelled, dropping her hands.

Genesis went still and closed her mind to Callen.

Callen took deep, steadying breaths. He saw her swallow hard as if she could swallow down the fear bubbling up inside of her, and his heart ached. She had become his closest companion. Elohim had said she was his greatest gift, but all she did was say things that cut him up inside. She tried his patience, but he had seen how broken she was inside. She was her own worst enemy. "I won't let you go back," he repeated calmly.

"But—"

"There is absolutely nothing that can be said or done by anyone that will change my mind," he said firmly.

Genesis clenched her fists so tight her knuckles turned white.

Callen gathered them into his once more and gently rubbed them between his palms. She didn't relax for a long time. *Why won't she trust me?*

∞

Eaerien tilted his head, studying his quickly maturing eyases. Their teamwork had greatly improved since their first trek out of the desert, but something had gone wrong at the last village. At first, he thought they were taking advantage of Callen's ability to communicate through thoughts, but now he wasn't so sure. "Did you two disagree about something again?" he finally demanded.

Genesis's expression became stormy.

Callen's eyes flashed, and he opened his mouth.

"Don't!" Genesis stopped him.

Callen looked offended but remained silent.

Eaerien glanced at Genesis and wondered at the miserable expression she wore. "We're meeting Shiloh and Tuolene at the next community. Jaden's influence is heavy there, and he was spotted in the vicinity a few weeks ago. I hope you will resolve your issues before we arrive."

Genesis's blood chilled at the name of her previous master. She had not faced him for years, and Eaerien had sheltered her from his influence as best he could. Now it sounded like they were walking straight into his domain. A strong hand took her cold one and warmed it. She looked up and saw Callen watching her with compassion. She squeezed his hand briefly to acknowledge his support then pulled away. She hated being weak.

They arrived at the outskirts of the community and found Shiloh's fledglings setting up camp. Dar whooped and gave them hugs. More reserved, Mead raised a hand in greeting. Genesis gave Dar a withering glare when he released her.

Dar held out his hands in surrender. "I'm sorry, but I kind of missed you."

"Where's Shiloh?" Eaerien asked.

"Scouting the area," he answered.

Mead beckoned them to a makeshift rock table. "Have something to eat. It's cold, but we decided against a fire."

"Madden can help with that," Callen offered. He patted the bulge at his chest, and Madden poked his head out. "Can you warm up our meal?" The little dog jumped onto the rock and glowed.

Eaerien grinned. "We haven't needed a fire since Madden joined the team."

"Does he ever run out of heat?" Dar wondered.

"He draws from Callen if he does."

Shiloh arrived as they were finishing their meal. He ate his portion quickly then departed with Eaerien. Callen cleared up the meal, and Dar wiped all trace of their presence off the ground, while Genesis and Mead found trees to sleep in for the night.

"Did Callen and Genesis fight?" Mead wondered when his teammate joined him. "They haven't said a word to each other since they arrived."

"I was thinking they were communicating through here." Dar tapped his temple. "Until that look Eaerien gave them before he left."

Mead glanced toward Genesis's tree. "I don't see Callen."

"I'll go find him," Dar offered. "You can stay with Genesis." He ran into their mentors before he found Callen. He was on the verge of asking about Callen, but the expression on their faces quieted his tongue.

Eaerien took one glance at Dar and his eyes turned ice blue. He located his eyas and called to him. *Callen, come quickly. See if you can reach Tuolene and Pax on your way. They must avoid the southern border at all costs.*

Dar led them to where Genesis and Mead were perched in the trees. Eaerien and Shiloh gathered them close and spread their wings around them, cutting off outside eyes and ears.

"Jaden is approaching from the south with a small army of followers," Shiloh spoke quietly. "Either there's enough people in this village resisting his influence, or he's aiming to engage us."

A shiver ran down Genesis's spine, and she locked eyes Eaerien. She hadn't lost control since Callen had confronted Moriana, but one word from Jaden could be her undoing.

"Where's Callen?" Mead asked.

I'm here, Callen answered. A moment later, he alighted in the tree and joined their circle, spreading his wings to widen it. "Tuolene and Pax already know about Jaden. They've been in and out of his trail all season. They flew by just to warn us, but they have an urgent message for Loren, so they aren't staying."

Shiloh rubbed his chin stubble. "Jaden had to have known we were coming. What's his aim?"

Eaerien sighed heavily. "He wants a fight. My guess is he wants either Callen or Genesis, or both."

"My team will stay," Shiloh volunteered. "We'll delay him until you are out of reach."

Genesis shook her head. "If we run, he'll decimate the community just to grab our attention."

Dar looked thunderstruck. "But most of them are his followers!"

"He doesn't care. He'll call it 'a necessary sacrifice.'"

Dar paled. They had been hatchlings the last time Jaden had gone on a warpath, massacring entire communities in his quest to find Elohim's newborn son. Entire races were wiped from the earth forever. It had lasted six horrific years. They knew the histories, but only the elder Caledons had witnessed the violence. "You were there?" he realized, seeing Genesis's haunted eyes.

Genesis felt sick. At six years old, she hadn't been old enough to witness the violence, but she had seen the aftermath firsthand. She had just been given to Jaden, and he had proudly shown her the devastation he had caused.

Mead put a gentle hand on Genesis's shoulder and steered the conversation away from her. "We need a plan."

They laid out several plans deep into the night then settled into the trees to rest. Eaerien sat with his arm draped protectively around Genesis. It was easy to forget how small and vulnerable she was behind her mask of anger. His mind wandered to the days they had met in secret at the outer edge of Jaden's property. She had been even smaller then, but somehow less vulnerable.

"I hate that faraway look in your eyes," Genesis muttered, bringing his nostalgia to an end.

"What's that?"

She looked dolefully at him.

"I'm not going to float away," he teased.

"Sometimes you look like you're about to," she remarked. "What were you thinking about?"

Eaerien ruffled her hair with his free hand. "Having Callen around has been good for you. The stronger he becomes, the more at peace I am about letting you go."

She tilted her head out of his reach. "Where are you going?"

"Not me," he corrected. "You."

"I don't understand."

"You and Callen will fly the nest eventually," he said, resting his cheek against her head. "Elohim has great plans for you both."

"What about you?"

"I will also follow the path Elohim has laid out for me."

Genesis looked rebellious.

Eaerien patted her soothingly. "Elohim never sends us out unprepared. When that time comes, we'll be ready for it." He closed his eyes and drifted to sleep.

Genesis turned her eyes to her teammate. He was fast asleep in the tree next to them. Madden was nestled on his chest, keeping watchful eyes on their surroundings. She tried to envision Callen defeating Jaden, but her stomach kept twisting into anxious knots. She pressed her palms into her temples. He was definitely going to try to get to Callen through her.

25.

The following day Shiloh led his team into the village to meet with the community leaders as originally planned, while Eaerien and his team remained hidden in the trees. Genesis had been suffering the effects of Jaden's nearness since the early hours of the morning. The closer he drew, the harder it was for her to resist his influence.

"Don't push yourself," Eaerien warned repeatedly.

"I'm fine." It was a lie that she wanted to believe. She felt herself tottering on the edge of control. As the hours stretched, and they waited for Jaden to make a move, her consciousness slipped. Moriana wasn't there to torment her anymore, but Jaden's influence was still strong enough to drag her down.

∞

Callen watched her slowly slip away again. It grieved him to stand by and do nothing, but his father had been very clear that Genesis had to make the decision on her own each and every time. He searched for his mentor, whose eyes told the same story. *She's always chosen us before,* he tried to reassure himself.

∞

Genesis couldn't block out Jaden's voice any longer. He was calling her, and he was nearby. She took a step forward, and Eaerien's face flashed in her mind, making her hesitate. Then her feet carried her forward again. She thought of Callen, and her steps faltered once more. They had had a plan, and she was about to ruin it. *I have to go back.* Genesis looked around and saw that she was alone. Fear gripped her.

"Moriana," a voice called softly.

Genesis broke out in a cold sweat. Jaden stepped out from the shadows with a sinister smile, and a panicked sob rose in her throat, but she forced it back down. For each step he took toward her, she took two back, and his smile faded into a snarl. Genesis trembled, and her talons came out unbidden.

"Do you want to kill me?" Jaden asked slowly, tauntingly.

"Leave me alone," she choked out in a small voice.

Jaden smirked. "It's not you I want, my little failure. I want the boy."

She froze. "No." *Not Callen.*

His eyes narrowed murderously. "I take what I want."

Genesis reined in her fear but could not stop shaking. "Not him."

"You can't stop me," Jaden said derisively, propping a hand on his hip. He grew uncannily still, sizing her up, and then he lunged. He had her by the throat before she could blink. He bent his mouth to her ear. "Caught you." He squeezed his hands until she was wheezing for air. "How pathetic. All this time you feared I'd want you back. I never wanted you. No one does. You're just everyone's bait."

Genesis's eyes glazed. She saw a face leering at her from the safety of the shadows. *Aeron.*

"Let her go!"

Jaden's eyes gleamed. He flung Genesis away from him and lunged for Callen.

Genesis twisted back in mid-air, still choking, and tackled Jaden to the ground before he reached the boy. "Don't touch him," she coughed out.

Jaden lashed out at Genesis, intending to maim her, but Callen deflected it as he ran toward them, forcing their enemy back. He slid to Genesis's side and dragged her to her feet. Jaden unleashed a shower of poisonous barbs while retreating into the shadows.

Callen threw himself over Genesis, shielding her with his body. She felt Madden burning through his tunic. *Where's Eaerien?* she wondered. She couldn't seem to stop shaking, and her throat was on fire.

Lacquers, Callen told her. He sat up, holding her close, and faced the shadows. "Let her go, Jaden."

Jaden laughed diabolically. "As long as she hates me, she will never be free. Come, Moriana!"

Genesis loathed herself for responding, but Callen held her fast. *There's someone else here.* He acknowledged that he'd heard her with a small nod.

Jaden walked a slow circle around them, careful to remain in the shadows. It was not lost on him that Genesis had not hesitated to defend Callen with her life. "We've met before, son of Elohim," he growled. "A Caledon without wings. You are quite unremarkable."

Genesis and Callen exchanged glances.

I told you, she said. *You have weird habits.* Even now, his wings remained sheathed.

Callen gave her a meaningful look. *If he doesn't think I have wings, we can use it to surprise him.*

Jaden attacked again with murderous intent. Callen threw up another shield, but Jaden pushed through with ease. Genesis shoved Callen out of his reach, leaving her back defenseless. With a wicked grin, Jaden ran his talons down the length of her back before being punched through the air by an invisible fist.

"Run!" Genesis gasped.

Callen scooped her up and swung into the trees.

∞

From the shadows, Aeron watched the battle with amusement. He had no intention of helping his master. His half-breed sister was even more impossible to deal with than before, and the Caledon boy was unpredictable and reckless. Somehow, he was facing Jaden head-on and surviving. Aeron was pretty confident his master was not going to win this battle.

∞

Callen set Genesis down in a tree and put his hand on the large gashes in her back, employing her skill and amplifying it. When he removed his hand, large puckered scars remained.

"I haven't gotten the hang of remodeling skin," Genesis remarked.

He took his outer tunic off and draped it over her. Then he scooped the little dog onto his shoulder, and Madden huddled next to his neck. "Stay here, Genesis."

"Callen—"

"This isn't your fight anymore," he said gently. "Stay, please."

∞

Jaden ripped through the trees, hunting for them. His anger blistered. The half-breed had shown more loyalty to this wingless Caledon in five minutes than she had ever shown to him all the years he had raised her. "Aeron," he hissed. "Make yourself useful. Find the half-breed."

Aeron lowered his eyes in obeisance. "When I find her?"

Kill her.

Leaping from tree to tree, Callen found Jaden's trail easily. He dropped to the ground and surveyed the path of destruction around him. He brushed the earth beneath a dying tree and shook his head. Jaden didn't simply kill; he poisoned so there was no chance of revival.

Madden bristled.

They had walked into an ambush.

∞

Aeron regretted not staying to watch his master's ambush fail. He half-heartedly flew through the forest looking for Genesis. He didn't care about finding her, and if he did, he wouldn't kill her. He was tired of Jaden's maniacal ways. He halted abruptly. There she was, blatantly staring at him with the same dark eyes as his mother. He crouched slowly where he stood. "You have our mother's eyes," he said without nuance. When she didn't answer, he relaxed. "I suppose you're not going to kill me, but Jaden gave me instructions to kill you."

"Get on with it then," she replied, equally toneless.

Aeron watched her carefully and saw her wince in pain with the smallest movement. His master inflicted wounds that burned long after the scars disappeared. "Jaden ambushed him."

"I know."

Aeron shrugged and brushed himself off. "I'm not going to kill you, dear sister, but I gave your position away." He gave her a hard look before turning his back on her and flying away.

∞

In the shade of the trees, Jaden whirled and attacked vehemently from all sides, but Callen held his ground. He burned with a righteous fury that matched the intensity of Jaden's hate. He advanced on Jaden, who yielded in surprise. His eyes pierced the darkness that Jaden's presence made with bright light. He saw the Lacquers descending around Genesis, overpowering Eaerien, and overrunning the village where Shiloh, Mead, and Dar fought for their lives. His fury expanded overwhelmingly, and with an easy breath, he gave it release.

Within seconds, silence reigned.

Jaden and Aeron were nowhere to be found, but his followers lay in smoldering ashes and the landscape violently altered. Callen lay in a heap on the ground. Safely cocooned in pockets of air, Genesis, Eaerien, Shiloh, Mead, and Dar stared wide-eyed at the total destruction around them.

Genesis stumbled to her teammate's side. Blood was oozing from tiny cuts all over his arms, and she moved quickly to stop the bleeding. She brushed the hair and ash from his face, and his eyelids fluttered. "You're quite destructive when you're angry."

Callen opened his eyes and searched hers.

"I'm okay," she replied to the unspoken question.

Callen responded with a small smile and closed his eyes.

Genesis healed as many cuts as she could, focusing on the few deep ones on his palms and wrists. She tried to concentrate on minimizing the scars, but her energy was spent. She had lost a lot of blood, and her body still burned from the poison inflicted by Jaden's talons. Even as her hands continued working, her eyelids closed and her chin drooped to her chest. The last thing she felt was a small, soft bundle work its way between her arms, spreading warmth through her.

∞

Genesis opened her eyes and found herself cradled in Eaerien's arms. "Eaerien?"

"How are you feeling, Genii?"

She glanced around. "Where's Callen?"

"Shiloh's got him."

"You're not hurt?" she asked anxiously.

Eaerien grinned down at her. "Nothing that will kill me."

"The village …"

Eaerien frowned. "Rest now. I'll explain everything when we get home."

∞

"Callen is in a coma?" Aria asked her brother.

Eaerien massaged his aching temples. He had just come from his aerie where both of his eyases slept.

"What happened?"

"He took Jaden on by himself."

"Why?" she asked in alarm. "He's not ready for that."

"He was protecting us. It's a miracle he wasn't killed."

"And Genesis?"

"Jaden went after Callen, and she got in between them." He closed his eyes and shuddered at the image of the scars running down the girl's back.

"Oh, Eaerien." Aria's face twisted sympathetically.

"I'd better go." He pulled his sister in for a quick hug. "I just wanted to check in."

"Do you need anything?" she asked, holding him tight.

"No, but thank you, Aria." He turned to go.

"Eaerien," she called.

He turned back.

"I'm thankful you returned unharmed."

He flashed her a smile and ducked out the door.

∞

Hours later, as dawn peeked over the horizon, Callen slowly came to life. His eyes cracked open, and his breathing grew shallow. Something warm drew across his cheek and whined softly. The boy turned his head slowly to see the small dog crouched near his head, wagging his tail slowly. *Madden.*

The little dog ran his tongue over the boy's nose happily and wagged his tail harder.

Callen closed his eyes again and tried to gather his muddled senses. Slowly, he became aware of a slight pressure against his hand. Opening his eyes again, he recognized his sleeping teammate. "Genesis ..." She didn't stir, and Callen sensed the residual poison working its way through her. He flipped his hand and curled his fingers around hers.

26.

The village had been decimated. Not one survivor.

Loren rubbed his hands over his face in an effort to collect himself. He had an uncanny ability to remain calm and levelheaded in the worst situations, which was why Elohim had chosen him to shepherd the Academy. But this … Loren drew in a shaky breath. This calculated level of destruction had not been seen since the last great conflict for the land.

"Callen does not yet know." Eaerien spoke quietly, hoping not to further addle the man.

"How many children?" Loren forced himself to ask.

Eaerien gave him an odd look. "There were no children."

Loren recognized the disappointment in the young mentor's eyes. "I am not above doubting, Eaerien," he said wearily. "Forgive me."

Eaerien dropped his gaze. "I'm sorry, Loren. I shouldn't have judged you."

The older man smiled. "You were right to rebuke me." He stood and paced the room as his demeanor returned to normal. "It's difficult for me to believe that an entire village existed without a single child in the midst. It's just not possible … unless …" He stopped short, turned, and went to his desk. He picked up an off-white, frayed piece of paper and walked back to Eaerien. "I received this, along with an urgent message, from Tuolene a couple of days before you and Shiloh returned to the Academy," he said, handing it to him.

"Jaden creating holy villages," Eaerien read aloud. "Priesthood already formed." He flipped the paper over several times and gave Loren a confused look. "This looks like it was written years ago."

"It was," Loren affirmed. "Pax found it buried in the ground beside a tree stump, near what appeared to be a mass gravesite … of children. A date was etched onto the tree stump."

Eaerien blanched. "Are you telling me that this 'Priesthood' has something to do with that?"

Loren clasped his hands together. "There is a rumor floating around that Jaden is rewarding his most loyal subjects with Caledon-like abilities. One way to prove your loyalty is to give up your offspring."

"What do you mean by 'give up'?"

"Abandon them, or murder them."

Tears filled the young mentor's eyes.

"Eaerien," Loren continued, "the date on the tree stump is the date Genesis's father disappeared."

Eaerien stared at him in disbelief. "He disappeared when she was four years old, Loren."

"No," the old Caledon cut in. "He was sent on a mission when she was four years old. In her mind, he disappeared and never returned. In truth, he had been maintaining communication with your father, here, at the Academy, and Raine asked him to look into something, which he did. Unfortunately, it took him a couple of years to return, and when he did, his wife and daughter were gone."

Eaerien held his head in his hands, reeling from the information. "So," he said, struggling to form a coherent thought. "When did he really disappear?"

"Three years ago; not long after Genesis came to the Academy."

Eaerien inhaled a long, slow, deep breath and sat back slowly, allowing his arms to fall to his side. "What is the connection between Genesis's father and that gravesite, other than the date? And how is that connected to this 'Priesthood'?"

"I sent Tuolene and Pax to find that out." Loren gave him a tight smile. "I'm sending you and Shiloh out to help them, after you speak to your father."

"You want me to find out what my father asked him to look into all those years ago," Eaerien stated knowingly. "When do Shiloh and I leave?"

"Tomorrow."

"What about Callen?" Eaerien asked. "Did you think he would have turned the children to ash, as well, if there had been any in the village?"

Loren grimaced. "For a moment, I was afraid he did."

"But he's Elohim's son," Eaerien protested. "Why would he do that?"

"Jaden was Elohim's right hand," Loren pointed out. "Or so we thought, until we learned that he was the one who had instigated the unrest that led to the war. We all get to choose sides, Eaerien. Callen, Genesis, and Jaden are evidence that no one is exempted."

"I understand," Eaerien said carefully, "but Callen had already made his choice when he left home to come to the Academy earlier this year."

"Which is why I said you were right to rebuke me," Loren said amiably. "Now, are you certain Callen does not know what he did to that village?"

Eaerien raised his shoulders slightly and dropped them again. "He tried to ask, but none of us have the heart to tell him, and Shiloh has been keeping Mead and Dar away in case they give it away."

"And Genesis?"

"She was still asleep when I left the aerie. She has quite a bit of Jaden's poison to work out of her system unless—" He stopped suddenly as if a sudden thought crossed his mind.

"Unless?" Loren prompted.

"I wouldn't be surprised if Callen found a way of clearing it out of her."

Loren paused by the window and gazed thoughtfully at the landscape. "I wouldn't be surprised either."

∞

Genesis pressed her ear against the door. *Why did they stop talking?* A voice called her name loudly, startling her. She whirled toward it and agitatedly gestured for silence.

Callen grinned self-consciously and complied. He watched curiously as she pressed her ear to the door once more. *Why are you eavesdropping?*

None of your business. Her eyes connected briefly with his. *I mean, I'll tell you later.*

Callen frowned. *Why are you shutting me out again?*

I'm not. But she was. She was afraid he would see the images tormenting her mind. Images he had unintentionally placed there. Thankfully, Callen didn't press her. He never did, and that only made her feel worse.

Have you seen Dar or Mead?

Not since we got back.

Callen leaned against the door. *Would Loren have sent them on another assignment so soon?*

Genesis gave up trying to hear anything more and walked partway down the hall so they could speak without being overheard through the door. "Neither of them, nor Shiloh, was seriously injured during the attack so I don't see why not."

"Everyone seems to be avoiding me." He peered at her, and she averted her eyes. "See what I mean?"

Genesis fixed her gaze on a point above his shoulder. "Do you remember what happened after the attack?"

"I fainted. Shiloh carried me the whole way home."

Home? She met his gaze, and the edge of his mouth tipped into a smile. At some point, the Academy had indeed become their home.

Callen's smile faded. She was guarding something from him. "Are you trying to protect me from something?" He appeared amused by the idea. An image flashed through Genesis's mind, and the amusement vanished from his face and was replaced with sorrow. "I know what I did," he said in a voice barely above a whisper.

Loren's door swung open, and he and Eaerien stepped out. They spotted the pair.

"Can't say I'm surprised to see you both up and about," their mentor said lightly, stepping toward them. He gave Genesis a once over.

"Callen healed—" she started to explain.

"I figured," Eaerien interrupted her. He turned to the boy. "Let me see your hands," he commanded gently.

Callen held his hands up. Faint scars crisscrossed his palms and traveled up his wrists, disappearing with his skin beneath his long sleeves.

Concern lined Eaerien's brow. "Are you in pain?" he asked.

"It burns a little," Callen admitted quietly.

All over? Eaerien ran his fingers lightly across the scars.

Callen hesitated a moment, then nodded affirmatively.

Loren put a hand on the boy's shoulder.

"He knows," Genesis blurted out. She glanced at her teammate. "He knew the whole time."

"I suggest we take a walk," Loren said. "I have questions that require answers." He led the way, leaving them no choice but to follow.

∞

Callen recognized the path as the one that eventually led to the city below. He had never gotten the chance to go back, and he brightened at the possibility of seeing Petra again. She would be discovering her wings soon if she hadn't already.

"Can you tell us what happened?" Loren's question cut through his thoughts.

Callen paused his steps. "I can show you." He gestured to a cluster of boulders lining the path. "Please, sit."

Genesis hung back, but when Callen held out his hand to her, she didn't hesitate to grab hold.

He gave her hand a gentle squeeze. *Don't worry. I've got you.* Then he took a deep breath and closed his eyes.

For several minutes, the only sound was nature. Then Loren gave a sharp intake of breath, and the images faded from their minds. He walked a few paces down the path, stopping to stare at the treetops below them.

Eaerien gave Callen an encouraging smile.

Loren ambled thoughtfully back. "Not one of the villagers would bend toward Elohim?" he asked more to himself than anyone. "Has it really come to this?"

"Inevitably so," Eaerien answered.

Genesis's eyes dropped to her hand still resting in Callen's. She was about to pull away when Loren's next words recaptured her attention.

"It seems that the war has finally begun."

27.

Eaerien observed Callen interacting with the earth-bound Caledons. A fond grin crossed his face when Callen wrapped his arms around a child peering up at Madden, who was sitting on top of his head. A small sound of displeasure drew Eaerien's attention to Genesis standing beside him. He studied the emotions playing out across her face. "You're jealous."

Genesis's brow knit together as she repeated the word. "Jealous?"

Eaerien tipped his head toward Callen. "You're used to always being the center of his attention, and it irritates you when he pays attention to others. Am I right?"

Genesis grudgingly nodded.

He swallowed his laughter. "You don't need to worry. Callen has this unique ability to make everyone he meets feel special in their own way at the same time."

"The same way you can see everyone individually all at once?"

Eaerien chuckled. "You can put it that way."

Genesis fell silent and crossed her arms.

"What's on your mind?" he asked.

"Is jealousy a Caledon or Lacquer trait?" she wondered, dropping her eyes.

"Both," Eaerien answered, stepping in front of her and tipping her chin up. "It's a trait common to all living creatures."

"What makes you jealous?"

He folded his hands together. "Thankfully, jealousy is not something I struggle with."

"But arrogance is," she retorted sarcastically.

Eaerien laughed heartily. She grew quiet again, and he elbowed her softly. "What now?"

Genesis scuffed the toe of her moccasin into the dirt. "Do you think Callen gets jealous about anything?"

"I know one thing he is extremely jealous over," he said teasingly. She looked at him with curiosity. "You, Genesis."

"Me?" she repeated with disbelief.

Eaerien lifted one shoulder nonchalantly. "Just because you don't believe it doesn't make it untrue." She spun around abruptly and started to walk away, but he put a hand on her shoulder to stop her. "Don't forget that you and Callen have classes tomorrow morning."

She glanced over her shoulder with a frown. "Why are you reminding me of that now?" When he didn't reply, she turned to face him. "I know that look, Eaerien."

"What look?" he teased.

"You're leaving," she said accusingly.

"I'm not leaving," he corrected. "Loren is sending a few of us on a reconnaissance mission."

"For how long?" she asked through gritted teeth.

"Ten days at the most."

"Ten days?" Genesis's temper flamed to life. "When were you going to tell us? Or were you just going to disappear?"

Eaerien chucked her lightly under the chin. "You know I wouldn't do that to you."

"What are we supposed to do for ten days?" she demanded testily.

"Attend your classes. Run your drills."

Callen wandered over, glancing back and forth between them. Genesis felt him projecting a sense of calm over her, and she threw him an irritated glance. His quick nod in the direction of the children was enough for her to understand, and she allowed the calm to cool her temper.

Eaerien rested his hand on Genesis's head for a brief moment. "I'm going to visit my parents. I'll see you two at the aerie."

Genesis stared moodily at their mentor's departing back.

Callen took her hand and tugged her in the opposite direction. "Come on. Last time you said you'd walk that path with me."

The scenery was beautiful, but Genesis barely saw any of it. Eaerien had never left her before, and now he would be gone for days. Would Callen be enough to keep her from returning to the darkness?

∞

Eaerien left before dawn the following morning. He hugged Genesis and told her not to be afraid. He cupped Callen's cheek and smiled. "See you in a few days."

At first, the days passed by fairly normal. They made it through their classes in the mornings. In the afternoons, they trained with Dar and Mead, whose mentor was also gone. In the evenings, they sat on the cliffs and watched the stars come out.

"What did we used to do at night?" Mead asked.

"Besides sleep?" Dar joked.

Callen grinned and elbowed Genesis. "We ran drills."

Genesis gave him a small smile. "Maybe we should run a few right now."

Dar groaned. "Please, no. Night patrols are bad enough."

"We're at war, Dar," Mead chided. "Now would be the best time to stay in shape. Where do you think they sent our mentors off to?"

"Pax is with them, so they couldn't have gone anywhere too dangerous," Dar stated reasonably.

"Eaerien said it was a reconnaissance mission," Callen volunteered.

"They went to scout out Jaden's movements," Genesis said quietly. "He's been preparing for this war for ten years."

Mead let loose a low whistle.

"So have we," Dar piped up. "And we've got Callen, king of destruction and Elohim's son, on our side." Genesis snarled, and Mead hit him. "I was joking!" he protested. "Callen, you know I meant no offense, right?"

Callen grinned. "None taken."

"We'd better get to bed," Mead suggested, rising to his feet. "If you're good on that offer, Genesis, Dar and I will run some of Eaerien's drills with you tomorrow afternoon."

Genesis smirked, and Callen laughed.

Dar grimaced. "We'd all better get some rest tonight then."

∞

Callen had just fallen asleep when he heard the aerie door slam shut. He bolted upright. *Genesis!* He ran out the aerie door, down the narrow tunnel leading to the cliff face, and saw her flying off into the distance. Pulling Madden off his shoulder, he hugged the little dog to his chest, back-tracked a few feet, and took a running leap off the edge, free falling down the cliff. He needed the momentum if he had any hope of catching up to her. At the last moment, he spread his wings and whistled through the air.

Genesis didn't stop until she reached the Lacquer side of the lake. Once there, she let her rage take over, attacking anything that crossed her path. The Lacquers shrieked in terror and fled from her, but their fear only fueled her rage. She chased them down and pulled them from their hiding spots. They surrounded her and attempted to dog pile her into submission, but they were no match for the anger that had been blazing hotter and hotter inside of her every day. By the time Callen reached her, she was standing in the midst of an entire community of quaking, injured Lacquers.

Callen grabbed her by the shoulders. "Genesis, what have you done?" The sadness in his eyes quelled her rage, and she shrank from him. "Who are you fighting?" he demanded softly.

She gave him a despairing look. *Why was I born a half-breed?*

Why do you let it define you? Callen asked instead.

Genesis shook his hands off. "We've been here before."

"Yes, we have." His expression hardened with determination. "We'll go through it over and over again until you understand."

She shut her eyes and backed into the darkness.

214

Callen pursued her. He wasn't going to lose her now. Not when her heart had already turned to his, and her mind was on its way. It wasn't easy finding his way, but he had been there before. It was the same barren darkness he had encountered in her mind. Only this time, Moriana wasn't the one dragging her back; Genesis was running there on her own.

∞

Genesis ran blindly through the forest, her mind consumed in darkness. *Why does this keep happening?* she thought hopelessly. *Why?* If only Eaerien hadn't left her behind. Genesis slipped, tumbled down a short cliff and lay motionless. She couldn't see past her darkness.

Callen knelt beside her. "Genesis."

"Why do you keep dragging me back," she yelled angrily. "Over and over again!"

Because you're worth it.

She covered her face. *I just want to be free!*

"Then be free," he commanded gently.

"How?" she cried.

"Trust me."

I want to! Genesis groped around the darkness. "Where are you?"

Callen grasped her hand. "Right beside you."

"You'll leave me too eventually," she whispered.

"No, I won't." He spread his wings over her, lighting the darkness surrounding her. "I will be with you, always."

28.

Eaerien, Shiloh, Tuolene, and Pax returned to the Academy at the end of ten days. Their reconnaissance mission had been a bittersweet success. They discovered that Jaden's most avid followers had instituted the 'Priesthood' Loren had heard about. Initiation into the elite group included offspring sacrifice and an oath to fight to the death. These priests of Jaden isolated themselves from the rest of the Lacquer community and conducted experiments on each other in an effort to reawaken the Caledon-like skills they were thought to once have.

The village that Callen had decimated was one of those holy villages, and Jaden hadn't attacked the company of Caledons because he wanted Genesis or Callen; he had been defending the village. Stumbling on Callen and Genesis had been purely incidental, and an opportunity he had taken advantage of.

Pax also discovered that a Caledon had been killed at that village, and one of the experiments the priests were conducting was the transplantation of that Caledon's skills into Lacquer hosts. After piecing together the information Eaerien had learned from his father, Pax came to the conclusion that the mass gravesite was most likely the priests' children.

Loren announced several days later that he was assembling a company to travel with him next year on a yearlong diplomatic excursion to the desert communities. The fledglings were to undergo specialized training, after which they would be tested. The ones who passed would join Loren's company.

Callen's mind raced backward in time to a young girl and an even younger boy he had left behind. *Marian, Caed, I'm coming.*

∞

The instructor glared at the four students before him. Not one of them bore an expression with any semblance of remorse. Worse yet, two of them had outright defiance in their eyes.

"Genesis," the middle-aged wingless Caledon spoke gruffly. "Why were you and Dar fighting?"

"We weren't fighting," she replied obstinately.

"You weren't fighting?" He directed a stern look at Dar.

"That's just how we are," Dar retorted. "We were getting along."

"Then it's time to re-evaluate your behavior. You can't expect to cultivate peace talks with communities if you're conducting yourselves like addled children. Come along!"

Mead caught Callen's eye and mouthed, "Addled children?"

More like male geese in the springtime, Callen commented, maintaining a straight face.

Heat crept up Dar's neck as images of male geese fighting over a mate invaded his mind, while Mead fought to suppress a smile. Genesis threw them both a glare that brought a grin to Callen's face.

The instructor led them to a classroom and spent all morning educating them on etiquette. Afterward, he led them back outside and turned them over to their mentors. For six months, their routine rotated between academic classes, social etiquette and cultural classes, training sessions, an occasional mission, and simulations. At the start of the summer, they were put through an extra week of simulations to determine their placement in Loren's company.

∞

"An evaluation every day for one week?" Dar complained. "There's no way I have the stamina for that. I'm going to fail, and I'll get cut from Loren's company!"

Callen gave his friend an encouraging pat on the shoulder. No matter how much Dar complained, he always came out one of the top in the class.

"Don't patronize me, Callen," Dar grumbled. "If I had half your endurance, I'd make it."

"What are you talking about? You're always second to Genesis."

"He's not talking about ranks," Mead explained. "According to the numbers, you're still at the bottom of the class, but we all know that your skills are way out of our league. Genesis, too."

Callen gave them a baffled look.

Dar sighed. "Of course you wouldn't know. No offense, Callen, but you and Genesis are like machines. You don't ever seem to run out of steam. Don't you ever take a break?"

"We don't have that luxury," Callen answered simply. "Jaden wants to destroy everything my father's created, and he wants Genesis. I won't let him have either."

Dar gritted his teeth. "When you put it that way, these evals are a piece of cake."

Callen grinned. "You sure about that?"

"I'm not sure about anything anymore, Callen, except I'm going wherever you go. What do you say, Mead?"

Mead shoved his teammate good-naturedly. "For a second, I thought I was going to have to find a new team."

Callen threw his head back and laughed.

∞

Genesis's anger was spiraling out of control. If the exam proctor didn't interfere soon, this simple test of skills was going to take a complicated turn.

Watching the girl struggle brought a sneer to the stranger's face. He was one of the wingless Caledons invited to participate in the new training regimen. "What's the matter, Genesis?" he taunted for her ears alone. "Isn't this what you've been training for all your life? Show me that bloodthirsty reputation you're famous for."

Genesis clenched her fists. *This can't be happening. Not here. Not right at home.*

"You're just dying to know, aren't you?" the stranger continued. "I can see you tearing yourself up inside. Come on, Moriana. Give up the act. You don't belong here. I'm actually surprised they let you stay this long, considering all the—"

"Shut up!" Genesis yelled. "I'm not like that anymore! I'm not going back!"

The stranger looked startled for a moment. Then he laughed.

∞

Callen frowned from his seat in the stands. *What's going on?* He glanced at his mentor's vacant seat. Where was Eaerien? The stranger's voice drew his attention back to the arena.

"Well, little girl. Are you going to show me what you're made of, or what?"

Come on, Genesis. You can do this. Don't let him get to you, Callen cheered silently. The pup on his shoulder barked in agreement.

Dar reached out and scratched the pup between the shoulder blades. "She's better at these exams than all of us."

Mead shuffled his feet restlessly. "I'm not sure I ever want to step foot in the city again. Not if they all act like that."

"Not all of them do," Callen reminded them.

"I used to," Dar stated in a voice filled with regret. "No wonder she hated all of us for so long."

"Genesis," the proctor's voice rang out. "If you are not able to continue the exam, you will forfeit. Understood?" She didn't answer.

"What's she doing?" Dar muttered.

Callen leaned forward in his seat and fixed his eyes on her. *Don't give in, Genesis.*

∞

Callen's voice cut through Genesis's haze of anger. She glanced into the crowd and found him. Hope surged through her, and she nodded to the proctor that she was ready to continue.

"Three minutes!" the proctor's voice rang out. "When time is called, all attacks must be stopped immediately."

Genesis leveled her gaze at her opponent.

"Moriana, why are you resisting?" the stranger queried. "You'll never be fully accepted as a Caledon. Give it up and come home."

"I'm already home," she retorted.

He stretched out his hand. "Your **real** home."

Genesis forced herself to step back. "You don't control me anymore."

"Are you always this difficult?"

Genesis backed up another step, trembling from the effort of resisting. An intense pounding began inside her head. "Get away from me!"

The stranger attacked immediately, catching her off guard and pinning her to the ground. "Surprised you, didn't I? Didn't think someone without wings and training could move so fast, did you?"

Genesis struggled to escape from his grasp, unable to think coherently with the hammering in her brain.

"Let's put on a good show for them, eh, Moriana?"

"Stop calling me that," she gasped, shoving the stranger away with all the force she could muster. With relief, she watched as his body flew across the arena.

He came at her again, and the darkness in his eyes paralyzed her.

I can't ... do this ... anymore, she thought weakly as the stranger raised his fists. Closing her eyes, she waited for the blow that would end her. No one would be able to stop it.

∞

"Genesis," a gentle voice spoke. "You can open your eyes now. You're safe."

Genesis opened her eyes and looked straight into Callen's.

He smiled, and there was a touch of amusement in it. "I promised, didn't I?"

"Is she hurt, Callen?"

Genesis peered over her teammate's shoulder and saw Eaerien with his back to them, standing guard over the stranger.

"She's not hurt," Callen replied.

"Eaerien, you're interfering?" she asked incredulously.

"Of course," he answered. "This is a simple test of skills. No physical contact is supposed to be involved." He turned frigid blue eyes on the proctor. "The match should have ended before you were even pinned to the ground."

The proctor looked embarrassed. "I didn't think any harm would come to her. She's a Lacquer, after all."

A familiar sadness filled Callen. Gathering Genesis into his arms, he faced both the stranger and the proctor. "She did everything she could to avoid conflict. Don't you realize that you two are more Lacquer than she has ever been?"

Do you really believe that? she wondered as Callen carried her off the field.

He glanced down at her. *Yes.*

Genesis fisted her hands. *You made them angry.*

He shrugged unconcernedly.

What if they turn the entire city against you? she demanded heatedly.

Callen abruptly spread his wings and took off, leaving the Academy and the evaluations behind. He soared high into the sky and floated among the clouds above the city. "Why are you angry with me?" he asked aloud.

You can't keep choosing me over your own people. Elohim—

"My father happens to agree with me," he said, intercepting her train of thought. "Besides, I'm not the one choosing sides." He tilted his head toward the city below. "They are."

"Defending me doesn't exactly work in your favor," she argued.

Callen gave her a look she couldn't interpret. "You chose me, Genesis, and you became mine when you did. Why would I not defend you?"

TWO YEARS LATER

29.

From the safety of the shade of his home, a young boy watched his father welcome a group of Caledons into their community. It had been three years since the last visit. The boy shut his eyes for a moment and allowed the painful memory to surface. Along with the memories, his father's words to him last night came to mind.

There are five Caledons to keep an eye out for: Loren, Kaven, Shiloh, Eaerien, and Tuolene.

Eaerien. His father had said something more, but Caeden had lost him at Eaerien. It was the name of the Caledon who had taken his brother away, and he was desperate to find out what had happened to him.

His sister was turning sixteen—marriageable age—in a few days, and her intended would come for her. Caeden was hoping to spare her from that, and the Caledons' arrival could not have been timed more perfectly. Mind made up, he sprinted for the kitchen. "Marian?"

"In here," a cheerful voice answered.

Caeden followed the voice and found her elbow deep in dough. "How's dinner coming along?"

"I just have to boil these and pop them into the stew. How much time do I have?"

"Father's greeting the Caledons now. Where's Mother?"

"Checking on the guest apartments. Did you know she's planning to house all of them?"

Caeden swiped one of the dough balls. "Where else would they stay? We have the largest dwelling."

Marian sighed. "You aren't the one who cooks and cleans for everyone."

He chose to ignore her statement and asked another question instead. "Have you decided what you'll do when you turn sixteen?"

She gave him a shrewd look. "What are you plotting, little brother?"

"I'm offended!"

"And I'm suspicious! You know I don't get to decide anything. None of us do."

"Callen decided," he said matter-of-factly.

Marian stilled.

"Recognize the name Eaerien?" He watched his sister squeeze the dough in her hands until it oozed between her fingers. "I thought he might be able to tell us where Callen is."

"Quiet, Caed!" she scolded in a hushed tone. "You know we're not allowed to say his name!"

The younger boy shrugged. "It never stopped you before. Don't you want to know what happened to him?"

Her hands started moving double time. "You should know from school that the Caledons have special talents. What if they have super hearing? Besides, the council made it very clear to Father that what happened to—*him*—is not our business anymore. Now get out of here so I can finish this dish before you eat all the ingredients!"

Caeden backed away slowly. "You don't fool me, sis. You're dying to know if he's with them."

"Did you see him?" she asked in a tight voice.

"No," he answered reluctantly. "Their faces were covered. What if he is?"

"*Caed.*"

"I just thought he might come back to us. At least to visit." He hated the whine in his voice.

Marian took a deep breath before facing her younger brother. "He will."

"You still believe that?"

"Of course. He's our brother—he's never broken his word."

"There's a first time for everything."

Marian shook her head. "You don't mean that."

"And if I do?" he insisted.

She regarded him with sympathy. "He hasn't forgotten about us, little brother. I promise."

Caeden tried to feign indifference. "I don't really care. I was just hoping he would rescue you."

"I don't need rescuing," she said with amusement.

He forced a grin to his face and said, before ducking out of the house, "But your future husband does." *From me. From Callen. Because we won't let Jaden have you.*

∞

In general, it was easy to forget how young Caledon warriors were. Once training started at Elo's Academy, they were expected to forgo childhood fantasies for a greater sense of responsibility, and even the smallest fledglings embraced their duty to the world. Only rarely did their youth pose an issue.

Kael studied the group before him and fought back an urge to shake his head from disappointment. The only one who had left a hint of a good impression on the village council was Loren. The rest of them were barely men and certainly not physically imposing, even as a group. He held his arm out to their leader. "I don't think that went over very well, Loren."

Loren grasped the man's forearm. "It went as expected. You haven't aged a day, Kael, while I've become an elder."

Kael's rigid expression softened. "I almost lost hope that you would ever return."

"It must have been difficult." He tilted his head toward the disappearing backs of the councilmen.

"We have much to catch up on."

Loren nodded to his company. "You are acquainted with Eaerien, yes?"

Kael extended his arm toward Eaerien. "We are. My apologies for the less than warm welcome." He glanced curiously around.

Eaerien grasped his forearm and smiled reassuringly. "Don't worry about it. Ah, we left our fledglings in the courtyard of your guest home. I hope that wasn't presumptuous of us."

It was a presumptuous albeit wise move, Kael thought to himself. He wasn't ready to face the son he had so easily relinquished to them three years ago. "Think nothing of it," he said aloud. "We have some time before the evening meal."

Loren nodded his assent. "Kael and I have much to discuss. We will see you all at dinner."

An unspoken word of communication passed between Loren and Kaven, who dipped his chin and left with the mentors.

"Kael, your son—"

Kael put a hand on Loren's arm. "He was never mine to call my own, and I am afraid I was rather cold to him. Still I am grateful for the years we had."

"None of us are perfect, my friend. Callen knows that. But come; we don't have much time."

Kael led his old friend into his study. He secured the door, and they both paused to listen. Loren nodded, signaling no one was within earshot. Kael then lifted a section of the rug beneath his desk, revealing a trap door that opened into Kael's real office.

"Tell me," Loren spoke without preamble once inside. "How deeply has Jaden infiltrated the council in this village?"

"Completely," Kael admitted with a weary sigh. "Three years ago, he formally requested my daughter as wife for his son. The rumors are true then?"

"Yes, he adopted a son to raise as his heir. Members of my company verified it a couple of summers ago. You agreed to the marriage?"

Kael gestured for Loren to sit then rounded the desk and sat on the other side. "Officially no, but the council is pressuring me heavily to. She is not yet sixteen, so I have been able to hold them off for now. Loren, you *must* take her with you. She was found with Callen, so she may well be a Caledon."

"I don't doubt Elohim's timing, old friend," Loren agreed. "He must have intended her to join us, Caledon or not. What of your youngest?"

"Caeden is ours through and through." Kael spoke with a hint of pride. "He will be a great leader someday, and I can see in his eyes that he isn't fooled by Jaden's lies. He is still clinging to boyhood, however. He's always had trouble restraining his emotions."

"He feels abandoned by Callen."

Kael looked frustrated. "I know this. Marian leaving may well destroy him, but I will not allow her to fall into Jaden's clutches."

Loren put a calming hand on the man's shoulder. "Kael, why have you not confided in your son? Why do you insist on bearing the burden alone?"

"He is not ready."

"He *is* ready."

Kael leaned forward earnestly. "You know this?"

Loren nodded. "I have faith in Elohim. He sets the stage, and we follow."

Kael still hesitated.

"Tell me, friend," Loren pressed, relaxing into his seat. "Why do you doubt?"

Kael frowned. "Caeden is not full Caledon. How can I guarantee he will be under Elohim's protection?"

"What is a Caledon, Kael?"

"A follower of Elohim."

Loren raised his brows. "Does your son follow Jaden?"

"No!"

"Then who does he follow?"

"I …" Kael blinked, realizing where Loren's line of thought was taking him. "I do not know. I have not thought to ask him where his loyalties lie."

Loren glanced upward. "We've run out of time, old friend, but let me assure you that Caeden has always held his siblings in the highest regard."

30.

The fledglings sat together in the courtyard of the head household's guest home, swapping stories, while their mentors, Loren, and Kaven were meeting with the village council. After traveling together for almost a year, they had become quite comfortable around each other.

Dar finished sharing one of his stories and looked across at Genesis. "Don't you have any childhood memories?"

"I don't remember any," she answered automatically.

Sitting beside her, Callen chuckled. "You weren't born twelve, Genesis."

She ignored him.

Dar stood up to move closer. "Where were you before Eaerien brought you to the Academy?" he asked.

"Maybe she doesn't want to talk about it," Mead commented, snagging the back of his outer tunic and pulling him to a stop.

Dar swatted his teammate's hand away and retorted irritably, "You're always rising to her defense, Mead."

Callen propped an elbow on his knee and rested his chin in his hand, watching Genesis. He could read her inner turmoil.

Without looking at him, she reached over and pulled Callen's hood over his face. *Stop that.*

Laughing, he straightened and pulled his hood off.

Genesis squared her shoulders and locked eyes with Dar. "The rumors aren't that far-fetched."

Dar, Mead, and Pax exchanged questioning glances and looked to Callen for confirmation. He merely smiled.

"You're not going to say anything either?" Dar snorted. "I *know* you know the whole story."

"It's not my story to tell," he replied cheekily.

"Then tell us your story, Callen," Pax suggested, jumping down from the wall he had been sitting on. "It's been three years, and I hardly know anything about your past."

Mead snorted. "It's been five years, and we know even less about Genesis's real one."

"There you go again, Mead!" Dar burst out. "Whose side are you on?"

Pax sighed and sat in-between Dar and Mead, forcing space between them. "We're all on the same side. Callen, your past?"

"Hmm," Callen mused, scooting closer to them and dragging Genesis with him. "I grew up here actually. I have a younger brother and sister."

Genesis waited expectantly for a reaction, but none of them caught on, and she released a breath of disappointment.

"We already know you came out of the desert," Dar remarked. "Tell us about your siblings. Where are they now?"

"Right where I left them."

Mead turned suddenly to Genesis. "You said the rumors about you aren't far-fetched. Is it true, then, that you have siblings?"

"A half-brother."

Dar's eyes popped out of his head.

"I saw him," Pax announced quietly. "Last summer. He went everywhere with Jaden. Is Jaden your father?"

"No," she answered defensively, half-rising from her seat. Callen touched her sleeve lightly, and she continued in a more subdued voice. "We have the same mother."

"Well, I've got four older brothers," Mead volunteered, breaking the sudden tension.

Callen grinned. "And Dar's an only child." He turned to Pax with a warm smile. "How's Petra?"

Pax's eyes widened imperceptibly. "You know my sister?"

232

"Petra?" Dar questioned, looking back and forth between Callen and Pax. "The little girl Aria's taken under her wing?"

"Uh-huh," Pax nodded. "She's my little sister."

Mead gave the boy a congratulatory smack on the back, driving him to his knees by accident. "Looks like genius runs in your family, Pax! Why didn't you tell us?"

Pax coughed and shook his head at the absurdity. "The only genius thing about her is that she recognized Callen before any of us did. The first time you went into the valley, you met her?"

Callen dipped his chin slightly.

"Before my sister left the house that day, she told my parents she was going to show Elohim's son the city." Pax looked at Callen. "Petra knew even before you did, didn't she?"

"But how?" Dar interjected.

"My father told her," Callen explained simply.

"I have a question for you," Pax voiced suddenly with a glance in Genesis's direction. "You said you grew up here, and Dar took it to mean the desert in general, but are you saying that *this community* is where came from?"

"Yes." Callen swept his gaze over the familiar structure. "This was my home."

∞

The mentors entered the courtyard to the sound of quiet bickering. Eaerien and Shiloh exchanged a glance. Kaven sighed heavily.

"Pax," Tuolene called sharply.

Pax jumped to his feet and stood shamefacedly.

Tuolene strode forward, stopping in front of his fledgling. "You surprise me, Pax," he said with disappointment.

"Not me," Shiloh remarked, coming up behind the mentor and patting him on the shoulder. He aimed a glare at his own fledglings, who were conveniently distracted by nothing in particular. "Dar and Mead know how to rile anyone up. What is it this time?"

Pax tucked his hands into his pockets. "We don't know as much about each other as we thought we did."

Eaerien walked up to the base of a large tree and looked up into the branches. "Where's Callen?"

"He said he'd be right back," Genesis answered.

"How long ago?"

She glanced in the direction of the sun. "Maybe fifteen minutes."

Kaven, who had followed Eaerien to the tree, peered up in the direction of Genesis's voice. He dropped his eyes to Eaerien and asked, "You don't keep tabs on him anymore?"

"No need to," Eaerien replied. He glanced up at Genesis again. "I'll be inside. Please don't wander off."

She rolled her eyes.

He chuckled and followed Kaven into the home.

∞

Genesis relaxed against the tree trunk and directed her thoughts to Callen. *If Marian doesn't want to go with us, what will you do?* she wondered.

Why wouldn't she want to? Callen questioned in surprise.

Genesis's eyes sprang wide. *You've never even considered the possibility?*

Of course I've considered it, he answered. *It's plagued me nearly every day for the past three years.*

Callen …

There's no point in worrying, he said. *Come here, I want to show you something.*

Eaerien asked me not to wander off.

Callen expanded his thoughts to include their mentor. *Eaerien, is it all right if I take Genesis with me for a moment?*

They both heard their mentor's amused chuckle.

Just please come back in time to clean up for the evening meal, Eaerien admonished them. *We are here on important business.*

Genesis leaped lightly to the ground and took off in a sprint. She didn't know why they weren't allowed to use their wings, or why they had had to walk the last two miles to the village, but Callen hadn't questioned it and following his lead was quickly becoming a habit. She followed the path he laid out before her and found him sitting at the edge of a wide, grassy clearing with Madden perched on his shoulder. *This is?*

Callen nodded. "Do you remember this place?"

She smirked at the memory. "I thought you were a fool for sitting out in the open in the middle of the night."

He grinned and ran headlong into the center of the field, flipping once or twice. Madden bounded gleefully around him.

Genesis shook her head and walked slowly after him. When she reached him, he was on his back staring at the sky, and she leaned over to block his view. "Callen, honestly. What are you?"

"Don't you mean, *who* am I?" he replied cheerfully.

"I know who you are."

He gave her a warm smile.

She stretched out on her stomach and relaxed her head in the crook of her elbow. "Well? What's on your mind?"

Callen frowned slightly. He turned so he could lean his head against her back. "Do you ever think about your parents?"

Genesis was quiet for a long time. Then, very softly, she answered, "All the time."

"What do you think about?"

Her lip curled. "How much I hate them, and how much I miss them. And what I would say if I ever saw them again."

"What would you say?" he asked quietly.

Genesis clenched her fists. "Nothing. I have no words for them."

Callen mulled over her answer. He said, "If I meet your parents, I'll tell them, 'Thank you for bringing Genesis into this world. I hope one day you'll know her the way I know her—a little rough around the edges, but full of hope and life.'

"Then I'll tell them, 'We used to fight an awful lot, but I wouldn't change one moment of it because through those fights, we learned to understand each other. Every day I get to see a little more of that wall around her crumble, and if you could just see how precious that girl behind the wall is, you'd thank Elohim for the privilege of being her parents.'"

"Only you would say something disgusting like that," Genesis muttered as tears pooled unbidden in her eyes.

Callen and Genesis remained in the field, in companionable silence, until the sun began to slip into the horizon. As promised, they returned with plenty of time to clean up and change.

"Eaerien, does my father know I'm here?" Callen wondered as they assembled back in the courtyard.

"He knows."

Was he with my brother and sister?

Eaerien's eyes twinkled. "No, but I did see a young boy spying on us."

A bright smile lit up Callen's face. *Caed?*

Eaerien winked at him. *He's grown quite a bit since we were here last.*

Mead tapped his shoulder. "Callen, are you bringing Madden to dinner too?"

"I am." He patted the sleeping dog inside his jacket.

"Is that allowed?" Pax piped up.

"He's part of the team," Eaerien said, guiding Pax back to his place. "Quiet now."

Loren gazed approvingly at his company. His eyes rested briefly on the lump in Callen's jacket and a hint of a smile formed. The little dog had indeed proved useful. Funny how Elohim's plans were sometimes. His nostalgia dissipated when an attendant showed up to lead them to the dining hall.

Kael greeted them at the entrance. He exchanged a friendly greeting with Loren and tipped his chin welcomingly at Kaven and the mentors. He walked beside Loren as the old Caledon introduced him to the fledglings.

When they stopped at Eaerien's team, Kael's face unmistakably lit up. "Welcome back, Callen," he greeted.

"Hello, Father," he greeted politely.

Kael surprised them all with a deep sigh. "You have a father, Callen, and it was never me."

The stiffness in Callen's shoulders relaxed. "You raised me for fourteen years, so in a way, you are a father to me."

"Loren tells me that most of the Caledons have been training at the Academy since they were children, and only the best graduate." Kael looked at him admiringly. "The past three years must not have been easy, Callen. You've worked hard."

"Father—"

Kael silenced him with an almost reverent touch to his shoulder. "Later, ask me anything you want to know." His gaze fell on Genesis. "I believe you and I have met before as well."

"This is Genesis," Eaerien spoke up. "She came with me to the village three years ago."

"I remember." He tilted his head thoughtfully. "Something is different about you."

Eaerien chortled. "Callen tends to have that effect on everyone around him."

"I see." He moved to the last team. "Shiloh, this is your team?"

Shiloh nodded to his fledglings. "Dar and Mead."

Kael returned their greeting and stepped back. "Welcome, everyone." He held his arm out for his family. "My wife; our daughter, Marian; and Caeden, our son. You all are aware now that Callen is our eldest."

∞

Marian stared, frozen and wide-eyed, at Callen. He was home: her brother, her best friend.

Ignoring everyone else, Caeden gritted his teeth and marched right up to his brother.

237

Callen angled his head in a familiar way and smiled. "Hello, Caed."

"I thought I'd never see you again," Caeden blurted out.

"I told you I'd come back." Callen lifted his eyes and connected with Marian's.

Her face broke into a thousand smiles, and casting aside formality, she flung her arms around him. "I've missed you so much, Callen!"

He embraced her warmly. "Marian."

Kael cleared his throat, and Marian quickly stepped back.

Their mother reached out and placed her palm affectionately on Callen's cheek, and he covered her hand briefly with his. "Please, come and sit," she invited. "You must all be hungry after traveling so far."

31.

It was hard to ignore the lump on Callen's chest. It moved around occasionally, and Callen would pat it until it grew still again. Caeden couldn't stop staring at it during the meal. Even Kael glanced at it once or twice. Only Marian successfully ignored it. She had felt it yield against her body when she hugged her brother earlier, so she knew it was soft and possibly alive. Caeden tried to ask about it during the meal, but his father gave him a stern look, and the boy dropped the subject.

When the meal was over, their host led them to a large common room with an attached study. Loren, the mentors, and Kael disappeared into the study, leaving their charges under Kaven's supervision.

"What's that lump on your chest?" Caeden wasted no time in asking.

Callen put a hand over the lump at his chest and patted it gently. "This is Madden."

"What is it?"

"*It* is a *he.*" He nudged the lump, and Madden emerged slowly from his hiding place.

"A dog?"

"Of sorts," Callen replied with a twinkle in his eyes.

Caeden approached with his hand outstretched.

"Watch it," Dar warned. "Or he'll light you on fire."

"Or blow you up," Mead added with a rumbling laugh.

"Blow *us* up," Dar emphasized with his arms stretched wide.

"He won't," Callen reassured him. He took his brother's wrist and guided his hand toward the dog's back. "You see?"

Caeden gave a sharp intake as his hand made contact with the heat of Madden's fur.

Marian slid close and held up a hand. "May I?"

Callen grinned and placed Madden in her lap.

"He's so warm!" she exclaimed with delight, cuddling the dog closer.

Caeden sat gingerly next to Callen. "Why do you keep him inside your tunic?" he asked.

"He helps me."

"How?"

Callen glanced between his siblings. *There's so much to tell them. I don't know where to start.*

Genesis heard his thoughts. "Show them," she suggested.

Caeden narrowed his eyes suspiciously. "Show us what?"

Callen took a deep breath and held out a hand to each of them.

Marian took it without hesitation. "Caed?" she prompted.

The younger boy gazed at the outstretched palm with his heart pounding. Part of him was dying of curiosity, but the other part didn't want to know.

Caed.

His eyes flew to Callen, startled by the gentle voice in his mind. *Callen?* he asked tentatively.

Trust me?

It was now or never. Caeden took his brother's hand.

∞

Genesis relaxed into her seat, watching the emotions chase each other across the brother's and sister's faces. She knew what Callen was showing them. She had been with him each step of the way, but it was fascinating to see it from a stranger's eyes. A ghost of a smile played on the corners of her mouth when images of his first evaluation came up. She wasn't surprised when he omitted their encounters with Jaden and his followers.

"I don't think this is a good idea," Kaven said quietly.

Genesis glanced around the room, realizing then that Callen was showing all of them what had transpired. Pax, Mead, and Dar sat transfixed as events they had heard about, but not seen until today, played out in their minds' eyes.

When recent images of the Academy surfaced, Kaven stood abruptly. "Callen," he called sharply and with an urgency none of them had heard from him before.

Dar and Mead blinked rapidly as the memories faded into a blur, and Pax turned questioning eyes toward Kaven. All of them were used to his regimental adherence to policy, but something in his manner was off.

Genesis's gaze collided with Pax's. She didn't have to read his mind to know what he was thinking. Kaven was hiding something.

Callen was still holding his siblings' hands and grinning at them.

"That was …" Caeden swallowed hard and slipped his hand out of his brother's grasp. "How long have you been able to do that?"

"Not long."

The boy's gaze swept the room. "Everyone saw what we saw?"

"Yes."

"Then why did you have to hold our hands?"

"In case you tried to run."

Dar choked on his laugh.

Marian bounced excitedly in her seat. "That was amazing! The council incorporated some Caledon history into our education after you left, brother." She turned bright eyes to everyone in the room. "What special gifts do all of you have?" Her eyes rested on the stone-faced girl beside Callen. "I bet your gifts are the most unique."

Genesis bristled.

She means no harm, Callen said.

"Marian, you never think before you speak," Caeden muttered.

"And you do?" she clipped back. Kaven cleared his throat, and her face flamed with embarrassment. "I apologize."

"We can show you," Mead volunteered. "Not the way Callen can, but a demonstration."

"Tomorrow," Kaven stated firmly. "Tonight, we retire early."

Dar groaned.

Pax stood up and stretched. "One good night of rest won't hurt." He tossed the briefest glance at Genesis.

What was that? Callen asked her.

Genesis shrugged and stepped away. *What was what?*

"Callen, you must greet Faye," Marian said, drawing his attention back to her. "She's been so lonely since you and Liam left, and I have been too busy to attend school."

He stopped short. "You stopped going to school?"

"Yes, but I have kept up on my studies." She held Madden out, and the little dog sprang from her hands and onto Callen's shoulder. "Father and Mother give me time in the evenings with some exceptions, such as today. Will you greet her?"

"Of course," he answered, tickling Madden behind the ears.

"Then I'll go get her!"

Caeden stayed her with a hand on her arm. "I'll get her, Marian. Why don't you take them back to the apartments? We'll meet you there."

"All right, little brother. Thank you." She looped her arm with Callen's as they made their way to the guest rooms. "You have no idea how wonderful it is to have you home again."

Callen grinned at her. "I have a pretty good idea actually."

Reading her mind? Genesis inquired wryly from in front of them.

No, of course not, Callen returned.

She twisted her body to the side as she climbed the stairs and smirked at him. *Sure.*

What's with you? he questioned. *And what was that look Pax gave you?*

Who's Faye? She reached the top of the stairs and paused in front of a curtained doorway.

Answer my question, and I'll answer yours.

Genesis curled her fingers into a fist and whipped her head around to glare at Callen. *Pax and I think Kaven's hiding something, and we're going to figure out what it is.*

Callen raised his eyebrows as he passed by her. *You and Pax can read each other's minds too, now?*

Yanking aside the heavy curtain, Genesis stepped inside and inhaled deeply, making an effort to rein in her temper.

Marian glanced from her brother to the curtain that Genesis had disappeared behind and pulled him to a stop. "What is it?" she inquired.

"They always do that," Dar answered as he squeezed by them. He stopped in front of a second curtained doorway and tapped his temple. "They talk to each other in here."

Marian's eyes grew round. "You can hear each other's thoughts?"

"He can hear yours too, if you let him," Mead added, reaching around his teammate to lift the curtain. "It was nice meeting you, Marian. Good night." He stepped inside, followed closely by Dar.

"Good night," she called. Turning to Callen she asked, "How do I share my thoughts to you?"

"You just talk to me," he explained. "But inside your head instead of out loud."

∞

Kaven climbed the stairs slowly after the fledglings, trying not to listen to their conversation, but he caught the last bit of Callen and Marian's. He stopped at the top of the stairs and rolled his eyes to the heavens. *You are giving all our secrets away,* he admonished.

Callen, Pax called, skirting around Loren's apprentice and making a beeline for the room he was sharing with Dar, Mead, and Callen. *Kaven doesn't seem happy with you.*

Callen looked over from where he still stood with Marian and gave Kaven an apologetic smile. *He thinks we're compromising Loren's mission by revealing everything to my siblings.*

*You **are** compromising it!* Kaven retorted, crossing his arms and studying the boy.

How? Mead wondered from inside their guest room. *Jaden's already aware of what each of us can do.*

*He has an **idea,*** Kaven corrected. *He doesn't need to know specifics!*

Were we giving away specifics? Dar questioned.

Kaven clenched his jaw. *Enough.* He crossed the hall to the room he would share with the mentors and was about to duck inside when a new voice caught them all by surprise.

∞

Callen? Can you hear me?

A grin spread across Callen's face as he looked at his sister. *I hear you, Marian.*

I've really missed you, she said, gazing up at him. *We all have, including Faye.*

Callen's smile dimmed. *I can't stay, Marian.*

She twisted her hands shyly. *I ... I didn't think you would ... But what if you had a better reason to stay?*

No, sister, he stated firmly.

You won't even give it a chance?

Callen could feel his friends holding their breaths, and he realized too late that he had allowed them all to hear his sister's thoughts. Chagrined, he put his arm around her and pulled her close. "Marian," he whispered into her hair. "That road has never been an option for me."

"Is it because of ...?" Her gaze drifted in Genesis's direction.

Callen shook his head and smiled gently. "You'll understand someday, Marian." He released her and tilted his head invitingly back toward the stairs. "Let's wait for Faye and Caed in the courtyard."

Marian smiled and threaded her arm back through his. "I don't know what you mean by 'someday' but I'll wait for it."

Callen shook the curtain in front of Genesis's room. "Genesis," he called. "Meet us in the courtyard."

∞

Faye easily kept pace with her best friend's little brother's long strides. "You've grown, Caed," she commented.

"Of course I have," he retorted.

"But your attitude hasn't changed," she quipped.

Caeden sighed and shorted his steps. "I'm sorry. I'm a little on edge."

"You? On edge?" she mocked good-naturedly without slacking her pace. "This is a first!"

He shook his head and lengthened his steps once more.

She nudged him with her elbow. "So ... where are you taking me in the dead of night?"

He gave her an irritated look. "It's hardly the dead of night, and like I said before, Marian has a surprise for you."

"Does this have anything to do with the company of Caledons at your house?"

He gave her a surprised look. "How did you know?"

"Oh, come on, Caed." She counted off her fingers. "One, I'm not blind. Two, I'm not deaf. Three, I have a brain."

"And you actually used it this time," he mocked. Her jaw dropped, and he burst into laughter.

She narrowed her eyes at him. "You win this round, but I'll get you next time."

He was still chuckling as he led her to the guest home.

Marian met them at the entrance to the courtyard. "Faye!"

"Marian! What is so important that you sent your annoying little brother to come get me this late in the evening?"

"Did your father mind very much?"

Faye waved her friend's concern away. "He trusts me."

"Good, because there's someone here you'll be glad to see."

Her mind immediately went to her brother. Just as quickly, she brushed the idea aside. Liam wouldn't have come here first, and he had no business traveling with Caledons. Could it be ...?

"Have you decided to use that brain of yours again?" Caeden teased.

"Oh, hush," she said then gave them a conflicted look. "I have to admit. I'm a little jealous that your brother came back, and mine didn't."

Marian took her hand and patted it sympathetically. "Come inside."

Faye followed her, looking around inquisitively. Her gaze rested on a young woman with long black hair and a slight build, who glanced at them as they approached. At the same time, the young man next to her stood.

"Faye!" he greeted warmly.

Faye ran forward and grasped his outstretched hands. "Callen! You came back."

"I wanted to at least make it to your wedding."

She rolled her eyes. "You know me better than that, Callen."

He grinned. "Still the same, aren't you?" He turned to his teammate. "I'd like you to meet Genesis. Genesis, this is Faye." *We grew up together.*

Took you long enough to answer, Genesis retorted, stepping forward.

Faye stuck her hand out impulsively. "Hello."

Genesis cautiously took her hand.

"I have something for you," Callen said, pulling out a letter. "A message from your brother."

"You saw Liam?" Faye exclaimed, taking the letter. "When?"

"A few days ago," Callen explained. "He really enjoys farming."

"How surprised was he to see you?"

"He wasn't."

"Of course he wasn't," Faye murmured, turning the letter over in her hand. "He always took your promises to heart."

Callen rested his eyes on his sister. "He wishes you well, Marian."

Marian took a deep breath and forced a smile to her face. "Thank you."

Callen sensed Genesis's confusion. *Our fathers had an understanding once, before we found out that Marian and I are Caledons,* he quickly filled her in.

What kind of understanding?

That Liam and Marian would be married.

Understanding dawned on Genesis's face. *Is that also what you and Faye had?*

Callen looked over at Genesis with surprise. "No."

"What?" Caeden asked.

Callen shook his head. "Sorry, I didn't mean to say that out loud." He shot his teammate an annoyed look. *There were discussions, but nothing was set in stone.*

Genesis shrugged.

"Callen can communicate with his mind," Marian explained to Faye.

Caeden hastily covered his head with his arms. "You're not reading minds too, are you?"

Faye sputtered. "What could you possibly be thinking for you to react that way, Caed?"

"I don't read minds," Callen explained, resisting the urge to tease his younger brother. "I only hear your thoughts if you allow me to, and you can also hear mine if you want to."

"I see. That explains earlier."

Faye fingered the letter in her hand.

Callen met her eyes. "You'd better take Faye home, Caed. We can catch up more tomorrow."

Faye smiled gratefully at him. "It was good seeing you, Callen." She turned to Genesis. "It was nice to meet you, Genesis."

"I'll walk with you too," Marian offered. She gave Callen a quick hug. "Good night, dear brother. Good night, Genesis."

"Good night, Marian." Callen locked eyes with Caeden for a moment. *Good night, brother.*

A small smile lifted Caeden's mouth. *It's good to have you here, however long you decide to stay.*

32.

Pax was sitting in bed reading when a soft rustle drew his attention to the window. He didn't appear surprised to see Genesis, but his eyes widened when he saw Callen climb up beside her.

"I can't keep him out of my head," Genesis whispered.

Callen still couldn't figure out when the two of them had grown close. "What's up, Pax?"

Pax scrambled out of bed to join them, stepping carefully around Dar and Mead's sleeping forms. "I'm glad both of you came," he said in a hushed voice. He glanced at the curtain. *Are any of the mentors back?*

Callen followed his gaze. *Not yet.*

Can you do that thing you do? Pax asked.

He smiled with amusement and expanded their conversation to include Genesis. *This thing?*

Yes! Pax nodded appreciatively. *Thank you.* He pointed out the window. *Shall we?*

Finally, Genesis grumbled, leaping into a tree.

What shall we do? Callen wondered, leaping up behind her.

Spy on Kaven, she replied.

Callen halted, and Pax collided into him from behind, toppling out of the tree. Callen and Genesis grabbed his arms and held him suspended between the branches.

Whew, that was close, Pax sighed.

Sorry, Pax, Callen apologized as they hauled him back onto the branch.

Not a problem.

Callen picked a leaf from the boy's hair. *Why are we spying on Loren's apprentice?*

Genesis shifted impatiently. *He's hiding something.*

He's always hiding something, Callen reasoned. *He's privy to everything Loren knows.*

Pax exchanged another look with Genesis. *You trust Kaven, Callen?*

*I'm surprised that **you** don't.*

I ... Pax seated himself comfortably on a branch and lost himself in thought.

Genesis flopped against the trunk and stared into the sky, muttering, "This might take a while."

Callen sat beside her. *Genesis.*

Hm? She turned her head to face him.

What do you think of Marian and Caed?

Genesis brought her eyes down to her hands. *She's definitely coming back with us?*

Yes, but that doesn't answer my question.

She bunched her hands into her tunic.

Callen snagged one of them and smoothed her fingers open between his hands. He repeated the gesture with her other hand, all the while patiently waiting for her reply.

They seemed relieved to see you, she finally answered.

That's the impression I got too. What do you think happened?

*Something to do with **him** most likely.*

Callen tightened his hold on her hands. *I won't let him take you from me.*

Genesis pulled her hands out of his grasp. *I wasn't worried.*

All right, Pax declared standing up and brushing his tunic off. *I've decided to agree with you, Callen. Good night.*

Genesis scrambled to her feet and stared as Pax retreated into the room. *What just happened?*

He decided to trust Kaven too. Callen said, stretching leisurely.

Just like that?

Just like that. He took her hand and gave her a smirk. *Let's go exploring.*

Wait a minute. Genesis pulled her hand from his grasp and crossed her arms. *I want to know what you did that made Pax change his mind so suddenly.*

Callen gazed at her for several moments. "Fine," he conceded. He motioned her further away from the window and sat down, pulling her down next to him. "I didn't tell Pax anything," he explained, "I just reminded him that Kaven's never done anything to make us *not* believe he has our best interests in mind. Don't you think so?"

"I wouldn't know."

Callen chuckled. "Think about it, Genesis. Eaerien trusts him. Loren obviously does, and so do I." He tilted his head and looked sideways at her. "Why don't you?"

Genesis squinted her eyes at him. "When you went on that trip with him and Loren, did you two have a life-changing heart-to-heart, or something?"

A grin split his face. *Maybe.* "Did I answer your question?"

"Barely."

"Will you come with me, now?" He held out his hand, and she took it without a word.

∞

Callen gave her a tour of the village, inviting her to share in all his memories. Overwhelmed by the emotions accompanying the memories, Genesis withdrew into herself.

Sorry, he apologized. *I haven't learned to curb it.*

Learn faster then, she grumbled.

Why are you so afraid of feeling? he asked curiously.

"I'm not afraid!"

He held a finger to his lips and pointed at the barn-like structure they had stopped in front of. "You'll wake the raptors," he explained quietly.

"I'm not afraid," she repeated.

"You sure?"

Why can't you just leave me be? she demanded.

Because I want to know everything about you. He glanced at her clenched fists and raised his eyebrows. "That scares you, doesn't it?"

"Emotions make you weak," she hissed. "They make you vulnerable."

Callen shrugged slightly. "Only if you let them."

"You're saying they make you strong?" she challenged.

"If you let them," he repeated. "They're like my energy levels. If I don't control them, they'll control me. With discipline and someone—" He patted the little dog at his shoulder. "—keeping me accountable, my power does great things. Unchecked, terrible things can happen."

"Does it scare you?"

"In the beginning it did," he admitted. "I didn't understand what was happening, and I was afraid I'd hurt someone." He closed his eyes and leaned against the barn. "When Jaden went after all of you that first time, I didn't have time to worry about what was happening to my body and whether or not I would lose control. I focused on saving anyone who wanted to be saved and ending Jaden's influence. That's when I realized controlling my energy isn't the key to my gifts. It's my intentions."

Genesis nodded slowly as understanding dawned.

"Light bulb?" Callen teased, pulling on an imaginary light switch.

She made a face and swatted his hand away.

Callen laughed.

I thought you said we had to be quiet, she reminded him.

He saw the tiny smile lurking around her eyes and grinned. "Too late, they're awake." He tilted his head toward the barn. "Come on, I have an old friend you need to meet."

They spent the next hour with the raptors. All of the birds he'd grown up training with were still there, but few new juveniles. Callen introduced Genesis to the eagle he had raised from an egg, and his heart filled with warmth when they immediately took to each other.

"He likes you."

Genesis stroked the eagle's breast feathers lightly. She didn't agree with keeping birds in cages.

"He knocked out Jaden when he came to visit the village the first time," Callen recalled.

"Did you tell him to?"

"No."

A satisfied smile appeared on her face. "Good."

He nudged her with his elbow. "Why are you sad?"

"Birds aren't meant to live in cages. Elohim wouldn't have given them wings if they were."

"I agree," another voice spoke up.

Callen tossed a grin over his shoulder. "Couldn't sleep, Caed?"

"I was about to when I heard you talking outside," he explained, hooking his fingers onto the cage. "Then I saw you go into the barn. You aren't surprised to see me?"

"We heard you," Genesis stated.

Caeden snorted. "That shouldn't surprise me."

"Have you gotten better with the birds?" Callen asked him. His little brother's falconry skills had been a disaster from the beginning.

"Nope. I've actually gotten worse since you left." He gestured helplessly to the eagle before them. "We like each other just fine, but I can't get him, or any of them, to do anything for me."

A merry laugh escaped Callen. "What do you do with them?"

"I let them out and pray they come back after they've had their exercise. Most of them return with a full crop, so at least I don't have to feed them when they do."

"Why keep them then?" Genesis wanted to know.

"Because this is their home, technically. They've lived here their whole lives, and birds are pretty loyal to their nests." Caeden shrugged. "It wouldn't be fair to them to lose their home just because I'm not a competent handler."

"If they want to leave, you would let them?"

He pointed in the direction of the other cages. "Do you not see how few juveniles there are? None of them were trained, and when they're ready, they leave."

"What does Father say about that?" Callen wondered.

"Nothing, but he gets this amused look on his face when he sees them in the sky."

Genesis fiddled with the bird's jesses. "What about this one? He doesn't seem like he would stay."

Caeden entered the enclosure and stroked the bird's feathers thoughtfully. "He was the first one I expected to leave. I let him out first thing every morning, and he goes off into the forest and disappears. But every night he comes back, and if I'm already in bed, he roosts on my window."

"What about Marian? She knows how to handle the birds," Callen said.

"She still does, but she doesn't have enough time to take them out every day. I asked Father if we could give them to her as a wedding present. He said no."

Genesis exhaled in relief. "It would be cruel to expose them to Jaden."

"She's not going to Jaden," the brothers declared at the same time. They exchanged glances, and Genesis read the determination in their eyes.

"Callen," Caeden said in a desperate voice. "We can't let him have her."

Callen draped his arm around his younger brother. "We're not going to, Caed." *Elohim help us.*

33.

The Caledons had only been in the village for one full day when things started to fall apart.

It started when Genesis had a terrifying nightmare. It was past midnight, and everyone was sleeping soundly when a loud crash reverberated through the guesthouse.

Eaerien and Callen burst into the room Genesis was occupying and found her crumpled on the floor in a corner, clutching her head between her hands.

"Genesis, look at me," Eaerien instructed gently. "Give me your hands." Trembling with the effort, she extended her hands toward him. They were ice cold. He turned to Callen, who had remained at the doorway to keep anyone who showed up at bay. "Callen, can I borrow Madden?"

Callen touched the little dog at his chest, and he hopped out and over to Eaerien, who placed him on Genesis's outstretched hands. Understanding the man's intent, Madden increased his body temperature until the girl's hands warmed to her normal level of heat.

"What's happening?" Kaven asked, keeping his distance while attempting to peer over the boy's shoulder.

Callen slipped out and let the curtain fall back. *Eaerien's got her.* He gazed around at the concerned faces of the company and nodded reassuringly. *She'll be all right.*

Mead's tight expression didn't relax immediately. *Is there anything we can do to help?*

She knows you're all here. That helps.

Pax had a faraway look in his eyes. "All these years she's been right beside us, and we ..." He shook his head. "I'm ... ashamed."

Tuolene put a comforting hand on his fledgling. "The fault starts with us, your mentors. We failed Elohim's command to treat her as one of own. I am sorry, Callen."

Callen shook his head. "It's time to move on," he said, filling them with hope and lightening the heaving atmosphere.

Dar stiffened and angled toward the stairs. *They're coming.*

∞

Caeden reached the top of the stairs first, followed closely by Marian. "Callen!" He slowed at the sight of the Caledons gathered together.

Marian sidestepped him and made a beeline for her older brother, who held his arm out and drew her close. *What happened?*

He let her search his eyes. *Everything will be fine.*

Kael stepped into the crowded hallway with a couple of the village elders at his heels.

Callen narrowed his eyes. *A secret meeting?*

Kael's expression was unreadable and his mind silent, but the brief moment he locked eyes with his eldest was enough to convey the warning. The elders were against Elohim.

Callen projected the warning to the rest of the company. Where was Loren?

"I trust, Kael, that all is under order?" one of the elders inquired with false politeness.

"It appears so." Kael's gaze landed once more on Callen. "Is there anything you need assistance with?"

"Thank you, but no."

"Don't you think you ought to know what exactly is happening under your own roof, Kael?" the other elder insinuated, and the tension in the air increased.

"I am inclined to believe my son," Kael replied smoothly.

"The boy who came home is not the same boy who left, Kael. You would do well to remember that, or you may end up proving yourself the fool."

"How can you say that?" Marian demanded in an outraged tone. "Father has been a trusted and wise member of the council for years. Has there been one instance when he has not made a sound decision for the best interest of the village?"

The elder eyed her with disdain. "There is but one."

"Father?" Caeden stepped forward, drawing their attention. "I'd like a word with you, if I may?"

"Certainly." Kael held his arm toward the stairs. "I will bid the elders good night and meet you in my study." He gave a nod to the Caledons. *My friends, goodnight, and keep your guard up.*

After their father and the elders left, Caeden reached for his sister's hand. "Marian, can you never keep your mouth shut?"

She opened her mouth to retort, but closed it again when Callen sighed. "Marian, I happen to agree with Caed on this," he said, loosening his arm around her shoulders when their younger brother tugged on her hand.

"Caed, please," she protested.

"I'm talking to Father about *you*," Caed said impatiently. "If you want to have a say in your future, this will likely be your only chance."

"Oh, all right, I'll come." She grasped Callen's hand and gave it a squeeze. "See you in the morning, brother."

"Good night, Marian. Good night, Caed."

Caed inclined his head in Callen's direction. "Good night, brother." *Will you please listen in on our discussion?*

Callen nodded. *If Father allows.*

He will. You heard him earlier, didn't you? I don't think I would have heard him if you hadn't opened up the connection.

A smile crinkled the corners of Callen's eyes. Kael's inward voice had been a pleasant surprise. He had so many questions for the man.

Back inside the room, Eaerien was unsuccessfully trying to rouse Genesis from the trance she had fallen into. *Callen,* he called.

Callen entered immediately. *Loren never showed up.*

Later. I need your help bringing her back.

He knelt beside them and put one hand on his exhausted pup and the other on Genesis's head. "Where is she?"

"Lost somewhere in her mind."

∞

Genesis was trapped in her subconscious. Metal bars surrounded her as far as her eyes could see. She ran along the length of one side and came across the door. It swung open on her approach, and she walked out only to find herself inside another cage. "What is this place?"

"Haven't you figured it out yet?" Moriana queried from beside her.

Genesis turned to her questioningly. For some reason, she wasn't surprised to see her.

"It's a maze of cages," Moriana explained. "Don't you recognize it? You created this place and locked me in it."

"But why am I in here too?"

"I've been trying to find a way out ever since," Moriana continued, ignoring Genesis's question. "Sometimes I think I'm close, but all I find is another locked door. Other times, *you* show me the way out. But my absolute favorite is when I find my own way out because I get to sneak into your soul and surprise you." She laughed sharply at Genesis's bewilderment. "You really are obtuse, aren't you?"

Genesis stared at her blankly.

Moriana shook her head. "Stupid."

"Answer my question," Genesis returned calmly.

"I don't know, okay? Maybe you weren't strong enough to keep the door shut. I was pushing hard, and you were slipping."

"So I locked myself in here to keep you from getting out? I see. Now how do I get out again?"

Moriana shrugged. "Either you figure it out on your own, or someone comes and gets you."

Genesis knit her brows together. "Who would do that?"

"That big old half-human Caledon got in one time. He had help though. The pathetic one you stick with tried many times, but you never let him in."

"Why not?"

Moriana scratched her head, muttering, "You're annoying." But she continued answering Genesis's questions anyway. "I can't say for sure, but it's probably because he won't be able to get out once he gets in."

Genesis furrowed her brow in thought. "How come I don't consciously know all this?"

"You know, Genesis, I'm actually surprised to see you here." Moriana lounged lazily against the metal bars. I never imagined we'd be locked in together."

"Why?"

"Because you'd only do this if you were out of options." She jutted her chin at nothing in particular. "What happened out there?"

"You don't know?"

"How can I? You keep me pretty isolated. Is Jaden nearby?"

Genesis glanced away. "Can you feel him, Moriana?"

"No," she answered with sadness. "I haven't been able to feel his presence in a long time. As stupid as you are, you're doing a good job of making me forget the power I get from him. All I remember is his name."

Genesis nodded. "Soon you'll forget that too."

Moriana turned pale with fright. "You wouldn't!"

"Yes. I'll do whatever it takes to obliterate you and him from my life forever."

∞

Callen was having a hard time getting into Genesis's mind. There were so many things in the way. Closing his eyes, he concentrated harder and called her name. Sweat broke over his brow as he poured all his energy into locating her. *Genesis!*

He found himself inside a locked cage. "Genesis?"

Still no answer.

Without hesitation, he strode forward, and the door swung open unbidden. "Genesis!" he called loudly. All the doors swung open at once, and he saw her. She was running toward him. He saw another girl, identical in looks, running close behind her. He shut all the doors, stopping both of them.

"What are you doing?" one of them yelled. "Let me out! I'm scared!"

"Callen?" the other one inquired. "How did you get in here?"

Callen stepped toward the girl closest to him, and the bars between them vanished. "Genesis, I've been looking for you. Why didn't you answer my call?"

"I tried to," she replied. "But I don't feel like myself." She held her hands in front of her and studied them. "I feel like a shadow."

Callen took her hand. "Stay with me," he entreated.

She gave him a surprised look. "Where would I go? I'm locked inside here."

He glanced at her look-a-like.

"That's Moriana," Genesis explained.

"We've met."

Moriana sneered at them.

"How did you know which one was me?" Genesis wondered.

Callen smiled tenderly at her. "I know you. I don't know her."

"How do we get out of here?"

"Walk beside me and don't let go of my hand. I'll show you the way."

Genesis gazed up at him. "How did you get in here?" she asked again.

Moriana snickered. "Her mind is slipping."

Genesis started to turn around, but Callen stopped her.

"Don't look back," he warned.

Her eyes grew round with fear.

"Trust me."

The fear departed from her eyes, and an amused smile graced her face. "I do."

34.

Genesis opened her eyes slowly. Where was she?

"Genesis?" Eaerien prompted gently.

The girl sat up. "Eaerien," she greeted groggily.

The young mentor hugged her tightly.

"I'm all right," she tried to reassure him. "I'm sorry, Eaerien. I tried not to go."

"I know you did. All that matters is that you came back safe and sound."

"Where's Callen?"

"Resting." A slow, admiring grin spread across Eaerien's face. "He's really something, isn't he?"

"Well, he *is* Elohim's son."

Eaerien scrutinized her face. "Can I get you anything?"

She shook her head. "There's something … I felt something … while he was in there with me." Genesis frowned. "I think it was … pain."

"Pain?"

"I don't know how to explain it, but I felt it. The whole time he was in there, he was in pain. As if … as if …"

"As if his life was being drained out of him?" Eaerien finished for her. She gave him a wide-eyed look, and he sighed heavily. "That explains why he collapsed."

"He collapsed?!"

"Shh," he soothed. "Loren's with him. You need to rest."

"I want to see him."

"First thing in the morning," he promised.

Genesis nodded and lay back down. She didn't have the energy to argue, and soon her eyelids grew heavy. "Will you stay?" she asked Eaerien. "Until I fall asleep."

"I'll be right beside you, Genii." He brushed the hair from her brow. *Oh Elohim,* he thought. *I'm not ready to let her go.*

∞

Callen valiantly tried to stay awake. He'd promised Caed, but delving into Genesis's tortured mind had taken a lot out of him. He caught pieces of sentences as he drifted between sleep and wakefulness.

Marry her off to a distant village ...

Someone kind ...

Go with the Caledons ...

Marian ...

His eyes popped open. *Marian!*

Caed's eye roll was palpable even through his thoughts.

Sorry, little brother. You've got my full attention now.

Our sister's singleness is the 'blemish' those old fossils were referring to, Caed filled him in. *They want her married to Jaden's son yesterday.*

That doesn't surprise me, he said.

Will you take her with you? Caed asked.

I had planned to.

What do you mean 'had'? Caed asked suspiciously.

You might want to include Father in this.

*Father **is** included.* Caed glanced at Kael behind his desk, looking serene. *I mean, he's giving me that look like he knows what I'm doing.*

Callen chuckled and expanded his thoughts. *Father?*

I'm listening, Callen, Kael replied.

Again, Callen was struck by the depth of Kael's involvement in Elohim's workings. *I have so many questions for you.*

I expected that.

Can we stick to the topic at hand please? Caed interrupted.

I may not be able to keep my mouth shut, little brother, but you are interminably rude, Marian's voice piped up.

Callen laughed weakly. *Back to the topic of your marriage, sister.*

Marian's inward sigh was long. *I understand I have two options: marry Jaden's son or run away with you. I'd rather not do either. Callen, I have missed you these past three years more than I can possibly say. But I don't think my place is by your side any longer.*

Callen was silent for a few moments. His sister was right. Elohim had work for her to do, but it wouldn't be with him.

Finally Kael spoke. *There is another option, but let me first clarify a few things. Marian, you are also Caledon, but one without wings—as am I. That makes you, Caeden, half human like Loren. The irony of the world we live in is that we shun half-lings when the majority are one. After the great conflict, my parents were among those sent by Elohim to the desert to establish communities among the wandering humans.*

Your mother and I found you both hanging from baskets in a tree. I traced Marian's parents back to the Academy. They were instructors there, traveling to the coast on a mission after you were born. They were murdered by Jaden's followers. We still don't know who found you. I wonder sometimes if it was Elohim, himself.

As for your third option, daughter, I propose you do marry, but to someone else I've chosen for you. He paused. *Callen, I understand you can project images, but can you also see those in others' minds?*

I've never tried, he admitted, intrigued by the idea.

Try now.

Callen bolted upright as images flooded his mind—memories, as well as current images filtering in from Kael's eyes. Callen's jaw went slack when he realized Kael had given him full access to his mind.

Overwhelmed? The man sounded entertained.

Very. Are Caed and Marian seeing this too?

I believe you may have shut them out inadvertently.

Callen slipped a hand over his sleeping pup. He had plenty of energy, but his mind was already worn from earlier.

A moment longer, Callen. Do you see the young man working with his hands?

Callen focused on Kael's memory of a man, who was not much older than himself, and who had kindness in his features. His body was lean and strong from years of hard work.

His name is Jeb, Kael explained. *He is one of the few wanderers remaining. He is a craftsman of all trades. His family lives in the city beneath the shadow of the Academy. I spoke to him about Marian the last time he was here. He is willing to take her as wife on the condition Elohim wills it.*

He follows Elohim?

Wholeheartedly.

Callen closed his eyes and snuggled Madden closer. He felt a weight lifted off his chest. His sister's future was secure, and he was free to carry on his father's work without further delay.

∞

Callen was sitting up in bed when Eaerien and Genesis walked into his room later that day. His eyes lit up as they entered.

"Glad to see you finally up," Eaerien commented. "How are you feeling?"

"A little drained mentally, otherwise fine," he responded cheerfully. "How's your mind, Genesis?"

She shrugged carelessly. "Back to normal, I guess." She hesitated briefly, then stepped close and scooped up his hand in both of hers. "Thank you."

He beamed at her.

Genesis dropped his hand and took a step back. "Your siblings are wondering why you aren't up."

Callen glanced between her and Eaerien. "I learned how to do something last night. Well, early this morning," he corrected.

Eaerien raised his eyebrows. "A new talent?"

"Not new, just another dimension to one I already have. May I show you?" At Eaerien's nod, Callen leaned forward and drew his teammate to his side once more. "Genesis?"

Genesis studied his expression. He was asking her to trust him again. Even though she'd already said she did. Did he expect her to have to make that choice every single time?

At her consent, Callen held her hand and stared intently into her eyes.

It was unnerving, and Genesis had to fight against herself to leave her mind open. If he hadn't been holding her hand, she might have bolted. Some of the intensity faded from his eyes, and he released her hand. She moved to look out the window. She wasn't sure what was going on, but judging from Eaerien's slacked jaw, something incredible was happening.

Callen took a couple of deep breaths and fell back onto his pillow, exhausted.

"He looked through your eyes, Genii," Eaerien whispered in awe. "He let me see the world through your eyes! What's your range, Callen?"

"I don't know," Callen answered slowly. "A hundred yards maybe?" I don't need you here with me to initiate it, but it's certainly easier.

"Amazing!" Eaerien exclaimed.

"Eaerien, I think we should keep this skill quiet for now," Genesis said quietly. She nodded at the boy fading out of consciousness.

"It does leave him pretty vulnerable," he murmured. "Come, let's let him rest. We need to get back to Loren."

35.

Loren was sitting in the courtyard with his apprentice, looking much too relaxed.

Eaerien approached, tilting his head with curiosity. He was certain the chancellor was aware of the overnight events.

"Beautiful day, isn't it, Eaerien?" Loren greeted.

"It's perfect," he agreed.

"Perfect for what?" Kaven wondered.

Eaerien smirked at his friend. "Wouldn't you like to know?"

Kaven released an exaggerated sigh. "Permission to pummel him to the ground, Loren?"

Loren chuckled. "That won't be necessary. You have come to speak to me about something?" At Eaerien's nod, the old Caledon stood. "Let's take a walk, shall we? Kaven, you know what to do."

"Doesn't matter," he grumbled uncharacteristically. "No one ever listens to me."

Eaerien winked at Genesis. "Keep Kaven company, will you? This won't take long."

∞

Genesis crossed her arms and stared at the man. She had always assumed he disliked her as much as the next Caledon, but Callen's confidence in him as Loren's apprentice had her re-evaluating that.

Kaven gave her a sidelong glance. "What is it?"

"You're nothing like Loren."

"Tell me something I don't know, child," he replied with a bored expression.

Genesis's defenses went up. "I'm not a child."

"Fledgling then," he amended.

Genesis moved to stand in front of him. "When I first came to the Academy, you marked me down as an eyas. Everyone else you referred to as a fledgling. Why?"

Kaven glanced at her with interest. "You're bitter about it, aren't you?"

She leveled her gaze at him.

He leaned forward unperturbed. "I marked Callen the same way when he arrived. Do you even know what an eyas is?"

"It's a falconry term. For domesticated birds."

"It's the word used to describe young hawks that were taken from their nest before they could fly and raised in captivity." He shook his head. "There's nothing domestic about them. Do you not think that is an accurate description of both you and Callen?"

"It's not a derogatory term?" she asked skeptically.

"Oh for heaven's sake, Genesis!" Kaven flipped his hands into the air and let them fall limp to his sides. "Contrary to popular belief, I actually *like* all of you. I am harder on you than your mentors are because someone has to be. Shepherding young, impressionable Caledons is no easy feat. If Elohim himself hadn't asked me to do this, I would not be here. Believe me."

Genesis softened toward the man. She recognized insecurity when she saw it. "Just because we don't like you doesn't mean you aren't qualified."

Kaven's jaw dropped slightly.

She shrugged. "You said it yourself. Elohim chose you."

"As he chose you," he returned kindly.

Genesis withdrew and left him without another word. He wasn't so bad after all, but she didn't need another person trying to convince her of her worth. Not after all the trouble she caused wherever she went.

∞

Kaven watched her retreat. A rare, amused smile played across his face. He had always been Genesis's biggest, albeit silent, advocate. Since his earliest days as Loren's apprentice, he had been in charge of setting the pairs for the evaluations, and he had done his best to set her up for success while still being fair to the others.

She was right in her assessment—he was nothing like the current chancellor. If anything, he was more like Genesis than anyone. Loren was loved by everyone he encountered, while Kaven rubbed them all the wrong way. He often wondered why Elohim had picked him to be the future shepherd of his Academy, but Loren always said the best diamonds had the roughest edges. Kaven wasn't inclined to believe that, but watching Genesis grow each passing day was teaching him the value of grace toward others, as well as himself.

∞

Callen was awake and pulling on his boots when Genesis walked back into his room. She eyed him critically, and he grinned. "Where's Eaerien?" he asked.

"With Loren."

He took her hand and led her out the window. "There's something I have to do, and I want you to come with me."

"What is it?" she questioned, following him.

"Take Marian to her new home and …" He held her hand a little tighter. "Find your brother."

Find my … Her expression darkened. "Why in the *world* do you have to find that monster?"

"He's not a monster, Genesis."

"He's Jaden's heir!"

He gave her a pointed look. "So were you at one point."

She planted her feet and pulled her hand out of his grasp. "No."

Callen turned to her. "No, you're not going to come with me, or no, you don't want me to find him?"

Her frustration mounted. "I'll go with you to help your sister, but not—just *why*, Callen?"

269

"Because he wants to be found." He smiled at her and added, "Do you know how nice it is to hear you say my name?"

Genesis blinked, taken aback, then remembered her train of thought. "How do you know he wants to be found?"

"I heard him."

She shook her head slowly. It was a trap. Another one of Jaden's ploys meant to sink his claws into Callen. Well, she wasn't going to let him.

Genesis, Callen said imploringly.

"What?" she asked flatly.

Elohim wants me to find Aeron, and I want you to come with me. He tugged gently on her hand.

She sighed, knowing she was going to give in. "Why me?"

"Because we're stronger together," he reminded her. "And you're supposed to be my helper. Elohim said so."

Genesis rolled her eyes. "What about Eaerien?"

"What about me?"

She spun around and found herself face to face with their mentor.

Eaerien caught Callen's eye, and an understanding passed between them. His gaze settled on Genesis, and he gave her a woeful smile. "I knew this day was coming."

"What day?" she asked.

"The day I graduate you from fledgling to juvenile," he sighed. He shot an exaggerated frown at Callen, who stifled a laugh.

"You mean …?"

Eaerien's smile reappeared. "I won't be joining you on this mission."

Genesis looked over her shoulder at Callen, whose expression had sobered. Leave Eaerien behind?

∞

Marian stood in her room, staring at the piles of belongings on her bed. It had been decided overnight. She was leaving to get married. Today. She fell face forward onto her bed and groaned.

"Need some help?"

Her head snapped up in surprise as Callen and Genesis climbed in through her window. "Callen! Genesis?" She glanced wildly between them. "I have a door!"

Callen laughed and held his palms up. "It's a habit."

"A bad one!"

Genesis eyed the various items on the bed suspiciously. "What's all this?"

"My stuff. I'm trying to pack."

Callen shook his head sadly. "I'm sorry, Marian. You can only bring what you can carry on your back."

"How am I supposed to pack sixteen years of my life into one bag?" she asked incredulously.

"I'll help you."

Her eyes filled with tears.

"Don't act like you're the only one who's ever done it," Genesis said stiffly.

Marian's temper flared to life. "At least you had nothing to lose by leaving your first home. I, on the other hand, don't *want* to leave."

"I wasn't speaking of myself," Genesis growled back. "I was talking about your brother!"

"Callen had a choice!"

"So do you!"

Marian shook her head. "No, I didn't. Not really. Either way, I have to get married to a stranger!"

Genesis clamped her mouth shut and took a deep, steadying breath. *Selfish, ignorant girl,* she ranted to herself.

Genesis. Callen tipped his head to the side and gazed at her.

Don't you dare take her side, she retorted, stomping angrily back to the window.

I'm not taking anyone's side, he said, smoothly blocking her path. *I'm asking you to see the situation from her point of view.*

Marian narrowed her eyes. "If you have something to say, Genesis, then say it."

"Marian," Callen intervened. "You know Caed, Father, and I want what's best for you, don't you?"

"I know that," she sighed. "That's why I agreed—"

"See," Genesis was quick to point out. "You chose!"

"Oh!" Marian flung a piece of her clothing onto her bed. "You are infuriating!"

Callen gave Genesis a reproachful look. *Not helping.* To Marian, he said, "Have I ever asked you to do anything that you ended up regretting later?"

"No, never."

"Then don't be afraid. We all have to take a leap of faith, or we'll never move forward."

Marian gestured to her belongings. "I still don't understand why I can't take my things."

"Because all this extra stuff will weigh you down. Everything you need from your past is already in here." He lightly touched the side of her head then pointed to her heart.

"What do I pack?"

"Practical items that will ease your transition into the next season of your life."

"All I really need is food, water, and a few articles of clothing …" Realization dawned on Marian. "That's all Father and Mother packed for you when you left for the Academy."

"It's all any of us leave with when we come of age."

∞

Goodbye was bittersweet. As soon as Marian finished packing, they prepared to leave.

Caeden hugged Marian for a long time. He was twelve years old, as tall as his sister, and his father's apprentice, but he felt like crying like a baby. "Watch your tongue, sister," he tried to joke through the lump in his throat.

Marian let her tears flow free and retorted with, "Watch your attitude, little brother. I love you."

"I love you too."

Callen put a hand on both their shoulders. "You'll see each other again," he reassured them.

"Soon, I hope?" Marian asked. "I wish we didn't have to leave right away."

"It's better this way," Callen softly reminded her. "Father will have less trouble with the village elders if it looks like we disappeared without warning."

"I'd like to see them try and make us accept Jaden," Caed stated forcefully. "I'll finally have an excuse to tell them off."

Callen chuckled and squeezed his brother's shoulder affectionately.

"Will we see you too, Callen?" Caed asked with a furrow in his brow.

Callen put his fingertip to the furrow. "Brother, don't forget to enjoy life. Hm?"

Caeden relaxed his expression. "Is that a yes?"

"Of course you will see me again." He tapped his temple. "Remember, you can always talk to me here."

Genesis walked up with a sack of food and tucked it into her pack. "Ready to go?"

Marian gave her mother and father quick hugs as Eaerien came to see them off.

Callen handed Madden to Genesis, who tucked the little dog into the hood of her tunic, and picked Marian up and spread his wings. He kept his back out of view and shook his feathers before any blood stained his tunic.

Genesis followed suit. *Why do you hide it from everyone?* she asked him.

Now is not the time.

If you say so. She looked at Eaerien, who smiled encouragingly. She gave him a little nod and took off.

Callen raised his hand in a final farewell.

Eaerien watched them long after they had disappeared from view. *Elohim go with you.*

273

36.

Jeb was setting up camp for the night when two winged humans, along with several birds of prey, descended on him. He'd seen them in the air several miles away and had wondered if they would join him. The tallest one—a young man—set the young woman he was carrying on her feet and pulled his face protector off, raising his hand in a friendly greeting.

∞

Callen couldn't help the swell of admiration toward his earthly father as he appraised his sister's future husband. Kael certainly had a knack for finding the right people. The human man was early in his twenties and carried himself with an easygoing confidence. His movements spoke of strength tempered with kindness.

∞

"Good evening," Jeb said as the Caledons approached.

"Hi, Jeb," Callen greeted.

Jeb raised his eyebrows. "You know me?"

"I do. I am Callen." He put a hand on his companion's shoulder. "This is my sister, Marian. Those are her birds." He gestured to his teammate behind him. "And this is Genesis."

"Ah." A bright grin lit up Jeb's features. "Elohim's son. Welcome." He pointed to his meager camp. "It doesn't look like much, but I have plenty to share. Will you join me?"

Callen nodded. "Thank you. My father sent us to find you."

"Elohim did?" Jeb asked incredulously, pausing in his search for more bowls to stare at them.

"My human father, Kael," Callen clarified. "You met with him not too long ago. He's the head of one of the larger desert communities."

"I remember Kael. He asked me if I would consider marrying his daughter—er, your sister." Jeb's eyes settled on Marian. "I said I would not if you did not also agree to it." He didn't wait for an answer and instead turned back to dig in his bags. "Here they are! More bowls." He passed them each a bowl filled with dates, fruits, nuts, an assortment of vegetables, and bread. "I don't carry meat or cheese with me across the desert," he explained. "Hard to keep those fresh."

"Neither do we," Callen grinned.

Jeb chewed quietly, studying the raptors perched on his belongings before turning to Marian. "What shall I give your birds?"

"They will hunt for themselves if they get hungry," she answered quietly. "All they need is a place to roost for the night."

"Where do you sleep?" Genesis asked suddenly. The sun had set, but there was no tent or shelter of any sort put up.

"Wrapped in a blanket under the stars," Jeb answered. He glanced at Marian. "I have a tent, but I seldom use it for myself. I'll set it up as soon as we're finished eating."

Marian stiffened. "I think I'm the only one here who's never slept outside, but I don't mind trying. You don't have to set up the tent for just me to use."

Jeb shook his head. "It doesn't take long. You should use it, Marian." He studied her eyes carefully. "Have you come because you agreed to marry me?"

Marian turned a bright shade of red.

Genesis dropped her eyes to her empty bowl. *Here we go.*

It will work out, Callen assured her.

Maybe we should give them some privacy.

We will in a minute.

276

"To be honest, I haven't decided yet," Marian answered honestly. "I wanted to at least meet you first."

Jeb smiled gently. "That's fair."

Her eyes snapped to his. "Did you feel the same?"

"Mm," he hummed. "If Elohim hadn't prompted me first, I would have."

"You knew you were going to marry me?"

He nodded slowly. "In a way, yes. I don't normally travel past your father's village this time of the year, but something urged me to. Then I met Kael, and he said he'd been waiting for me. That's when I knew that ultimately this was orchestrated by Elohim. It's the only explanation that makes sense."

"Did you also know that I wouldn't have another option?" Marian demanded.

"There's always another way," he answered evenly.

"What other way could there be?" She set her food aside and started pacing. "If I don't marry you, I have to marry Jaden's heir. And I **won't** marry Jaden's heir. But if I marry you ..." She flung her arms into the air. "I don't know what's going to happen!"

Jeb stood up and faced her. "Marian," he said calmly. "Is it so terrible not knowing what your future will be?"

"You don't know what it's like to not have control of it."

"Don't I?" His brow tilted ever so slightly.

Marian hesitated. "I don't understand."

Jeb glanced at Callen and Genesis, briefly wondering if he was overstepping his bounds. He didn't exactly know them, although he'd known *of* them for a while. "Do you think I grew up in the valley of the Academy dreaming of becoming a wanderer? Or did Callen know he was going to save the planet from decay? And what about Genesis?"

"What about me?" Genesis couldn't refrain from asking.

Jeb looked her square in the eyes. "If you could change your past—control the outcomes—would you?"

Genesis surprised herself with her immediate, "No."

"Why do you say that?"

"I wouldn't be where I am today if I did." She looked over at her Callen. He caught her eye and gave her that knowing smile that made people believe he understood them completely.

"None of us can control our future," Jeb was telling Marian. "What we can control is who we entrust it to."

Marian studied his features. "You trust Elohim with yours?"

"Wholeheartedly."

"That's why you agreed to this plan? Even though you'd never met me before?"

"That's the beauty of following Elohim. You never know where he will send you, but you know he won't send you there to fail."

∞

"You said I had other options?"

Jeb gave Marian a slightly wounded look. They were huddled by the fire still talking after Genesis and Callen had left to patrol the vicinity.

"I've already made up my mind," she hastily explained. "I was just curious about it."

"You could say no."

"I never thought about that."

He smiled teasingly. "You're a smart girl, Marian, but you seem to have trouble thinking outside of the box."

"I was raised that way."

"So was your brother."

A blush stole across her cheeks. More from her wounded pride than embarrassment. "Are you going to lecture me again?"

Jeb laughed. "I'm sorry. I'll be more aware of that."

"If you forget, I'll remind you."

He laughed again. "Please do."

Marian ducked her head. "I appreciate advice, Jeb. But if I'm going to be your wife, I'd rather you give it gently and not in a way that makes me feel like you're my father."

He blanched. "I definitely don't want to be a father figure to you."

∞

Marian blinked slowly and stretched. Her muscles didn't ache as much as she expected after sleeping on the ground three nights in a row. She stared at the fabric of the tent above her.

Marian, are you awake?

I'm awake! She threw her blankets off and lifted the entrance.

Callen stepped into view with a smile. "Good morning."

"Good morning!"

His smile widened.

"Sleeping in has been wonderful," she admitted. "And Jeb is not what I imagined him to be."

Her brother laughed. "So we're on the same page now?"

"Yes. Thank you, Callen, for giving me the past three days. I know you have much bigger things to take care of."

He stopped her with a hand on her arm. "I always have time for you."

Genesis drew up next to them. "So today's the day."

"Are you glad to finally be rid of me?" Marian teased.

The tiniest smirk formed at the corners of Genesis's mouth. "You have no idea."

Impulsively, Marian hugged her new friend. "I'm beginning to understand why Callen says you're so special. You're extraordinary, you know that?"

Genesis wiggled out of her arms.

"You don't believe me," Marian noted.

"You don't know me that well," she pointed out.

"True, but I do know my brother, and if he says you're special, then you are."

Genesis sighed. "Everyone is special to him."

Marian tilted her head and squinted one eye at Genesis. "Also true, but he has an extra special fondness for you. Whether you believe it or not doesn't make it untrue."

"I've heard that before," she muttered.

Callen nudged Marian with his elbow. "Are you ready, sister?"

"I'm ready."

∞

Jeb and Marian were married before Elohim with Callen and Genesis as witnesses. It was a simple ceremony, and their camp was packed up and ready to move by early afternoon.

"Are you sure you don't want to travel with us a few more days?" Jeb offered. "I'm sure Marian would appreciate it."

Callen shook his head. "There is something Genesis and I must do. We'll meet again at the Academy." He wrapped his sister up in a warm hug. "You know how to reach me if you need me."

Marian held him tightly. Oh how she loved him. She moved to where Genesis stood off to the side. "Do you mind if I give you a hug?"

"You've already given me one."

"Well, here's another one."

Genesis stiffened slightly but held still and even patted her awkwardly on the back in return. "I don't envy you, Marian."

Marian laughed lightly. "And I don't envy you, Genesis. Take care of my brother, please."

Genesis nodded.

Jeb and Callen shook hands.

"I meant my vows, Callen. I'll take care of her."

Love her, Jeb. Obey Elohim, and love my sister. That's all I ask.

I already love her, and I will keep doing so. Thank you, Callen. "Elohim be with you."

"Always. You and Marian, as well."

∞

Marian stood beside her husband watching Callen and Genesis disappear into the horizon. Her heart threatened to quail at the uncertainty of her future. She liked Jeb, and she trusted Callen's judgment, but they were still little more than strangers, and she had never been away from home before.

Jeb slipped an arm comfortingly around his new wife's shoulders. "Marian, we have a lifetime to look forward to together. Let's take it day by day, what do you say?"

She nodded, relaxing. "How far will we travel today?"

"Not far," he answered with a smile. "There is a small oasis we'll head for. We can spend a day or two there if you would like."

"I'd like that. It'll be good for my birds, as well."

"I'd better learn how to get along with them, especially that one eying me." He pointed to the large grey-feathered one.

Marian laughed. "Callen trained that one. He's an eagle—just coming into adulthood. He went up against Jaden and won."

Jeb grinned. "You'll have to teach me soon then. Shall we go?"

Marian returned the smile, feeling lighthearted once more. "Let's go."

37.

It was the dead of night when Genesis rolled over and shook Callen awake.

He sat up quickly, causing Madden to tumble into his lap. "What is it? Did something happen? Are you all right?"

She made a face. "I'm fine. I just wanted to ask you something."

Callen yawned and lay back down. Madden crawled into his tunic and snuggled close. "What is it?"

"Why did Eaerien send us on this mission alone?"

"I don't know," he answered groggily. "He's trying to teach us something."

"Obviously," she scoffed. "But what?"

"Probably the same thing he's been trying to teach us for the last three years," he suggested with a lazy grin. "Teamwork."

"We work fine together," she countered.

"And you trust me."

Genesis frowned. It wasn't a question.

"And I trust you too."

She huffed.

Callen craned his neck to look her in the eyes without having to sit up.

Genesis averted her gaze.

"I can always read your mind—"

"Read it then."

He laughed. *I'll wait for you to tell me when you're ready.*

She gave him a smug look. *I knew you'd say that.*

Callen chuckled again. *I don't know why Eaerien allowed you to come with me, but I'm glad he did. I feel better with you by my side.*

Why me?

He put his hands behind his head and stared up at the stars. *You watch my back like no one else does. You drive me to be better. You remind me of what I'm fighting for. And you're always there when I need you.*

"That's ... you," she said in surprise. "To me."

"Now do you know why I say we're better together?"

"But it doesn't make any sense."

"It doesn't have to. You just have to believe me when I say it."

Genesis rolled back and stared into the night sky. "Eaerien made a similar promise years ago, and it's brought him nothing but suffering."

"You're wrong," he answered softly. "It's brought him more joy than suffering. Eaerien told me what makes him sad is his own inability to break the hold Jaden still has on you."

"No one can break that," she said sadly.

"I can, and I will," he promised. *Even if it costs me my life.*

∞

They left early in the morning after a few hours of sleep. They flew above the clouds with the rising sun at their backs, looking for any signs of Jaden's heir, and all the while, Genesis couldn't shake the feeling they were flying into a trap. Days blended into weeks then months, and the further from the Academy they flew, the higher her anxiety mounted. They travelled deep into unfamiliar territory, following Lacquer trails. Genesis couldn't make rhyme or reason out of the paths they were taking, but when she had asked, Callen had merely smiled and told her to trust him.

Just after sunset one day, they crested a mountaintop and dove low, keeping within the treetops. Instantly, the hair on the back of Genesis's neck went up. She could sense him now. *He's here.*

Callen slowed and dropped a few feet behind her, giving her the lead.

Genesis weaved side to side, testing where his presence was strongest. She drew in a sharp breath as they crossed a fresh trail. Narrowing her eyes, she plunged blindly through the dark forest, ignoring the rough branches and sharp leaves. The nearer she drew to him, the angrier she felt and the wilder her eyes became. Memories flashed through her mind—memories she had nearly succeeded in erasing. She lowered her head and uncurled her fists. *I found you.*

∞

Callen felt absurd. The further he went into the forest, the harder the plants fought to keep him out. "What is this?" he asked aloud.

Perched anxiously on his shoulder, Madden whined.

"I'm going as fast as I can," he protested. "I think the forest is actually pushing me back."

The little dog tipped his head doubtfully.

Ignoring him, Callen struggled on. A short time later, he stopped again, completely frustrated. Genesis had disappeared from sight, and she wasn't answering his call. "Madden, go and seek her scent."

The little dog immediately disappeared into the thick undergrowth. He reappeared a few minutes later, somersaulting out of the brush and onto his master's shoulder. He was trembling, and his fur was letting off sparks.

Callen smoothed the bristled fur comfortingly. "Calm down. You'll light me on fire." The animal growled angrily, facing the way he had come. Setting the dog down, Callen said, "Show me."

Madden led him to the edge of a wide clearing, and Callen immediately caught sight of his teammate crumpled on the ground at the roots of a giant redwood. Stepping out from the shelter of the trees, he knelt and turned her over. "Genesis, wake up."

She opened her eyes slowly and winced. "My head ..."

"Are you all right?" he asked, brushing the hair off her face.

Suddenly she jerked awake. "He's here! You have to run!"

An obstinate look appeared in Callen's eyes as he helped her stand. She put a hand to head and swayed. Callen caught her and swung her into his arms. "What happened?" he asked as they took refuge within a thick stand of trees.

"I had him," she answered as if in a fog.

"Who?"

"Aeron."

"And then?"

"Out of nowhere ..." Her head lolled. "Jaden ... hit me."

Callen braced her across his knees and gently cupped her cheek, spreading his fingers across her temple. Genesis leaned into his palm as the throbbing in her head gradually subsided. He checked her scalp for blood and found none. What had Jaden hit her with?

"I shouldn't have let you out of my sight," he murmured.

"I knew you'd get tangled up," she said, taking deep, steady breaths. "This forest is home to Lacquers. The plants aren't normal. They've been poisoned and deranged." She groaned. "What did he hit me with? I can't find your voice."

"I don't know." He touched his forehead to hers. Whatever it was, it was trying to block him out. "I need you to fight it."

"Trying to."

Callen threw up a hedge of protection around them and concentrated on sifting the poison out of Genesis's mind. She was fighting valiantly, and he felt a touch of pride for her. At last the darkness receded and her mind cleared.

Callen?

I'm here. He grinned, lifting his head to look into her eyes. *Welcome back.*

Her dark eyes regarded him somberly. *We knew this was a trap.*

Then we must not get caught. He lifted her and set her carefully on her feet. *Can you sense anything?*

Genesis took a careful step, testing her balance, and studied their surroundings. *Aeron's close by. You were right. He's trying to get away, and Jaden used him as bait.*

We've got to find him.

She shook her head. *You won't get to him without going through Jaden first.*

Then point me to Jaden, he insisted.

That's suicide!

You don't believe in me?

Genesis gritted her teeth and strode away. *Why do you always have to do that?*

Callen walked up behind her and spun her gently around to face him. *Elohim sent us here in victory, remember?*

She dropped her eyes. *He didn't say you wouldn't get hurt.*

That's why he had Loren teach you how to heal. He touched her cheek, drawing her eyes back to his, and waggled his eyebrows.

All right, she relented with a heavy sigh. *Let's go.*

He grinned. *Stay inside my shields.*

38.

Genesis was breathing hard. The fight was lasting longer than she had expected. Callen wasn't moving, and she was starting to worry. He'd taken Jaden one-on-one again and won, but at what cost?

"Hey!" her opponent called. "Don't get so easily distracted or you might get hurt."

"Doubt it," she answered back. "We've been fighting this long, and you still haven't put a scratch on me."

∞

Aeron clenched his jaw. She was right, he noted with frustration. She was too quick for him—always evading his reach—and she didn't seem to have a weakness. Unless … His eyes darted to her unconscious companion. The little dog stationed on Callen's chest might pose a problem, but Aeron seriously doubted he would combust and risk burning his master.

∞

Genesis saw where Aeron's gaze rested, and she shifted her feet ever so slightly as her talons unsheathed. No one was getting near her friend.

He curled his lip into an ugly expression and lunged at Callen. Genesis intercepted him, and they toppled to the ground grappling, wings flapping, and with the unmistakable sound of blows hitting their marks. When they parted, they were both breathing hard and bleeding.

"Why are you trying so hard to protect him?" Aeron demanded. "You know you won't be able to keep it up."

"Try me," she growled.

"I don't want to have to kill you, sis."

"You couldn't even if you tried."

Aeron's hackles rose. "You'll regret that! I have skills no one has ever seen before!"

Genesis spread her wings and crouched. "Bring it on."

The battle ended minutes later. Genesis stumbled to Callen's side and collapsed. She touched his arm and felt a degree of relief to find it still warm. She pulled some large branches over them and curled into a fetal position. She'd called Aeron's bluff and sent him running, but he would be back soon enough. She didn't have the time or the energy to move Callen far enough away that he wouldn't be able to track them. Even if her half-brother wasn't a killer, he was persistent and determined. But determined to do what exactly?

She studied her teammate's still form as her eyelids grew heavier and heavier. The last time Callen had fallen into this deep of a slumber, it had taken Elohim's intervention to wake him up again. She reached for the edge of his sleeve and gripped tight.

Night had fallen when Genesis woke again. She sat up stiffly and checked Callen for any injuries she might have missed before and found none. Lifting the sleeves of her tunic, she turned her arms over. Her cuts and bruises had disappeared while she slept, but there was nothing to eliminate the fatigue she felt all the way to her bones. Since there was no sign of Aeron yet, Genesis lay back down again to rest. Madden slid off Callen's chest and stretched out between them, sharing his warmth, and she drifted into an uneasy slumber. *Callen, please come back soon.*

∞

Tucked within the safety of his mind, Callen rested in Elohim's presence. Jaden's poison had no physical effects on him, but combating the darkness the demented Caledon spread drained immense amounts of energy from Callen, plunging him into a comatose state in the aftermath. It was in this state, however, that Callen found peace. Elohim always came to him, bringing healing and restoration, as well as answers to his questions.

Elohim had just finished explaining the divide between the Lacquers and Caledons when they heard Genesis's voice. "She's calling to you."

"I'd better go back." Callen paused. "Father, how much longer are we to let Jaden rampage the land?"

"You will come into your own, Callen, and you will know when the time is right. Until then, you must change as many hearts as the people will allow."

"What will become of those who refuse?"

Elohim's eyes filled with grief. "I will not force their hand, my son. I gave them the will to choose, and I will honor it." He put his great hand on his son's head. "Go now, Callen. Your work is not yet finished."

∞

Callen opened his eyes and took in the faint streaks of dawn breaking the night sky. He turned his head and saw Genesis curled around Madden, snoring softly. The dog blinked at him but made no attempt to move. Callen sat up and rested his hand on Madden's chilled fur, letting the animal replenish his depleted energy. "Genesis," he whispered. He ran his other hand over her hair, and she stirred.

Genesis wrestled against the heaviness of her eyelids and squinted. Her eyes went wide at the sight of Callen. "You're awake!" she exclaimed.

"So are you," he remarked with a playful grin.

"Are you all right?"

He jumped to his feet and stretched his arms out. "Good as new. What about you?"

"I'm ..." She turned her arms over slowly, and a corner of her mouth tilted up. "I'm not surprised that I'm also refreshed."

Callen chuckled then squatted close. "What happened after—" He paused to settle the turbulent emotions rising. "I decimated everything."

A shadow passed over her face. "Aeron showed himself. Twice." She glanced around. "He's coming back again if he isn't already here."

"Why?"

Genesis shrugged. "We fought." *See for yourself,* she invited.

Callen watched a replay of her battles with Aeron through her memories. Afterward, he moved out of their flimsy shelter and sat contemplatively watching the sunrise.

∞

Pain gripped Callen as he gazed at the desolation around them. Madden whined and slipped out of his hiding spot to nuzzle his master. Callen dropped to his knees and placed his palms on the ground. This was his father's world—his inheritance—and it saddened him to see the state it was becoming. If this was what cleansing the world of Jaden's poison amounted to, how was Callen's method any better? He brushed a palm over the earth, and to his surprise, a bud popped up.

Genesis came up and knelt beside him. She glanced at him with her brows raised and gently caressed the tiny bud. Suddenly, the bud grew and sprouted a leaf, reaching toward the sun. She gasped with wonder. *Callen?*

A gentle grin split his face. He swept his other palm over the ground, and new buds sprang up all around them. Laughing now, Callen grabbed Genesis's hand and pulled her along with him as he stood, and his little dog clambered onto his shoulder. He spread his wings, and the small spray of blood that always accompanied that action scattered and soaked into the ground. Where the drops of blood landed, the earth blossomed to life. Trees, flowers, and shrubs shot out of the ground fully grown. Callen pulled Genesis against his chest, tucking her close, as he flew into the sky.

∞

Hope so powerful engulfed Genesis as she watched the ground fill with foliage of all shapes and sizes, and with a variety she had never encountered in all their travels.

Callen was redeeming the land.

∞

Aeron peeked over a downed redwood—one of the few not turned to ash by Callen's righteous fury. His sister and her teammate piqued his interest more than his master ever could. He was inexplicably drawn to them, and ever since their first encounter years ago, he hadn't been able to put the two from his mind. Who was this Callen, son of Elohim, who had earned Genesis's loyalty so fully, who struck fear into the heart of Jaden, and whose name alone brought entire communities to their knees? And what kind of energy did he hold in the palms of his hands that gave him the power to both destroy *and* restore?

∞

Callen settled Genesis back on her feet and sighed deep with contentment.

She watched him with a vaguely amused expression. *You are full of surprises.*

He turned to her with a grin. "That sounds like something Eaerien would say."

Her expression sobered. *Aeron's here.*

I know.

Genesis narrowed her gaze in the direction of Aeron's hiding spot and unsheathed her talons.

Callen put a reassuring hand on her shoulder and called out, "Aeron."

A figure emerged from behind a great log and stepped away from its shadow. "I wish to speak to Callen alone," Aeron demanded.

Callen looked at Genesis, who very reluctantly returned his gaze. "I'll go speak to him."

She bristled but sheathed her talons. "What am I supposed to do in the meantime?" His stomach growled, reminding her of the ache within hers, and she rolled her eyes.

A little smirk appeared on his mouth. *I won't take too long, and then we can eat.*

Genesis watched him approach Aeron, who eyed them warily but maintained a relaxed stance. Satisfied that he wasn't going to engage Callen in a fight, she walked off in search of food.

Aeron waited until Callen was close enough that he wouldn't have to speak loudly. "You must know why I was sent here." He held out his hand to show his enemy the weapon in his palm. "I guess my master didn't trust me to do it and came to finish the job himself."

"You came to kill me?"

"Obviously."

Callen planted himself within arm's reach and tilted his head. "That's not the way I see it."

Aeron sneered. "Enlighten me then, oh son of Elohim."

Callen was undeterred. "Jaden used you as bait. You were looking for me, but not to kill me." He held his arms a small distance away from his body with his palms up. "Here I am."

"Fine," Aeron growled. "You want the truth?"

"That would be a good start."

"I was supposed to *try* to kill you, but only if you wouldn't give Moriana up. My master wants her back."

"He's not getting her back," Callen stated firmly.

Aeron chuckled darkly. "I figured as much." He flung the weapon aside. "Tell Moriana I wasn't trying to hurt her."

"Her name is Genesis," Callen corrected.

"Ah, I see," he commented sarcastically. "So nice of you to give her a new name."

"Her name has always been Genesis," Callen explained patiently. "Jaden was the one who attempted to change it."

"He tried to change mine too, into something demented-sounding. I didn't let him." He shrugged. "Well, I guess you can keep her."

"Why the change in heart?"

"No particular reason. I'm not that fond of my master."

Callen's gaze bore into him. "The truth, Aeron."

Aeron swallowed with difficulty. The truth was that he was discontent and disillusioned with Jaden. He was also incredibly lonely. "I don't want to inherit whatever it is that Jaden thinks he can give me," he finally admitted. "He's a maniac. I'm pretty sure I know why my sister ran away."

Callen's expression softened. "Well, you're free, Aeron. What will you do now?"

"Eat something for a start. I'm starved."

A smile crossed Callen's face. "Come with me."

39.

A eron followed Callen back to Genesis, who had gathered an assortment
of fruits, nuts, dates, and fish during the short time they had been
conversing. She sat cross-legged with her back against a tree trunk, popping
berries into her mouth. She eyed their new companion with open hostility.

Callen folded his legs down beside her and studied the large rock she'd
placed off to the side before throwing her a glance. She pointedly kept her
focus on Aeron. With a small sigh and swipe of his hand, Callen split the
top off the rock cleanly, leaving a smooth, flat surface. He arranged a pile of
tinder in the center that Madden promptly lit on fire. He added a few more
pieces of wood and laid the fish directly on the flame.

Madden stayed on the edge of the rock, adjusting the temperature
accordingly. The resulting fish was cooked perfectly—charred and crispy on
the outside with smoky white meat on the inside. His job done, the little
dog stepped off the rock and dug into a pile of raw fish Callen had set aside
for him.

Aeron wordlessly accepted the fish offered to him, understanding the
intentional show of power Genesis had backed her friend into. His master
was beyond salvation if he thought he could stand against someone half his
age, who split rocks with the blink of an eye, and who reshaped entire
landscapes in a day. All this, and Callen was not yet in his prime. The more
Aeron dwelled on the absurdity of Jaden's greed, the more humorous it was.
He started to laugh.

"Aeron," Genesis said warningly.

"Sis, I see now that you had the right idea, running away from our
master."

"He's not—"

Aeron held up his hand and cut her off. "Whatever. You're smart enough to know what I mean." He turned a dark look on Callen. "You are just a son of Elohim, yet you wield such amazing power. How much more powerful is your father?"

"Callen is not just a son of Elohim," Genesis cut in fiercely. "He is his one and only son."

"What turned you to him?" Aeron demanded. His stood up and paced, flicking his wings in agitation.

Genesis jumped up with him and followed his movements with a tense expression.

"You always scoff at other people's skills, and power doesn't impress you," Aeron continued his tirade. "So what did it?"

What turned me? Genesis looked at Callen. He met her gaze with his steady one, a little intrigued and a little amused. "He's … good."

"Good?" Aeron scratched his head. "What's that?"

"It's Callen."

"Curious?" Callen inquired, packing up the remainder of their meal. "Then come with me."

"I'm already here," Aeron shot back.

"Not just to eat one meal."

Aeron's eyes darkened at the subtle challenge in Callen's voice. With a sneer, he folded his wings and stalked back to them.

Callen straightened and took a few steps toward home. He held his hand out to Genesis, who reluctantly put her back to Aeron and walked to his side.

Aeron had an instinctive urge to tear at their exposed backs, but he quickly dispelled it. He knew when he was defeated.

∞

After travelling several hours, they took respite in a cave they found along a sandy cliff.

Aeron woke up in the middle of the night to find Genesis hovering over him and gave a startled cry.

"Shut up," she whispered crossly, clamping her hand over his mouth. "Callen's asleep."

Aeron shoved away from her and answered sarcastically. "Well, excuse me for being afraid, considering I woke up to the face of the person who tried to kill me!"

"If I had wanted to kill you, brother," she spat. "I would have."

"What were you doing then?" he asked wearily.

Genesis scooted close again. "Healing you. Some of your wounds started bleeding again."

"You gave me these wounds," he retorted drily.

"Because you went after Callen."

Aeron gave her back his arm and tried to relax. "Who taught you how to heal?"

"Loren did." She glanced up from her work. "He's the chancellor of Elo's Academy."

"I don't know what Elo's Academy is."

"Did Jaden have you living under a rock?" she asked drily.

"Close," he snorted. "He kept me on a short leash after you left. I never saw anyone except for him and our targets. Even the other Lacquers kept their distance."

Must have been lonely, she thought inadvertently.

Aeron quietly watched her work. When she was almost finished, he asked in a low voice, "Aren't you going to ask about her?"

Her eyes flicked up at him for a brief moment. "Who?"

"Our mother."

Genesis's hand faltered. Did she dare?

Aeron pulled his sleeve over his newly healed wounds and stretched out on his side. "Well, I'm sticking around for a while, so ask whenever."

"Why did you leave?" Genesis demanded.

"I want peace, sis," he answered honestly. "I'm tired of living a pointless life. Tired of doing some maniac's bidding. Tired of watching people tear each other apart for no apparent reason. I want more."

"So did I," she admitted.

He studied her expression. "Did you find what you were looking for?"

"Little by little." Genesis's thoughts went to her mentor. It had been four months since she had last seen him, and she missed him. "Eaerien taught me what family, friends, love, and happiness are." Her gaze strayed to Callen. "Then he showed up and showed me what they mean. He gave me everything I was looking for, everything I ever needed." She paused, weighing the verity in her next words. "And he gave it willingly."

"It sounds too good to be true."

She smirked. "That's what I said too."

His expression brightened suddenly. "Do you remember when we used to run around together, destroying everything in sight?"

"I remember."

"I used to think that was a lot of fun." His eyes slid to Callen. "I saw what he did to the land both before and after Jaden spread his poison over it. *That* looked like fun."

Genesis smiled. "It was. It's like he can do anything once he's made up his mind to do it."

Aeron curled into a ball. "You mean he didn't know he had that particular skill?"

Genesis nodded. "He gets it into his mind that something needs to be done, and he goes and does it."

"Just like that?" Aeron shivered. "Sounds like Jaden."

"No," she defended immediately. "Nothing like Jaden. He's never cruel. He's …"

"Good," Aeron finished for her. "That's what you meant earlier, isn't it?"

"Yeah."

"Do you think he'll let me stick around?" he wondered. "I'm a full-fledged Lacquer after all."

"One thing you'll learn quickly," Genesis said, moving back to her spot and laying down. "There's no such thing as Lacquer or Caledon to Callen. There's only for him or against him."

∞

Aeron stared at Callen's sleeping form and contemplated her words. He still had questions about the unknown entity known as Elohim, but he determined in his heart that night, as a seed of hope was planted, that he was definitely for Callen.

∞

Days later, in the early hours of dawn when the sky was just beginning to lighten, but before the first rays of sun broke over the horizon, they returned to the Academy. Eaerien was waiting for them, having seen them approaching hours before.

Genesis didn't bother landing, instead barreling straight into the mentor and wrapping her arms around him in a rare display of affection.

Eaerien's grin was as wide as the valley, and he held her tight. Letting his juveniles go had been expected, yet sudden, and he'd felt their absence acutely. Although he trusted Elohim to bring them home safe, he hadn't been able to wipe his mind free of all the worry.

Callen joined them, throwing his arms over both of them. *I'm sorry for not checking in as frequently as I should have.*

There was no need to.

Callen lifted his head to look at Eaerien. *You weren't worried?*

Oh, I was! I have to remember that Elohim has you in his sights the whole time. Still, it's good to have you home. Out loud, he asked, "Who is our new friend?"

Genesis slid out from between them and tilted her head at the boy. "My brother, Aeron."

Aeron threw her a questioning look and stepped closer.

"Ah." Eaerien's eyes twinkled. "Welcome home, Aeron."

40.

Their friends accosted Callen and Genesis as soon as they entered their aerie.

"Finally!" Dar exclaimed.

Mead grinned widely. "Welcome home."

Callen's answering grin was tired, but just as wide. "How did you know we were coming?"

"We kept on the lookout," Pax explained. He paused to fight the grin forming on his face.

"Basically, we stalked Eaerien," Dar announced. "We knew he'd see you coming long before any of us would."

Callen laughed.

Genesis shook her head, but there was humor in her eyes. "Bet Eaerien loved that."

Mead's rich guffaw was answer enough for them.

"This is Aeron," Callen said, pulling him forward. "He's not much older than you, Pax."

Pax stepped forward and held his arm out.

Aeron frowned and drew back defensively.

Genesis rolled her eyes and clasped Pax's arm with her own. "It's just a greeting."

Aeron mimicked her and stuck both his arms out toward Dar and Mead. Dar raised an eyebrow, but Mead didn't hesitate. An awkward, crooked smile spread across Aeron's face when they clasped his arms with theirs.

Callen's eyes lit up with delight. What his friends had offered Aeron wasn't a simple greeting. It was one reserved for the most trusted of friends.

∞

Aeron's life with Jaden had been harsh and empty, so he quickly embraced Academy life. He loved the grounds, the freedom, and not having to look over his shoulder at every breath. He even loved going to classes and sleeping on the couch inside Eaerien's now over-crowded aerie. He followed Callen around like a puppy much to Genesis's chagrin.

"I did that to you when I first came here," Callen reminisced on their way to their midday meal.

"Did she try to kill you?" Aeron asked curiously.

"No," he chuckled. "But she tried very hard to run away."

"Why?"

"Because it was annoying!" Genesis retorted.

"Aeron!" Pax called, hurrying to them and waving excitedly.

Aeron jumped up and waved his arms back. "What's up, Pax?" he hollered.

"You're so over the top," Genesis muttered under her breath, causing Callen to choke on a laugh.

Pax skid to a stop and caught his breath. "The council made their decision. You're moving into Tuolene's aerie. We're going to be teammates!"

Aeron frowned. "I thought it took months to make a decision."

"Elohim intervened," Pax explained. "I'm the only one Tuolene is mentoring, and everyone else already has two, so the obvious place for you is with us."

Aeron swallowed hard. "Elohim knows I'm here? How?"

"Elohim knows everything," Genesis stated.

Callen put a reassuring hand on his shoulder. "You're part of the family, Aeron. You don't have to be afraid."

"What if I screw up?"

"You will," Genesis stated confidently.

"Thanks a lot, sis!"

"Elohim doesn't expect us to be perfect," Pax said. "Respect him, obey him, and stick close to him. Callen will take care of the rest and fix whatever we screw up."

"That's it?"

Genesis shared a look with Callen, who quirked a corner of his mouth into a smile. "That's it."

∞

"You know he reads people," Dar teased Aeron over their midday meal, pointing his utensil at Pax. "That's the talent Elohim gave him."

"What do you mean?" Aeron asked.

"Body language," explained Pax. "I see subtle changes in expressions and the smallest twitches, and I interpret them."

"How?"

"I don't know." Pax lifted his palms to the sky. "It's a gift from Elohim."

"Well, *why* then?"

Pax lifted his shoulders. "I don't know that either."

"What *do* you know?" Aeron mocked.

"I know he meant for me to use it for good. That I'm to develop it and maximize my potential. It's pretty handy for someone of my stature—keeps me one step ahead of my opponents."

"Is that why Elohim put me on your team?" Aeron questioned accusingly. "So you can keep an eye on me and warn everyone if I turn out to be a spy for Jaden?"

"No." He said it with such finality that Aeron's follow-up questions dissipated into nothing.

"So," Dar spoke up. "You and Genesis have the same mother. What's she like?"

"A nightmare."

"Aeron," Callen chided.

His eyes hardened. "She sold her children to that monster trying to ruin the world, Callen. Tell me why I'm wrong to hate her."

"You said you wanted freedom," Callen pointed out. "Then forgive her, or you'll always be slave to your past."

"What would you know about my past?" Aeron snarled. "You're Elohim's son! You were born for glory and power!"

"The parents he grew up with threw him out!" Genesis yelled, her temper besting her. "Before he knew he was Elohim's son. Before he knew he was a Caledon. Before he knew he had a future. They were prepared to turn him out into the desert with nothing more than the clothes on his back!"

Madden leapt out of his hiding spot and balanced on her shoulder, spitting fire.

"He went back anyway," she continued, "and still, the village rejected him. *You* led him into a trap, knowing Jaden wanted him dead. He went after you anyway because you called him. And I—I—" Anguish filled her. "I tried to kill him myself." She took a calming breath and looked at Callen. "He fought for me anyway. He's fighting for all of us, even when we're not ready to accept him. Where's the glory in that?"

"We had to learn the hard way that it's easier to follow Callen's lead than to question him," Dar said quietly. He smiled apologetically at Genesis. "I hated Genesis at first. Don't ask me why because there was never a good reason to. Turns out she's the best one out of all of us."

Genesis gave him a startled look.

"You are," Mead agreed. "You always sell yourself short, but you've shown more faith and loyalty toward Elohim than the entire valley combined. Everyone credits Pax's little sister for recognizing Callen as Elohim's son, but technically you were the first to."

Callen's mind touched hers. *Now will you believe me when I say you're special?*

Genesis looked distinctly uncomfortable with the attention.

"Okay, let's not talk about your mother," Pax said, coming to her rescue. He nudged Aeron. "What about your father?"

"I never knew him." Aeron threw his sister a guarded look. "But I knew yours."

41.

"You knew my father?"

"That's not what he said you used to call him."

"What did he say I called him?"

"Daddy."

Genesis's blood ran cold. No one—not even her mother—knew she had called her father that. "Where ... How?"

Aeron leaned close, and everyone followed suit—the midday meal long forgotten. "I don't know how much the rest of you know about Lacquer hatchlings, but a family can have up to six young ones at a time. New ones are born every year, versus you lot who get—what, three per lifetime? Anyway. The older ones pick on the younger ones until they either run away or die. Not long after Genesis left, a rumor started going around that if you ran far enough, someone would find you and take you to a safe place. It went on for years. Hatchlings would vanish without a trace."

"Maybe something was eating them," Pax suggested, and Dar grimaced.

Aeron and Genesis locked eyes. "Uhm, we're not edible."

"Everything's edible to something," Dar said.

"Not us."

Genesis stared at her brother. "Just tell them, Aeron."

"But it's a Lacquer's secret weapon," he protested.

"You're not a Lacquer anymore," she reminded him. "You're just Aeron now."

"So what's the secret?" Mead prompted.

Aeron still hesitated.

"It's time everyone knows," Callen spoke up.

"*You* know?" he asked incredulously, leaning away from the table.

Half of Callen's mouth tilted up. "Of course."

"Sis, you told him?" Aeron demanded, rising to his feet.

"Yes, I did." She pointed to his seat. "Stop being overly dramatic and sit down."

"Can someone please fill us in?" Dar insisted.

"We're poisonous," Aeron announced with a hint of pride in his voice. He unsheathed a wing and pointed to the feathers. "If you pluck one, poison comes out of the shaft. One is enough to kill a two-hundred-pound ... anything. When we die, our feathers fall out, and the poison seeps into the ground and kills everything it touches. The soil becomes toxic forever." He paused to wink at Callen. "Well, apparently not forever."

Pax stared at Callen. "What does he mean by that?"

"I can bring the earth back to life."

"I can't wait to see that!" Mead whooped.

Dar stood up. "Can we see it now?" He tipped his chin toward Aeron's unsheathed wing. "Do you mind?"

Aeron frowned at Callen. "They're allowed to test you?"

"They're not asking me to prove myself. They're asking me if I'll show it to them." He grinned at his friends. "Come on, I'll show you, but let's leave the poison out of it."

They went out to the arena Callen had destroyed a few years before. It had never been rebuilt. He spread his fingers over the earth, and they watched in amazement as he raised a miniature forest.

Aeron looked disappointed. "You can do more," he urged. "Bigger. Grander!"

Genesis held her breath. Aeron must have missed the part where Callen's spilled blood was the cure to Jaden's poison.

Callen looked pensive. "I don't need to."

Aeron's eyes bulged. "So what? You have the power! Use it!"

The atmosphere around them tightened. "Power without self-control is another form of poison." *Do not try me, Aeron.*

He blanched. "I'm sorry," he mumbled. "I didn't realize. I'm sorry."

Callen gentled, and the atmosphere softened. He swung into one of the trees and patted the wood beside him. "Will you finish telling us about Genesis's father?"

Aeron followed him into the tree and waited until everyone had settled around them. "As I was saying, no one could have eaten them, and their bodies would have been found if they'd died. There had to be some truth to the rumors, so Jaden sent someone to investigate." His gaze found Genesis's. "Take a wild guess who he sent."

Her stomach dropped. "Our mother."

He nodded. "I'm sure you can figure out what happened from there."

"She found him." Genesis closed her eyes. "Did she turn him in?"

"She did." His voice grew weary. "She sold him out to Jaden, and he was tortured for days. Jaden wanted to know what he did with the hatchlings, but he wouldn't say. I snuck in every day to talk to him. I was curious why anyone would save a Lacquer hatchling, but all he wanted to know was if his daughter had finally escaped Jaden. He said Elohim made him a promise that he would save his daughter, and that promise was the only thing that kept him going.

"I asked him who his daughter was, and he told her me her name was Genesis. I didn't realize that was you at first. I asked him why she would be with Jaden if she was a Caledon. He said his wife was a Lacquer, and that's when I put two and two together. I told him a Caledon had come asking to take you to some Academy, but Jaden had chased him off. Then an older one came by, and Jaden got scared and handed you over to him.

"Your father asked me how long ago that had happened, and when I told him, he got this weird, calm look about him. He couldn't smile because his face was so swollen, but you could tell he was smiling with his entire body. He said you used to call him Daddy and had the sweetest smile. Don't worry, I didn't tell him that you stopped smiling a long time ago."

"What happened to him?"

"He died." Aeron balled his hands into fists. "Jaden left his bones to rot in that hell hole."

"Is that what made you want to leave?" Genesis wanted to know.

Her brother nodded.

"What happened to the hatchlings?"

"I don't know." He hung his head in shame. "I was afraid to ask."

Callen buried his face in his hands and disappeared into his mind.

"What's he doing?" Aeron asked.

Genesis leaned against the trunk tiredly, trying to process what she'd just heard. "He's talking to Elohim."

They waited several minutes for Callen to re-emerge from his mind. When he did, his eyes were alight with hope. "The hatchlings were saved." He pulled Genesis toward him and hugged her. "Elohim didn't leave your dad's body to rot. He sent his eagle, and it carried him home."

42.

Jaden was on the move and somehow—insanely—his powers had increased. He was claiming dominion over the earth and demanding the allegiance due to a king. Any creature that resisted was quickly eliminated—male, female, and young alike. Entire species were being wiped from the earth. A few days after Callen, Genesis, and Aeron returned, Loren quickly set Elohim's plan into motion. He commissioned all Elohim's loyal followers in the name of their king and dispersed them across the land. The mentors he gathered and appointed a special task. The madman was hellbent on defiling Elohim's sacred mountain—the mountain that sheltered Elohim's Academy and Valley. Their mission was to divert Jaden's advancing army away from the mountain. It was a dangerous one, and the likelihood of all three of them returning was low. Still they accepted, made their preparations, and left.

Eaerien shook his head to clear his thoughts—a habit he had managed to impart on Genesis. A wistful smile briefly crossed his face as he thought of the young woman. Over the years she had become more than his eyas. She was a family now—his precious younger sister. "I wonder what she's up to?" he said aloud.

"Thinking about Genesis?" Tuolene asked from beside him.

"Mhmm."

"I hope you're not worried," he said. "After all, she's with Callen."

Eaerien squatted down and rested his arms on his knees. "I'm not worried. I miss them."

"This was supposed to be a simple diversion." Shiloh exhaled tensely and joined them.

"Yet here we are," Tuolene stated philosophically.

"Do you think they've reached their destination yet?" Shiloh wondered aloud.

Eaerien toyed with the idea of looking for his juveniles. It would be fairly easy. His eyes could see far and wide, and searching took little physical effort on his part. But no, he dismissed the idea. Loren needed them in top form for the upcoming confrontation. He stood and brushed himself off.

"Eaerien?" Shiloh prompted.

"I'm more concerned about Kaven wrangling your soon-to-be juveniles than I am about mine being off on their own," he remarked.

The three of them shared a laugh.

"I don't understand why Kaven's less popular than the three of us," Shiloh remarked.

"Pax tells me it's because he's the least seen out in the field," Tuolene mentioned. "Being Loren's apprentice doesn't carry as much weight with them as it does with us."

"It can't help that we tease him so much ourselves," Eaerien added with a smirk.

"Kaven wanted to come with us," Tuolene reminded them. "It's the first time I've seen him argue with Loren."

"His place is at the Academy, and he knows it," Shiloh replied. "Elohim didn't choose him to be Loren's successor for nothing."

Eaerien breathed deep and spread his wings to their full span. Everything was falling into place. *Can you sense it, Callen? Elohim is calling you home.*

∞

Two young Caledons were basking in the morning air. As usual, Callen was at peace—fading in and out of sleep. Genesis was contemplative and unnaturally still.

"What do you think Eaerien's doing right now?" she asked him. The finality in his goodbye had shaken her to the core.

"Thinking of you" was Callen's immediate reply.

Genesis remained quiet.

Callen sat up and stretched. "Nothing's happened yet."

"Has Loren contacted you?"

"Not yet." He took her hand. "You'll know it the moment he does."

She nodded slowly. There were more things she wanted to say, but Eaerien had taught her that some things were better left unspoken.

∞

Tuolene pointed toward the horizon where small dark spots began to multiply and grow. They didn't need Eaerien's special eyes to know it was Jaden's army coming for them. There would be no diverting them. The only way to stop them from reaching Elohim's mountain was to face them head on. The three of them fanned out wingtip to wingtip. All their years of training were boiling down to this one crucial moment.

Eaerien's mind flashed to Genesis and Callen again. What he wouldn't give to gather them into the safety of his wings one more time and shield them from the pain and cruelty of the fallen world around them. *Take care of each other,* he breathed.

"Well, old friends," Tuolene rallied them with a rare grin. "Let's have one more go at them, shall we?"

"For Elohim," Shiloh stated.

"For Elohim," they echoed.

∞

Loren watched with a mixture of sorrow and pride as first Eaerien, then Tuolene and Shiloh together leapt from the top of the cliff. They kept their wings tucked loosely to their sides, gathering speed and momentum until they were nothing more than a fast-moving blur riding on the wind. Three against a multitude.

The odds were stacked against them, but Elohim was on their side. Surely, he wouldn't call those three to a needless sacrifice. The war was just beginning, and the Caledons needed the three mentors' skills. Didn't they?

Loren flinched as a Lacquer hit its mark, and Shiloh wobbled. They didn't break form, however, testifying to the strength of their bond. Tuolene dipped low for a harrowing moment and came right back up. They were halfway across the endless wave, and the enemy was dropping like flies. As one, they spread their wings and barreled through—twisting, dodging, fighting back, moving forward, and never giving ground.

Loren's heart twisted and fractured as he watched them reach the end of the line. They slowly descended to the ground and lay still, wingtips still touching wingtips. At a glance, they could have been resting. Not one of them had turned back to see their accomplishment. Jaden's vast army had been reduced to a handful, forcing the cruel leader to retreat. Loren's eyelids slid shut as grief overwhelmed him, belatedly remembering the juveniles watching the scene through his eyes from a hundred miles away.

∞

Eaerien was dead.

Callen couldn't believe it. As he stood motionless with Madden, he thought of the man who had become more than a mentor to him the past several years. A soft knock on the door interrupted his thoughts.

"Callen?"

He took a steadying breath and reluctantly emerged from his room. His composure cracked at the sight of Genesis gazing aimlessly into space.

Aria touched the young man's shoulder, momentarily drawing his attention away. "Loren is asking if you'll say a few words to the people."

He nodded and returned his gaze to his teammate.

"She's taking it harder than anyone else," Aria stated quietly.

"He was the first person she learned to love."

"What happens now?"

"We continue forward." He took Aria's hand and gave it a gentle squeeze, comforting and encouraging her.

Aria wiped the tears from her eyes and gave him a brave smile. "I'll see you at the assembly."

Callen waited until she'd left before moving to Genesis's side. *Genesis.*

She faced him—her eyes awash with unshed tears. "Why?" she asked in a strangled voice. Her eyes darted back and forth across his face, looking for answers he didn't have. "Callen, why?"

He didn't know why either, and the pain was almost too hard to bear. He pulled her into his arms and held her. "I'm going to end this war," he vowed. "And wipe out Jaden's influence once and for all."

43.

All eyes arrested on Callen when he stood before Elohim's—his—people. They all knew him and had interacted with him at one point or another, but he had never stood before them and formally addressed them as the son of Elohim their king. He connected his mind to Genesis's.

Nervous? she asked before he even had a chance to speak.

Yeah. I never imagined this—

Eaerien would be proud of you, she cut in.

Callen took a deep, steadying breath and looked out at the crowd gazing expectantly at him. "My people." He didn't shout, but his voice was strong and carried across the valley. "We grieve for our brethren, but do not be disheartened. My father's promise still stands. We will be reunited again one day. Eaerien's, Shiloh's, and Tuolene's lives were not in vain, nor will their deaths be." He looked deep into each one of their hearts. "Each of you has been given a task either from my father or myself. Obey it." He paused, and his expression gentled. "When you come to the end of yourself, rest assured that I will be there to aid you. My father and I will never forsake you. And know that whatever sacrifice we have asked or will ask of you, I give also."

Then he comforted everyone by playing in their minds memories of the three mentors from their hatchling days to their last on the earth. He projected peace and a sense of unity onto them before stepping out of sight.

∞

"You're leaving?" Mead asked. He, Dar, Pax, and Aeron had followed Callen and Genesis back to their aerie. With their mentors gone, they suddenly found themselves promoted to juveniles. This meant they would be sent on missions without the guide of an older, more experienced Caledon.

Callen paused in his packing and turned to his friend. "We don't have a lot of time left."

"What will you do?" Dar wondered.

Callen gave him a teasing smile. "Didn't you hear what I said earlier? We all have a job to do—Genesis and myself included."

"All you have to do is ask, and we'd be right there with you," Dar offered.

"Not yet, Dar, but someday after the war, we'll all be together."

Mead looked slightly depressed.

Aeron attempted a joke. "You're becoming like your old man—leaving, coming back, and leaving again. I was under the impression this place was supposed to be home, and we—a family."

Callen laughed, but his expression was pained. "This is home, and we are a family."

"What are we going to do without your influence over our emotions?" Pax asked nervously. "You know how fickle we can be, and without our mentors to guide us, we could be led astray."

Callen went and sat beside the boy, who really wasn't much older than Caed. "Don't forget that your thoughts will still reach me. The longer you leave our connection unbroken, the easier it will be for you to exist in whatever state of mind I am in."

Relief coursed through Pax. Dwelling in Callen's state of mind was easy because it was always light.

Always the practical one, Mead asked, "How long will you be gone?"

Callen took in the aerie he had grown so fond of returning to. He knew without a doubt he wouldn't be coming home for a very long time.

"You are coming home, right?" Pax questioned.

Genesis sighed deeply and left her perch at the nook to sit beside the boy. "Pax," she said quietly and matter-of-factly. "If we don't succeed, there won't be a home to come back to."

∞

Genesis sat at the top of the mountain and gazed thoughtfully into the vast expanse of the night sky. The stars seemed to burn brighter up here.

"What are you thinking about?" Callen asked, climbing up to join her.

"Eaerien. He loved the stars."

"He's not bound by the laws of this world any longer," Callen observed. "Nothing's stopping him from seeing them up close and personal."

A small smile turned up the corner of her mouth. "He won't get near them. He doesn't like the heat."

Callen chuckled.

"What do you like best about the sky?" she asked him.

"It's the same no matter where you go." He tucked his hands behind his head. "I used to wonder if Elohim was also lord of the heavens, and if I would inherit them as well."

"Now you know."

He nodded. "Now I know."

"Eaerien loved to retell how Elohim spoke the earth and sky into being," she reminisced. "How he simply thought of their existence, and there they were." She swiveled her head to look at him. "Kind of like you."

Callen raised his brows questioningly.

Genesis quoted, "I had half a thought …"

He laughed.

"Imagine what kind of things you could accomplish if you had a whole thought."

Callen couldn't stop laughing—partly out of wonder that Genesis was joking with him, especially considering the circumstances.

"I can read your mind too, you know," Genesis remarked.

"Can you?"

"You're wondering why I'm not falling to pieces," she stated calmly.

"Actually, I'm wondering if you know why you're not."

Because of you, she admitted simply.

Callen studied the night sky with a light heart. Tomorrow they would embark on their greatest mission to date. They were going to pursue Jaden from one end of the earth to the other. It was time to break his hold on the land once and for all. It was going to be a difficult and costly journey. It would test their strengths and push them past their endurance, but that was tomorrow. Tonight, they basked in the comfort of Elohim's presence.

44.

Relentless. There was no other way to describe it. It wore on Jaden. It broke him down and struck fear into his heart. Everywhere he turned, no matter where he ran, they pursued him. If he didn't run fast enough, they caught him and engaged him in battle. Battles that he had no hope of winning.

Callen's influence alone was frightening. His presence—absolutely terrifying. Every time they fought, new mountains, deserts, valleys, and plains were formed. Everything Jaden poisoned, Callen healed and remade stronger and more resilient with his blood, and Jaden couldn't conquer the same place twice.

For three years, Jaden ran. His followers were dwindling, either joining sides with the son of Elohim or being reduced to ash by his righteous anger. Jaden's only choice now was to make one last stand. He wouldn't survive, but if he could take Elohim's son with him, it would all be worth it.

∞

Caeden called out to his brother. *Your friends were just here,* he explained in a rush. *Pax, Mead, Dar, and Aeron. They brought Marian and Jeb in from the desert. They were attacked!*

Slow down, Caed. Who was attacked?

Caed took a deep breath. *Jeb and Marian. Marian's fine, but Jeb is dying. We've done everything we can for him. Will you come?*

He won't live until then.

You can still help him. You're Elohim's son!

Callen's heart warmed at his brother's unwavering faith. *I'll give you the power to heal Jeb.*

Caed stiffened. *How?*

Do you trust me?

I do.

Then put your hands on him and heal him.

Caeden swallowed hard. Before any doubts could take root, he spun on his heel and ran to Jeb's side. He inhaled deeply to quiet his nerves and exhaled slowly, positioning his hands over the worst of the man's injuries.

"What are you doing?" Marian questioned.

"Trusting Callen."

Brother and sister watched in fascination as Callen's energy flowed through his brother's hands, and Jeb's wounds began to close right before their eyes.

Marian, Callen called to her. *When the poison comes out, collect it in a jar and bring it to Faye.*

Sure enough, a thick, sinister-looking fluid began seeping out of the wounds.

Marian grabbed the closest empty jar and collected the poison. She tore herself away from her husband's side and quickly made her way to her friend's home.

Faye met her at the gate. "I saw you coming. What happened? Why were there Caledons here?"

"They brought us here. We were attacked, and Jeb was injured. I don't know how, or if the Caledons knew we needed help. It had to have been Elohim's doing." She held out the jar. "Callen told me to bring this to you. It's the poison that was inside Jeb's wounds."

Faye's eyes went wide. She took the jar and hurried into her house, giving Marian little choice but to follow her. "I've been working on an antidote," she explained. "Unsuccessfully. By the time we extract the poison out of someone's system, it's lost its potency. I suspect it wanes after its done its job, but I haven't figured out how. This is exactly what I need to find that answer."

Marian watched curiously as her childhood friend mixed varying amounts of herbs in powder and liquid forms, finishing with several drops of the poison. Faye counted the number of drops it took before the antidote failed—eight. She quickly mixed another sample and placed seven drops of poison in it. Pleased that the antidote remained clear, she gave it to Marian.

"Have your husband drink this. It will neutralize any remaining toxins in his body. He'll still need a few days to rest before you can leave, but that will give me enough time to make a large batch to send with you."

Marian was already making her way out the door. "We'll spread the antidote to all the villages! Thank you, Faye!"

Faye took a deep breath. *Thank you, Callen.*

∞

Callen was all smiles when he and Genesis touched down at their friends' campsite after a long, hard day of travel.

"You're here!" Pax ran up and threw his arms around the pair.

Madden hopped from shoulder to shoulder, shooting off harmless sparks. Even Dar and Genesis hugged. While Callen and Genesis had been chasing after Jaden, their Academy mates had followed in their wake, recruiting people to Elohim's side.

They settled themselves around the campsite.

"How goes everything?" Mead inquired, passing around sandwiches.

"Everywhere we go, we hear about you two," Pax said excitedly. "Makes our jobs easier if the people we're trying to reach have already witnessed what you can do."

"Well, they'd be complete fools not to believe after seeing what Callen can do," Dar retorted.

"It doesn't matter," Genesis reminded them. "As long as they're saved from Jaden."

"Do you give them one last chance?" Mead wondered. "Before you ... you know?"

"Before he turns them into dust, you mean," Aeron stated.

Genesis gave him a scathing look.

"What?"

"Of course he gives them a chance!"

Pax moved closer to their leader. "You're awfully quiet, Callen."

Callen finished the sandwich in his hand before speaking. "I was hungry," he said with a grin.

"How's Jeb faring?" Pax asked.

"Recovering well. Faye came up with an antidote from the poison extracted from his wounds."

"Faye is the young woman betrothed to Caeden?" Dar asked.

Callen nodded. "She's the one."

"And Caeden?" Mead inquired. "How is he?"

"Tall," Callen said fondly. His expression fell. "Like Loren was."

Pax rubbed his face. "I can't believe we lost Loren too."

Dar shook his head. "We didn't lose him, Pax. Elohim showed up and took him home. Ask Mead. He saw them."

"I did," Mead spoke up. "They went for a walk as the sun was setting. Then an eagle flew by, and they were gone. I think Elohim walked him from earth to heaven."

"Just like that?" Aeron insisted

Mead nodded. "Just like that."

Aeron shrugged his acceptance. "I guess anything is possible with Callen and Elohim."

"Has anyone been back to the Academy and the valley?" Dar questioned. "It's been so long since Mead and I have been back."

Genesis's heart constricted at the memories that surfaced. She and Callen hadn't been home since Eaerien had passed.

"We just came from there," Pax informed them. "It was nice to come home, but it was also difficult."

"It wasn't the same," Aeron added. "Not that I spent a lot of time there."

"Different, how?" Mead wondered.

"It still feels like home, and it's obviously the safest place to be right now, but the atmosphere is quite somber."

"How's Petra?" Callen asked.

"Growing up and demanding to join the fight. Every time we visit, she asks to come with us." He threw a sidelong glance at his teammate. "She's developing a crush on Aeron."

Aeron's face heated, drawing a snicker from his sister. He threw a bread crust at her, which Madden smoothly intercepted. "Petra's a kid!"

"So are you," Genesis retorted.

"Maybe when you're both older," Mead joined in. "We'll consider it."

"I will consider it," Pax clarified.

"We'll set up a panel of judges," Dar offered. "Aeron has to accumulate a certain number of points by completing a series of obstacles—" He dodged the body flying at him. "Watch it!"

Pax tackled Dar from behind while his eyes were focused on Aeron sprawled in the dirt. "Who asked for your input?" he jokingly yelled.

Mead stood up and eyed Aeron, who immediately raised his hands in surrender. "I just want to get off the dirt." But then he tackled Mead as soon as he turned his back. "Can't believe you fell for that, Mead!"

Genesis rolled her eyes. "Hatchlings. All of you."

Callen's gaze roamed over them. "I've missed this—" He spread his arms wide. "—us all together. Its been a long time, hasn't it?"

"Too long," Mead agreed, pulling Aeron to his feet.

Pax released Dar from a chokehold. "We should run into each other more often."

"How long will you and Genesis be staying this time?" Dar wanted to know.

Genesis felt the weight of Callen's longing, sadness, and pain mingled with hope.

"I have one more task for you," he said. "Will you do it?"

"Yes," they answered unanimously.

A tender expression appeared on his face. "Jaden is going to make one last stand. Genesis and I will tail him, and I would like all of you to accompany us."

All four sets of eyes went wide. They had been waiting years for Callen to ask them to join him.

"I'm in," Dar said immediately.

"So am I," Mead echoed.

"And I!" Pax nearly shouted.

Aeron grinned his crooked, happy grin.

Genesis smiled. *You just made their day.*

It will be so much more interesting having them around.

Are you calling me boring?

You know what I mean.

Sounds like you're saying I'm boring.

Callen chuckled. "For the record, I'm not bored with you, Genesis. It's time for our friends to come with us."

Pax sighed quietly. "I will finally get a reprieve from their—" He jutted his chin at Mead and Dar. "—constant bickering."

"Hey," Mead said.

"We don't bicker!" Dar protested.

"We discuss our differences," Mead explained.

They bicker, Aeron reaffirmed.

Callen bit back a laugh. *You two might not get as much reprieve as you're expecting.*

You and Genesis are different, Pax noted. He dug the toe of his boot into the dirt. *Those two 'discuss' the same issues over and over again and never reach a compromise.*

Sounds frustrating.

Very!

But you love them anyway.

Pax's head came up sharply. *I do. Sorry, Callen. I was merely venting.*

Callen clapped the younger man on the back encouragingly. *And I will always listen before reminding you of what's important.*

"I've really missed having you physically here with us," Pax said aloud. "Even though I know what is true in my mind, my heart still feels lost sometimes."

"So does mine," Genesis reluctantly agreed. "And I'm with Callen all the time."

"It's the consequence of Jaden's hold on the land," Callen explained with sadness. "Until his influence is completely obliterated from the earth, we will continue to struggle with that."

"You too, Callen?" Dar asked in surprise.

"To some extent, yes. The more time I spend in Elohim's presence, the easier it is to resist."

"Is that the same as me dwelling in your state of mind?"

"Yes," Callen answered with a smile.

Pax was ashamed of himself. He often recalled Callen's invitation, but he had not acted on it.

It's not too late, Pax.

I'm sorry, Callen.

Don't worry about it.

I'll do better!

Callen caught his eye and dipped his chin in a subtle motion. *I'll hold you to that.*

45.

Jaden took his last stand in the shadow of the mountain, beneath the Academy and in full view of the valley. He sent his last remaining followers to ambush the company of Caledons that refused to leave Callen's side. The Lacquers played as dirty as they dared, pulling out their own feathers in an effort to poison their enemies. Thwarted at every turn, Jaden took his frustrations out on the beautiful landscape, daring to mar the sanctuary created by Elohim himself.

Callen's fury burned brighter and hotter than ever. Three very special people had given their lives to protect the land gifted to them by Elohim. Enough was enough.

∞

Callen called his people, and they answered. He brought them together to witness the final battle with Jaden.

"I don't understand," someone said. "If the son of Elohim doesn't want us to participate in the actual fight, why did he call us here?"

"He needs our support."

"He wants an audience!"

"He wants witnesses."

"Why?"

"Who knows?"

∞

Genesis walked away from the crowds before she lost her temper. How could they still not understand? How could they not see the loneliness plaguing Callen? She looked for her friends, and a sigh of relief escaped her when she found them.

"There you are!" Dar hailed her.

Mead took one look at her expression and asked, "What happened?"

Pax patted the ground beside him. "They said something about Callen."

Aeron and Dar smirked, and even Mead couldn't hide his smile. Ever since Eaerien's death, the only thing that could still rile Genesis up was a slight to Callen.

"They don't know anything," she forced out. "After all this time, they still know nothing."

"Well, some of them do," reasoned Mead. "But yes, a lot of them still don't."

"They're here though," Dar pointed out. "They responded to Callen's call. That's how it begins."

Pax bumped her shoulder to get her attention. "Don't forget that only a few of us have the privilege of knowing him the way we do."

"But they could know him as well as we do," she argued. "They just don't make the time to. They're too obsessed with glory and victory."

"We hear you, sis," Aeron said impatiently. "But think about it. Why else would Callen call them to witness the battle if not to right their priorities?"

Genesis glued her eyes to the sky above them and nodded. They were right, of course. She found a measure of comfort from their company, but nothing could compare to the total security she had in Callen. She reached out to him with her mind, and he answered immediately.

I'm here.

A sense of peace filled her. *Can I go to you?*

She heard his smile in his reply. *I need you right where you are.*

Why can't I stand with you?

You already are.

Is there nothing more I can do?

Love so profound flooded her mind, sending goosebumps across her skin and forcing her eyelids shut to hold back tears.

This battle is for you, for our friends, for everyone desperate to escape Jaden's power. It is mine alone to fight. Callen looked down at the little dog nestled in his tunic. He patted the little animal fondly. "It's time for you to go too, my little friend." Madden turned large, trusting eyes to him, and he stroked the warm, dark brindle fur. "You've been a wonderful little friend, Madden. Now go and stay with Genesis."

Madden briefly pressed his nose into Callen's hand before climbing out. He settled on the puff of air Callen created for him and fixed his eyes on his master as a gentle breeze carried him away.

∞

Jaden faced his arch nemesis and grinned tauntingly.

Grounded, Callen did not physically appear daunting. He had just reached maturity and was slight of build as all Caledons were. His eyes, however, spoke volumes and carried a depth of understanding reflective of his father, Elohim.

He gazed at the man opposite him. Jaden was hopelessly lost, and now he was also at the end of his road. Callen let go of the sadness he felt for the man and replaced it with judgment. In every battle before, he had allowed Jaden to take the initiative, hoping against hope that one more life would be spared. Today, there were no more second chances.

Callen unsheathed his wings and shook off the stray drops of blood from his feathers. His wingspan spread wider than any Caledon's had before and shone with a brilliance that was blinding. He rose majestically into the air and raised his arms, blanketing his people with an impenetrable seal of protection. Not one of his beloved followers would lose their lives today.

Jaden launched an attack while Callen's arms were still raised. He sped through the air toward him with talons outstretched and dripping with poison.

Callen deflected the attack.

Jaden made a U-turn and attacked from above.

Callen dodged it.

Jaden arched around from behind and threw poisonous darts at him, then circled back around and threw some more. Without pause, he dipped low and launched an acid death cloud that obscured Callen from view. He flew backward to watch the son of Elohim fall.

Callen dispersed the cloud and darts with a flick of his wrist, and the poison fell on Jaden's followers instead. He did not flinch as their agonizing cries of pain filled the air. An eerie silence descended when the last one quieted and turned to dust.

Jaden was utterly alone. He looked into Callen's eyes and realization struck. "You were playing with me!" he snarled. "All this time!"

Callen swept his arm over the people. "I was giving them a chance. Your time on earth is ended, Jaden."

No. He turned to flee.

Callen closed an invisible fist around him and held him there. He tightened his fist until Jaden, screaming, was ground into dust. Callen then took the dust and disintegrated it into absolutely nothing. He took a deep breath and flew high into the atmosphere.

∞

Genesis watched in awe with the people around her. When Callen flew into the heavens, her awe turned into dread. He meant to wipe out the poison from the earth in one go, and that would require his blood—a whole lot of it.

The sky turned black. Thunder roared and lightning flashed. A torrent of rain came down tinted with blood, pounding into the earth and cleansing it. Callen's people watched in frightened amazement, safely cocooned within their seals. After several intense hours, the heavens cleared, and the sun shone bright and promising. While people turned to each other and whooped in victory, Genesis kept her eyes fixed on the last place she had seen Callen. Her heart skipped a beat when a figure slipped from the clouds, and then it dropped into her stomach as her teammate, her best friend, her savior, and the king of her mind and heart plummeted from the sky.

Genesis sprinted through the air toward Callen, flying faster than she had ever flown before. She pushed herself even faster. *Please, no,* she begged. *Callen!* She caught his limp form and glided awkwardly to the ground. "Callen," she prompted.

His eyes flickered open. "Genesis."

Her feet touched the ground, and she sank to her knees with him in her arms. "I've got you," she whispered. "You're going to be okay."

Callen's breaths came in shallow gasps. "It's over," he breathed.

"Yes, it is. The darkness is gone. I can feel it. You saved us all."

"I am … tired."

"You can rest now." Her voice caught. "I've got Madden here, and I can heal you."

Nothing to heal.

"Don't say that," she pleaded.

Genesis.

"I'm here. Tell me what to do."

A gentle smile appeared on his face. "You have been my closest friend," he said in a voice barely audible.

Her grip tightened and tears streamed from her eyes. *Please, Elohim. Please!*

My greatest help.

An eagle cried in the distance.

"Don't leave me, Callen," she whispered. "You promised."

I will still be with you. He lifted his hand weakly and pointed at her heart. "In there."

Genesis cupped his hand with hers and pressed his palm to the side of her face. *And in here.*

Callen regarded her tenderness as the eagle's cry drew nearer.

Genesis's eyes filled with tears. "Callen!"

Wait for me, beloved. He smiled gently, closed his eyes, and breathed his last.

A dam broke inside Genesis, and she wept.

EPILOGUE.

Elohim's people scattered throughout the land, and the Caledons were once more guardians of the earth. The Academy prospered under Kaven's leadership. Caeden became head of his village. Marian and Jeb continued to traverse the land with their little ones in tow.

Callen's company also went their separate ways, although they met up often to fellowship and remember. Genesis looked for traces of Callen everywhere she and Madden went. Without realizing it, she also left traces of him for others to find wherever she went.

"He feels so far away," Genesis thought to herself. She closed her eyes and reached out with her mind, and her hand inadvertently reached out as well.

A warm hand suddenly took hold of hers and her eyes flew open. "Mead."

The young man let go of her hand and smiled. "What were you reaching for?"

"Nothing," she answered, averting her gaze.

"You were looking for Callen again," he said knowingly.

Genesis bristled. "I know he's with Elohim."

Mead held his hands up in surrender. "I understand, Genesis. I want to see him again too. We all do." He dropped his hands. "You know better than we do that Callen won't come back until he's ready."

Genesis closed her eyes for a moment. "He won't come back until *we're* ready, Mead. This is our last task."

"Our final mission," Dar echoed from beside Mead.

"Don't cry, sis," Aeron teased, drawing close. "You've still got us."

Pax snorted. "We're poor replacements of him, Aeron."

Genesis smiled. "But we're family."

And you love each other anyway, right?

GLOSSARY.

Academy: also known as Elohim's Academy or Elo's Academy; a school developed by Elohim to train young Caledons

Aerie: Caledon homes built into a mountain cliff

Caledon: a winged-creature, who serve as guardians over the world. Some have wings, some do not.

Crop: a bird's food pouch

Eyas (plural eyases): young bird(s) or winged-creature taken from its parents and raised by another

Fledgling: a bird or winged-creature that has flown from the but still dependent on adults for survival

Hatchling: a bird or winged-creature that does not yet know how to fly

Juvenile: a bird that is independent of adults but has not yet grown its mature feathers

Lacquer: a Caledon whose talents become tainted and warped by evil

CHARACTERS
(IN ORDER OF APPEARANCE).

Elohim: creator of the world, Caledon king

Loren: chancellor of Elohim's Academy, half human-half Caledon

Jaden: warped Caledon, leader of the Lacquers

Moriana/Genesis: half Caledon-half Lacquer, Jaden's original heir, Eaerien's eyas/fledgling

Aeron: Lacquer, Genesis's half brother, poses as Jaden's son and becomes his heir

Eaerien: Caledon mentor to Genesis and Callen, Genesis's guardian, brother to Aria, son of Raine

Callen: Elohim's son, Eaerien's eyas/fledgling

Kael: Caledon, Caeden's birth father, Callen and Marian's adoptive father, Mother's husband, head of a desert community

Marian: Caledon, Callen and Caeden's adoptive sister

Caeden: son of Kael, Marian and Callen's adoptive brother
Mother: human, Kael's wife, adoptive mother to Callen, Marian, and Caeden

Faye: human, Marian's childhood friend, Liam's sister

Sara: human, Marian's childhood friend

Liam: human, Callen's childhood friend, Marian's betrothed

Flander & Creed: dromedaries

Kaven: Caledon, Loren's apprentice

Shiloh: Caledon mentor to Mead and Dar

Aria: Caledon, Academy instructor, sister to Eaerien, daughter to Raine

Raine: Caledon elder, father to Eaerien and Aria

Tuolene: Caledon mentor to Bruno and Pax

Mead: Caledon, Shiloh's fledgling

Bruno: Caledon, Tuolene's fledgling

Petra: Caledon hatchling, sister to Pax

Madden: Callen's dog

Dar: Caledon, Shiloh's fledgling

Pax: Caledon, Tuolene's fledgling, brother to Petra

Jeb: human, desert wanderer

Elohim's eagle